A GOOD START, CONSIDERING

Peter Ryde

A Good Start, Considering

THE GAY MEN'S PRESS

First published 1999 by The Gay Men's Press,
GMP Publishers Ltd in association with Prowler Press Ltd,
3 Broadbent Close, London N6 5GG

World Copyright © 1999 Peter Ryde

A CIP catalogue record for this book is available
from the British Library

ISBN 0 85449 281 X

Distributed in Europe by Central Books,
99 Wallis Rd, London E9 5LN

Distributed in North America by InBook/LPC Group,
1436 West Randolph, Chicago, IL 60607

Distributed in Australia by Bulldog Books,
P O Box 300, Beaconsfield, NSW 2014

Printed and bound in the EU by WSOY, Juva, Finland

A GOOD START, CONSIDERING

1

As soon as I turned the corner, I could see that our street door was standing open, a thing impossible to account for. Gran wouldn't be home yet. Mackenzie's didn't close for dinner till one o'clock, and when I'd left the Pascoe's two or three minutes earlier, it was only half past twelve; I knew by the wireless. So who was in our house, and what were they doing there?

Rival instincts battled for supremacy.

Plan A (Roy Rogers): Charge in with both guns blazing, flush out the intruders, recapture the premises.

Plan B (cowardice, masquerading as realism): Back off discreetly, and keep out of the way.

Plan C (adult, responsible, as befitted a soon-to-be Grammar School boy): Scout round for a bit, then approach with caution.

While I was crossing the road, Mrs Nicholson appeared in the open doorway and waved to me. Ninety per cent relief. The Nicholsons were our neighbours. Even so...

'Hallo?' I said; half greeting, half challenge.

She smiled. 'Hallo, love.' Something wrong with the way she said it, though.

I made straight for the kitchen. 'Got to get the potatoes on.' During the holidays that was one of my jobs. They had to be nearly ready when Gran got in.

'No, love.' Mrs Nicholson reached out and caught my arm.

I knew, then. I'd had enough practice. People's faces; particular tones of voice that warned you before the actual words were spoken.

Very sudden, apparently, very sudden indeed. Right in the middle of snipping the coupons out of old Miss Partridge's Ration Book.

I tried to visualise the scene but found it impossible. 'So is she...?'

'Yes, my love. I'm afraid so.'

I glanced hurriedly round the room for tell-tale signs, furniture pushed aside as something bulky and awkward was carried through. 'No, I meant, is she here?' You'd need to know, or you wouldn't dare open a door.

Mrs Nicholson shook her head. 'They'll let you see her later if you want.'

'No!' Impossible to keep the horror out of my voice.

She pretended not to notice. Instead, after a suitable pause, she leant forward tentatively, as if preparing to broach an even more delicate subject. 'Alan, my love, there's just one thing. They asked at the Hospital. Do you happen to know if she'd sewn her own shrouds?'

'Shrouds? I didn't know you were supposed to.' Infinite disgrace loomed over the house. Would I have to look for them? Upstairs, there was this big mahogany chest of drawers, full of untouchable women's things with a strange uncomfortable smell.

'Don't worry about it. It's just that some people are very particular. I thought I ought to mention it.'

I couldn't think what to say.

She glanced briskly at the clock on the mantelpiece. 'I expect you're hungry.'

I thought about it. 'Not specially.'

'We can't have you going without your dinner. You come next door with me. I'll make you something.'

'No. It's all right.'

'Well, come anyway. You don't want to be sat here on your own.'

Didn't I? After all the time Gran and I had spent shackled together, trapped in the same house, I knew very well what I didn't want. I didn't want to be chivvied out of the place just when I'd finally got it all to myself.

In the old days, Gran's house in Havelock Street had been a nice safe distance away. Especially on a Sunday, the journey from Barnes to Harrow in two buses and two trains could stretch to a couple of hours. It made a good excuse for limiting social contact to a minimum, but the truth was that she never took to my father and she didn't much care who knew it. 'I don't see why he couldn't have been a butcher, or a grocer. An ironmonger, even. Messing about with ribbons and buttons and bits of knicker elastic. Whatever sort of a job is that, for a man?' When he was killed in the Western Desert, her attitude probably softened a little, but not so as you'd notice. Once, she remarked to Paul, 'Your mother was such a sensible girl till she went and fell for your father.'

We never discovered for certain what the trouble was, but it can't have been helped by the fact that the wedding cake and Paul's christening cake were very nearly baked in the wrong order. After the buzz-bomb, when I had to move in with her, she was fond of mentioning in my hearing that as the one member of the family left untainted by these nuptial irregularities, I was now its only survivor. Which made you think, she said.

It was plain from the day I moved in that her scheme of things had little room for a nine year old. Barring emergencies, and early closing, her days were spent at Mackenzie's Corner Shop (Est. 1906), and her evenings in the Lounge at the Wheel & Anchor, whose name in vernacular form was my introduction to Spoonerisms. The prospect of a second stab at motherhood did not appeal to her. 'I thought I was finished with all this,' she would sigh, confronted with measles or muddy football boots.

Most of the time, I did sincerely try to be as little trouble as possible. With only a token show of resistance, I would see to a whole range of domestic tasks, such as grinding up the big rectangular blocks of cooking salt on the cheese grater, or carrying the accumulators for the wireless set down to the bicycle shop each week to be recharged. But there was too much latent friction in the household for it to stay beneath the surface for very long, and since it was chiefly at meal times that we came into close contact, the kitchen table was our principal battleground.

The worst debacle occurred over the subject of spinach. At the back of her terraced house was a tiny patch of cultivated ground, about six feet by twenty, where we Dug For Victory and raised a depressing selection of vegetables. Unfortunately, whatever we grew, there was always something the matter with it. Potatoes rotted in the ground or were eaten by slugs; pea-pods remained totally flat; and the carrots, through some defect in the seed or soil, developed into hideous twisted mutants with arms and legs.

The one thing which grew in luxuriant and unblemished abundance was spinach. But I drew the line at this; I would sooner have eaten raw seaweed. One dinner time, as the regulation dollop of green slime remained untasted on my plate, and our battle of wills was clearly approaching crisis point, she came out with a remark which totally baffled me.

'With Paul gone,' she said, 'it's going to be up to you to have enough kids for both of you.'

'What?' I said, my fork frozen in mid-air halfway to my mouth.

She gave me a shrewd, penetrating stare, as if this was a moment long foreseen and now finally upon us. 'You'll never get lead in your pencil if you don't eat greens.'

I was speechless. In the first place, I thought it was absolutely none of her business; and in any case, I had made up my mind a number of years earlier that I would never marry or have any children. I had even gone so far as to ask Paul if this would be illegal.

She pointed towards my plate with the blade of her knife. 'You'll eat that spinach, and you'll eat nothing else in this house until you do.'

Argument was impossible. I knew no words to express my sense of outrage. But next day, I vowed to settle the matter, and enlisted Richard Pascoe's help. Having borrowed an old dustsheet from their outhouse, we pegged it down loosely over the growing spinach crop, and imprisoned the Nicholsons' cat beneath it. After that, it was simply a matter of letting nature take its course.

When Gran came home and saw the destruction, she dragged me outside by the scruff of the neck, pointed to the vegetable patch, and said in a smoking fury, 'You did that, you wicked little sod.'

'I never. It was a cat.'

'No bloody cat did that,' she said, jerking my head back and forth as hard as she could.

When she stopped, I merely pointed in silence to the mass of feline footprints in the soft earth. She stooped forward for a closer look, then stood up and walked slowly back into the house without a word. It was three days before we spoke to each other again.

All the same, I had my uses, and when I passed for Bishop Inglis School in 1946, she put on airs no end in front of the neighbours. I was whisked off importantly to a Bring & Buy sale at the school to pick up a second-hand cap and blazer, and she made me wear them all the way home so that everybody would know that Her Alan had Got Grammar. It was an embarrassing journey. The school colour was a shade of green that took some coming to terms with, and I felt like an impostor, wearing the uniform when I hadn't actually started yet. As for being Hers, I hadn't been anybody's since 1944, and I thought she had the cheek of the devil to call me that, after some of the things she'd said.

But now what? How was I going to manage? As master in my own house, I ate some jam straight from the pot, smoked a couple of Gran's fags and curled up on the big sofa without taking my shoes off. But after an hour or two the glamour of undisputed possession was wearing a trifle thin, so at tea time I capitulated and moved in unofficially with the Nicholsons. There was a kindly, undemanding warmth about them, like old brass by candlelight, and I shouldn't have minded staying there, if they'd have me, in exchange for my rations. But my independence proved to be short-lived.

Most of the next day I spent at the Council Offices, hanging about in corridors or waiting in tall empty rooms while decisions were reached about my future. It was clear that from now on I was going to be Occupied Territory, ruled under mandate by a foreign power, with all my sovereign rights extinguished.

'Strip. Everything.'

'Why?'

'Don't argue.'

Authority inspected my naked body as if I was livestock that might have to be put down.

'Cough.'

Somebody's hands where they had no business to be.

'Head back. Open wide.'

All the way round my teeth in twenty seconds.

Every official I stood in front of started a new file on me, and most of the time was taken up with copying details into it out of the others. Until this had been done, I was expected to keep silence, so I counted the number of ink stains on the desk-top, or worked out methods of moving all the way round the room without my feet touching the floor. I soon stopped trying to read what they were writing about me. I knew it by heart.

CAREY, Alan George: d.o.b. 15/2/35. Yngr s of Thos. Carey, Hbrdshr & Drpr S.W.13 (k. in action, 1942). Fllwg d. of mthr, brthr, (enemy action 6/44) domcld Gmthr (d. 8/46). Barton Ho. 8/46 –. Educ: Bshp Inglis Gr Sch 1946 –.

To finish with, my photo had to be taken, so they could stick a copy into the special rectangle on the front of every folder.

A day or two later, I caught sight of the picture. Incredibly, it was stamped 'Crown Copyright' – as if even my own face was now the property of somebody else.

2

Barton House was a gaunt Victorian mansion with stone reinforcements at every corner, and windows with pointed tops. Along the ridge tiles there were little decorative fences made out of cast iron, and a fancy monogram was carved into the wall above the entrance. Somebody splashing out a bit in the 1890s.

Miss Bentley had gone back to the car to fetch some papers. I felt extremely conspicuous, waiting on the front step in my green cap and blazer, and I prayed fervently that no one was watching.

The solid outer door stood open. Beyond it was an inner door with etched glass panels and a small, inconvenient handle at about knee height. A brass bell-pull was set into the brickwork, but Miss Bentley ignored it. 'We can go straight in,' she said, sweeping past me. So I picked up the cauliflower crate containing my worldly goods, and followed her into the hall.

The whole place had the makeshift air of a building requisitioned for the duration. Naked light bulbs dangled from ceiling roses four feet in diameter, and except for the stained edges the floors were of bare untreated wood where carpets had once been. The black Lincrusta dado was scuffed and peeling; above it, the walls were a greenish-brown colour that defied analysis, as if someone had bought a consignment of paint remnants, and mixed them all together in one pot.

Miss Bentley and I had nothing to say to each other. Miss Carswell was supposed to have brought me. I'd met her several times at the Council offices, and thought she was quite nice. But when it was time to leave, a woman I'd never seen before had turned up at the Nicholsons', and said she was there to collect me.

'Where's the proper lady?' I said.

'Miss Carswell is otherwise engaged,' she snapped, as if I had no business to be asking.

Mrs Nicholson had offered to come with me, but this had been briskly discouraged. 'Best not, I think. Hop in, Alan. We haven't got all day.'

We drove the two and a half miles in silence. I kept hoping the car would break down, or that time would somehow come to a dead stop, so that we never arrived.

I tried to guess in advance what the Wilkinsons would be like, but found it impossible. When we actually met, I hardly knew what to make of them. Mrs Wilkinson seemed amiable enough, with grey hair straggling out of a bun, and a coloured apron fastened loosely around her waist. But Mr Wilkinson was wearing a dark suit and a wing collar like Neville Chamberlain; he was tall and spare, and spoke very precisely, as if you'd better hear him the first time because any re-transmissions would have to be paid for.

'It'll take you a day or two to learn your way around,' he told me, during a lightning tour of the premises. 'But the others will show you.'

The cauliflower crate was left on one of the beds in a large room upstairs. On the way down again, we encountered another man who was coming up, and we all paused briefly on the half-landing while I was introduced.

'Aha,' he said. 'A new addition to the family.'

He had a bow tie and a drinker's nose, bulbous at the tip, and threaded all over with tiny purple veins, finer than fuse wire. Unlike the Wilkinsons, he sounded very smooth and sophisticated, so I just looked out from inside myself, and said nothing.

When we got downstairs again, Mr Wilkinson waved vaguely in the direction of two doors. 'Those are the rooms you'll use in the daytime. That one's the Quiet Room; the other's the Club Room. Take your pick. Get to know people.' As he walked away, he said as an afterthought, 'Tea's at five-thirty. You remember your way to the Dining Room?'

The door of the Quiet Room was closed. I looked inside briefly, but it was deserted. There were two or three shelves of battered books, and some ancient armchairs covered in brown rexine. The air smelt musty, as if no one had sat in there for a hundred years, so I backed out again and decided to try my luck next door.

The Club Room was long and narrow, obviously made by knocking two rooms into one. There were a couple of large tables with benches and chairs round them, and several delapidated sofas with torn covers and lumpy stuffing. Part of one wall was occupied by cupboards, all padlocked, and there were shelves here and there with piles of miscellaneous belongings. Just inside the door was a notice board with some lists pinned to it, and a large green poster with DON'T written at the top in big letters and two or three dozen lines of typing underneath.

I was reading this without taking it in, when a much older boy with cropped red hair approached and started looking me over. His face was freckled, the skin pale and eerily translucent. There was a hard look to him that I didn't fancy.

'You got a name?'

'Alan Carey.'

He reached out and felt the edge of my blazer, testing it suspiciously between his finger and thumb. 'What the hell is this?'

'What's it look like?'

He glanced away disdainfully. 'Got any dough?'

'No,' I said. Or I may have put it a bit more forcefully.

Without warning, he lifted me bodily off the ground, swung me upside down, and shook me till a pencil and three pennies fell out of my pocket. Dropping me onto the floor, he picked up the pennies and held them securely in his clenched fist.

I stood up again and tried unsuccessfully to grab hold of his wrist. He fended me off each time, and taunted me by jingling the pennies in his palm.

From somewhere behind me, a voice said, slowly and deliberately, as if reading instructions aloud, 'To Get Your Money Back, Press Button B.' I didn't know whether it was a hint or a sarcastic comment, but it seemed like a good idea, so I punched the red-haired boy as hard as I could in the stomach. He dropped the pennies in surprise, and came for me angrily with both fists flying. In the effort to dodge him, I tripped and fell backwards, bringing him down on top of me.

It wasn't one of my better fights. But it was mercifully brief. After a couple of minutes, he stood up, kicked me, and walked off, leaving the pennies where they had fallen. While I was retrieving them one at a time, the same voice as before said, 'Anyfing else you want to know, ask your Uncle Ocky.'

From down on the floor amongst the chair legs, I could see a boy of my own age sitting at a table on the far side of the room. As I approached, he made a space for me on the bench beside him. His hair, I noticed, was cropped short, like the other boy's.

'Who was that?' I asked, getting my breath back.

'Tom Shales. He's all right, really.'

'Glad you think so.'

'You got your money back. What more d'you want?' He sniffed. 'Keep clear of Eddie, though. He shits in the bath.'

'Which is Eddie?'

'You'll know him when you see him.' He glanced rather doubtfully at my green blazer and said, 'D'you normally go round dressed like Robin 'Ood?'

'Not if I can help it.'

He jerked his head towards some pegs on the wall beside us. Thankfully, I took the blazer off and hung it up. Ditto my garters, an irritating novelty that went with the uniform, and made my legs itch. Socks, if worn at all, were best left to find their own level.

Ocky yawned and stretched his arms. 'Met the Wilkies?'

'Yes. And some other bloke. I didn't exactly get who he was.'

'Jacko. He wants watching.'

'Why?'

'You'll see. Met Hurly?'

'Who's Hurly?'

He struck a preposterous attitude, hands on hips. 'Bejasus,' he said, in a farcical Oirish accent. 'You'll not be one of these soddin Catholics?'

I burst out laughing. 'You're kidding!'

'I am *not*,' he said, and then, reverting to his normal voice, he added, 'C'mon. See for yourself.'

I followed him down a long passage that took us towards the very back of the house. Eventually, we stopped outside a broad wooden door made of stripped pine. He stuck his head round it, whistled softly between his teeth, and said, 'Wotcher Hurly.'

'Is it yourself, Ocky!' said a gravelly voice from inside. 'I've no biscuits for you, my love. It's the rationing.'

Ocky pushed the door open, and I followed him in. He jerked his thumb at me and said. 'Alan. Just come.'

We were in a large dark kitchen with an Aga and a gas cooker installed along one side, and tall cupboards all the way down the other. At a big scrubbed table in the middle sat an ample figure dressed in a short-sleeved white overall.

'Alan, is it?' she said, studying me with interest over the top of her *Daily Mirror*. 'My, but you're a fine lookin boy. I bet you'll break the heart of many a poor girl and leave her sighing for the feel of you between her legs.' She put her paper down, and hauled herself out of her chair for a better look at me. Her body was vast and sagging, like a balloon filled with porridge. 'Did Hitler kill your Mommy and Daddy?' she demanded suddenly.

'Well, I suppose...'

'Anyone else in your family?'

'My brother.'

She shook her head as if scandalised. 'Your own brother? And your Mommy? And your Daddy? Hitler killed them?'

I shrugged. 'In a way.' I couldn't see where all this was getting us.

Tilting her head shrewdly to one side, she remarked, 'Hitler was a Catholic. Did you know that? There's a lot don't, and there's a lot try to deny it. But it's God's truth, and wouldn't you know it? It was a Catholic killed your Mommy and your Daddy and your own brother. So now you'll know what a Catholic is, if you know nothing else.'

Ocky had positioned himself behind her and was making faces at me round her huge overalled body. I was losing two battles at the same time, one against a violent attack of the giggles, and the other against a recurring nightmare image of Paul's hand sticking out from under a pile of rubble. Two and a quarter years had done nothing to diminish its vividness. Eventually, I had to turn away and stare very hard at the big iron kettle on top of the Aga.

She clicked her tongue in self-reproach. 'There now, I've upset the boy. Never you mind, my love. I'll see if I haven't a biscuit after all.' She opened one of the cupboards and took out a big square tin. 'Just the one each, mind,' she said, removing the lid.

I took a biscuit and started to eat it, but the moment Ocky reached for the tin, she slapped the back of his hand. 'What do you say, now?'

Ocky looked up at her, all innocent. 'Please?' he suggested.

'You're a wicked boy, teasin a poor old woman,' she said, ruffling his hair. 'Say it, now. Say it.'

'I don't like to.'

'Then you'll go without,' she said, making as if to put the lid back on the tin.

I caught Ocky's eye, but he didn't so much as twitch a muscle. Clasping both hands behind his back like a choirboy, he said sweetly, 'Fuck the Pope.'

'There, now,' she said. 'It's not so difficult.' And she let him take a biscuit.

Out in the passage again, we leant against opposite walls to recover. 'Did I lie?' he demanded. Just then, there was a great shout from somewhere outside. 'Ock–y!' It sounded a bit like Tom.

'Got to go,' he said, and ran off down the corridor.

I found my way back to the Club Room, but there was no one there. To fill in some time, I read my way round the notice board. There was a ping-pong ladder, a typed washing-up rota, another headed 'Baths', and the month's programme for the local cinema. I thought about having a second crack at the DON'T list, but gave it up and decided to stay ignorant.

There was a wireless set on a bracket fixed to the wall, but I couldn't get it to work, so I drifted away to explore the rest of the house. I must have spent the best part of an hour wandering aimlessly from room to room, gazing out of windows, and filling the time in pointless ways such as counting the banisters, or walking a tight-rope the length of the upstairs corridor, placing my feet precisely heel to toe. There didn't seem to be anyone else about. The others were still at work, presumably. Or perhaps they were down at the Recreation Ground; I remembered us passing it on the journey.

Halfway up the main stairs was a door marked W.C. Inside, the Victorian plumbing was still preserved intact. On a plinth, with three steps leading up to it, stood a massive pedestal, built to withstand a giant, and covered all over, inside and out, with a blue floral design under the glaze. High above it, almost lost in the gloom, was a massive cast-iron cistern with an ornamental chain and handle. It looked as if anyone actually using it would risk being swept away in the deluge; but I went inside, locked the door behind me, and sat for a while on the stout mahogany seat, relieved to have found a refuge.

By around five, unmistakable boy noises were starting to filter up from the ground floor, so I emerged cautiously and went downstairs to the Club Room, hoping to find Ocky. There was no sign of him, but a couple of boys were in there playing ping-pong, and another was kneeling in front of an open cupboard. On the inside of the cupboard door was a nude torn out of *Lilliput*, with a drawing pin transfixing each of her tits.

Eventually, a small handbell tinkled feebly in the distance, and after the signal had been relayed by somebody giving a good sharp whistle between their teeth, there was a general movement towards the dining room. I followed the others and waited just inside the doorway for someone to tell me where to sit.

There were about twenty boys, seated at three long tables, roughly according to age, the youngest about nine or ten, the oldest around fourteen, and every one of them with the regulation bog-brush haircut. I spotted Ocky at the middle table, but he was deep in conversation with the boys around him and didn't notice me. So far as I could see, there weren't any spare places.

Mrs Wilkinson came in, pushing a big trolley.

'Where shall I sit?' I asked her.

'Anywhere.'

'There isn't a place.'

'Are you sure? I told Mrs O'Herlihy.'

'I'm sorry, I can't see one.'

She glanced about her, and said impatiently, 'All right, wait a minute.' She left the room and came back with some cutlery and a mug. 'You'd better go there for now,' she said, pointing to the end of the bottom table, 'and in future, for Heaven's sake learn to fend for yourself.'

It didn't seem like the moment to tell her there weren't any spare chairs, either. When a plate arrived in front of me with a piece of fried bread on it, and a spoonful of beans, I wondered vaguely whether to kneel on the floor, or eat them standing up. I couldn't decide. For some reason, my brain simply refused to function.

I stood there motionless for two or three minutes, gazing down at the plate. Eventually, the boy on my right said blankly, 'You going to eat that?'

'I haven't got anything to sit on.'

'Try your arse,' he suggested.

A boy further along looked up and said quietly, 'You can fetch a chair from the Club Room, if you know where that is.'

By the time I returned, the plate of beans had gone.

'Got cleared away,' said the boy on the end.

'Well, thanks for nothing. You could have said I was coming back.'

He shrugged.

'Is that it, or will there be anything else?'

He pointed towards the trolley, where Mrs Wilkinson was cutting apples in half with a big knife. There were plates of bread and marge on the lower deck. We were given a slice each to go with our half apple.

The boys next to me ate theirs quickly and left, stacking their empty mugs and plates on the trolley. When they were gone, the boy who told me about the chair moved to the end of the table and sat beside me. He had finished his apple, but still had half his bread left. Without a word, he put it onto my plate.

I looked up in surprise.

'It's okay. She feeds me where I work.' He was wearing a singlet that left his arms and shoulders bare; they were brown and strong. He looked about the same age as me, but a lot tougher and more experienced.

'What sort of work do you do?'

'Dig her old man's allotment, mostly. Or the garden. Anything out of doors. I'm not fussy.'

'You don't like stopping inside, then?'

He shook his head. 'Makes you feel trapped.'

I finished the bread. 'What's it like here?' I asked, glancing cautiously over my shoulder. Careless Talk Costs Lives.

'Like?' The question seemed to puzzle him. 'It isn't like anything.' He frowned slightly, as if he was searching for a better answer.

'You coming, Ronnie?' someone called from the doorway.

'Yeah. In a bit.' He turned back to me, obviously still thinking. At last he said in a flat, expressionless voice, 'It's like school dinners. Only all the time. And for ever.'

'How do you make the wireless work?' I asked the boy with the nude.

He looked at me as if I was a half-wit. 'You switch it on.'

'I have.'

He elbowed me aside, and turned the knob back and forth several times; but there was no sound, and no light came on behind the dial.

'Perhaps the accumulator's flat,' I said.

'Accumulator?'

'For the valves.' Mr Pascoe had explained it to us.

'It doesn't need one.' You'd think I'd insulted him.

There was no point in discussing it any further, so I went outside. A group of boys, including Ocky and Ronnie, were playing football in the street. As I came down the steps, the ball shot towards me, heading straight for the inner door with its glass panels. A one-handed save, a quick throw-in, and without any more ado I was part of the game.

We stayed out there till dusk, pausing now and then for a passing vehicle. There weren't many at that time of night; a bus every half hour or so, a few cyclists. Most of the private cars still had their wheels off, and their axles propped on piles of bricks.

Welton Road was long and straight; you could see for a good quarter-mile in either direction. Most of the way, it was built up with a mixture of semis and small commercial premises, but next to Barton House was a patch of waste ground, rampantly overgrown with thistles and dock plants, four or five feet high. In the middle of this stood a long wooden shed with several windows, and a Yale lock on the door. It looked like a small workshop, and by the sound of it, there was some kind of machinery being used inside.

At about the time the gas lamps in the street were coming on, the lights inside the shed went out, and a man appeared, slamming the door behind him, testing it two or three times, just to be certain. He looked quite old, with a white moustache, and a calm, unhurried way of moving. He was wearing a cap and jacket, but no collar; looped across the front of his waistcoat was a watch-chain you could have anchored a ship with.

He waited patiently until the ball went out of play. Then he fished a bag of boiled sweets out of his pocket and offered them

round, addressing everybody by name. 'Ronnie..., Joe..., Ocky...'
It was clearly a regular thing.

Not being known to him, I hung back, in case I wasn't included. But he thrust the bag at me without making any distinction. When we had each taken a sweet, he put the rest back in his pocket and shuffled away slowly along the road.

'Who was that?' I asked.

'Mr Pond,' said Ocky. 'Everyone's grandad.'

'What does he do in there?'

Another boy said, 'He makes hundreds and hundreds of little metal parts, all the same. He showed me once.'

Somebody whistled to us from the doorway.

'Supper,' said Ronnie.

'What will it be?'

'Bread And.'

'And what?'

Everyone laughed. Officially, it was bread and dripping; but the dripping was actually mashed potato mixed with enough bacon fat to cover a sixpence. There was cocoa, too, if you wanted it, or at any rate boiling water mixed with a gritty, pinkish powder the colour of wall plaster. Much was made of its transatlantic origins. 'There, now,' Hurly announced importantly, sliding the mug towards me, 'President Truman sent you that.'

By this time I was looking forward to bed, the ultimate safe haven in time of trouble. Whatever you had to put up with during the day, darkness and solitude set you free. In the secret world of your own imagination, you could think and act as you pleased. At Gran's in Havelock Street, when things were bad, I would even pull the pillow down into the bed beside me, and lie curled up with my back pressing against it and my face towards the wall. In the old days, Paul and I would frequently double up, especially when there were visitors, and that's how we used to lie, arse to cock, with me on the inside, safe.

But at Barton, with seven beds crammed into one room like some sort of makeshift shelter during the Blitz, retreating into a private world was impossible. You might as well have been in a school changing room after a football match. For a long time I sat on the edge of my bed, watching the others undress, as if the scene had nothing to do with me. I wasn't shy about taking my clothes off in public, but the loss of privacy at the close of day was something I hadn't bargained for.

Ocky turned out to have the next bed to mine, so that was all right, and Ronnie was in the room with us as well. But on the other side of me was the boy with the nude, who thought I was a half-wit, and he seemed pretty disgusted at finding me next to him. I hadn't discovered his proper name, but everyone called him Snapper, or simply Snap, on account of his false front teeth.

'Are you planning to sit there all night?'

I looked up. Ocky was standing in front of me, stripped down to his underpants, ready for bed. 'I wouldn't let Jacko catch you,' he said, as he wriggled his slender body between the sheets. 'You're supposed to be laid down by ten.'

This gave me about thirty seconds. With a frenetic burst of energy, I slipped out of my clothes and started to get into bed. As I pulled the covers back, Snap said, 'You're not supposed to do that.'

'Do what?'

'You've got to get in without untucking anything.'

'Says who?'

He shrugged and rolled over, turning his back to me, so I took no notice. It was my bed, and I'd get into it any way I chose.

I lay on my back for a couple of minutes, feeling extremely tense and uneasy. Instead of a pillowcase, the end of the bottom sheet was folded over the pillow and tucked in, an arrangement which saved on laundry but made the pillow a virtual fixture. The sheet had been sides-to-middled, so a lumpy seam came directly under my head. For greater comfort, I tried clasping my hands behind my neck. In this position, I could see right down to the foot of the bed, which was tall, with vertical bars. It felt as if I was lying inside a cage.

Jacko came in to turn the lights off, his bow-tie slightly askew. 'Good night, animals,' he said, checking all round the room, his fingers resting gently against the switch. As he glanced in my direction, he paused, and then crossed the room towards me.

'Expecting visitors?' he said.

'What?' I was completely baffled.

He gazed pointedly at the side of the bed. 'Not properly tucked in. Hop out and see to it.'

It was the stupidest thing I had ever heard. But he stood there watching intently, so I had to get out of bed, tuck in the sheet and blanket as tight as possible, and wriggle back in again from the top, like Ocky. Snap, who still had his back to me and his head half under the bedclothes, nevertheless contrived to register 'I told you so'.

After the light was out, I lay for a long time, trying to get to sleep. With no curtains, it wasn't many minutes before I could make out every separate leaf of the ceiling rose, and count the teeth along the plaster cornice. I could have done with having the pillow against my back, but there was no chance.

In a way, it felt like being in the hospital. Strangers in charge. Lots of beds in the one room, and kids who I didn't know. Asking when Mum was coming to see me, and not getting an answer. Asking where Paul was, and still not getting an answer. Finding my head bandaged and my arm in plaster; not understanding, not quite remembering. Sometimes, Gran sitting beside the bed, looking down at my face with her lips compressed as if it was all my fault. What was wrong with me? What had I done?

But no, not really the same. I'd slept okay at the hospital. Doped, probably. It was mostly during the day that the bad thoughts came. The horror flashes, momentary, brutal, endlessly repeated: Paul's hand, quite still, yet somehow clawing its way upwards out of the rubble. Sudden gaps in the fog: a face at an upstairs window, the sound of boots scampering over the asphalt.

We'd seen it coming. You did, with a doodlebug. Not like the V2s. You'd hear the sound of its motor, and gaze up at the sky, keeping your fingers crossed until it was out of sight. After that, it was somebody else's problem. Sometimes, you heard it cutting out while you could still see it. The nose would suddenly dip down, and you'd think: Supposing it was you that was underneath? What would you do? Not just in a general way, like taking cover, and keeping your mouth open to stop your ears from popping. Suppose you were playing out, and you looked up and saw it coming for you, what would you actually do?

And then one day, if you drew the short straw, you found out. Not that it left you any the wiser, because even if you survived, you couldn't remember. You tried and tried, but whatever controlled your memory wouldn't allow it. There was just the blackness; and then you were lying in hospital without knowing how you got there.

So there was no resemblance, really. Being at Barton wasn't a bit like that. No brainfog. Just facts, undeniable, but impossible to accept. Like having your arm cut off and seeing it thrown onto the ground in front of you.

What now? Surely there must be an office, where you could fill in a form, and a man would look at it and say, 'Good gracious, yes, you've been given the wrong future. I'll see you get your grandmother back immediately.' Or perhaps he would shake his head and say, 'No. I'm sorry. We've got you down as making certain remarks.' And he would show you a list of all the bad things you had ever said about her; your form would be torn up, and back you would go to Barton House.

I must have dozed off eventually, because I dreamt about my mother and woke with a sudden jolt. From the sounds of regular breathing, I could tell that nobody else was awake to hear me, so I finally did what any sensible boy would have done already, and cried myself to sleep.

3

After dinner the next day, Miss Carswell came to collect me. Five minutes' notice was all I had, barely time to put on my uniform.

Wilkie found me waiting in the hall. 'You can't go to a funeral in a coat that colour,' he snapped. 'Whatever will people think? And haven't you got a tie?'

'No.'

'Not even a school one?'

'There weren't any.'

He sighed. 'Wait there. I'll try and find you something more suitable. And at least button your collar.'

Two or three minutes later, he came back carrying an ordinary black school blazer. 'You'd better wear this.'

It was second or third hand, but there was a brand new piece of tape inside the collar, with 'Fielden' written on it in marking ink. I wondered who he was. Nothing in the pockets, not even fluff, so he couldn't have worn it yet. Perhaps he was starting the following week, like me.

'How are you getting on?' Miss Carswell said, in the car.

'I thought there'd be girls.'

'You're lucky, you know. Lots of children are sent to places miles and miles away, with their own schools and everything, and they have to stay there all the time.'

'I wasn't complaining.'

She tried again. 'And there's Jack Crofting, too. A very cultivated man. You'll be able to learn a lot from him, a boy like you.'

I wondered what I was like.

'He once met Lawrence of Arabia. Did you know that?'

'Gosh! Really? Then what's he doing in a place like Barton House?'

There was a pause, while she negotiated a right turn. 'It was a long time ago,' she conceded.

When we got to the Crematorium, the Nicholsons were there, and Mrs Pascoe, and one or two other people from Havelock Street. I thought we should both be going inside to join them, but Miss Carswell said that as chief mourner it was my job to follow the coffin. So I hung about in the vestibule, waiting for something to happen. I didn't know what you did at funerals.

After about five minutes, the coffin was wheeled up to me on a little trolley. It seemed a lot too small to have a person inside it. But according to Richard Pascoe, bodies had to be cut up to find out what they died of, and presumably when they were all in bits they didn't take so much room.

A man in a black overcoat looked at his watch, and said, 'All right, Sunny Jim, let's get on with it.' He started to push the trolley up the aisle, so I walked in after him, head down, keeping my eyes fixed firmly on his heels.

When we got to the front, some other men in overcoats lifted the coffin onto the catafalque, and then moved aside, leaving me standing there in Fielden's blazer, uncertain what to do next. All the seats at the front were marked Reserved, so in spite of what Miss Carswell had said, it didn't seem right to sit there. After an awkward pause, I glanced back over my shoulder in desperation, and somebody steered me from behind towards a chair in the front row.

A clergyman appeared. There was a hymn and some prayers.

'Forasmuch as it hath pleased Almighty God of his great mercy to take unto himself the soul of our dear sister...,' he consulted his notes, 'of our dear sister, Edna Brookhouse...'

I looked at the coffin, and imagined her lying inside it, still wearing her wrap-over pinafore, with her special right-angled scissors for cutting the coupons out of ration books dangling from her belt on a long string. Perhaps she mightn't recognise me, dressed as I was. But there's no fooling the dead. 'I'm sorry about the spinach,' I told her privately.

All of a sudden, there was a dreadful grinding noise as if someone had set some machinery going. Glancing about in amazement, I noticed a huge bicycle chain revolving slowly under the coffin. A block of some sort was fixed to the lower half of it, and was gradually travelling towards us. I realised that as the chain came round the pulley, the block would flip up and catch hold of the coffin, pushing it away from us over the rollers, and through the swing doors at the back. I watched, fascinated, and felt a glow of satisfaction as my prediction was proved correct.

Afterwards, we all went out through a side door, and everyone shook my hand.

'Have you seen all the lovely flowers that people have sent?' Mrs Nicholson said, and drew me aside to look at them. However, it turned out that most of them belonged to a different funeral. Only three bouquets were ours; one from the neighbours, one from Mr Mackenzie, and one from the regulars at the Wheel & Anchor.

'Which is your bunch?' somebody asked, doubtless hoping to please me.

Mrs Nicholson took my arm and walked me towards the gate. 'Are they taking care of you properly? I worried about you half the night.'

'I'm all right,' I told her.

She gave me a doubtful look. 'You'll come and see us, won't you? You know you'll always be welcome.'

'Yes,' I said.

I knew she meant it. I meant it, too. But already, it seemed like half a lifetime since I'd left their house, and in some mysterious way which I couldn't explain, I knew that Havelock Street had ceased to be part of my world.

She stroked the arm of Fielden's black blazer, her fingers full of regret. 'So you won't be going to Grammar School after all? What a shame. Edna was so proud of you.'

'Oh yes,' I said, 'we start on Tuesday.'

Miss Carswell beckoned impatiently, so there was no time for explanations. I waved goodbye out of the car window, and kept on waving until we were out of sight.

Ocky was in the hall when I got back. 'Oh,' he said, pointing to the blazer, 'you're going to Mount Street. That's good. I thought you was one of these Grammar snobs.'

'It's not mine,' I told him. 'And why call me a Grammar snob? I didn't choose which school to go to.'

He eyed me suspiciously. 'So what are you wearing that for, if it ain't yours?'

'Wilkie told me to. He said I couldn't go to a funeral in the green.'

'Whose is it, then?'

I took the blazer off, and showed him the name tape.

'Bloomin cheek!' he exclaimed indignantly. 'Don't bother to bloody ask me!'

'Keep your hair on. I told you, Wilkie gave it to me. Anyway, I wasn't to know you were called Fielden. You've never even told me your first name. It can't really be Ocky.'

'If you must know,' he said sulkily, 'it's Oliver. Oliver Claud. O.C., get it?'

'Claud!'

'All right, so what if it is? Fairy Carey.'

I gave him a sour look. I couldn't see how we'd got into this.

But he hadn't finished. There was the whole alphabet to try. 'Hairy Carey.'

'Shut your gob.'

'Mary Carey. That's it. Mary Carey, the Grammar snob.'

After kicking and punching each other the full length of the hall in both directions, we backed off by tacit consent and stood glaring at each other from opposite sides of the passage.

I picked the blazer up. 'I was told to put this back in the Sewing Room,' I said, making for the stairs.

'Scarey Carey.'

'On second thoughts,' I said, 'I'll probably bung it down the toilet.'

Ocky turned his back contemptuously and walked away.

I badly needed a little time to myself, so I hung the blazer up and made for the W.C. on the half-landing. Even behind a locked door, it took me a good ten minutes to calm down.

As I emerged, Jacko was coming upstairs. Exhaling smoke through his nostrils in precisely regulated jets, he remarked, 'You're only supposed to use the halfway house at night. Other times, you go out the back.'

'I didn't know.'

'Fair enough; but remember another time. Anyway, come along to my flat. I wanted a word with you.'

At the far end of the main upstairs passage, he produced a latchkey and opened a heavy panelled door. Inside, there was a thick red carpet your feet sank into, and enough furniture for a whole house all crammed into the one room; armchairs, bookcases, two or three nests of side tables, a knee-hole desk with a leather top, a china cabinet full of delicate crockery, and an old-fashioned gramophone with a papier-maché horn. Pictures in gilt frames hung two or three rows deep on every wall, and wherever you looked there were ornaments perched, like flocks of gulls on a cliff.

Through an open doorway on the far side, I glimpsed another room that seemed to be equally crowded, but Jacko swiftly pulled the door shut before I had time for a proper look.

'How are you getting on?' he said, turning back to face me.

'All right.'

'Try not to make too many comparisons. They'll only depress you.'

I nodded.

He flicked his ash casually into an ornamental brass bowl. 'How do you feel about starting at Bishop Inglis?'

'I wish I wasn't the only one from here.'

He acknowledged the point through a cloud of smoke. 'You'll soon make plenty of friends, though. A boy like you.'

That made twice in a single afternoon. How could people who scarcely knew me be so certain? Not for the first time, I pictured myself walking alone through the big wrought-iron gateway at Bishop Inglis, being jeered at by hundreds of other boys who knew I didn't belong. I suppose I must have shivered, or something, because Jacko suddenly said, 'What's the matter?'

'Nothing. Just a bit cold.'

'Cold? Well, that's a change. Ten minutes ago, you were slogging away like Jack Dempsey.'

He'd seen us, then. I looked down at my feet. 'A small disagreement,' I said.

'Yes. But don't fight in the house, there's a good chap. You'll only break something. Go outside if you feel the need.'

For no reason I could think of, I felt my whole body starting to shake. With the cigarette still between his fingers, Jacko placed his hands squarely on my shoulders. 'Steady on,' he said. After twenty or thirty seconds, he stepped back. 'Now, hold your hands out.'

As I brought them up in front of me, I was puzzled and irritated to find them quivering as if they were on springs.

'Looks like a case of the D.T.s,' he said.

You should know, I thought.

He grasped my hands in his to steady them. 'Don't worry. You're just a little overwrought. It's been a difficult time.'

As I pulled my fingers free, the lighted end of his cigarette brushed all along my left hand from the wrist to the knuckles. I shot backwards with a yelp, and doubled over, clutching my left hand in my right. Except that it wasn't possible, you'd almost think he'd done it on purpose.

'You'll live,' he said, glancing at the burn. 'But another time, watch how you wave your hands around when people are smoking.'

I stood there, staring at him in disbelief.

He nodded towards the door. 'All right. Run along now. We'll talk another time.'

I hoped not.

As soon as I reached the stairs, I sat down on the top step and looked at my hand again. A blister was forming along the burn. At first, I thought the pain was starting to ease off, but almost at once it was back again, in great throbbing surges that brought the sweat out onto my brow.

I was sitting with my head well down on my knees and my teeth gritted against the next eruption of pain, when I suddenly heard Mrs Wilkie asking me what the matter was. She must have come up the stairs without my noticing. I showed her my hand.

'What's that?' she said curtly.

'A cigarette burn.'

'Been smoking, have you? Serves you right.'

'No, Miss,' I said, 'Mr Crofting done it.'

She stared at me with her face all hard and menacing.

'Did it, I mean. Mr Crofting did it.'

She continued to stare at me.

Further explanation seemed to be called for. 'He was holding my hand, and the end of his fag went right across the back of it.'

Mrs Wilkie pushed me against the wall and held me there with one hand while she slapped my face with the other, once forehand and once backhand. 'Now just you listen to me, my lad,' she said. 'I don't know what you've been getting away with where you were before, but don't you dare go telling a tale like that.' And she repeated, 'Don't – you – dare,' slapping my face again in time with the words.

It was a sharp lesson, and cured me of honesty.

In a blur of misery, I wandered down to the Club Room, sucking the back of my hand to ease the pain. It was a toss-up whether to run away or start a revolution. The first thing that caught my eye was the DON'T poster.

'Sod it,' I said, kicking the wall below the notice board as hard as I could. 'Sod it; sod it; sod it.'

This outburst was greeted by a slow handclap from behind. I

turned round angrily. It was Ocky. I should have walked out again, only I needed to sit down; so I flung myself onto one of the lumpy sofas with my back to him.

A moment or two later, I found him standing beside me. 'You want to put that in cold water,' he said.

'I thought you were supposed to put grease on burns.'

'Suit yourself.' He turned away, and went back to his place.

The pain was starting to well up badly again. Keeping my head down, I gripped my left hand as hard as I could with my right, and thrust them both down between my knees. The pressure seemed to help for a little while, then made it worse.

After about five minutes, Ocky folded up the comic he was reading, stuffed it into his pocket, and positioned himself in front of me. 'Come on,' he said, nodding towards the door. I followed him like a zombie, all the way to the washroom. He put a plug in one of the basins and ran some water from the cold tap. 'In there,' he said.

The relief was total, and practically instantaneous. I could feel the knots in my stomach start to untie themselves, and in less than a minute, my breathing was back to normal.

I glanced at Ocky, and found him looking at me. He seemed to hesitate, then nodded towards my hand and said, quite simply, 'Jacko?'

'How did you know?'

'I told you he wanted watching. Did he hit your face as well?'

'No. Mrs Wilkie.'

He was appalled. 'You never went and told her?'

'Only because she asked.'

He shook his head. 'Don't ever do that. Don't ever, ever do that.'

'No fear. Not after the way she created.'

He shrugged. 'What do you expect? He's her brother.'

It took a few moments for all the implications to sink in. 'I could have done with knowing that earlier,' I said.

'You know now.'

I took my hand out of the basin to see if it had stopped hurting. It hadn't. 'How long does it take?' I asked.

'Give it another ten minutes. If it still hurts, run some fresh water, nice and cold.'

He moved towards the doorway, and stood there uncertainly, as if he was trying to make up his mind about something. Eventually, he pulled the comic from his pocket and held it out to me.

'You can have a read of this if you want. Only don't let anyone else get their thieving paws on it.' It was a *Film Fun*, my favourite. Stepping quickly forward, he thrust it into my dry hand. 'Got to go,' he said, and ran out of the room.

I was still upstairs, reading, when the bell rang for tea. By the time I reached the dining room, the only empty place was next to Snap and directly opposite Tom Shales. It looked like being an uncomfortable meal.

And that wasn't all. Next to Tom sat Eddie. Until now, I'd kept out of his way, though it was impossible not to be aware of him. Instead of the plimsolls most of us wore, he clumped about in army boots, with a curious lurching motion as if the nuts and bolts in his knees had come undone. He had a flat round face, hair like straw stubble, and extremely pale blue eyes. His trouser legs looked as if he spent most of his time kneeling in cow dung. That morning, in the washroom, when we were still in our underpants, I had seen him pissing into one of the basins.

I perched awkwardly on the end of the bench, and pretended to be invisible. All through the sausage and mash, I kept my head well down to avoid catching anyone's eye, including Mrs Wilkie's as she stood at the trolley cutting the apples up.

When she gave them out, Eddie glanced rapidly round, comparing sizes. Suddenly, without a word, he reached across the table, snatched my apple, and munched it up in two huge bites, core and all, like a horse.

'Christ, Eddie!' said Snap.

By that time, there wasn't much fight left in me. I simply wanted the meal to be over. But Eddie's apple was still on his plate, so I grabbed hold of it before he could stop me.

In pre-Barton days, I should have been flayed alive if I had sunk my teeth into an apple when I was sitting at table. So from sheer force of habit, I sliced the captured half into two and started to cut the cores out with my knife. Immediately, Tom nudged Eddie, and together they stared at me as if I was a French poodle with a ribbon tied in its hair.

I bolted the apple down as fast as I could, and fled.

Afterwards, in the Club Room, Snap tried switching the wireless on. But it still wasn't working. 'Shit!' he said. 'I wanted to listen to Arthur Askey.'

By chance, during the morning, I had seen Eddie pulling a plug from its socket by yanking the wire, and it had given me an idea; only what with the funeral, and various other things, I'd forgotten about it till now.

Kneeling beside the skirting board, I pulled out the wireless plug and unscrewed the top. Sure enough, one of the wires was disconnected. A minute's work with a pocket knife was all it took to mend it. 'Try it now,' I said.

The dial light came on, and as the set warmed up, the sound swelled out loud and clear. For a moment, Snap looked quite surprised. Then he recovered. 'You see? I told you there was nothing the matter with it.'

So I left him to it.

But later on, he beckoned me over. 'Seen this?' he said. 'It's good.'

On a small sheet of paper, he drew the back view of a naked woman sitting on a chamber pot. With the point of his knife, he carefully cut her bottom away, leaving a square hole directly above the pot. Then he held the picture up with two fingers behind it, side by side, so that the fleshy tips were showing through the hole. The effect was staggeringly realistic. Snap glanced round at me expectantly, and we both collapsed across the table, helpless with laughter.

'Who showed you that?' I said.

'A boy at school.'

'Mount Street?'

'Where else? Oh, of course, you're Grammar, aren't you? What's it like?'

'I'll tell you on Tuesday.'

I suppose I must have sounded rather subdued. Snap gave me a shrewd look. 'You'll be all right,' he said. 'Bound to be. A bloke like you.'

4

I had to set off for school much earlier than the others. It was only a ten-minute walk to Mount Street or the Hambledon Road Primary, but getting to Bishop Inglis was an exercise in itself.

For a start, my season ticket was still written out for the old station, but now I had two more stops to travel. 'If anyone asks,' Wilkie remarked impatiently, 'just explain.'

At the barrier, I flashed my ticket holder with guilty nonchalance, and made for the platforms like a seasoned traveller. The next instant, I was seized by the collar and unceremoniously hauled back again. After a brief scrutiny, the inspector held the ticket out with his big flat thumbnail pressed hard against the station name. 'What does that say?' he demanded.

'I know,' I said. 'I moved last week, and they never gave me another.'

He had heard it all before.

'They said it would be all right,' I added.

'Well it isn't.'

I heard the train come in. Hopefully, I started edging towards the barrier, but he placed his hand squarely against my chest and pushed me back again.

'That's my train,' I pleaded.

'Yours, is it? When did you buy it?'

'I've got to be on it, or I'll be late.'

'You should have thought of that before you decided to go on the fiddle.'

From the platform came the sound of the doors closing. In despair, I watched the train pull out of the station, carrying with it my whole future.

'But what am I supposed to do?' I said.

'I wouldn't know. You can't travel from here on that ticket. You'll have to pay the difference, or walk to the right station and go from there.'

I hadn't the money or the time.

'When's the next train?' I asked.

'Fifteen minutes. But you're not getting on it without a ticket. I'll still be here.'

I wandered out again into the street, without the least idea what to do next. I should never make it to Barton and back in the time, and our old station was at least three miles away, through unknown territory. It was hopeless. On practically any other day of my life, a cast-iron excuse for missing school would have seemed heaven-sent. But today, of all days!

Paul, for God's sake, what am I going to do?

I was standing outside the newsagent's a few doors along from the station entrance, when I spotted a familar figure approaching; or at any rate, as familiar as I was likely to find. But would he remember me?

'Mr Pond?' I said, stepping out in front of him.

He looked down in surprise.

'I don't expect you remember, but I'm at Barton House. You

came past in the street the other night. I was playing football with Ocky and Ronnie and that lot.'

He looked me carefully up and down. 'I reckon to know most of the Barton boys,' he said.

'It was my first day.'

'Was it, now?' He flicked the ends of his moustache with the tip of his forefinger. 'Well, that would explain it.'

'I don't know what to do,' I said, and gave him a rather frantic summary.

He heard me out in silence. When I had finished, he eased his cap gently away from his forehead and scratched the front of his scalp. 'I expect they'll sort it out for you at school,' he suggested.

'But how am I to get there? The train'll be here any minute.'

He pulled a handful of change out of his pocket and reckoned it up. 'We'd better buy you a ticket. I'll pop in for a word with Mr Wilkinson when I'm up at the workshop.'

At the sight of us, the man in the Booking Office raised his eyebrows. I suppose he must have been watching me earlier on. With maddening slowness, my extra ticket was date stamped and cut in half diagonally with a big pair of scissors. In those days, if you paid half fare, you only got half a ticket, which was logical.

By the time I returned to the barrier, the next train was already approaching.

'Huh,' said the ticket inspector, nipping the angled edge vindictively with his clippers. 'That'll teach you.'

Till then, in my second-hand uniform, I'd been kidding myself that I didn't look much like a new boy – a vain delusion, which evaporated as the train came to a standstill. I scanned the carriages warily, hoping for one where there weren't any other green caps and blazers. Fat chance. But at least when we all got out, I had plenty of people to follow. With green caps dotted along the road in twos and threes all the way from the station, I couldn't have got lost if I'd tried.

Just inside the school gate a blackboard and easel were lying flat on the ground, where the wind had blown them over. The board had NEW BOYS chalked on it, and a big arrow; ironically, this was now pointing straight back towards the station. It was tempting.

But instead, after a brief exploration, I joined a group of fifty or sixty other boys who were waiting outside some double doors, and looking as if their uniforms didn't belong to them. I searched anxiously for someone I recognised. Richard Pascoe hadn't passed, but there should have been two or three from my old school.

Glancing round, I saw two other boys approaching. One was an obvious new boy; the other, in long trousers and quite a bit older, was showing him where to go. They stood for a moment, talking; then the older boy walked off in another direction, leaving the younger to join the waiting group. As he came towards us, I caught his eye, and we both made the same split-second decision.

'Wotcher,' I said.

'You new as well?'

I nodded. 'Alan Carey.'

'Robert Whitman. But everyone calls me Toddy.'

'Was that your brother?'

'Yes. Why?'

'No reason. What happens now?'

He shrugged. 'We wait, I suppose.'

'I didn't see you on the train.'

'No. Dad brought us.'

I was amazed. 'In a car?'

'Yes.'

Mr Whitman was evidently the sort of person who could get petrol even when there wasn't any.

At this point there came the sound of bolts being shot back, and the double doors were opened from inside by a teacher out of a story book, complete with gown and mortarboard. We followed him into the empty hall and stood at the front, meekly eager to carry out his instructions. Six feet from the platform, there was a painted line on the floor. The toes of Row One were to touch it, and succeeding rows were to space themselves back at arm's length, parade-ground fashion. For several minutes, we shuffled about nervously, trying to achieve the required degree of precision.

The hall seemed vast and subduing, with tall windows and a ceiling so high it was practically out of sight. At intervals along each wall, hymn sheets printed in huge type hung from special brackets; but apart from these, and a number of grimy wooden shields with painted crests on them, there was no furniture or decoration of any kind. Compared with the teacher in his authentic regalia, it was rather a disappointment; you felt there should have been carved oak, and antiquity.

A distant bell rang. Before long, other groups of boys started to file noisily into the empty space behind us, and teachers, most of them in gowns like the first, took up strategic positions along the walls. One glance over my shoulder was all I felt like risking;

but I noticed with bewilderment that the back of the hall appeared to be filled by men dressed as schoolboys, and when it was time for the hymn, the sheer volume of rich, masculine sound was over-whelming. At a stroke, the world of Primary School was annihilated. This was the real thing, like joining your regiment.

After Assembly, we were led away to a row of classrooms, and divided up into forms according to a typed list. Toddy and I were both in 1B, but the rule about sitting in alphabetical order swept us apart into opposite corners.

Ours was the middle slice of an old Victorian schoolroom cut into three by slatted wooden shutters that rolled up and down like the front of a fishmonger's. The windows were tall and narrow, with iron bars across them to discourage thoughts of escape, and along the side walls ran a dado of glazed brown lavatory tiles, which together with the high, vaulted ceiling ensured a rich and fruity echo.

In the front corner, opposite the door, the teacher's table stood on a small raised platform; beside it was a hefty blackboard with its pegs securely chained to the easel for the better avoidance of sabotage. Our own desks were in long, solid rows supported on cast-iron pillars screwed to the floor, with movable benches behind them. The wood of the desk lids was gouged and scored all over with inscriptions ancient and modern, some of them dating back to before the First World War. Here at least were the signs of antiquity so unaccountably missing from the hall.

But it was a moot point which of the two was older, our class-room or our form teacher. Conferring later, we decided that Mr Hedger must be at least ninety. He had short white hair brushed forwards over his forehead, and a vast straggling white moustache that was stained a dirty yellow at the tips. He wore black boots and a suit of brown herring-bone tweed, with a matching cap for out of doors. Above his starched collar, his throat and neck were as creased and leathery as a turtle's.

His eyes looked rheumy, but he could read the mischief in a boy's mind and kill it dead with a single warning look. It was just as well. On the table in front of him stood a large rectangular box covered in black leatherette. Connected to this by a length of ma-roon twin-flex was a telephone earpiece on a springy metal band. Once we were all seated in order, he put on the headset, clipped a microphone to his coat lapel, and crouched intently over the box as if he was picking up signals from Occupied France.

For several minutes, we watched in silent amazement, while

he turned the grooved bakelite knobs this way and that, and re-settled the headset over his huge, flat ear. Having adjusted every-thing to his satisfaction, he pointed to the boy who was sitting next to me at the start of the front row and demanded brusquely, 'Name?'

'Anderson, sir.'

He nodded, then pointed at Toddy in the far corner.

'Whitman, sir.'

'Speak up.'

'Whitman, sir.'

'Wickham?' He consulted the form list, looking slightly puz-zled.

'No sir. Whitman.'

The knobs were readjusted. 'Again?'

Toddy's voice was getting a desperate edge to it. '*Whitman*, sir.' The sound echoed round and round the room.

'Again?'

'Whitman, sir.' Toddy was practically in tears. 'Whit Man.'

At last, a grim smile of satisfaction flickered across Mr Hedger's face. 'A poet, then,' he commented drily, and withdrawing a single sheet from amongst his papers, he began to dictate our timetable.

Finding a different room for every lesson was an even more de-moralising experience than our first encounter with Mr Hedger's deaf aid. 'You can't miss it,' people would breezily assert, as they sent us off to wander folornly round the corridors for the next ten or fifteen minutes.

Latin, our last period of the morning, began with a folk mi-gration of positively epic proportions. As we finally hove in sight, our teacher was standing in the doorway glowering at his watch. 'Classes arriving late,' he announced querulously, 'will make up the time in the dinner hour.'

'Please, sir, we got lost,' somebody said.

'Lost?' He seemed to take it as a personal insult.

He was a little rat-faced man in a clerical collar. It was odd, finding a reverend in a classroom; you wondered what he was do-ing there, instead of looking after his church.

Once we were all in our places, I glanced up and found him standing close in front of me, his hands clasped neatly behind his back. He stared at me for some time with evident displeasure, sway-ing hypnotically to and fro like a cobra, rising up on his toes and then dropping his heels to the floor again. At last, he moistened his lips and said icily, 'Where is it?'

'What, sir?'

'You know perfectly well.'

'No, sir.'

He tilted his head back, and stared at me down his nose, his chin jutting forward imperiously. After ten or fifteen seconds he said, 'What is your name?'

'Alan Carey, sir.'

'Very well, Carey. What have the others got that you haven't?'

It didn't seem like the time or place to be discussing it. I shouldn't have minded telling Toddy after a day or two, but I couldn't see why I should have to submit to a public interrogation.

'Well?'

'I don't know, sir.' Self-Defence for Schoolboys, Chapter One.

'Don't pretend to be an imbecile. I shall ask you once again, and this time I expect you to answer me. What have the others got that you haven't?'

I said nothing, and stared hard at my desk again, fixing my gaze on one particular groove in the wood.

'Stand up.'

This was quite difficult, because there were four of us sitting on the same bench. I couldn't push it back, so I clambered awkwardly over it, one leg at a time, and stood behind it.

'Now, Carey,' he said, his voice sharp as a razor blade. 'For the last time. What haven't you got?'

In desperation, I fixed my eyes on the groove; but they were beginning to blur over.

'Answer me.'

It was no good. I couldn't hold out any longer. 'Parents, sir,' I said.

A terrible silence covered the whole earth. At last he said, 'Your personal circumstances are not of the slightest concern to me. Or to anyone else in this room,' he added, raking each row of desks with a bleak stare. 'But I insist on everyone attending my lessons properly dressed. Where is your tie?'

'I haven't got one, sir.'

'So I can see. Where is it?'

'I haven't got one, sir.'

'You left it at home, I suppose?'

'I haven't got one, sir.' How many more times did I have to say it?

'Why not?'

'They didn't give me one, sir.'

'"They"? Who are "they"?'

'I don't know, sir.'

'You can't go through life expecting to have everything done for you. When you're accepted for a place here, you're under an obligation to equip yourself with the correct uniform, and that includes a tie. This isn't a Central School,' he spat the words out with contempt, 'it's an ancient and venerable foundation, and no boy has a right to be here unless he comes properly dressed.'

He stepped back, as if confident that the ghost of Bishop Inglis would shortly rise through the floor to pronounce a formal excommunication. When this failed to happen, he went on, 'You will report to me at the Common Room at half past one, wearing a school uniform tie. Is that clear?'

'Yes, sir.'

Actually, it was touch and go whether I'd still be there by that time. For two pins I'd have walked out during the dinner hour, and headed north on the first lorry that stopped for me – an idea I didn't so much abandon as postpone. But at twenty-five past one, I made my way to the Common Room corridor wearing Toddy's tie, and joined a line of boys who were waiting side by side along the wall. The boy ahead of me looked huge, and so did the one who arrived next. Standing between them was like riding a bike between two double-decker buses; any moment, you could be squashed flat without them even noticing.

They swapped glances over my head. 'First day?' one of them asked, looking down at me.

I nodded.

'You're soon in trouble, then. Who sent for you?'

'The Latin teacher.'

'Which one?'

'A reverend.'

The other boy gave a sardonic laugh. 'Evans. What an arsehole.'

'Wants shagging with the rough end of a pineapple,' the first boy said.

The Common Room door opened, and the Reverend Evans appeared. Several boys stepped forward from the line, so I tagged on behind them. When it was my turn, he looked me up and down as if he didn't recognise me.

'You are...?'

'Carey, sir.'

'Why are you here?'

'You told me to come wearing a tie, sir.'

He glanced down at my collar, and nodded. 'So you had one all along. I thought as much. In future, please make sure you wear it. And Carey...'

'Sir?'

'At Bishop Inglis, we demand the same high standards from everybody, whatever their personal circumstances.' He paused, as if expecting an answer. 'Do you hear me?'

'Yes, sir.'

As I was walking away, looking fairly hard at my feet, I heard my name called.

'Oi. Carey.' It was the same boys as before. One of them reached out to rumple my hair, and turning towards the Common Room, directed a vigorous V sign at the Reverend Evans's back. 'Have that on me,' he said.

When four o'clock finally came, Toddy was off in a great rush; his mother was coming to fetch him in the car. But several minutes later, as I left for the station, he and his brother were still standing at the gate. I wouldn't have stopped, only I noticed him pointing me out, and then they both looked in my direction as if they expected me to join them.

'Wotcher,' Toddy said. 'I was telling Mike about you and Evans.'

'Oh.' I didn't see any point in discussing it.

You could tell they were brothers, but Mike was slimmer, and dark instead of fair. I guessed he was in the third form. Maybe the fourth.

He looked me over without much interest. 'Evans is a shit,' he said, disdainfully. 'First time with a new class, he always picks on a perfectly decent kid and scorches him to a cinder.'

'Why?' said Toddy.

'Gives him a thrill, I suppose. What he really likes is to make them cry, and then jeer at them for it.'

'So how long are we stuck with him?' I asked.

'Only a year. Then you'll change.'

'Thank God for that,' said Toddy.

It was nearly five by the time I got back to Barton House. Ocky was kicking a ball about in the road and looking rather subdued. When I asked him how he'd got on at Mount Street, he said, vaguely, 'It's big. You keep getting lost.'

I nodded. 'Same here.' To keep the conversation going, I added,

'All our teachers wear gowns.'

'What, dressing gowns?'

'No, twerp. Black things. Like in pictures.'

He shrugged. 'What did you expect? Toff school, toff teachers.'

I thought about kicking his shins, but I couldn't be bothered. In any case, he jerked his thumb at the front door and told me, 'Wilkie wants you.'

'Now?'

'He said, as soon as you get in.'

When I poked my head round the door of the office, Wilkie looked up sharply.

'I understand you've been begging in the street,' he said.

'No.'

'Mr Pond came to see me. He says you stopped him outside the newsagents and asked for money.'

'I never. I asked him what I should do. They wouldn't let me get on the train.'

'Didn't you have your ticket?'

'Yes, but it's no good. I explained like you said, only they wouldn't listen.'

'Why didn't you telephone me from the station, instead of pestering other people?'

'Telephone?' I was nonplussed. All I knew about telephone boxes was how to get tuppence for nothing. He might as well have said, why didn't I sell my clothes, or force my way past the ticket inspector at pistol point.

We stared at each other in mutual accusation.

'What shall I do in the morning?' I said.

'About what?'

'About my ticket.'

With lofty restraint, he drew a sheet of official headed paper onto the blotter, and unscrewed the top from his fountain pen.

To Whom It May Concern.

I couldn't read the rest from where I was standing, but I could guess the drift from the look on his face and the whole set of his body.

Alan George Carey: Owing to the fact that this boy is an imbecile, incapable of explaining himself or sorting out the smallest difficulty on his own, I, who have a great many more important things to be doing, am obliged to waste my valuable time...etc., etc.

He laid the sheet face down on the blotter, pressing it firmly with three precise strokes of his hand; the top, the middle, the bottom. Without re-reading it, he folded the page into four and held it out to me.

'That should do for the time being,' he said.

The moment I left the room, I remembered about the tie; but I wasn't going back for another note. Perhaps the same one would do. Any enquiries, kindly refer to the undersigned.

After tea, Jacko sent for me. He hadn't forgotten that I was still due for a little chat. This time, I was invited to sit down, which made escape more difficult. As usual, he was smoking, so I kept my hands well out of his reach.

'Is there anything you'd like to ask me?' he said with an expansive gesture, placing a lifetime's experience at my disposal.

I shrugged. 'Not really.' You can't ask questions when you don't even speak the language.

He raised his eyebrows in gentle disbelief. 'What, nothing at all?'

Something was obviously called for, if only to get him off my back. 'Is it true about Lawrence of Arabia?' I said. It was the only thing that occurred to me.

His head jerked round in surprise. 'Is what true?'

'Miss Carswell says you knew him.'

'Ah.' He sounded relieved. For a moment or two he stared vaguely out of the window, as if he needed time to think of an answer. 'For a brief period, our respective latitudes and longitudes happened to coincide. I wouldn't say more than that. Why do you ask?'

'He was in our reading book.'

'At your old school?'

'Yes. Don Bradman was in it too. When he was a boy, he used to hit a golf ball against the side of the house with a cricket stump for hours and hours, just for the practice.'

Jacko nodded, distantly. 'I can imagine. And your new school, what about that?'

'I wish I could go to Mount Street.'

'What on earth do you mean?'

'I'm not cut out for Latin and things like that. Anyway, they don't want me at Bishop Inglis.'

'I'm sure that isn't true.'

'Oh, yes. One of the teachers told me I'd no right to be there.'

He leant forward, his hands clasped on his knees. 'Look, too many things have been happening to you all at once. It's not surprising you feel like a cork on the water. But what do corks do?'

I thought about it. 'Stop up bottles?'

'They float, Alan. Whatever else may happen, they float. They don't sink. All right?'

I nodded.

'Any time you're bothered about your school work, let me know. I'll help you.' He reached out, brushing his fingers lightly against my cheek. 'And try not to worry. You're not a bad little chap; I'm sure we'll manage to make something of you.'

I didn't especially fancy being anyone's raw material, certainly not Jacko's. All the same, I was intrigued to think I actually knew someone who'd known someone whose name was printed in books.

Next morning, the awkward ticket collector was back on duty. 'You again?' he said.

I showed him my note. He read it all through several times, and handed it back without a word, jerking his head reluctantly towards the platform.

While I was waiting for the train, I read all the posters very thoroughly, so as not to think about Latin and the Rev Ev. As it happened, though, the situation resolved itself in a totally unexpected fashion. When I got to school, Toddy was waiting for me in the yard. Rather sheepishly, he pulled a crumpled paper bag from his pocket and held it out to me.

I looked at him in surprise. 'What is it?'

He seemed embarrassed. 'We just thought... In case you got into trouble again.'

Cautiously, I looked inside. Coiled up at the bottom was a Bishop Inglis tie.

'It's an old one of Mike's,' he said. 'He was sick all over it, so Mum got him another.'

I didn't know what to say.

'It's been washed,' he added hastily.

I took the tie out of the bag and put it on. The smaller end was a bit stained, but I tucked it inside my shirt, and it hardly showed.

'You've saved my life, Toddy. It was really decent of you to think of it.'

'Oh,' he said, looking away, 'it wasn't my idea. It was Mike's.'

5

Between them, lessons with Mr Hedger and the Rev Ev accounted for almost half our timetable, so I spent my early days at Bishop Inglis in a state of permanent apprehension.

The Rev Ev was a great believer in tests; nasty, nit-picking little affairs at the start of every Latin and Scripture lesson. They were done on tiny scraps of paper which he manufactured by cutting up old envelopes. The pass mark was four out of ten, otherwise you had to write out so many verses from the Bible, or a page of *Kennedy's Latin Primer* – a constipated, mean little book, whose cover I should recognise to this day at a hundred paces.

Mr Hedger also went in for tests – History seemed to consist of little else – but his speciality was terrorism by poetry. Every week, he set us twenty or thirty lines to learn for homework, and the following morning we spent the entire lesson repeating them on demand as he called our names. You had to be ready to take over without warning in the middle of a verse, or even the middle of a line, and there was no knowing how long your turn would last.

It was a dreadful business. Mr Hedger sat at his table with the headphone on and the volume control turned up to maximum. In front of him was the Form List and the Poetry book. When everything was arranged to his satisfaction, he would solemnly shoot his cuffs and pick up a ruler.

'Thompson.'

'All the world's a stage the men and women...'

'No.' Down came the ruler against the table top.

'All the world's a stage... and all the men and women in it...'

'No.'

'And all the men and women... men and women... are...'

'See me afterwards. Anderson.'

'And all the men and women merely players they have their exits and their entrances and one man in his time – '

'Lang.'

'Plays many parts his acts – '

'Carpenter.'

'Being seven ages – '

And so it would go on. As soon as you reached the end of the last line you simply started again at the beginning. The odd lapse was overlooked so long as you corrected yourself, but if you floundered seriously or dried up altogether you were condemned to recite the whole piece at a quarter to nine the following morning. Homework was a thing barely countenanced at Barton House, so it looked as if these early-day appointments were set to become a regular fixture.

To counteract the tedium and the constant sense of anxiety, I clung to the thought that being at Bishop Inglis was actually a sign of normality. I'd still have been going there even if Gran hadn't died. At Barton House, on the other hand, normality was conspicuously absent.

At breakfast time my second or third Sunday, there was no food in sight, and no sign of the Wilkies. We sat at table for ten or fifteen minutes, with nothing to do but rattle the cutlery and wait for something to happen. After a very long time indeed, Jacko appeared with the trolley, and a look on his face that disclaimed any responsibility for what we were about to receive. Stirring the porridge pan with a ladle, he announced grimly, 'All right, Animals; this is breakfast.'

As he filled our bowls, we received them in stunned silence. He seemed to be giving us nothing but dirty water with a few coarse husks drifting about on the surface.

'Oh Gawd!' somebody said. 'Hurly's Brahms and Liszt again.'

We sat down to investigate the cloudy grey liquid. I tasted a little; it was bitter and slightly salty. Cautiously, Ocky lowered his spoon beneath the surface and dredged up a small collection of sodden granules which had sunk to the bottom. He sniffed them suspiciously, and tested one of them between his teeth; it was as hard as lead shot, and when he flicked it clear of his fingers, it skittered off the table and onto the floor.

Incredulous, we turned to look at Jacko. 'If you don't want it,' he said, 'you can tip it back.'

By this time, angry voices could be heard approaching along the corridor. All of a sudden, Mrs Wilkie rushed in with her hands over her ears, pursued by Hurly brandishing a potato masher. They made their way all round the room and out again, with Hurly shouting, 'Have I not told you a dozen times already? It wouldn't have happened if you didn't go feeding the childer on fuckin horse oats.'

'Jesus!' said Snap, who was sitting next to me.

'Surely she'll get the sack?' I asked.

'Don't be daft,' he said. 'Who else would work here?'

Even with less drama and a fuller breakfast, Sundays were apt to be pretty demoralising. At around a quarter to ten, Jacko or one of the Wilkies would marshal us into a ragged crocodile for the walk to Church. On the journey, which took us through one of the better neighbourhoods, we generally came under fire from a fat-faced boy with a pushed up nose who sat at an upstairs window armed with a catapult. He went to a posh school on the other side of the railway line, and seemed to think it gave him the right to use us for target practice. Our plans for retaliation, if ever we managed to catch him, were detailed and obscene.

In the church itself, we always sat in a side aisle, separated from the rest of the congregation by a thick coloured rope with brass hooks on the end, which was looped across the ends of our pews. Adults generally ignored us, but children sitting with their parents kept glancing in our direction with a sort of fascinated horror, as if they were visiting the reptile house at the zoo.

The Reverend Hawkhurst, who took the services, had one of the oddest speech impediments ever encountered, a total inability to pronounce the letter W. Instead, he would make an extraordinary gasping sound, as if someone had punched him in the guts. 'Our Father, UHHich art in Heaven...' Most weekends, Joe and Snap ran a ha'penny sweep on how many times he'd do it, so we all kept a careful tally.

Afterwards, in the churchyard, as we waited to walk home, we were often accosted by a strange old lady, who was never seen on any other occasion, and who turned out, incredibly, to be Wilkie's mother. Her face was all seamed and sunk in like a last year's potato, and her going-to-church outfit included one of those dreadful fox furs that was virtually the complete animal. When she engaged you in conversation, it was impossible to escape the hypnotic stare of its malevolent little eyes.

'You do believe in the love of God, don't you, Alan?' she would say.

'Oh yes, miss, definitely.'

A moment's hesitation, and the fox would have had your balls off.

On Sunday afternoons you could go visiting, if you were lucky enough to get invited. One time, I went to Barry Anderson's. I liked him a lot, but the visit wasn't a success; tea was eaten in ten degrees of frost, and they didn't ask me again. Mrs A was a bit in the twin-set and pearls direction, so I probably didn't come up to scratch. Or perhaps she'd been grilling Barry about the stains on his pyjamas, and found out it was me who told him how.

'Why don't you come to ours?' Toddy said, when I mentioned about the Andersons. We looked at one of the street maps they sold in his father's shops, and it turned out that his house was only a bus ride away.

I was very nervous about it in case his parents didn't like me. But when I arrived, Mrs Whitman looked up from her knitting, and said 'Hallo, love,' as if I belonged there. Mr Whitman I wasn't so sure about. He was a big, no-nonsense man, who owned this chain of stationer's shops all round the district, and a printing works as well. He looked me over as if I'd come for a job, and wasn't likely to get it. But later, when Toddy and I were kicking a ball about in the road, he came out to work in the front garden, and when the ball flew over the fence he picked it up and handed it back to me with a quick, friendly nod, as if to say, 'You'll do'.

Their house was comfortable and nicely furnished, but it wasn't the sort of place where you daren't sit down for fear of dirtying the chairs. Upstairs, as well as the main bedroom and the one which Toddy shared with Mike, there was a little extra one at the back which they called the Radio Room. Mike and his father used it, but Toddy said it would be all right to look inside. There was a workbench with electrical instruments on it, and rows of shelving stacked with valves and boxes and half dismantled wireless sets. Several big printed charts had been fixed to the walls.

'What do they do in there?' I asked.

Toddy shrugged. 'Build radio sets.'

'Do they broadcast?'

'Good God, no! They mess about with loudspeakers and soldering irons; that sort of thing.'

When it was time for tea, I started to feel nervous again. But Mrs Whitman said, 'Just wash your hands, love, before you come to the table. Dry them on this, look.' And that was the secret. You knew exactly what was expected of you, instead of having to guess and then getting looked at as if you were something the dog had done on the carpet.

The Whitman family seemed completely at ease with one another. Not like me and Gran. As we all sat round the kitchen table chatting after tea, I had the curious feeling that instead of it being my first visit, I'd been there dozens of times before. I even told them about Mackenzie's, and the shop in Barnes, although I hadn't meant to.

On the kitchen wall next to the dresser was a cork noticeboard with snapshots pinned all over it. Mike and Toddy, much younger, riding a bike in the garden; somebody's birthday party; a family group, taken at the swimming baths. For some reason, the sight of them filled me with a strange yearning that I couldn't exactly put a name to. It was as if I ought to have been in the photos too, and couldn't think why I wasn't. I thought Toddy was very lucky.

'What's the matter?' Mike said, all of a sudden.

I hadn't realised anybody was watching me. 'Nothing. I was just... looking at your pictures.'

Leaving was such a wrench that I almost wished I'd never gone there in the first place. No point reminding yourself of things best forgotten.

But when I was fetching my coat from the hall, Mrs Whitman followed me out. 'You must come again, Alan,' she said. 'Soon.' Glancing quickly round to make sure we were still alone, she added, 'Toddy knows you can't ask him back, so there's no need to feel bad about it.' And she slipped me a couple of barley sugars to eat on the way home.

At Barton House, brush and comb were superfluous. Once a month, our hair was cut by a visiting barber, who mowed it down with the clippers to a uniform quarter-inch length all over, and the little he left us with was maintenance-free.

Having missed his August visit, I first encountered Sam Barnett one Friday night towards the end of September. He was a bitter, wizened little man, with the pinched remains of a roll-up drooping permanently from the left-hand corner of his mouth. According to Snap, he was a Communist.

As I perched awkwardly on the stool, he flicked the sheet round me with obvious irritation. 'I oughter get paid double for new boys,' he said.

Grievances were his staple topic of conversation. 'Waste of a skilled man, this,' he grumbled, as he set to work. 'Had me own place once, three people under me. Hot and cold in the basins, bevelled mirrors, the lot. Where's it all gone, eh? Where's it all gone?'

'Were you bombed out?'

Ignoring the question, he flicked a handful of cut hair away with a gesture of mild distaste. 'Kids nowadays. Everything done for you. At your age, I was earning my own living.'

'Better than going to school.'

He made a contemptuous little noise. 'What would you know

about it? Keep still.'

After shearing away resentfully for nearly a minute, he went on, 'Man like me shouldn't be working at all. Not in my condition.'

'Why? Aren't you well?'

He gestured vaguely towards his middle. 'Mass of scars. Make you sick to look at it.' Standing back for a moment, he surveyed me with a sort of impersonal hostility. 'Listen,' he said. 'A grown man's supposed to have fifty foot of toobing in him, if it was laid out end to end. What d'you reckon I've got, then? Go on, have a guess.'

'Forty?' I ventured.

He gave a bitter laugh. 'Twenty. And you ask me if I'm ill.'

'What happened to all the rest?'

'Bin took,' he said, but declined to elaborate.

Having by now reduced my hair to the regulation length, he whipped the sheet away and jerked his head towards the communicating door. 'In there,' he said.

Sitting in the next room was Mrs Wilkie, equipped with a bug rake and a bowl of disinfectant. 'I know they do you at school,' she said. 'But we like to be on the safe side.'

As I quickly discovered, a Sam Barnett haircut marked you out as a Barton boy throughout the neighbourhood. At dinner time the next day, when I was walking home from the Rec, I saw a couple of boys I didn't know coming towards me. As the gap between us narrowed, I noticed them glance significantly at each other. Next thing I knew, they had me spreadeagled against the wall of the clothing factory with my wrists held and my feet pinned down securely under theirs.

'Barton oik,' said one of them, leering into my face, and bringing his knee up sharply between my legs. The other produced a pocket knife and started to reach for my braces buttons. 'Oik, oik, oik,' he repeated. They had pink caps and posh accents. The boy with the knife was fat, and his piggish face looked vaguely familiar.

I struggled to break free, but couldn't manage it. Fixing my gaze on a spot six feet behind their heads, I grinned as if in relief, and said, 'Wotcher, Paul. You take the fat one.' Amazingly, they fell for it. Glancing behind them, they slackened their grip enough for me to duck down and butt my way out between them. I landed one good kick on the fat boy's ankle, and turned to deal with his friend. But apparently, this part wasn't in the script. Without more ado, they made off up the road and took the path that ran alongside Mr Pond's; it led to the footbridge over the railway. At the last moment, when they were almost out of sight, they looked back at me and the pig-faced one shouted, 'We'll get you, Barton oik. Just wait till tomorrow.' I realised then that he was the boy with the catapult.

'Bloody cheek,' said Ocky, when I mentioned the pink caps. 'They're supposed to stay their own side of the bridge.'

'Who are they, anyway?'

He made a sour face. 'St Andrew's. They get school Saturday mornings. Serve the buggers right.'

'Do we often get trouble with them, then?' The 'we' was experimental, and lacked conviction.

He shook his head. 'Not on our own patch. Lucky for them you was on your own.'

Next day, as we passed the pig boy's house on our way to church, I thought we'd be sitting ducks as usual; but for once, his bedroom window was closed.

The Whitmans had asked me round again that afternoon, and when I arrived they pretended not to know me because of the haircut. Toddy practically choked himself with laughing, but Mike was intrigued. 'Hallo, Fuzzypeg,' he said, and ran his hand over the top of my head as if he was stroking a cat.

'Get off!' I told him, ducking away. I hated being handled.

He grinned, and stood back to judge the effect better. After a moment or two, he said, 'It suits you, though. Seriously. If you ask me, it's actually rather...' He shrugged, suddenly at a loss, and left the sentence in mid-air.

At Bishop Inglis on Monday morning, the new look was generally reckoned to be hilarious. But the Rev Ev considered it an affront to decency. At one point during the morning, I was sent round all the classrooms with a message, and had the misfortune to find him teaching a fifth form. He stared at me with supercilious disdain as I walked nervously across the room towards him, sweating under the gaze of thirty seniors whose broad shoulders dwarfed their desks into doll's furniture. When I held out my piece of paper, he ignored it. 'Are you a member of this school?' he enquired.

'Yes, sir.'

'You amaze me. I thought you'd probably wandered in from the street.' He glanced round at the class, and collected a few dutiful titters. 'Be that as it may,' he went on, 'I don't like having my lessons disturbed by little boys.'

'It's a message, sir. I was told to bring it.'

'Indeed? What is your name?'

'Carey, sir.'

'Surely it ought to be Lepidus?' He glanced at the class again with a slimy smile.

'No, sir. Carey, sir.'

'Do you know who Lepidus was?' he said, taking the paper at last, and running his eye over it condescendingly.

I stared as hard as I could at the floor beneath his feet. 'No, sir.' I was uncomfortably aware of a very faint hissing noise, coming from somewhere towards the back of the room. It was all I needed. The Rev Ev was bad enough on his own, without his fifth formers giving me the bird.

'In Shakespeare's *Julius Caesar*...' His head snapped round to face the class again, and the hissing immediately stopped. 'In Shakespeare's *Julius Caesar,* Mark Antony says of Lepidus: This is a slight, unmeritable man, meet to be sent on errands.' I was still looking down at the floor, but I could sense the smirk on his face. 'Rather appropriate, don't you think? Though I fancy even a Roman would have managed a more respectable head of hair than yours.'

By this time, the hissing was gradually being overlaid by some sort of softly whispered chant. Whatever they were saying about me, it had two syllables and was followed by three taps of a shoe sole against the floor.

'Have you ever read *Julius Caesar*, Carey?'

'No, sir.'

The chant grew louder, and more insistent. All I could make out was the vowel sounds: oo-ee, tap tap tap; oo-ee, tap tap tap. Unable to ignore it, the Rev Ev looked round at the class, his eyebrows raised in challenge. The chant died down again.

Please, God, I prayed, let this come to an end and I swear I will go for a whole week without doing it.

The Rev Ev addressed me again. 'It is a play. By Shakespeare. I take it even you have heard of Shakespeare?'

'Yes, sir.' The chant began again, so I upped my offer. Two weeks.

'Suppose you tell us who he was, then?'

'A play-writer, sir.'

'One does not say "play-writer". What does one say?'

'I don't know, sir.'

The chant was now being taken up all round the room. Suddenly, for the first time, I could make out what they were saying. 'Bul-ly,' tap tap tap; 'Bul-ly', tap tap tap.

Incredulous, I raised my head a little, and recognised in the back row the boys who had queued beside me outside the Common Room.

'One says "play*wright*".' The Rev Ev was starting to look distinctly red in the face. 'However, perhaps we'd better acquaint ourselves with the message which Lepidus has brought us.' As he looked down at the paper, the chant began again, softly, but absolutely distinct. 'Bul-*ly*', tap tap tap.

The Rev Ev quickly ticked his initials and room number at the bottom of the note, and handed it back to me. 'Be off with you,' he said. 'You've wasted quite enough of our time already.'

I fled.

But outside in the corridor, as I leant against the wall for a moment to stop my knees from shaking, I began to think that possibly, after all, the world would just about do.

6

At Barton House, it didn't pay to be seen hanging around on Saturday mornings as if you had nothing to occupy yourself with.

'I'd find a regular job if I was you,' said Ronnie. 'Quick as you can.'

After a two-hour stint of extra spud-bashing, I didn't need much convincing; and a surreptitious peep through the workshop window was enough to settle the matter.

The following Saturday, when I finally summoned up courage to knock at the door and poke my head inside, Mr Pond was bending over the stove, coaxing it back to life after the night. A thin haze of coke fumes was rising around his head, and the air was rich with the smell of tallow and lubricating oil.

'Come for a look round?' he said.

'Please. If you wouldn't mind.'

On the right-hand side of the hut stood a row of machines bolted to the floor and driven by leather belts from an overhead shaft. When the stove was drawing properly, Mr Pond switched on the big electric motor and let me throw the lever that set the lathe running. As the belts went round, there was a rhythmic clicking sound from the metal fasteners hitting the drive pulleys and I knew at once with an absolute certainty that I had found my spiritual home.

'I'm doing a run of these,' he said, scooping a handful of bright little metal parts from a box, and letting them trickle back between his fingers.

I fell in love with them, without even knowing what they were. 'Can I?' I said, my hand poised over the box.

He nodded, so I picked up a couple of specimens for a closer look. 'Whatever are they?'

'Just terminals. Nothing very exciting.'

In the far corner by the stove there was a little nook with a gas ring and a sink with running water. In the opposite corner, behind a low partition, was the Office; it consisted of little more than a table, a stack of wire trays full of papers, a shelf stuffed with files, and some oil-spotted ledgers with marbled covers and well-worn leather spines. At the front of the table stood a big typewriter with a long roll of paper feeding into it. It was much the same as a regular office Remington, but the print was huge, about half an inch high, for making box labels.

Between the sink and the Office stood a series of racks with strips of steel and brass in them of various sizes and shapes – angle, flat, round, square, hexagon. Some of the spaces were almost empty.

'It's a job, these days, getting the stock,' Mr Pond said. 'You have to make do with whatever they send.'

Along the left-hand side, which faced towards Barton, were benches with more machines on them. The rest of the floor space was stacked to waist height with crates and boxes, and there were shelves everywhere, crammed with hundreds and hundreds of old tobacco tins full of screws, nuts, washers, ball bearings, and countless miscellaneous oddments.

Mr Pond slipped his watch out of his waistcoat pocket and checked it against the clock on the Office wall. 'Time I got to work,' he said. 'Was there anything else you wanted?'

So I asked straight out if there was any chance of a job.

He shook his head. 'I've got a boy already. He'll be here any minute.'

'Couldn't you do with another?'

'No. You'd only muck about together and waste each other's time.'

'We wouldn't. Honest.'

'You mightn't mean to, but you would. When I was a lad, the farmers had a very true saying: One boy is one boy; but two boys is half a boy, and three boys is no boys at all. In any case,' he went on, 'I need a special kind of boy, and it takes a long while to train them.'

'I could sweep up, clean the windows; things like that. And watch.'

But Mr Pond was not to be persuaded. 'I'm sorry, Alan. I don't promise what I can't deliver. I've nothing to offer you.'

'Nothing at all? I'd really like to learn. Really and truly.'

He eased his cap back, and scratched at his hairline with his thumbnail. 'I'll keep you in mind,' he said. 'That's the best I can do.'

So I tried asking at some of the local shops. It seemed the next best thing. Strictly speaking, I must have been under age, but nobody seemed to bother. With a Grammar School uniform, and previous experience to recommend me, I twice made it as far as the back office. But thanks to Sam Barnett, that was the end of it. The moment I took my cap off, people looked round anxiously in case the till had been left open. 'Sorry, we don't take Barton boys.'

There was said to be money in horse manure, so another Saturday, complete with bucket and shovel, I set off in pursuit of the United Dairies. But the milkman had his sons with him, and I was rapidly put to flight. Rights in the Express Dairy's horse were uncontested, but proved to be worthless, so the scope for becoming a manure baron seemed extremely limited. You could make more money with less effort by doing the phone boxes. It was amazing how many people forgot to claim their money back when they couldn't get through. Snap reckoned they didn't like pressing Button B because of the noise it made, a loud, portentous ticking, like the prelude to an immense explosion.

As a stop-gap, Ronnie got me a morning's work helping him dig over one of the allotments on his list. I was glad, because I enjoyed his company and I needed the money; but we both knew within half an hour that I shouldn't be any use to him.

Like most beginners, I tried to work too quickly.

'Go steady,' he said, pausing for a moment, and resting on his spade. 'You'll be knackered in ten minutes at that rate.'

He dug with the calm unhurried rhythm of long practice, and was clearly set to keep going the whole morning. I envied his stamina and expertise, knowing I could never match them. To me, soil was something you scraped off your boots, an alien element to be attacked and disposed of; whereas to Ronnie it was a trusted friend, strong, and resourceful, but in need of elaborate grooming like a horse.

By dinner time, my patch of ground looked ravaged rather

than cultivated, as if wild animals had fought all over it; but Ronnie's had a rugged, satisfying beauty which made it good to look at although there was nothing to see but the bare earth.

Clearly, I wasn't cut out for horticulture; but he accepted my inadequacy without the slightest hint of scorn or criticism, and we walked home in amicable silence. That was the thing about Ronnie. He never talked much, but he made you feel it was all right to be the person you were.

The following Saturday, as I was slipping discreetly away from the house, the Reverend Hawkhurst drew up outside in a battered estate car.

'Ah!' he said, with an ingratiating smile. 'How very kind. You've come to help me unload.' He had a way of gripping you by the arm, which I didn't care for. I suppose he thought he was reaching out to people.

The back of the car was crammed full of big cardboard boxes, inefficiently tied round with string. Mrs Wilkie appeared while I was still struggling to manoeuvre them into the hall, and before I could think of a suitable excuse, I found myself conscripted to lug the whole lot upstairs and help her sort through the contents. It looked like being a morning's work.

Ocky leered at me from the Club Room door. 'You're doing a grand job,' he said.

In the corridor outside the Sewing Room, I undid the boxes and looked inside. They were full of old clothes, donated to us by the parishioners. Mrs Wilkie listed the items as I took them out, and between us we sorted them into piles along the wall, one for shirts, another for jerseys, and so on.

Several of the shirts were put on one side so that Mrs Dooley, who came in three days a week, could cut the sleeves off. All shirts at Barton were required to be short-sleeved, on the principle that your bare arms were cheaper to wash and didn't need ironing. If a long-sleeved shirt appeared on the premises it was given immediate surgery, and the spare material made into handkerchieves or saved for patching. The cuffs, minus the buttons, were used as polishing rags or dishcloths.

Before the woollens were taken into the Sewing Room, I had to arrange them over the back of a chair, one at a time, so that Mrs Wilkie could blast them with a Flit Gun. It was a job that seemed to appeal to her. Each time she forced the plunger along the yellow barrel, sending a cloud of droplets billowing up like smoke all round the garment, the corners of her mouth turned slightly upwards in a tiny secret smile, as if she enjoyed exterminating things.

Before long, the vapour was making my nose run.

'For Heaven's sake, stop sniffing,' she said. 'Haven't you got a hanky?'

It was downstairs, in my blazer pocket, so she sent me to fetch it. I'd taken the blazer off while I dealt with the boxes, and I knew for a certainty that I'd left it lying in the Club Room; but to my surprise there was no sign of it.

'You've taken your time,' she said, when I came back empty handed. My explanation failed to please her. 'You're supposed to be intelligent,' she snapped. 'It beats me why you can't look after your things.'

When the woollens had all been dealt with, I thought I might be allowed to go. But there were still the reject items to be stored away in the broom cupboard for use as cleaning rags, and before that, the buttons had to be salvaged. Mrs Wilkie handed me a pair of scissors. 'You may as well finish the job,' she said. 'And mind you pull all the bits of thread out before the buttons go in the tin.'

By the time I got downstairs again, it was nearly a quarter to twelve, and there was still no sign of my blazer; but ten or fifteen minutes later, I was amazed to see Ocky slip through the back entrance with something green and familiar bundled under his arm.

'You borrowed mine,' he said, when I confronted him.

'I didn't just walk off with it. Anyway, you hadn't even worn it, then. Mine's got all my things in the pockets.'

'Keep your hair on,' he said crossly. 'You won't find nothin missing.'

'But what did you want it for?'

He shrugged, and turned towards the door.

'Look! It's my blazer. Surely I'm entitled to know.'

He stood in the doorway, shaking his head slowly from side to side in exaggerated disbelief. 'Blimey,' he said at last, 'What a bleedin fuss you do make.'

At dinner, Mrs Wilkie noticed me wearing the blazer. 'You've found it, then,' she said.

'Someone had moved it.'

'You mean, you'd forgotten where you put it.'

As I left the dining room, Tom and Eddie appeared from nowhere, and frog-marched me out of the back door. When we were out of sight beyond the toilets, Eddie gripped my arms from behind and held me close in front of him.

'What did you tell her?' Tom demanded.

'About what?'

He punched me once in the stomach, and once in the mouth.

'Shit!' I said angrily. 'What was that for?'

At a signal from Tom, Eddie jerked his knee up under my backside, and then pushed me suddenly forward so that I fell to the ground. Before I had time to get up, one of his army boots came in hard against my ribs. As I rolled over, Tom lifted his heel directly above my face. I gritted my teeth, and waited for the crunch; but at the last minute, he seemed to change his mind. 'Next time,' he said.

He jerked his head at Eddie, and they started to walk away, leaving me on the ground. After a few steps, Tom looked back over his shoulder. 'Just a friendly warning,' he said.

It was lucky the toilets were close at hand.

When I emerged,Ocky was nowhere to be found. It was tea time before I could corner him and demand an explanation.

'Don't blame me,' he said. 'It wasn't my idea.'

'At least you can tell me what the hell's going on.'

'Work it out for yourself. You're the clever one.'

Whatever it was, the incident seemed to be over. But that night, Snap happened to find me alone in the washroom. 'If you know what's good for you,' he muttered hastily, 'you'll take care before you get into bed.'

'Meaning?'

He shrugged noncommittally, and resisted further questioning; but after the last time, I knew better than to ignore his warning. It was hard to know what to expect, though.

While I was undressing, Ocky sat with his back to me. But his casual disregard was a little too studied to be altogether convincing. I made as if to get into bed, but at the last minute I stripped the covers back. Halfway down was a dead rat, lying on its side with its tail stretched out behind it. I stood quite still, staring at it with a mixture of panic and disbelief, acutely aware of its little pink feet, so tiny, and so intricately formed. Amazing to think of all those miniature joints and muscles.

Within seconds, the word spread, and everyone gathered round for a closer look. Ocky stayed where he was, but a couple of times I saw him glancing over his shoulder.

'Any blood?' said Joe.

Snap leant forward and cautiously prodded the rat with an outstretched finger. 'No. Poisoned, by the look of it.'

'Watch out,' Joe said. 'There'll be fleas.'

'Not if it's dead.'

Ronnie pushed past the others and lifted the bottom window sash. Catching my eye, he jerked his head curtly towards the opening.

Everyone looked at me, and waited. My rat: my job to get rid of it. I felt a strong urge to run out of the room, but the crowd round the bed would have made it impossible. Taking a deep breath, I picked the rat up by its tail and moved slowly towards the window. I was afraid of the tail breaking if I wasn't careful, in which case the body would drop straight onto my pillow. With my head turned away, I reached up to the window, thrust my hand outside, and let go. Instinctively, we listened in silence, hoping to hear the body land; but there was no sound. One by one, we all relaxed again.

Ronnie shut the window, and pointed to the bed. 'You want to turn your sheets over,' he said. 'Less insanitary.'

Reluctantly, the crowd dispersed. While I was stripping the bedclothes, Jacko came in and wanted to know what was going on. 'Apple pie bed,' I muttered.

'Ah, well,' he said with a bleak smile, as he left the room again. 'Happens to the best of us.'

Ocky was lying with his eyes closed, pretending to be asleep. When I'd finished remaking the bed, I jumped on top of him, and forced his shoulders down hard against the mattress. 'Talk,' I said. 'Or do I have to take you apart one piece at a time?'

After a token attempt at wriggling free, he lay quite still. 'It wasn't me. Promise.'

'Tom?'

He shook his head.

'Eddie?'

No answer. Eddie, then.

'Why?'

Still no answer.

I increased the pressure. 'Why?'

'The blazer. You blabbed to Ma Wilkie.'

'I only said it had turned up again. She knew I'd lost it.'

'You shouldn't have told her in the first place.'

'She sent me to get it. How was I to know you'd pinched it?'

Ocky sighed, and shook his head in disgust. 'Don't you ever learn?'

'You still haven't told me why you took it.'

This time, he made a more determined effort to break free. 'None of your business.'

I could hear Jacko's footsteps returning, so I nipped smartly across to my own bed. As I was sliding reluctantly between the sheets, he popped his head round the door. 'All settled? Splendid. G'night, animals.'

'Well...?' I hissed to Ocky, through the darkness.

'Leave it, can't you?'

'Why should I?'

'Later, then. When we're on our own.'

I rolled over, then back again. Either way up, I didn't much care to think about which bits of me were closest to where the rat had been.

On the way down to breakfast, Ronnie said, 'Got any more out of Ocky?'

'Not yet. But I will.'

'Don't be too hard on him. He gets his arm twisted enough as it is.'

Afterwards, I manoeuvred Ocky into the washroom. He leant back against the wall with his hands behind him and his feet well forward, braced against the floor. Something about the look of him made it impossible to be angry. 'Well?' I said.

After a long silence, he gave a little shrug of resignation. 'Just doing a few shops, that's all. The usual. One of you keeps them talking, and the others get on with it.'

'But why the blazer?'

'The colour. If they ever twig, that's all they'll remember. Barton boy in a green blazer.'

'Yeah. In other words, me. Well, thanks a million, Ocky.'

He shook his head. 'No. Listen. You're in the clear. You was with Ma Wilkie.' He looked down at the floor. 'We'd all have been in the clear if you hadn't gone and loused it up. I don't wear a green blazer, and you can prove you wasn't there. Evidence unreliable; no case to answer.'

'Don't be daft. They'll just think we were both in it together.'

He leant his head back against the wall, his eyes closed, his breathing laboured and jerky. 'Look – it was a mistake; all right?'

'All right? Christ, Ocky! You frame me for shoplifting, you get me done over by Tom and Eddie, and a rat left in my bed, and you say "All right?"'

He sighed, and shook his head. 'You know your trouble? You think the whole world's like your stupid stuck-up Grammar School.

It wasn't my decision. I do whatever I have to, the same as anyone else.'

'So whose idea was it?'

'Do you have to have everything spelt out for you? Grow up, for God's sake, and get off my back.' He jerked himself upright, and made for the door.

'At least you could have warned me about the rat.'

He shrugged, as if it wouldn't have mattered to anyone normal, and walked out of the room. He was right, of course: being indignant only makes you ridiculous. But it bothered me that he could undermine my certainties so easily, while keeping his own intact.

Later in the day, when nobody was about, I slipped upstairs and went to work on Eddie's bed. The mattress was supported on a lattice of metal slats which were anchored to the bed-frame by flanged pegs. It was a simple matter to twist the pegs and lift the slats off, leaving the whole structure still in place but totally unsupported.

At bed time, we heard a muffled crash from the room opposite, followed by raucous laughter and a round of applause. A minute later, Eddie stormed into our bedroom half undressed, grabbed hold of me, and dragged me back with him across the corridor. Pointing to the wreckage, he shouted, 'Put that back together, you fuckin little turd.'

'Do it yourself. It's your bed.'

He tightened his grip and doubled me over the empty bed-frame, trying to force my head right down to the floor. The others were still laughing and jeering. 'Let him go, Eddie,' someone called. Eddie ignored them, and crushed me against the bed-frame with his knee. I knew I couldn't hold out much longer, but a crowd was beginning to gather in the doorway, and I wasn't going to yelp in front of so many people. Besides, the current of feeling seemed to be running my way.

Just as I was on the point of giving in, a voice cut sharply through the whistling and jeering. 'Let him go, Eddie.' It was Tom – of all people. Immediately, I felt the pressure slacken, and a moment later, I was able to break free.

When we were back in our own room, Ocky gave me an enigmatic look, as if he was wondering whether I'd worked things out yet. It occurred to me that Tom's intervention might have been Ocky's doing – though why Tom should listen to Ocky, I couldn't imagine. And another thing: Snap hadn't expected the rat; you could tell. Suppose he'd only acted as intermediary, and the warning had really been Ocky's all along? I didn't know what to believe any more; and I wondered – not for the first time – if I should ever manage to get the hang of things, and learn to think and feel like other people.

7

At half-term, just to be different, Bishop Inglis gave us the Monday and Tuesday off instead of the Friday and Monday like everyone else. So on Friday I was the only one from Barton going to school; and on Tuesday I had the house to myself.

The first part of the day I spent cleaning our outside toilets, a job which Mrs Wilkie liked to save for me to show that Grammar School boys were the same as everyone else.

It was a lengthy and malodorous business. To start with, you sluiced everything down using a long black rubber hose that had to be unwound from its drum and screwed to a standpipe in the yard. The resulting flood waters were supposed to flow into a central soakaway, but they needed prolonged encouragement with an old stiff broom. Then there were all the porcelain fittings to brush and sprinkle with bleach powder from big unlabelled tins supplied by the Council; and finally, you swabbed the concrete floor with a pungent brew of steaming hot water and Jeyes' fluid.

By the time I'd done all that, and wound up the hose again, I reckoned I was entitled to some refreshment, so I slung the mop and pail back in the cupboard, and made for the kitchen.

As I approached, I could hear raised voices and the sound of a door slamming. A sour-looking woman in green tweeds and thick stockings stormed past me in the corridor, cradling a sheaf of manilla document files against her arm. She was wearing brown brogues with tongues that folded right down over the laces, and a prim little felt hat like a caricature of a man's trilby.

'In the name of God!' Hurly shouted, as I opened the door. 'Will you get away to wherever you came from, and stop wastin the time of people with proper jobs to do.' Seeing me poised uncertainly in the doorway, she said, 'Ach! Is it yourself? I thought you were Fancy Madam back again.'

'In the green tweed? She's gone.'

'No loss,' Hurly said, positively steaming with fury, and

thumped her fist against the table. 'Would you credit it? Tellin me in my own kitchen I'm rollin the pastry out in the wrong direction. And her not even married!'

'Not married?'

'That one?' Hurly snorted contemptuously. 'She couldn't get a man if she walked naked into a barracks.'

There was a small brown teapot standing on the Aga. 'Any chance of a cuppa?' I asked hopefully.

Still quivering with rage, she poured me a mugful of tea and slopped some milk into it.

'Any biscuits?'

She waved me aside dismissively. 'Be off with you. Have you no place of your own to go to?'

So I carried the mug to the Club Room and switched the wireless on. To pass the time, I thought I might have a go at Snap's picture of the girl sitting on the chamber pot. As I cut out the hole for my fingers, 'Workers' Playtime' was finishing, so I hummed along with the signature tune.

I was just congratulating myself on a perfect result when the paper was suddenly whisked out of my hand.

'Where did you learn this dirty little trick?' It was Jacko.

I stared back at him in silence.

'You'd better come up to my flat. I think we need to have a bit of a talk.' He glanced at the picture again with obvious distaste. 'And you a Grammar School boy.'

In manifest disgrace, I followed him upstairs. Unlocking his front door, he stood aside to let me through, and then dropped the latch behind us, snapping the catch down firmly against intruders. He put the drawing on his desk, and pointed to it accusingly. 'Write your name on it. Works of art should always be signed. It increases their value.'

When I had done as he said, he folded the paper carefully and tucked it away in his wallet. Then he leant back in his chair with his hands clasped behind his neck, and looked me up and down. 'So. Interested in bottoms, are you?'

'No, Mr Crofting.'

'Not even,' he insisted, 'when the bottom in question is your own?'

He lit a cigarette, and glancing up quizzically to gauge my reaction, rested it carefully in the ash tray. 'We wouldn't want any accidents,' he said, baring his teeth like a crocodile. The message was not lost on me. Then he held up two fingers the way you did for the picture, and started to poke at them idly with the dead matchstick.

As I bent over his armchair with my shirt hitched up and my shorts and underpants round my ankles, I still thought he was going to wallop me for drawing a dirty picture. But this was not his intention.

There was a sudden whiff of Brylcreem, which puzzled me because neither of us was wearing any, and something cold and slimy was wiped onto me in a very intimate place.

'What are you doing?' I said in alarm, and tried to look behind me. I could scarcely believe what I saw.

He pushed my head back down again. 'Making it easier for you.'

As he bent over me, his hot tobacco breath came gusting around my ears, making me retch. 'Keep still,' he hissed, gripping my shoulders and thrusting suddenly into me with a convulsive movement of his hips.

It felt as if my whole body was going to be ripped in two like a log being split with a wedge, but he stifled my cries of pain by pressing my face so hard against the upholstery that I thought I should suffocate.

When at last he withdrew, I remained exactly where I was, not daring to move. 'You can get dressed now,' he said, as if the whole thing had been one of those routine medical indignities we were always having to put up with. His words seemed to be echoing down a tunnel, like when you're coming round from an anaesthetic.

I fumbled helplessly with my buttons; in the end, it was Jacko who did them up for me. Then the mist seemed to clear a little, and I surprised myself by walking quite calmly towards the door. As I reached for the handle, Jacko called my name. I paused, without answering or turning to look at him.

'Your drawing,' he said. 'Shall I show it to Mr and Mrs Wilkinson?'

I glanced back and tried to meet his gaze, but all I could manage was a slight shake of my head.

'This is between ourselves then. I thought you'd see it that way.'

For a long time, I lay on my bed, quite still, my brain feeling as bruised as my insides. The room was familiar in every detail; and yet it looked strangely different, as if I'd been jolted into a parallel universe where all the perspectives had been subtly altered.

I couldn't even be sure of what had really occurred in Jacko's flat. I wasn't so ill-informed as not to realise what he'd been doing. But it remained an obscenity beyond all comprehension, with no more sense to it than if he had stuffed my mouth with pencils or poured golden syrup into my ears. The simple facts were too inexplicable to be taken at face value, or even fully believed. You heard about such things; but they were strictly the province of changing-room talk, as remote from real life as Jack and the Beanstalk, and you could no more reconcile the experience with practical common sense than if you had actually met a Giant. So the natural tendency was to try and discount it. Pretending it couldn't have happened was easier than acknowledging that it had.

Apart from anything else, it wasn't the sort of incident you could possibly admit to without completely losing your self-respect. If you were any sort of a boy worth the name, and a bloke so much as tried to slip a hand up your shorts, he'd get your knee in his balls before he was in as far as the fingernails. So if word got round that you'd actually stood there with your clothes half off while he...

Thank God it had happened when everyone else was out, and they'd never know.

I spent the afternoon wandering round the neighbourhood, deliberately choosing streets that were unfamiliar. I needed to practise being myself in front of people who'd never seen me. It hurt a bit to walk, but so long as I kept moving, I had the illusion of being back in control, and gradually, the mental turmoil was replaced by a strange detachment.

Alan Carey, Elstree's answer to Freddie Bartholomew, was shooting his latest picture. Today, it's the bit where he wanders about in a sort of daze because of a thing that has happened; but it's only happened in the story, of course; it's only happened to the boy that Alan is acting.

Or: Unknown to everyone else, my father was something quite big in the Government, and needed the low-down on places like Barton House. The only way of getting it was to send me there for a while. Maybe quite a long while; several years, even. But my father was thinking about me all the time, and when it was over, I should be able to go home, and then he would say Well Done, and buy me lots of nice things to make up for it.

Not bad, that one. It got me through the afternoon, at any rate. But by tea time I was starting to wonder uneasily how I should manage if I had to go on like that; pretending, and pretending I wasn't pretending. You can't keep a vital part of your mind switched off indefinitely without going round the bend.

When I got back to Barton, I was nervous the others might notice something; but I needn't have worried. A bizarre domestic drama was completely absorbing everybody's attention. The visit by Fancy Madam had evidently proved too much for Hurly. Having spent the afternoon in her room, she had come downstairs again three sheets in the wind, and instead of putting our pies to bake in the oven, she had simply picked the whole lot up and thrown them out of the window.

Next morning, for no particular reason, I paused on my way down Welton Road to break the glass in the public fire alarm and pull the handle. It only took me a couple of seconds, and there was nobody there to see; moments later, I was heading for the station again, quite innocently, to catch the train for school.

It was one of our Scripture days. Divinity, rather; Scripture was what we had at the old place.

The Book of Job. Pronounced 'Jobe'. The Rev Ev leant forward in his seat with the look that meant he was going to challenge our intellects.

'The Book of Job...' He paused: someone had dropped a pencil. 'The Book of Job examines the relationship between sin and suffering.'

Just the thing for a class of twelve-year-olds.

'Here we have a person who seems in every sense to be a model citizen: righteous, law-abiding, deservedly prosperous. And then, suddenly, he suffers a devastating series of afflictions. He loses his home, his family, his possessions, his health, his peace of mind. Why? All these calamities seem completely unmerited. So what on earth are people to make of them? Surely, they must be a punishment. But for what? God wouldn't punish him for something he hadn't done. Has he committed a sin of which he is unaware, or which he refuses to acknowledge? Has he offended against God by his thoughts and attitudes? Or is he being put to the test, and if so, for what purpose?'

With a faint smile of satisfaction, the Rev Ev leant back for a moment so that the whole fascinating enigma had time to evolve in our minds. Unmoved, we sat in silence, waiting for him to continue.

'And then, of course, there's the really big question. How does Job himself react? How do his afflictions affect his attitude to

God? Is he angry? Does he blame God for his misfortunes: or does he accept that they must have been deserved? Or does he simply say, I don't understand all this, but if God wills it, it must be right?'

The corners of his mouth twitched back, and his eyes glittered expectantly, as if we must surely now admit that our curiosity was aroused.

'A heading, please, in your notebooks; remembering – Carey – to leave a line blank after the previous piece of work. I think we can still afford to keep up civilised standards, in spite of the paper shortage.'

Over the next three and a half weeks his notes on the Book of Job accounted for seventeen pages, so I dare say he was right.

And if Job hadn't a clue what it was all about, at least that gave us one thing in common. As for the story, it was a non-starter; the answer was given away in Chapter One. You knew from the very beginning that all Job's miseries came about so that God could win this bet with Satan. It didn't say much for God, or the way he looked after his own. All very well to claim that he made things right in the last chapter; but what about all the sons and daughters and manservants and maidservants who were casually done away with back at the start? Where was the justice in that?

Needless to say, this aspect of the matter was not discussed. But that was typical. There was no shortage of people to tell you about the third declension, or Eliphaz the Temanite. But nobody bothered to teach you the things you really needed to know; such as how to earn money when nobody would employ you; or what to do when someone like Jacko told you to grease his cock with Brylcreem and bend over, or you would get your bare arse burned with a cigarette end.

You didn't find that in the Bible, or *Kennedy's Latin Primer*.

By the time we'd finished the Book of Job, Jacko's little chats were getting to be a regular thing; not that chatting had much to do with it. When I walked into the room, he would simply point or nod to indicate his requirements, and the way he looked at me, you'd have thought I was there to be punished for something too despicable to be mentioned. Then, as I left, he would generally slip some sweets into my pocket, or maybe a half-empty packet of Navy Cut. Afterwards, every time, I used to despise myself for having been so compliant. But when it came to applying pressure, he was shrewd and infinitely resourceful. 'I'd like a word with you after lunch, Alan.'

'But I'm going to the Whitmans'.'

'Well now, that rather depends, doesn't it?'

Or another time, it might be a veiled remark about public fire alarms.

All the same, shouldn't I have gone down fighting? But Jacko seemed to enjoy resistance, for the sheer pleasure of forcing me into submission. Why give him the satisfaction? Besides, the less you struggled, the less it hurt and the sooner it was over.

Not that it was something you left behind by walking out of the room. There was a place inside me that was permanently tender; and morning visits to the toilet were becoming a nightmare, thanks to a problem too indelicate to discuss, but requiring half a roll per session to deal with it, and at least six flushes. Meanwhile, people queueing outside would be wondering what the hell was going on. Discretion was impossible. In those days the paper was not only bulkier, but incredibly noisy by Andrex standards. In desperation, I gradually trained myself to perform during non-social hours when I could have the place to myself. But Mrs Wilkie, who was extremely bowel conscious, used to check us in and out each morning against a list; so for the sake of domestic peace I was obliged to take my turn, and emerge a couple of minutes later after generating a few appropriate sound effects.

And there were other difficulties. Once, when I greased him a bit too vigorously, he came all over my hand. I held it away from me in disbelief as if it was reeking with corpse blood; that day alone, I washed it eleven times, and I ate my bread left-handed for a week. Lady Macbeth didn't know she was born. Even in bed, I didn't feel safe. Often, I would wake in the night, convinced that I could feel him stroking my bare legs.

At times, the whole business brought me close to despair. Eddie and Tom you could live with. They were everyone's problem, and at least they belonged to a world that a twelve-year-old could make sense of. But with Jacko, you were simply out of your league; there was nothing to relate to, except fear and physical pain, and no one to ask for advice.

Who could you tell? Not the Wilkies, that was for sure. Hedger, then? Imagine shouting that into his deaf-aid. The Whitmans? No fear. The whole idea of going there was to leave Barton behind. Besides, after admitting a thing like that, how would you ever be able to face them again?

Anyway, supposing you thought of someone, what would you actually say? The first sentence? The first word?

And just supposing you did finally manage to blurt it out,

what then?

You are a liar.

And you *let* him? Well, we don't want your sort here.

If you don't like it, tell him to stop. Why don't you learn to stick up for yourself?

Or possibly: My! Well, aren't you the lucky one! A man who used to know Lawrence of Arabia!

Or even: Good, well now you've had some practice, come round on Saturday.

Half the trouble was not knowing the rules. You had this feeling, deep down, that it couldn't be altogether right. But in a world where you could have a home and family one minute, and the next they were gone for ever, who was to say any longer what was reasonable, and what was not? Presumably, he wouldn't be doing it if he wasn't entitled to. And hadn't the Reverend Hawksworth said, on one of his monthly visits, that if any small services were expected of us by way of recompense for the benefits we received, he hoped we should carry them out with a willing spirit and a joyous heart?

One thing was certain: it would either be your fault it was going on, or your fault for complaining. Safer to say nothing. Pretend it wasn't happening.

Simple, really; easier than you'd think.

Except that deep inside, where the truth refused to be contradicted, you went on feeling more and more isolated, dirty, and afraid.

8

December was an anxious month. Secretly, I was dreading Christmas. At Gran's, it had always been a difficult time; too many memories reawakened and brought into sharp focus by the festivities. I used to wish I could hibernate until it was safely over.

But against all odds, Christmas at Barton turned out better than I'd expected.

On the first day of the holidays, the Reverend Hawkhurst arrived unexpectedly, bringing a big tree. We set it up at the foot of the stairs, its trunk wedged into a bucket which Snap cunningly disguised with a frill made out of pleated wallpaper. A foraging party collected a sack full of fir cones, which we painted red and silver with aeroplane dope and hung from the branches on loops of cotton. Tinsel was unobtainable. But someone gave us a big packet of anti-radar scatter foil. We cut the strips into two-inch lengths and Mrs Dooley fed them through the sewing machine, catching them between the threads like the bristles in a tea-pot brush. Somebody had to take hold of the cotton as soon as it cleared the needle, and then walk slowly backwards out of the sewing room, drawing the strip of tinsel away as it grew. Quite soon, we had a dozen or more pieces, eight or nine feet long. They didn't sparkle properly, because the foil had a frosted surface, but swagged criss-cross over the tree, they still looked pretty effective.

After that, it became a point of honour to decorate the entire house. A paper-chain production line was quickly set up in the Club Room. Hurly's *Daily Mirrors* were cut into strips, which were coloured with poster paints – courtesy of Hambledon Road Primary School – and their ends stuck down with flour paste. Output was brisk, but suffered a set-back when two of the chains caught fire. However, this was all in the cause of science. The dope we'd used on the fir cones had to be cleaned up with lighter fuel from little jelly capsules. There was one left over, and Joe said you could make a flame-thrower by squirting the fuel across a lighted match. He was right.

Visitors were amazed by our decorations, and said they had never seen anything like them. So we were well satisfied; and a convincing pre-Christmas snowfall added the final touch of seasonal perfection.

Jacko decided we ought to go carol-singing, and spent a whole hour rehearsing us in our repertoire. My voice being tuneless and rather husky, I was discouraged from joining in, but was given a lantern to carry. It hung from a pole, and looked quite picturesque. Jacko said it was a waste of time going from door to door; instead, he arranged a tour of all the pubs in the neighbourhood, half on the Monday night, and half on the Tuesday, which was Christmas Eve. This way, he said, we should play to full houses and make a quick killing every time.

For pure showmanship, you had to hand it to him. Whatever we sounded like, the sight of us proved irresistible. Kids in the snow, with lantern. We must have looked like a Christmas card come to life. As soon as we took up our places in the pub yards, people in both bars would put out the room lights and congregate round the windows. For once, we were just what they wanted to see, and our collecting tin, prominently labelled 'Barton House

Amenities Fund', whatever that meant, was filled to overflowing.

On Christmas Eve, we finished up at the Welton Arms, where they gave us hot mince pies and some sort of spiced grog that was heated up in a copper cone like a huge candle snuffer, thrust deep into the open fire. Afterwards, as we made our way home, I realised with a profound and sudden shock that I was happy.

On Christmas Day, the tables had snowmen on them, made out of milk bottles covered with cotton wool. There was a goose, of which I remember little, except for the prodigious amount of soft, rancid grease that came out of it and tainted our meals for weeks; also an odd vignette, glimpsed through the kitchen doorway, of Hurly, with one foot braced against the table, hauling the sinews out of the goose's legs with a pair of gas pliers.

After dinner, we all had presents out of a metaphorical bran tub. To Ocky's disgust, his parcel contained a magic crayon, for doing invisible writing which only appeared when you heated the paper; he swopped with one of the younger kids and ended up with a cardboard draughts set. The draughts turned out to be even better than milk-bottle tops for flicking across the room. Ronnie got one of those glass-topped puzzles with ball bearings in; and Snap had a propelling pencil with a sliding knob on the outside to move the lead. Up to the last minute, I'd been hoping a miracle would bring me a loose-leaf file like Barry Anderson's. A second-hand one would do; in fact, it might even be preferable, because people at school would assume I'd had it for ages. But my present was a packet of modelling wax, six pieces, all different colours. It was clearly a judgment on me for having celebrated the day in a very unholy manner. I could imagine Jesus thinking: Surely you could have waited until tomorrow?

To make things right, I volunteered for some of the extra washing up. There was no one else in the scullery, so I filled both halves of the wooden sink with water and switched the motor on, ready to make a start. The stack of dirty plates looked suitably daunting, but to tell the truth, my penance was somewhat equivocal; the dishwasher had a ponderous ingenuity that I found rather appealing. The right-hand sink was fitted with two cylindrical brushes, about a foot in diameter, mounted vertically, with the tips of their bristles touching. As they rotated under the water, you pushed a plate between them till its rim rested on two rubber rollers. The bristles scoured the plate on both sides, and also spun it round, so that after about five seconds it had been cleaned all over. You then transferred it to a wooden rack in the left-hand sink, and put in another.

I was just heaving a full rack of rinsed plates onto the draining board, when Jacko wandered in. Oh God, I thought, not now.

'No one helping you?'

'I can manage.'

He leant against the scullery wall and watched as I fed the next batch of plates through the machine. By putting them in with one hand and taking them out with the other, you could achieve an uninterrupted flow. After a couple of minutes, he said, 'You're quite a dab hand at that, aren't you?'

'It's not difficult.'

'You're too modest.' He paused, and moved in closer, resting his fingertips against the nape of my neck. I could guess what was coming. But before there was time for anything else to happen, Hurly came waddling in.

'Anyhow,' Jacko said, backing quickly away, 'don't be long. The filmshow's nearly ready.' And without more ado he wandered out again.

So in spite of everything, it looked as if God was on my side.

Mr Franklin, the Reverend Hawkhurst's daughter's fiancé, who wasn't a reverend yet, but only practising, had brought a projector, and six reels from the Wallace Heaton Film Library. The Dining Room furniture had all been rearranged, and a sheet hung on the wall to make a screen. The picture was rather dim, and the people seemed to buckle as they walked across the folds; but no one had ever seen a film except in a cinema, so the show was a big success, in spite of the fact that with the Wilkies sitting there, you couldn't whistle or throw things at the screen. There was a Felix cartoon, a travel film called *Going Up the Iguazu,* and a good Charlie Chaplin where they were all roller skating. I don't remember the others. To finish with, we saw some of the roller skating projected backwards, which was the best thing of all.

Actually, I was more interested in the projector than the films, and sat at the back so as to watch the way it worked. When the show was over, I edged cautiously towards the table where Mr Franklin was packing the films away in a fibre transit box. The projector was still set up on its special stand.

'Is that yours?' I asked.

He hesitated. 'My father's.'

'Are they expensive?' I thought perhaps we could buy one with the Christmas carol money, if Jacko hadn't spent it all getting pissed in the Welton Arms.

'I'm rather afraid so. Did you want a look?'

He showed me the motor switch, and the lamp switch, and the focussing; he was even going to unpack one of the films and let me try lacing it up, but Mrs Wilkie intervened.

'Come along, Alan. You're wasting Mr Franklin's time.'

He looked round in surprise. 'No, really. He's very welcome.' But he said it far too politely, and she took no notice. You could tell he hadn't had much experience with women. As I left the room, I couldn't help glancing back. He smiled a little ruefully, and said 'Some other time, perhaps.'

I saw him again at Church the following Sunday, and hoped he might be going to tell me when I could have a proper demonstration. I said hallo, and he said hallo back; but he looked rather startled, and you could see from his face that although it was only a day or two, he didn't even remember who I was.

It puzzled me why anyone got excited about New Year; you might as well celebrate Monday morning, or the start of a school term. It was sad to think of the old year slipping away. Something else that was gone for ever.

But I didn't have long to wait for my New Year's luck. The second or third morning in January, I came across Mr Pond standing forlornly in the road, gazing towards his workshop.

'Look at that,' he said, easing his cap back so as to scratch under the peak. 'Now what am I supposed to do?'

The snow was lying knee-deep all along his pathway, and the door was half hidden under a huge drift.

'Do you want it clearing?'

'Terry's supposed to look after things like that.'

'I can soon do it.'

He drew out his watch, consulted it thoughtfully, and then snapped it shut again. 'Well, I wouldn't say no.'

When the path was cleared, he invited me in. 'I've got some parcels to pack, if you feel like giving me a hand.'

In the end, I spent the whole morning at the workshop, sweeping up and doing various odd jobs. He even let me make some labels on the giant typewriter. 'Hm,' he said, when I showed him the results. 'You've got a good eye.'

While I was pasting the labels onto the cartons with Gloy from a large jar, he selected a short end of steel bar from an odds-and-ends box and locked it into the lathe chuck. 'Now then,' he said, beckoning me over.

I watched intently as he manoeuvred the cutting tool into position. 'Lesson Number One,' he said. 'Facing up. That end's been cut with a hacksaw. We want it nice and smooth.'

He set the chuck turning, and gradually wound the tool point across the rough face of the steel. There was a soft rattling sound, and little chips of metal flew off in various directions. At the second cut, with the tool set slightly further in, some bright little spirals came away. This time, he stopped the chuck to show me the result. The parts that had stuck out most were starting to look quite smooth, but the rest of the surface was still rough.

Standing behind the lathe was an old tin, streaked with oil. He splashed some cloudy liquid out of it with a paintbrush so that it ran all over the end of the steel bar. 'Flushes away the chips. Otherwise they jam under the tool and dig in. Cools things down as well.'

I sniffed the tin. 'Ugh. Whatever is it?'

'Suds. Oil and water.'

'I thought they didn't mix.'

'Special kind. Now, ready to have a go?'

He set the tool a little further in, and then stood back so that we could change places. I slid the belt across, and cautiously took my first-ever cut – an amazing sensation. As I turned the handle, the tool seemed to glide inwards, stripping the hard steel away with less effort than it took to sharpen a pencil. It was magical, intoxicating. Even before the lathe had stopped and I saw the face of the steel bar, smooth and clean, reflecting the light in a neat concentric pattern, my mind was made up; this was a skill I must master, come what may.

He let me spend the rest of the morning working my way through the oddments box, facing up various offcuts, and turning the ends down to smaller diameters. At midday, he sent me home with a shilling in my pocket and a smell of suds on my fingertips that I managed, with care, to preserve till bedtime.

Next day, there was a message for me. Mr Pond wanted a word, so would I go round to the workshop.

'I've found out what became of Terry,' he said. 'Hit a tree, tobogganing. Broken his collar bone. Six weeks, they reckon; minimum.'

Poor Terry. I waited, not breathing.

Mr Pond settled back on his stool and looked me straight in the eye. 'I'd have preferred somebody older, but at least I know you. So if you're still wanting a Saturday job...'

'Oh yes, Mr Pond. Yes, please.'

'I need someone dependable, mind.'

I nodded eagerly. There was just one thing. 'What happens when Terry gets better? I mean, with two boys being half a boy, and that.'

'We'd have to see. I don't make promises I can't be sure of keeping.'

For a time, the others were not aware that they had a mechanical engineer amongst them. It was a private satisfaction, not to be shared. I had learned to be guarded about my enthusiasms; in any case, you needed some good secrets, to make up for the shameful ones. Good secrets made you strong.

I did tell Ronnie, though. It was snowing again, and we stood at the Club Room window, side by side, gazing out into the street. He listened impassively, and then said 'Ah' with a little nod of approval, as if it was something altogether appropriate, and he'd been expecting it, right from the start.

1947 was already well on the way to becoming the definitive winter, with daily sights and situations that no one could have imagined: stupendous icicles, thicker than lamp posts; a man proceeding down Welton Road on skis; people stepping straight onto their garage roofs from adjacent snow drifts; crates of milk arriving by sledge, the cardboard closures lifted an inch and a half above the bottle necks on columns of creamy ice.

For a time, our outside toilets were kept from freezing solid by means of a paraffin heater which had to be left burning night and day. Then, as conditions worsened, only the cistern nearest the main building remained unfrozen, and when the supply of heating oil ran out, there was nothing left but the halfway house. Eventually, the Council found us some more oil, but by then, the coal was running out. There was only just enough to keep the Aga going, so the paraffin stove had to be moved to the Club Room. It was better than nothing; but pretty soon our meagre ration of oil gave out again, and we were left without any heating at all.

Wherever you went, you heard people agreeing that it was no way to run a country, and they'd known right from the start that the Socialists wouldn't be up to it. But we didn't concern ourselves with the politics of the fuel crisis: and the chaos, so richly exploitable, seemed nothing to complain about. On the contrary, our lives were gloriously disrupted for weeks on end, as one rule after another had to be abandoned.

At school, assuming you could get there, and assuming it was open if you did, the lessons were like the ones we used to have in air-raid shelters. With so many absentees each day, classes were often combined for general knowledge quizzes or community singing. Occasionally, if the broadcasts hadn't been cancelled to save power, we listened to the wireless. Not even the Rev Ev, absurdly resplendent in mittens and a balaclava helmet, could manage to carry on as normal.

At Barton, thanks to the Aga, there suddenly weren't enough kitchen jobs to go round.

'Me and Joe's doing the spuds.'

'Fuck off. You did 'em yesterday.'

'All right; you peel 'em, we'll cut 'em up.'

In the rest of the house, conditions were Arctic. We had to wear most of our outdoor clothes indoors, and most of our indoor clothes in bed. Visits to Jacko's flat, with its gas fire, began to seem almost welcome.

Coldest of all were the bedrooms, with blanket raids a nightly occurrence. One evening, after tea, Wilkie announced that there weren't any extra blankets left, so all but the oldest of us would have to double up and pool our bedclothes.

Immediately, Ocky nudged me in the ribs. 'You and me, all right?'

If it had to be anyone, I'd have preferred Ronnie, but there was no point in arguing.

For geometrical reasons, if no other, couples were instructed to lie with a head at each end, like the Jack of Diamonds. It was also specified that shared beds were to be made up with three sheets, one of you lying between the upper two, the other between the lower. The middle sheet, by preventing direct physical contact, was supposed to render the whole scheme more acceptable. But it was an insane arrangement, clearly devised by someone who had never had to put up with it. To prevent whoever was lying under the middle sheet from being completely immobilised, it had to be left slack; this meant that as the two of you stirred in your sleep, you would gradually wind yourselves up in the loose material, pinning your arms tightly against your sides as if you'd been sewn into a shroud.

Our first night, a glass of water drunk too close to bedtime led to a near disaster at 3 a.m.

'Ocky, wake up!'

'Uh?'

'I need a pee.'

'You fuckin woke me up to tell me that?'

'I'm stuck. I can't get out.'

'Stay where you are, then.' And in seconds, he was asleep again.

'Ocky! It's urgent! You'll have to do something. I can't move.'

I felt his feet and knees dig into me, then slide away a little. 'Sod it,' he muttered, a moment or two later. 'Neither can I.'

We thrashed about ineffectually in the darkness until something suddenly gave way, and Ocky fell out of bed, unwinding himself as he went. There was a muffled crash, and a stream of confused profanity from somewhere down on the floor.

Needless to say, it was all my fault. When I returned, shivering, from the halfway house, he muttered sourly, 'Tomorrow night, wear a balloon on your cock. Then we can both sleep easy.'

Re-making the bed to specification proved impossible in the darkness, so we spent the rest of the night side by side with the bedclothes in a jumbled heap on top of us.

'I can't believe we have to do this,' I said, as we burrowed down together amidst the wreckage, jostling for position.

'We done it in the war.'

'It's not the war now.'

'Freeze to death, then. See how you like that.'

In the morning, when I woke, it was rather a shock to feel somebody lying close beside me. 'Paul?' I mumbled drowsily, not quite believing it. Then I remembered.

Jacko didn't approve of our new arrangement. 'Good Gracious!' he said when he caught sight of us. 'What's this? The Babes in the Wood?'

We explained.

'Well, it's not to happen again. Do you understand?'

'Why not?' Ocky demanded. 'This is a much better way.'

Jacko hesitated. 'Just do as you're told,' he said at last, 'and don't ask so many questions.'

9

A few mornings later, at Bishop Inglis, we found ourselves confronting a total stranger.

'Where's Mr Hedger?' someone demanded.

'Not very well, I'm afraid. I'll be taking his place for the next few weeks.'

We eyed him warily, ready to close ranks against the intruder. He was a lot younger than Mr Hedger; thin, tall, angular, and not deaf.

He opened the Register, and started to call our names, glancing up each time to see who answered. 'By the way,' he said when he'd finished, 'I'm Mr Dudley. So now we know each other.'

At the start of our History lesson the same morning, he watched in silence as we shuffled into our places.

'Could you all find page 211, please.'

Prolonged leafing through tattered textbooks. Several hands went up. 'Ain't got it, sir.' Definite chaos potential.

'Never mind. Lang, share with Naylor and Norton. Taylor, share with Thompson and Whitman.'

He'd learnt our names, then. Already.

'Anyone else who can't see the picture?'

Picture? Mr Hedger didn't hold with pictures. They took up space that could have been occupied by facts.

It was a complicated drawing with several panels, showing some outlandish pieces of medieval machinery. Underneath, it just said, 'Siege Engines'.

'Who knows what a siege is?'

'It's when you attack a castle, sir.'

'Good. Can someone improve on that?'

No offers.

Mr Dudley waited a few seconds, and then went on. 'It comes from a French word that means "sitting down". Why would you sit down all round a castle?'

'Sir!'

'Yes, Everard?'

'To stop the people escaping, sir.'

'Ah. Now we're getting somewhere. What would happen if no one could get out? Or in?'

'They'd run out of food.'

'And...?'

'They'd starve.'

Mr Dudley smiled. 'I'm sorry. I meant, what else would they run out of?'

'Ammo,' said Naylor.

'Water,' said Edwards.

'That's right. Now, what about these siege engines? What were they for?' His finger sketched a trajectory in mid-air.

'Chucking things?' said Slater.

'What sort of things?'

'Big stones. Things like that.'

'Yes. Good. But why bother? Why not just sit and wait? Once they're down to eating the rats and drinking their own urine, they'll soon surrender.'

'Speed things up a bit,' Toddy suggested.

'Exactly. Starving them out could take a year or more. We want to break their spirit, make them decide it's not worth carrying on. What's the matter, Anderson?'

Barry had turned quite pale. 'Sir, did they really drink... what you said, sir?'

'If it's a matter of survival, you do whatever you have to. Now, how big were they, these machines?'

Who could tell?

'Have a look at the top left-hand picture. What else can you see?'

'A bloke.'

'Okay. So how tall is the machine?' He held his hand out flat, and kept raising it a few inches at a time.

We didn't stop him till his hand was way above his head.

'So high?,' he said. 'All right, let's try a little experiment. I think we could use the forms you're sitting on to build a sort of rough framework about the actual size. It won't be exactly like the real thing, but it'll give you the general feel.'

We carried the benches out to the front, placing them where he told us. In a couple of minutes, there was a large rectangle on the floor to show the size of the base; then we stood the two longest benches upright and balanced another across the top. It was a huge and cumbersome structure, roughly resembling the stout timbers of the original. We all stood back to admire our handiwork. For the first time ever, History was starting to make sense.

'Of course, this is only a little one,' he commented casually, glancing up at the ceiling. 'The bigger ones, you wouldn't fit into the room.'

Next question: how did they actually work?

'Let's start with the ones that fired a big spear. Who's got a pencil with a broken point?'

'Sir! Here, sir!'

'And who's got a good big pellet-flicking ruler?'

'Sir! Sir!'

He selected the one that suited him, and asked to borrow

Horton's pencil box as well. The lid had a handy groove in it.

'Now we're in business.'

He put the box on the edge of his desk, and rested the pencil in the groove, leaving about an inch sticking out at the rear. Holding the ruler upright, he bent the top back, and then released it suddenly. The pencil shot forward, but crash-landed four or five feet away.

'How can we make it go further?'

'Tilt the box, sir.'

This time, the pencil flew in a long smooth curve and landed on the far side of the room.

'Now have a look at the picture.'

And of course, it was all there. A springy upright plank, just like the ruler; a big spear resting in a grooved track, and a special little tilting device to alter the elevation. However, the spear in the picture seemed to have something wrapped around it, just behind the head. Rags dipped in tar, apparently, to be set alight just before you fired.

Mr Dudley glanced mischievously round the room as if to say, 'Well, shall we?' Producing a cigarette lighter from his waistcoat pocket, he unscrewed the plug from the bottom, and teased out a small piece of the wadding with a pin. He wound the wadding round the pencil tip, and prepared to fire. At the last minute, he held the lighter under it, and as soon as the flame caught, he shot the blazing spear right across the room. It landed in the waste bin and set fire to some screwed-up paper. Spontaneous applause.

'A fluke,' he said, with a deprecating gesture.

When the flames had been put out, and everyone's property returned, he started borrowing again.

'I'll bet there's someone who's bored a hole right through their ruler with a compass point.'

'Sir! Mine, sir!'

He held the compass leg with the point towards us, and slid the ruler over it so that it balanced horizontally.

'Suppose I fastened this bulldog clip on one end of the ruler, and then let go?'

'The clip would swing down.'

'And suppose we rested a paper pellet on the other end of the ruler?'

'It'll fire the pellet, sir.'

And it did. Not very far; but you could see the idea.

'Sir! It's the picture in the middle.'

'That's right. Only instead of the bulldog clip...?'

'A box full of stones and earth and things.'

'Sir,' said Toddy. 'You balanced the ruler in the middle; but in the picture, the place where it pivots is much nearer the weight.'

'Okay. So the part that does the throwing is much longer.'

'Sir,' Slater said. 'Is that why the pellet didn't go very far?'

Mr Dudley smiled. 'You're really getting the hang of this. You could practically build your own.'

Toddy and I had the same thought at the same moment, and exchanged glances across the room.

'*Can* we, sir?' Toddy asked. 'Can we build one? A working model?'

Mr Dudley looked doubtful. 'Oh, well, I didn't really... Do you think you could?'

'Yes, sir! Me and Carey. We'll make it at the weekend.'

'Can I as well, sir?' Carpenter said. 'With Anderson and Naylor?'

'Sir! Me and Everard...'

Marks and positions for the week: Dudley, 1st, 100%. Hedger (Absent, Not Placed), Will have to do much, much better.

Mr Whitman backed the car out of the garage so that Toddy and I could use the work bench at the end. The idea was to make a mangonel, a giant catapult with its throwing arm powered by twisted ropes. Toddy pointed out some pieces of timber, grey with age, that were leaning against the wall. 'Dad says we can have these.'

There was plenty there for a good-sized model. We could easily make it a couple of feet high.

'I'm not very good at sawing wood,' Toddy said. 'You'd better do it.'

I measured off the first length. 'We'll need a try-square.'

'Can't you manage?'

'We want it decent.'

He gave me an odd look, and wandered off into the house. 'Mike,' I heard him calling. 'He says he needs a try-square.' After about five minutes, he came back with the set-square from his pencil box. 'Will that do? It's all there is.'

'Yeah, better than nothing.'

I drew some pencil lines on the wood, and Toddy held it down while I sawed off the pieces for the base. It turned out he couldn't knock nails in, either, so I had to do that as well, and by the time we were ready to start on the uprights, he had wandered off again.

It wasn't easy, sawing the wood with no one to hold the end. 'Shit!' I said, out loud, as it slipped for about the twentieth time. Glancing round hurriedly to make sure no one had heard me, I saw Mike standing in the doorway.

'Do you want a hand with that?'

'Where's Toddy?'

'Indoors. It's his chest; he's not supposed to get cold.'

Mike held the wood while I finished the sawing, and together we nailed the uprights to the base. With the struts in position, you could suddenly see the whole thing taking shape.

'Classy job,' Mike said.

A slat of wood with a small baked beans tin nailed to the end served as the throwing arm. It didn't look very medieval, but it saved a lot of trouble.

'We'll need a couple of pegs for twisting the string,' I said.

Mike whittled away with his pocket knife. 'Something like this?'

'Yeah!'

There was still no sign of Toddy, so we wound the string as tight as it would go, ready for the first trial, and Mike put a pebble in the baked beans tin. I pulled the arm back, and let go. The pebble shot downwards, hitting the floor and skittering across to the far side of the garage.

I remembered Dudley's experiment with the spear. 'We need to raise the front.'

Mike nodded. 'Or you could fit a block to stop the arm coming up so far.'

That sounded much more professional. This time, the pebble flew straight across and hit the top of the doors with a sharp smack.

'Blimey!' Mike said. 'There's some power in that thing.'

We took it outside, and set it up on the drive, firing towards the road. The pebble went right over the gate, and we heard it land somewhere on the far pavement.

Mike darted indoors to fetch the others. 'Hey, come on out and look at Alan's model.'

It was dark by now, and getting very cold, but the field trials went on for quite a while. Mr Whitman watched with enthusiasm. 'Not bad,' he said. 'Not bad at all.'

On Monday, at the start of the History lesson, all the models were taken out in the yard. Barry Anderson's was bigger than ours, and more realistic, but it didn't fire as far; and anyway, Naylor told us afterwards that it was really Mr Anderson that had made it.

In spite of our baked beans tin, Dudley seemed impressed. 'You've made an excellent job of that, Whitman,' I heard him say, while I was gathering up a fresh supply of pebbles.

Afterwards, when I caught Toddy's eye, he grinned a little sheepishly. 'Well, anyway, it was my idea,' he said. 'And my wood.'

Mr Dudley brought some fresh air to our English lessons as well.

'Who do you think is the most important person in the world?' he asked, one morning.

There were a few tentative suggestions which he neither accepted nor rejected. Winston Churchill; President Truman; Jesus. After a while, he said diffidently, 'This isn't a guessing game. I was hoping some of you might be willing to risk a little honesty.'

We were intrigued, but still cautious.

'All right. Here's something else to think about. Six people in a plane. You're one of them. It's about to crash and there's only one parachute. Well...?'

Rather below the belt, that one.

'Now, try this. Out of all the people around you in your daily lives, who would you miss most if they suddenly weren't there any more?'

There was an anxious, inward-looking silence. After about thirty seconds, he stood up and clapped his hands together briskly. 'That's enough for the moment. But I want you to do a piece of writing for me, and I don't want to be served up with second-hand opinions. So think before you write, and don't turn your back on the truth.'

'What's the title, sir?'

'That I leave to you. But I want you to write about someone who matters to you. Someone you really care about.'

'Anyone, sir?'

'Yes. Anyone.'

'Can we start, sir?'

'No. It's for homework. Just keep your thoughts simmering gently until then.'

The power cut that evening lasted much longer than usual. On a normal night, I mightn't have taken the risk. But I was alone in the Quiet Room with darkness all around me, and by candle-light the blank page looked friendly and inviting.

Not that the words came easily. They were there in my mind but they fought hard to avoid capture. Getting your thoughts down on paper was like unwinding a huge spring and trying to hold it flat on the table; the moment you caught a grip of one bit, the rest started to slip away from you.

My brother is called Paul, and I talk to him quite often although he is dead. He is a year and a half older than me only with him been dead two year and a half I am a year older than him which is a hard thing to get accustomed to. He is all I've got and I don't want to leave him behind as I grow up. Apart from some tyresome habits we get on fine, he is a very good person to be with and talk to, I miss him a lot.

There was more I wanted to say, but it wouldn't come, and it was too cold in the Quiet Room to sit and wait for it. So I put the book safely away in my satchel, and got on with my Maths and French.

During the bad weather, we were allowed to have our supper in the kitchen. Especially by candlelight, there was a cosy tribal feeling about huddling close together round the Aga clutching our mugs and slices while Hurly, vast and aproned, hovered maternally in the background. Cave dwellers, roasting an ox over the camp fire, waited on by their womenfolk.

That evening was one of the best. Snap had his mouth organ with him, and Hurly taught us a lewd Irish ballad. But then when the lights came on it was all spoilt. We blinked resentfully, and felt exposed, like when you're having a pee behind a hedge, and suddenly notice somebody watching you. The singing quickly died, and pretty soon people began to drift away.

Ronnie and I stayed behind to rinse the mugs out; it made an excuse to linger a few more minutes in the warm. As we returned to the Club Room, sounds of derisive laughter could be heard coming from inside. I opened the door.

Someone was reading aloud. 'He is a year and a half older than me, only with him been dead two year and a half...'

Tom Shales was holding court at the far end of the room, surrounded by seven or eight of the others. He had my exercise book in his hand.

'That's private,' I shouted, barging forward through the group. 'You've no right to go looking at people's private things.'

There was a chorus of jeers. 'Tell your big brother, then!'

I tried to snatch the book back, but Tom held it high above his head, and every time I reached for it there was a fresh outbreak of whistling and jeering. Defiantly, I looked round the group to size up the opposition; and there, right in the midst of them, was Ocky.

At twelve, I didn't reckon to cry in public; but what with Jacko and everything, it was a close call.

'Give us it, Tom. I'm warning you.'

He held the book out and then snatched it away at the last moment, throwing it over my head to one of the others. Twice, I nearly got hold of it, but just missed. Someone threw it to Ocky, and I thought he was going to give it to me, but he changed his mind, and threw it back to Tom.

If I'd had any sense, I'd have simply walked away. But by now, it was Victory or Death. The others eased back a little to give us fighting room.

I stood in front of Tom with my hand held out, and did my best to look menacing. Once again, he dangled the book in front of me, and I lunged forward to snatch it from him. But all I managed to do was to rip the page out, and I was left standing there with the paper crumpled in my hand. Too late to save it now, but it hardly mattered. All I cared about was revenge; so I dropped the paper and went for him with everything I'd got. He landed one good punch right in my face and then made the mistake of stopping to admire his handiwork. I saw my chance, and while he was off his guard, I brought my knee up hard into his groin. He keeled over and lay doubled up on the floor, clutching himself between his thighs. After a moment or two, he gasped out, 'You dirty little sod! Is that what they teach you at Grammar School?'

There was absolute silence. None of the others moved or spoke. So I picked up my book and the torn page from where they had fallen, and looked round for my satchel. It was lying in the corner, with most of the contents spilled out of it. I put everything back in, buckled the straps up tight, and hung it over my shoulder.

Tom was still writhing about on the floor, his face white and clammy. Rolling onto his side, he sat up a little and looked round at the others. 'You saw that, didn't you?' he demanded. 'You saw him knee me in the balls?'

Still nobody spoke.

He looked across to the far end of the room. 'You saw him, Ronnie. You saw him, didn't you?'

Everyone turned to look at Ronnie. He stood there impassively, with his arms folded and his legs a little apart. He didn't answer. Instead, he glanced across at me and jerked his head towards the door. 'You're bleeding, Alan. You'd better get cleaned up.'

I left the room, feeling sick and humiliated. I wished I could be like Ronnie. People respected him because he was cool and calm, like someone a lot older. If anyone got across him, he didn't lose his temper or make himself ridiculous; he just looked at them with a sort of faint contempt that made them back off and keep out of his way. I wished he hadn't been there to see me make such a mess of things.

I managed to stop my nose bleeding, but I couldn't face going back to the Club Room. I just wanted to dig a hole in the ground and hide. The only other option was to go straight to bed. You were allowed to do that, any time after supper.

It must have been one of the coldest nights we'd had. All the same, I pulled Ocky's blankets off the bed and threw them onto his bare mattress, along with his pillow. I doubled one of my own blankets to make an extra layer, and spread my raincoat over it as well. Still wearing everything but my blazer and shoes, I burrowed down under the bedclothes and tried to stop shivering.

After a while, I heard some of the others come in, but I kept my eyes shut and pretended to be asleep. I wished I'd thought of stuffing something into my ears; I didn't want to hear what they were saying.

Before long, I recognised Ocky's footsteps. He stood for a few moments beside his bed, as if uncertain what to do.

'Alan?'

When I didn't answer, he leant across and shook me.

'Alan!'

'Fuck off.'

'We're supposed to be sharing.'

'We're supposed to be mates.'

Pause. 'It was only a schoolbook.'

I burrowed down again, and waited for him to go away.

'Alan, I'll freeze!'

'Good.'

'And so will you.'

'Who cares?'

I heard him turn away and walk out of the room.

About ten minutes later, he was back. 'Look, I'm sorry. All right?'

'You weren't sorry till you wanted something.'

I heard a creak as he sat down on his mattress. Then he said,

'It's different for you. You ain't like the rest of us.'

No need to rub it in.

'You and Ronnie...' He seemed to be searching for words. 'You're sort of... sort of strong inside.'

'What the hell are you on about?'

'You're the only ones who ain't afraid of Tom.'

'*What?*' In spite of myself, I turned to look at him.

'He can make the rest of us do whatever he wants.'

It was pointless arguing; the world was making even less sense than usual. But the bitterness was still seething inside me. 'You had the book in your hand and you wouldn't give us it.'

There was quite a long silence. Then he muttered, 'I said Sorry, didn't I? What more do you want?'

'I don't know.'

Nothing Ocky could give me, anyway. I just wanted things to be different, which was pointless because no one could alter them. He spread his blankets over the bed again, and a few minutes later I felt his feet tunnelling in through the bedclothes and coming to rest against my back.

In the morning, I set off for school in plenty of time. With luck, there might be a chance of copying out my composition before the books were taken in, except that it hardly seemed worth the trouble. I could see now that it wasn't any good. No wonder the others had laughed at it.

In any case, as it happened, the train came to a halt between two stations and stayed there for nearly fifteen minutes. By the time I walked into our form room, Slater was already collecting the homework, so I simply gave him my book and kept my fingers crossed. Trouble later was better than trouble now. Dudley couldn't possibly mark the books in time for the English lesson, so at least the matter would rest until tomorrow.

I was right about the lesson, but that was as far as it went. At going-home time, Dudley told me to wait behind, and I could see he had my exercise book on his desk. When all the others had gone, he opened it at the place where my composition wasn't, and looked at me expectantly. I stood beside him with my hands behind my back, and waited.

'Well?' he said at last.

'I tore it out, sir.' Pointless going into details.

'Why?'

'It wasn't any good, sir.'

He picked the book up, turning it this way and that. 'There seem to be what the police call "signs of a struggle". Also, if I'm not mistaken, I detect bloodstains.'

'Yes, sir.'

'Did this happen at school?'

'No, sir.'

'At home, then? I mean... the place where you live.'

'Yes, sir.' He knew about Barton, then.

He sat for a while with his chin resting on one hand. 'Tentative Reconstruction, based on the evidence. A boy is writing something in his book. Something very personal, not for public consumption. Another boy tries to read it, but the first boy doesn't want him to. The second boy snatches the book, the first boy snatches it back, and...' He gestured towards the torn page. 'How am I doing?'

'Pretty close.'

'And the missing page?'

'It was all screwed up, sir.'

'Yes, it would be. Have you still got it?'

'It wasn't any good, sir.'

'I'd very much like to see it.'

I fumbled about inside my satchel for as long as I dared; then I handed over the crumpled sheet and stood beside him, gritting my teeth, while he read it. At last, he put it down, but immediately picked it up again and read all through it a second time. My mouth had gone completely dry.

'Carey, I'm so glad this didn't get thrown away,' he said. 'That's a powerful opening sentence, with a real kick to it. And it's an interesting point you make about your ages. There's a poem – I wonder if you know it? Dreadful thing, really, but there's one superb stanza buried in the middle; it's all anyone remembers. About the dead not growing old.'

'Oh – Armistice Day?'

'That's probably when you've heard it. But about this work of yours. I can't give a mark to something in this condition. You do understand that, don't you?'

'Oh yes, sir.'

'Any chance you could copy it out tonight?'

'Yes, sir. Only...'

He waited patiently.

'I'd rather not do it at Barton.'

'I agree. Most unwise. What about Dinner Hour tomorrow?

You could sit in the School Library.'

'Can you do that? I mean, work in there?'

'Of course. Why ever not?'

'I thought it was just for the older boys.'

'You might find it a very useful place.'

'Yes, sir. And sir, is it all right if I put a bit more? On the end?'

He spread his hands accommodatingly. 'I look forward to reading it.'

The outside door of the Library was tall and pointed, with a wrought- iron handle and dozens of black metal studs; I had to put my shoulder to it to push it open. Inside, there were double swing doors covered in dusty, dark red baize with brass kicking plates at the bottom. A loud creak came from the hinges as I levered my way through.

It was like walking into a church; there was the same oppressive silence, the same feeling of sterile sanctity. You knew if you coughed, people would look up and frown at you as the sound echoed back and forth under the vast, vaulted ceiling.

I looked round cautiously, reluctant to move too far from the door. Rows of long tables, most of them occupied, stretched away into the distance. All round the walls were monumental bookcases of carved oak, inscribed 'To the Glory of God and in Memory of the Fallen, 1914–1918.' In the circumstances, you'd think it might have been better to put the Fallen first.

There seemed to be space at the second table, so I sat down tentatively and opened my exercise book. On a clean page, I ruled a margin and copied out my original composition word for word, except for putting right the mistakes which Mr Dudley had unobtrusively corrected. But the last full-stop was a threshhold, not an ending. I had always known it; the really important things had been left unsaid.

Starting a fresh line, I added: I wish I could remember.

And there, once again, I came to a halt. I knew what I wanted to say; but everything needed to be explained before everything else. My thoughts had locked themselves into a tight circle, with nowhere to break in, as if they were ganging up to keep me out.

Long before I was ready, the bell went for afternoon school. Panic. The composition looked ridiculous with one extra sentence tacked on the end, leading nowhere. Worse still, I suddenly noticed that I seemed to have written it twice. There was no time for the fearful alchemy of Sloan's Ink Eradicator, even if I'd had any.

Nothing for it but to cross out the abortive second paragraph and make my peace with Mr Dudley as best I could. I left my book on his desk, and hurried off to the first lesson.

After school, he kept me behind again.

'I've marked your book,' he said, and showed me the page. Five out of ten; better than I'd expected. 'I rather wondered about this, though.' He indicated the line I had crossed out.

I did my best to explain.

'This thing you can't remember,' he said. 'Is it something to do with the way your brother died?'

I was amazed. 'How did you know?'

'Just a guess.'

He waited patiently while I struggled to produce coherent thoughts out of the fog.

'The buzz-bomb came down on the house. Direct hit, practically. We were both of us playing out, but Paul was on the far side of the street, much further away than me. I blacked out, and then I was in the hospital. Only I must have come to for a moment, because I remember seeing his hand sticking out from under the rubble. But the thing is, he was in the wrong place. He was lying between me and the house.'

'The blast could have flung him across.'

'No. Wrong way.'

'Perhaps he started to run towards you.'

'Why would he do that? We heard it coming. He'd have gone down flat where he was.'

'And you did the same?'

'Must have done. First thing you learned.'

Mr Dudley frowned, his chin resting on clasped hands. Then he said, very gently, 'Your... mother was in the house?'

I nodded.

'Could Paul have been trying to reach her?'

That other memory; the face at an upstairs window.

When I didn't answer, he looked at me in concern. 'I'm sorry. I'm afraid I've upset you.'

'No. I'm glad. It's beginning to make sense.'

He leant back in his chair a little. 'Of course, there's another possible explanation. I know you're perfectly sure about what you saw, but given the circumstances... A blow on the head, a very stressful experience...'

I'm quite certain,' I said.

'Yes. But that's it; you would be.'

I didn't see any point in discussing it.

He looked at his watch. 'You'd better be getting along. Will you be all right?'

'I'm fine,' I told him.

He smiled, almost sheepishly, and watched me as I packed my things together. He was still sitting there at his desk as I turned to go.

10

The thaw, when it finally came, was a mixed blessing. The Rec, frozen for weeks, was flooded now, so we still couldn't use it, and although the unrivalled possession of our own beds was a luxury after the horrors of the three-sheet system, my night-time fears about Jacko quickly resurfaced once we were back on our own.

Another drawback was that our church parades began to come under fire again from Snorty Pig – for so I had secretly christened him. Now it wasn't so cold, he could afford to keep his bedroom window open, and a bull's eye scored on my right ear gave notice of the fact. Our chances of getting even seemed as remote as ever.

But it was at Bishop Inglis that the end of winter led to the worst calamity.

One Friday dinner time, I was kicking a stone about behind the Library when Mr Dudley suddenly came in view carrying a camera.

Photography was still my impossible dream. At that time, the only cameras I was acquainted with were the pocket Kodaks. My father had had one, and I used to study it longingly as a child, intrigued by its pleated bellows and intricate fold-away mechanism. You held it at waist level, and squinted down through a tiny viewfinder which showed you the scene inverted left to right. But Mr Dudley was using something infinitely more sophisticated. For a start, he was holding it up to his eye; and instead of peering in through a little red window in the back when he wound the film on, all it needed between exposures was one quick twist with his finger and thumb.

I drew near, and made overtures.

Courteous as always, he showed no sign of irritation at being interrupted. 'You know about cameras, do you?'

'A bit. I've never seen one like that, though.'

'It's a Leica. German. I picked it up at the end of the war.'

'Did you loot it?'

'Not exactly. But I sometimes feel as if I did.'

'Who did you get it off, then?'

He seemed to be considering how to answer. In the end, he simply said, 'A boy.'

I was astounded. 'A boy owned that? Lucky sod!'

'If you'd known him, I doubt you'd have called him lucky.' Mr Dudley sounded quite severe. 'Klaus, his name was. I came across him in Berlin, wandering amongst the ruins. He was carrying a paper bag with a few little possessions in, trying to swop them for food. They were junk, mostly; whatever he'd managed to salvage from his home. But the camera was in amongst them. His father's, I suppose. He was a nice kid. I did what I could for him.'

'But he was a German!'

Mr Dudley didn't answer. All the same, I sensed the sharp edge of his disapproval, and hastily tried to manoeuvre myself back into favour.

'How old was he?'

'Oh – your sort of age; but a lot less fortunate. There were kids like that all over the place, starving, dressed in rags. I tried to find him again next day, to give him some more food and money, but...' He shook his head.

'So you never knew what became of him?'

'No, I'm sorry to say.' There was an awkward pause; then he suddenly smiled again. 'Anyway, you wanted to look at the camera.'

I tried a few scenes through the viewfinder. 'You see it the right way round,' I said. He looked puzzled, so I explained.

'Why not try taking a picture?'

'Sir! Could I?'

'Do you know how to set the focus?'

He took the camera back to show me. It was simple enough, except that the distances were in metres, and I didn't know how you paced them out.

Mr Dudley laughed. 'Ah, no. You see, this camera's got a coupled rangefinder.'

He moved two or three steps away from me. 'I've been taking shots of the buildings, but suppose I was going to take a picture of you from about here.' He held the camera up to his eye and pointed it towards me, reaching round for the focussing lever under the lens. 'I just look through here, you see, and alter the focus till the rangefinder tells me it's right. And then I take the picture.' He pressed a button on top of the camera, and wound the film on with a quick twist. 'Now, if I move a bit further away, I just look through the rangefinder, adjust the focus, and... click.' Once again, he pressed the shutter release and wound the film on. 'Or I could come in for a really big close-up.' He stepped forwards to within about three feet of me. 'I'm just getting your head and shoulders now. So I re-focus again, and... click. Very easy; very quick.'

'You're not actually taking all these pictures?' I asked in alarm.

He looked mildly embarrassed. 'Yes.'

'But you'll run out of film. There's only eight.'

He shook his head. 'You're thinking of roll-film cameras. This sort give you thirty or forty pictures at one loading. Plenty left.'

He handed me the camera, and explained how to use the range-finder, adjusting the focus until the two images coincided. 'Now, what are you going to take a picture of?'

Anything. It didn't matter. 'Shall I do one of the Library?'

'Good idea. Leave the shutter speed and aperture as they are. Move about till you see what you want in the viewfinder, look through the rangefinder to focus, and then you're in business.'

I found a suitable position, and went through all the steps as instructed. 'Shall I take it now?'

'When you're ready.'

A deep breath, finger on the shutter release, and it was done. My first photograph; and what was more, I'd taken it on a looted German Leica. Definitely a moment to savour.

'When can I see it?' I said. 'My picture, I mean.'

It seemed a reasonable enough request, but his face suddenly clouded over. 'I'm not sure. It's my last day, you see.'

'Sir?'

'Mr Hedger's better now. He'll be back next week.'

I stared at him blankly, unable to register what he was saying. 'You mean you're leaving *today*, sir?'

He smiled a little awkwardly. 'That's why I was taking pictures. I wanted some souvenirs.'

'But sir, we need you.' It was appalling. All the wonderful doors he'd opened for us were being slammed in our faces.

'Don't look so glum. When I've developed the film, I'll post you your photograph; how's that?'

'Yes, sir. Thank you, sir,' I said. But I hardly cared any more.

I ran straight to our Form Room, and blurted the news out to Toddy. Slater and Barry Anderson overheard, and in ten seconds it was all round the room.

'I vote we give him a going-away present,' Slater said.

'Yeah!'

'But there's no time. Dinner break ends in five minutes.'

'We can still collect. We'll just have to give him the money.'

Everyone started dipping into their pockets, contributing pennies and halfpennies and threepenny bits. There were even one or two sixpences, but it didn't look very much. If only we'd known.

People coming in from the yard were told the news and added whatever they could. Meanwhile, I was searching desperately for some money. Having tried all my pockets twice without success, I had a look in my desk. You never knew. But it was no good. Not even a farthing.

'Can you lend us something?' I whispered to Toddy.

He shook his head. 'I put in all I could spare. I need the rest.'

'But I've nothing to give him.'

'He won't know.'

'I'll know.'

'Ask someone else, then.'

As if I could go round begging. Besides, who else would have cash to spare?

For want of a paper bag, the little collection of coins, to which I had not contributed, was wrapped in the back page of an old *Beano*. At the end of afternoon school, we all filed into the Form Room and sat down silently in our places. I doubt if we'd ever been so quiet. Mr Dudley looked up in surprise, and glanced enquiringly in my direction. I sat quite still, but I could feel my cheeks burning. We waited, expectantly. After a few moments, a faint smile flickered across his face, and he said, 'I gather you've heard my news already.'

We shifted uneasily in our seats.

'It's been nice knowing you. I shall miss you all very much.'

Slater stood up awkwardly and walked round to the front, carrying the little parcel. He was supposed to make a speech, but at the last moment his nerve failed him. 'For you,' he said huskily, and scuttled back to his place, leaving the present on Dudley's desk.

Dudley picked it up in cautious surprise, whereupon the wrapping split, and the little collection spilled out in front of him, rolling in all directions. But he carried the moment off magnificently. Gathering the coins together into a tidy heap, he looked up at us and said solemnly, 'This is enormously kind of you. I really do appreciate it very, very much.'

We cheered him till we were out of breath. Most of the others crowded round his desk to say goodbye, but not having given him anything, I couldn't have looked him in the face. Besides, if you want the truth, I was scared of crying. There had been so much to look forward to, and now there was nothing. It had even occurred to me that given the right circumstances, he was the one person with whom I might conceivably broach the delicate matter of Jacko. And now it was too late. So although I hated myself for doing it, I simply slipped away without a word.

On Sunday, when I was round at the Whitmans', Mike said, 'I expect you'll all miss Dudley. I gather you gave him quite a send-off. Even a present.'

We were up in the Radio Room, but as it happened, Toddy had gone downstairs for a minute. 'I was broke,' I said. 'I didn't have anything to give.' Pointless to mention it, really; but for some reason, Mike seemed like a good person to tell.

He put his screwdriver down. 'Look, according to Toddy, nobody even knew Dudley was going until you told them.'

I nodded.

'So if it wasn't for you, there'd never have been any present. Surely that counts for something?'

I managed a weak smile. Actually, I'd have liked us to talk some more, just him and me, but Toddy was coming upstairs again, so I left it at that.

Next day, Hedger was back, complete with deaf aid and a fresh set of batteries.

And the very same week, at Barton – Wednesday it must have been – there was amazing news: Ronnie had scarpered.

That was an evening to remember. His empty place; the word going round; the eyes-down silence, no one admitting anything. And then the individual grillings, in at one door, out the other, and no conferring. Later, we whispered furtively about how he'd managed it, and what his chances were. All we could piece together between us was that he'd set off for school that morning but hadn't arrived. What then? Into Central London to hide out on a bomb site? Easy enough to do. Or maybe down to the docks and onto a ship. Or would he have headed north, to another large town? Or out into open country somewhere? It was all rather exciting, like a prisoner-of-war escape story.

At bed time, Jacko sent for me. Hardly the ideal moment. But for once, it was something else he wanted.

'Thought we might just have a quiet word. Rather heavy-handed, all those interrogations earlier.' He looked me straight in the eye, and held up two fingers twisted tightly together. 'You and Ronnie, eh?'

'He didn't tell me anything.'

Jacko took a deep breath, and let it out again, long and slow. 'You do realise, don't you, that he could be in terrible danger?'

'I've told you. I don't know nothing about it.'

He lit a cigarette. I thought I was in for some third degree. But he hastily stubbed it out again when he saw the look on my face, and shook his head as if to dismiss the very idea. Instead, he started fidgeting with the ornaments, moving them round and trying them in different positions.

'Nothing? You're quite sure? Not even a hint?'

I shook my head. 'It wouldn't have been his way.'

But Jacko wasn't ready to give up. 'I want you to think back carefully over the last week or two. There might be some little thing, meaningless at the time, that starts to make sense in the light of what's happened.'

'Not really.'

He seemed reluctant to let me go. 'Very well. But if anything occurs to you, come and see me at once.'

I was dimly aware that it gave me a certain power over him if he thought I could tell him something he wanted to know. But I was too artless to exploit the situation effectively.

In any case, I didn't have time. Next evening, just after tea, a van drove round to the yard at the back of the house. Two men got out and opened the rear doors. Ronnie was inside, bundled up on the floor. They hauled him out, and dragged him into the building like a sack of carrots, with his heels scraping along the ground. It was one of those sights that burn themselves into your memory and stay there all the rest of your life.

Wilkie emerged briefly from his office, and glowered at the rest of us as if he would shoot the first person who spoke; so we retreated, and left Ronnie to his fate.

At bed time, there was no sign of him.

'He'll be in the Sick Room,' Ocky said.

'Yeah. He looked in pretty poor shape.'

Ocky glanced at me as if I would never learn.

Next morning, at breakfast, Wilkie made an Announcement. 'As most of you probably realise, Ronald Pearson is in the Sick Room, and that's where he'll stay for the time being.'

'Can we go up and see him?'

'No.'

'Has he got something catching, then?'

'No. He's being given the opportunity to consider the consequences of his behaviour. The rest of you are not to go to the Sick Room, or to communicate with him in any way. Now, get on with your meal.'

'Solitary,' Ocky said under his breath. 'I knew it.'

'He'll go crackers, all on his own,' I whispered back. 'He can't even stand being indoors, never mind locked in a room.'

Ocky shrugged. 'Lucky it ain't the cellar.'

All the way to school, I kept seeing Ronnie dragged along the corridor, limp and defeated. He should have been kicking, struggling, shouting obscenities, but there hadn't been a flicker of life in him; and that was the worst thing of all.

'Is he still up there?' I said to Ocky, when I got home.

He nodded.

'Anyone made contact?'

'You heard Wilkie.'

'Sod Wilkie. We can't just leave him to rot.'

The Sick Room was at the very top of the house, on the second floor. Unfortunately, the foot of the staircase was right outside the door of the Wilkies' flat. Risky. But later, when Mrs Wilkie was down in the kitchen, Joe and Snap kept Wilkie busy in his office, and Ocky stood guard on the landing while I crept upstairs.

I tapped softly at the Sick Room door. 'Sst! Ronnie?'

The bed creaked, and a moment later I heard him crouching down to whisper through the keyhole. 'Who is it?'

'Alan. Are you all right?'

'Yeah. I suppose so.'

'Are they feeding you?'

'Bread and water.'

'What do you do all the time?'

'Nothing. Jerk off.'

'There's books and jigsaws in the cupboard. I've seen them.'

'It's locked.'

'Do they let you out at all?'

'No.'

'Not even for the toilet?'

'There's a bucket.'

'Couldn't you get out of the window?'

'Bars. Anyway, they've took my clothes.'

'What, all of them?'

'Yeah. Just got a blanket.'

I didn't know what to do. He needed food, or something to read; but what could you push through a keyhole?

'I'd best be going,' I said. 'I'll try and come up tomorrow, but it may be difficult. We're not supposed to talk to you.'

'I know. Don't hang about.'

Ocky was peering anxiously up the stairs as I came down. I gave him a quick summary, and later we wandered round, inspecting keyholes. Too small for fags, even for roll-ups. Drinking straws were a possibility; we might be able to smuggle a mug of cocoa up at supper time. But straws came undone if the drink was hot. What about liquorice braid? Just the shape to go through a keyhole, but we couldn't go out and buy it. The Wilkies kept our coupons, and bought big tins of toffees and acid drops for selling to us in quarters. Gum would have been okay, but we needed the flat kind you could only get off the Yanks.

'Can't we push something under the door?' Ocky suggested.

'No. I checked. There's a draught excluder.'

It looked pretty hopeless. But next morning, when I was typing labels for Mr Pond, I had an idea.

'Is there any string I could have?'

He held up a huge ball of the white sisal we used for packaging. It was much too thick and hairy, though. He burrowed about for a while in the far corner, and fished out a part-used cob of smooth white parcel string. It was perfect.

'Can I borrow it?'

'What do you want it for? Something to do with school?'

'No. I can't really tell you. But it's important. It's not just for mucking about.'

With a benevolent grunt of resignation, he slipped the cob into my pocket.

After dinner, Ocky kept watch again while I slipped upstairs to the Sick Room. I ought to have brought some wire; the end of the string kept drooping, and getting caught in the lock. But after about six goes, I felt Ronnie catch hold of it from the other side. The cob spun round on my pencil as he hauled the whole length through, hand over hand.

'Okay,' I said. 'We'll whistle as soon as we're ready.'

For our first delivery, Ocky had wheedled some biscuits out of Hurly. Heaven knows what blasphemies he'd been made to utter, but she'd given him half a dozen, and we wrapped them up in Friday's *Daily Mirror*. As soon as we judged it safe, we slipped round to the side of the house, and Ocky gave the signal.

For a long time, nothing happened. We gazed upwards anxiously, but the Sick Room had a dormer window set high in the roof, and you couldn't see it from the ground.

'What the hell is he doing?' Ocky said. 'We can't stay here for ever.'

'Perhaps it needs a weight on the end of the string,' I said.

But at that moment, the coil shot outwards over the gutter, unwinding as it fell. We tied the relief supplies onto the end, and whistled to Ronnie to haul away. Everything went fine till the package reached the gutter, but it caught there, and wouldn't slide over onto the tiles. For two or three minutes, we watched helplessly as the parcel kept dropping and rising again, only to jam each time at the same place.

'Fine scheme this turned out to be,' Ocky remarked.

The package suddenly dropped again, a lot lower, and dangled outside one of the first-floor windows.

'For Christ's sake! What if somebody comes?'

'Keep your hair on,' I said. 'It's only teething troubles.'

The package hung in mid-air for several seconds, then shot upwards again, flipped suddenly outwards round the gutter, and disappeared from view. A moment later, we heard a distant whistle, and the sound of the Sick Room window closing.

'Whew!' said Ocky. 'That's took ten years off my life.'

As we slipped away towards the back of the house, I saw Mr Pond gazing at us out of the workshop window. I waved to him and then noticed he was beckoning. We needed to sound the All Clear to the others, so I held my arm up with the fingers spread wide to indicate five minutes, and he nodded.

He had the lathe going when I arrived, so I stood and waited just inside the door while he finished the cut and slid the belt across to the loose pulley. After a long pause, he jerked his head towards the house. 'Wasn't that Ronnie up there?'

I nodded. 'He did a bunk, but they caught him.'

Mr Pond seemed to be searching my face for something he couldn't find. I felt uneasy. He was probably on our side, but you never could tell with people.

'He's locked up there on bread and water with nothing to do,' I said at last. 'They've even took his clothes. Everything. All he's got is a blanket.'

Still he didn't say anything.

I reckoned the time had come for some plain speaking. 'It's

not right, Mr Pond. It's really not right.'

He nodded gravely. 'And when's the next load?'

'As soon as we get some things together.'

He turned back to the lathe. 'Do you think you can finish facing this up for me? I need to pop out for a bit.'

'I suppose so.' Sudden panic. I'd never used the machinery on my own. What if I couldn't manage? Terry's collar-bone was bound to be mended soon, so I couldn't afford any accidents. 'It's mild steel, isn't it?' I said.

'Yes. Not difficult. Light cuts, remember, and plenty of suds.'

Cautiously, I slid the belt across to the Drive position, and took a trial cut. There was a faint rattling sound that I didn't like, but I kept the handle turning as smoothly as possible and eventually reached centre without mishap. So far, so good. Now it was just a question of patience, repeating the process, over and over, trimming a little bit more off every time.

One last extra-careful cut to leave a nice smooth finish, and I was done. With relief, I disengaged the drive, and examined my handiwork. Somehow, the surface never looks quite so nice as it does when it's still spinning, but it wasn't too bad, I reckoned.

'Good lad.'

It was Mr Pond. I looked up in surprise. 'I thought you'd gone.'

'I had. And now I'm back.' He handed me a small package, wrapped in newspaper. 'For Ronnie, whenever you get the chance.'

Inside, there was an old cardboard tan-gram puzzle, and a whole bar of Fry's Chocolate Peppermint Cream. A boy would kill for a single piece of it, especially one of the ends.

'Gosh, Mr Pond, that's really...'

He reached out and placed a finger gently across my lips. 'I don't know anything about it. Understand?'

Ocky said we should pack the parcel straight away, but leave delivery until after dark. Because of the gutter problem, we wanted to make the bundle as round as possible, so Ocky went in search of some more papers to use as padding. I was still at the table, waiting for him, when Tom and Eddie wandered in.

'Ta very much,' Tom said, and before I could stop him, he picked up the chocolate bar, broke it in two, and threw half to Eddie. Hardly pausing to tear the paper off, they crammed the whole lot into their mouths at once, and it was gone.

'God, you're a turd, Tom. That was for Ronnie.'

'You can nick another.'

'It wasn't nicked. It was given to us, specially. Someone went to a lot of trouble to get him that. If you won't help, at least don't pinch the things other people contribute.'

The way they stood and looked at me, I wanted to smash their faces in. But I couldn't tackle them both, so for the time being I was powerless. That's the trouble with being properly brought up: you go through life expecting everyone else to be reasonable, and when they aren't, you've nothing to fall back on but indignation.

Ocky was no help, either. 'You don't want to take it so hard,' he said.

He was right, of course. That's how you survived – by not caring. But how did you learn the knack of it? There were Pitman books to teach you Accountancy, or Shorthand, or Electroplating; there should have been one about Not Caring.

We packed up the tan-gram puzzle and one or two other things that people had given us, odd sweets, mostly, and sent them up to Ronnie after tea. This time, the system worked without a hitch; the parcel rose to the gutter, dropped a couple of feet, and then shot upwards again and out of sight.

'How long will they keep him there?' I said.

'Who knows? Till he gives in.'

'Gives in? To what?'

'How should I know? Whatever it is they want.'

'He'll never give in; not Ronnie.'

'Oh, yes,' Ocky said. 'You'll see.'

In the morning, as per normal, we came under fire from Snorty Pig on our way to church. Something else for me not to care about. I tried repeating 'I don't care, I don't care,' under my breath, but it didn't make any difference. I'd have given a month's earnings to meet him face to face, when he wasn't skulking behind his parents, or a gang of his posh friends.

The sermon aroused a momentary flicker of interest. 'Why should I trust in God, when all around me I see iniquity triumph?' But the reasons offered were unconvincing, and I don't remember them.

Afterwards, one or two people gave me comics for Ronnie. I thought we'd better deliver them straight away; I was off to the Whitmans' immediately after dinner, and I wouldn't be back till late. Ocky seemed to have disappeared, but now we'd got the system down to a fine art, I thought I could manage without him. It was as good a time as any. Wilkie was taking his mother home from church, Mrs Wilkie was helping Hurly with the dinners, and Jacko for certain sure would be down at the Welton Arms.

I gave Ronnie our usual whistle, but either he didn't hear me, or he was having problems getting the string ready. I whistled again, and heard the window open. At the same moment, I suddenly noticed Wilkie coming along the road; and with faultless timing, the string dropped at my feet just as he turned in at the front entrance.

A couple of minutes later, I was standing in his office with my head down and my hands behind my back.

'I suppose you thought you were helping him?' Wilkie remarked scathingly, after one or two wholly predictable opening exchanges.

'Yes. I don't think it's right to keep him locked up like that.'

'So going to Grammar School makes you an expert on right and wrong? It's a pity it hasn't taught you obedience and a bit more common sense. He'll be on his own much longer, thanks to you. Is that what you wanted?'

'No.'

'Then I hope you finally realise you're not so clever as you think. Were any of the others involved in this?'

'Just me.'

'What about Oliver?'

'No.'

'Did he know about it?'

'Everyone knew about it.'

'I wonder what they'll all think of you now.'

The desk blotter was lying a little askew. He straightened it, as if it offended him not to have things in perfect order when he was passing sentence.

'You can spend the rest of the day making yourself useful for a change,' he said. 'There are plenty of jobs waiting to be done. Immediately after dinner, you can clean the baths. By the time you've finished that, I'll have made out a list of the other things.'

'I'm supposed to be going to the Whitmans',' I said.

'You're not going anywhere.'

'They're expecting me.'

In silence, he pointed to the telephone.

'But I don't know the number.'

Still without speaking, he passed me the L to Z. I put the book down on the floor and started fluttering through the pages, crouching low so as to read the small print. There were dozens of

Whitmans.

R.K.Whitman & Son, Prntrs & Statnrs, Ealing. Ditto, Eastcote. Ditto, Harrow. Ditto, Hayes. Ditto, Northwood. Ditto, Pinner. Ditto, Ruislip. Ditto, Uxbridge.

Wilkie clicked his tongue impatiently.

'I'm sorry, Mr Wilkinson. It's hard to find.'

Eventually, I located their home number. Keeping the place with my finger, I raised my head level with the desk top, uncertain what to do next.

Wilkie gestured irritably at the telephone. 'Lift the receiver. When you're asked for the number, say it slowly and clearly.'

Toddy answered. His voice sounded loud and odd. It was strange, talking to him in front of Wilkie; they belonged to different worlds.

'It's me, Alan. I can't come.'

'Why not?'

'I've got to clean the baths.'

'What?'

'I'll tell you tomorrow.'

'All right.' There was a tremendous clatter in the earpiece as he put the phone down.

That'll be twopence,' Wilkie said, when I stood up.

At dinner, Ocky was scathing. 'You should have waited. Anyway, it was a daft scheme. I said so all along. You want to learn to leave things alone.'

Afterwards, I fetched the scouring powder from the scullery, and set to work on the baths. Twenty minutes, Wilkie had given me, before he came to inspect them.

Having dealt with the round end of the first bath, I was just squatting down in a fresh position when Tom and Eddie arrived. To begin with, they stood and watched me through the open doorway, but after a while they came inside and lounged against the wall.

'I wouldn't call that clean,' Tom said. 'Would you, Eddie?'

Eddie lurched forward and ran the palms of his hands all round the inside of the bath, leaving trails of black grease on the clean enamel.

The cold tap was already running, so I brought my hand up hard under the outlet, and raked them both with spray till I'd driven them out. A moment later, Tom reappeared in the doorway. As I reached for the tap again, he shouted 'Catch', and with a contemptuous little sneer, threw something towards me. By the time it had come to rest in the bottom of the bath, he was gone. I reached forward in surprise to pick it up. It was an acid drop.

I hadn't long finished the second bath when Wilkie came in for a look.

'All right,' he said briskly. 'That'll do. In a minute, you can scrub the kitchen floor, but first of all I want to show you something. Come with me.'

He unlocked the door at the top of the cellar steps, and beckoned me inside. I couldn't imagine what we were doing there. I'd been down once or twice before, to carry stores for Mrs Wilkie – crates of soap and disinfectant, tins of polish, boxes of toilet rolls. The boiler was down there, for heating the radiators; and a big pile of coke, tipped in through a coal hole in the yard. There was an old wooden ladder, too, hanging on rusty brackets, with a row of buckets underneath it, each containing an A.R.P. stirrup pump. Perhaps my next-but-one job was to sweep out all the cobwebs. I didn't much fancy the idea. With only a twenty-five watt bulb, the cellar was dark and spooky; you wouldn't want to be left there on your own.

He switched another light on. At the very end, the passage turned to the left and ran a yard or two further, with a door on either side.

'Wait there.'

He unlocked the right-hand door, leaving it ajar, and then stepped back to join me.

'Come out here,' he called.

There was a soft scuffling noise, and the sound of bare feet on concrete. Slowly, as if in a trance, Ronnie emerged and stood in front of us, swaying slightly, his face completely expressionless. He was naked, and his whole body was streaked with grime.

'Turn round.'

As he slowly rotated, I saw there were ten or a dozen thick purple weals across his arse, some fresh, some older.

'All right. Back inside.'

Without registering any emotion, Ronnie obediently stepped back through the doorway. Wilkie locked him in again and switched the light off.

'That's your handiwork,' he said to me. 'I hope you're proud of it.'

I must have worn the kitchen floor down further with my scrubbing brush in a single afternoon than generations of trampling feet had managed in half a century. Sometimes, the brush went round and round over the same four tiles for minutes on end. But the wet spirals of soap froth could not obliterate the scene in the cellar, or my own part in bringing it about.

Wild schemes crossed my mind for breaking in through the coal hole, jemmying open Ronnie's door with one of the pump stirrups, and using the ladder to help us both escape. And then? Hadn't I done enough harm already?

Or suppose I rushed out into the street and said to a passer-by, 'Help! My friend has been stripped naked, beaten, and locked in a dark cellar like a vicious animal. What shall I do?' They would look about them, and they would see the front of the house, all neat and respectable, and the pillar box, and the bus stop, and the advertisements for Ovaltine and Zam Buk on the side of the clothing factory; and instead of Attila the Hun or a stevedore in a drunken stupor, they would encounter Wilkie with his starched collar and polished boots and official printed stationery; and they would say to themselves, 'This boy is out of his mind.'

There was no solution. If it had been Tom or Eddie down there, I'd have been glad. Serve them right. But Ronnie? I could find no way to accommodate what I had seen; and the only defence against the nightmare was to scrub and scrub.

11

At school on Monday morning, Toddy demanded, 'What was all that about baths?'

'Just a spot of bother,' I said, and to change the subject, I told him about Wilkie charging me twopence for the call.

'You were rooked, then. Twopence is from a box. It's only a penny on a private line.'

Wouldn't you know it? – as Hurly might have remarked.

When I got home that evening, Wilkie wanted to see me. Now what? More floors to scrub? He held up a brown envelope. 'This came for you by the second post.'

My photograph! Dudley had kept his promise. Perhaps he'd put his address in, too, and I'd be able to write back. I held my hand out eagerly, but instead of passing me the envelope, Wilkie withdrew the contents and placed them carefully on his desk.

'You've opened it!' I said indignantly.

'If people are writing to you, I need to know who they are and what they want.'

'It's only a photograph. I took a picture on somebody else's camera and they promised to send it when it was developed.'

Wilkie glanced at the photo without interest, and put it aside. Then he held up another. 'And this?'

'Oh, that's just one of the ones he took of me.'

'So I see. It's very good. Very good indeed. It must have been an expensive camera.'

'A Leica,' I said, importantly.

'A Leica? You've got a friend with a Leica? Good Heavens, they cost a hundred pounds or more.'

'It's one of our teachers.'

'I see.' Wilkie looked puzzled. 'But in that case, why not simply give you the pictures at school?'

'He's left.'

'In the middle of a term?'

'Yes. He went very suddenly. Nobody was expecting it. Mr Hedger...'

'Just a minute, Alan. I think I'd better have another look at this letter.'

'But it's mine. It's private.' I snatched the sheet of paper up from the desk, and backed away. Wilkie stood there holding his hand out, and looking extremely irritated. But I took no notice.

As soon as I unfolded the letter, I could see there was no address, just a line or two of Dudley's familiar handwriting:

Dear Alan,

    I was sorry not see you again before I went. I have printed your photograph, and I hope you like it. I also enclose one of yourself. I think it's the best, altho' they are all good, and I am glad to have them. It was nice knowing you, and I enjoyed our time together. Give my regards to the others.

Philip Dudley

'There you are,' I said, resentfully, handing Wilkie the note. 'That's all it is.'

He glanced quickly through it, and put it down on the desk. Pointing to an upright chair that was standing against the wall, he said, 'Just bring that over here, would you, and sit down.'

I was surprised; this was a courtesy not normally extended to us.

Wilkie picked up the letter again. 'This Mr Dudley. How many pictures did he take of you?'

'I lost count.'

'That many? Didn't it strike you as rather odd?'

I explained about him demonstrating the rangefinder.

'And where did this take place?'

'Behind the Library.'

'Was anyone else there?'

'No.'

Wilkie glanced at the letter. 'Then who are these others he speaks of?'

'The rest of the form, I should think.'

'But they weren't there when he was taking the photographs?'

'No.'

A significant pause.

'Did he do anything else, besides taking the pictures?'

'I told you. He showed me the camera. And he let me take a photo.'

Wilkie nodded. 'How did all this come about? Did he ask you to meet him behind the Library?'

'No.'

Another pause.

'Were you alone with him on any other occasions?'

'He used to keep me back after school.'

'Why was that?'

'It was about my work.'

'I expect you talked about other things as well?'

'Sometimes.'

'What sort of things?'

'Private things.' I wasn't prepared to go into all the details.

Wilkie leant forward intently. 'What things, Alan?'

'I'm not telling you.' If I'd known all this was going to happen, I'd have asked Dudley to write to me care of the Whitmans.

Wilkie observed me for some time in silence. The chair seat was slippery, and sloped downwards; you had to brace your feet against the floor to keep from sliding off.

'He says here he was sorry not to see you before he went. Was he expecting to?'

'I don't know. I suppose so.'

'Well, then?'

'I didn't want to. Why do I have to answer all these questions?'

'Why didn't you want to, Alan?'

I hadn't the least intention of explaining.

'Why didn't you want to, Alan? Was it because of something that had happened earlier?'

'It's none of your bloody business.'

'Don't speak like that.' Wilkie glowered at me, his eyebrows knitting across the frown lines.

'I don't understand,' I shouted back. 'What am I supposed to have done?'

'No one's accusing you of anything.'

'Then why won't you give me my letter and leave me alone?'

I thought he was going to hit me; but after a tight-lipped silence, he put the two photographs back in the envelope and handed them over. I snatched them from him angrily, though I hardly wanted them now. They had been defiled.

The letter was still on his desk. 'I shall need to keep this for a day or two,' he said.

'Why? It's mine. What right have you got to take my things?'

No answer. He simply opened a drawer and put the letter inside.

I stood up angrily. 'And about that phone call to the Whitmans. You chiselled me. It's only a penny, and you charged me twopence.'

He stared back bleakly.

'So you owe me a penny,' I said.

We confronted each other in silence across the desk for about half a minute. I made my mind up that if he gave me the penny back, I wouldn't keep it; I'd put it in one of those little net stockings for the Blind that hung in shops.

At last, he said stiffly. 'So you think I owe you a penny? Have you ever stopped to consider what you owe me, what you owe all of us here?' He crossed over to the window and stood looking out towards the clothing factory. 'All over Europe, there are children who lost their homes and families in the war. But unlike you, they have nowhere to live and no one to look after them.'

'I know,' I said, thinking of Klaus.

'Well, then, considering that you're fortunate enough to be fed and clothed and given a home at public expense, shouldn't you be a bit more co-operative? Whatever you may think, we're only trying to do what's best for you.'

It was pointless arguing, so I shrugged as insolently as I dared, and left it at that.

As soon as I got home the following evening, Jacko beckoned me surreptitiously into the Quiet Room. There was a notice pinned to the door, saying Keep Out.

'What, in here?' I said. We always did it in his flat.

But the moment I stepped inside, he walked out again, closing the door behind him. I thought he was locking me in. Utterly bewildered, I turned towards the window, and found that I was not alone. Slumped on a chair in the far corner was Ronnie, washed and dressed, but looking like someone the morning after an air raid.

I didn't know how it was going to be between us. After all, I was to blame. 'Are you all right?' I asked doubtfully.

He nodded, and the corners of his mouth twitched upwards into the vague semblance of a smile.

'Look, I'm really sorry about what happened.'

He shrugged philosophically.

'When did they let you out?'

He shrugged again, and stared blankly out of the window.

I thought I'd better explain about the chocolate bar, in case Mr Pond referred to it. After that, I ran out of things to say. There were all sorts of questions I wanted to ask him, but somehow I didn't like to, after what he'd been through. It made you feel pretty humble.

At tea, Ocky and I sat one each side of him, like bodyguards. Amidst the general chatter, I failed to register something that should have been obvious. Then there was my homework to finish, so it wasn't till supper time that I really became aware of it. Even then it needed Ocky to point it out.

'You know what?' he muttered, glancing at Ronnie over his shoulder, 'He ain't said nothin.'

'I don't blame him. Who'd want to talk about it?'

'No, I mean he ain't said *nothin*. Nothin at all.'

And it was true. He communicated after a fashion, nodding or shaking his head in reply to a question; he would point, if asked to choose, or shrug to convey indifference. But since he came out of the cellar, not once had anyone heard him actually speak.

It was the same all week.

'Cat got your tongue?' Mrs Wilkie said, unwisely, one day when he hadn't answered; and slowly turning his head to fix her with a gaze as cold and pitiless as a gun barrel, he simply stared her inch by inch into the ground.

'How's Ronnie?' said Mr Pond, on Saturday morning.

'I don't know. He's acting a bit strange. I messed things up with the string, you see, and we got caught. After that, they put him down in the bomb shelter. And...' I hesitated, uncertain how far to go.

Without comment, he slid a length of hexagon brass into the lathe. I got the feeling he wished he hadn't asked.

'It's pretty bad down there,' I said. 'They made me go and look. I saw what they'd done to him, the bruises and everything. And it was all my fault.'

He thrust a blueprint at me. 'See what you make of that. Terminals. For Morse keys. It'll be good practice for you.'

To hide my confusion, I studied the drawing extra hard. The job didn't look too complicated. 'How many off?' I asked.

'Only four hundred. Not worth anyone tooling up for properly. Now, what do we do first?'

'Cut off a piece the right length?'

'All right.'

I fitted the parting tool into the holder and measured up as accurately as I could. Parting off was my least favourite job; you could easily make a mess of it. But for once I was in luck; the piece came away quite neatly, and it was exactly the right length. Three-quarters of an inch, spot on.

'Good. Now do another the same.'

That one was okay as well, or so I thought. But when the two pieces were held against each other, the second was a fraction longer. 'Does it matter?' I asked.

He looked at me as if I'd said a really bad word.

Shall I trim it down to match?'

He nodded, so I changed to the other cutting tool and took just the tiniest whisker off. It wasn't enough, so I tried again and ended up making it shorter than the first. It took me fifteen or twenty minutes, trimming them down alternately, until I got them exactly the same length. 'There,' I said, holding them out for inspection. 'They match now.'

'Yes,' he conceded. 'But do they match the drawing?'

I measured, and of course I'd cut them back so much they were almost a sixteenth under size. 'Won't they do?' I said.

He pointed to the blueprint. 'Three-quarters means three-quarters.'

All that trouble for nothing. He might have warned me. I chucked the pieces angrily into the waste box. Another failure.

As usual, Mr Pond remained unruffled. 'There's many a job

that has to be done twice. The first time, you find out how not to do it. Now, fetch them back, and you can have a shot at the next stage.'

The terminals needed a crosswise hole for the wire to fit into. He watched intently as I took the pieces over to the drilling machine and fitted the first one into the vice.

Or, to be more precise, discovered that I couldn't. The trouble with hexagon bar is that you don't get a flat side facing upwards; but if you try and grip it across the corners, you chew them to bits. The only hope was to fit the terminal end-on between the vice jaws, but the grip wasn't secure enough and the drill immediately snatched it out.

'You can't do it,' I said at last. 'There isn't a way.'

He gave me an arch look. 'There's always a way. The trick is finding it. Have another think while you brew up.'

What I thought was: Terry would never have made such a fool of himself.

When I brought Mr Pond his tea, he beckoned me back to the lathe. 'Now you've discovered the questions, you'll understand the answers. I've set this to give us three-quarters of an inch.'

He slid the hex bar up to an adjustable stop, tightened the chuck jaws, and set the lathe going. In a few seconds, he had parted off a piece to exactly the right length without having had to measure it. A minute or two later, the whole of the first bar had been cut into pieces all precisely the same, and he was starting on a second.

Carrying a box full of cut lengths across to the drilling machine, he showed me a small jig made from a block of wood. With this arranged in the vice, you could quickly insert each terminal and lock it in exactly the right position. After a couple of minutes' practice, I was in production, drilling the pieces as fast as he cut them. By dinner time, we had notched up the whole four hundred.

Before I went, I watched him get things ready for drilling and tapping the screw holes. After one or two final adjustments, he started putting the pieces through at incredible speed. Even with all his special gadgets, I shouldn't have been a tenth as quick.

'Experience,' he said. 'That's what counts.'

'Yes, I can see. So when's Terry coming back?' That seemed to be where we were heading; I might as well know how things stood.

'Terry? He isn't. Now, go and get your dinner.'

After the meal, I was thinking of going back to the workshop, but Wilkie called me into his office and shut the door.

'Can I trust you, Alan?'

A pointless question, if ever there was one. What did he think I was going to say?

'Ronald Pearson needs some fresh air. But I'm only willing to let him go out if someone reliable stays with him all the time. And I mean, all the time. Do you understand?'

'Yes.'

Actually, I couldn't make any sense of it. Reliable? Me? After all he'd said? Anyway, why couldn't Wilkie go with him? Then I saw it. They thought that with just the two of us on our own, he might start talking again.

Most of the shops were shut on Saturday afternoons, so we made for the Green Belt. If you went over the footbridge and kept going for quite a way, you came out onto the golf links. About a mile further on, there was a stand of climbable trees, with several patches of dense undergrowth where you could lie low. It was better when there was plenty of foliage, but we found a suitable place without much difficulty, a tiny patch of clear ground in the middle of a thicket, with a tangle of branches over our heads and all around us.

We sat huddled together with our backs against a tree trunk, and shared a fag.

'I wish I could blow smoke rings,' I said, and we both tried for a while without success.

In the past, we'd always been quite at ease with each other's silences, but that was when we could still talk if we wanted to. I had a creepy feeling there was something very important I needed to do or say to break the spell; only it was up to me to guess what it was, and because I couldn't, I was letting him down.

To pass the time, I started a game of noughts and crosses, drawing the lines with my finger in the soft leaf mould. Toddy had once told me there was a way you could always win, but I couldn't remember it.

After about half an hour, we crawled out of the thicket and found a tree to climb. It was a good feeling, perched high in the branches, where you could take the piss out of unsuspecting golfers down below, the men in ridiculous plus fours, the women in pleated skirts and green celluloid eyeshades. But eventually they all moved out of earshot.

'D'you want to go back, now?' I said.

Ronnie nodded – a bit reluctantly, I thought, but there wasn't much point in staying.

When we were nearly back at the footbridge, we noticed four or five St Andrews boys coming towards us. Their sports field was further along the road; they must have been going home after a football match.

Technically, we were on their territory, and two against five would be tricky. If they got to the little wicket gate before us, they could simply stand in front of it and stop us reaching the bridge. By running flat out, we could probably get there first, and if I'd been with Ocky, I think that's what we'd have done. But I wasn't going to demean myself in front of Ronnie. Besides, as the distance between us narrowed, I saw that one of the five was Snorty Pig.

Sure enough, when we reached the wicket gate, they were leaning against the railings, blocking our way. 'The fat one's mine,' I murmured to Ronnie.

We planted ourselves in front of them, and for a time we all just stood there, sizing each other up. You could tell at once that two of them were starting to feel doubtful. We might be outnumbered, but one look at Ronnie was enough to convince most people that they'd better not take any chances.

Between us, we could certainly deal with Snorty Pig and the boy next to him; the waverers wouldn't be much trouble. That left the fifth. He was tall, and about my age, or a bit older. As we met each other's gaze, it seemed to me that he didn't belong with the rest. If he hadn't been a St Andrews boy, I'd have said he looked pretty decent. Everything just right about him, somehow, the way you'd have wanted yourself to be, given the choice.

He was studying me intently, as if I belonged to a species he'd heard about, but never actually seen. I tried hard to guess what he was thinking, but I couldn't fathom his expression. Not hostile, though. Uneasy, perhaps, but not afraid; definitely not afraid. Puzzled? Surprised? Intrigued? Impatient? I tried a whole list of words and none of them fitted.

All of a sudden, he seemed to reach a decision. Glancing at his wristwatch, he said curtly to the others, 'Oh, come on, this is ridiculous.' Without more ado, he hitched his bag over his shoulder, and set off down the road.

'Oi! Jessop!' Snorty Pig whined in dismay. 'Come back!'

The boy took no notice.

'Dave! Don't!'

But it was too late. The waverers were already picking their bags up and preparing to follow. That just left Snorty Pig and one other. Ronnie stepped forward towards the wicket gate, and the two of them sullenly moved aside for us.

We hadn't gone more than a dozen paces when I was hit on the back of the neck by a clod of earth. I spun round to see Snorty Pig leaning over the gate and giving me a V sign with his catapult. But the moment I set off after him, he dodged quickly away down the road, and by the time I was through the gate again, he'd caught up with the others and wasn't worth chasing.

It was a less than satisfactory encounter. Certainly not the defeat it might have been, but inconclusive. I didn't insist on drawing blood, or feeling the crunch of bone under my fist, but something more than a moral victory was called for before we could walk unhindered where we pleased.

Wilkie was on the lookout when we got back to Barton, and he gave me a small nod of acknowledgement. But next day, I was back in the doghouse.

On the way to church, we came under fire as usual, and something sharp caught me right on the cheek. It was too much. Just ahead of me, in the gutter, lay a handy stone of the perfect size and shape. I broke ranks and picked it up. As the others walked dutifully on, I stepped up to the fence and chucked the stone as hard as I could at Snorty Pig's bedroom window. By a happy fluke, I scored a bull's eye, and the whole pane disintegrated with a sound-effect the BBC would have paid a fortune for.

The column came to an abrupt halt. Concealment or denial were out of the question, so I simply stood by the fence like a suffragette waiting to be arrested. Jacko strode back and seized me by the collar. Seconds later, I was standing in chains beside him on the doorstep.

As he reached for the bell, the door opened, and a man stepped out to confront us. He was wearing a bow tie and a fawn cardigan. Snorty Pig himself could be seen skulking in the background.

Jacko and Mr Snorty Pig noticed each other's bow ties, and immediately locked horns.

'I take it this little hooligan is in your charge?'

'Yes,' Jacko admitted. 'He's one of ours.'

'Then it's a pity you don't keep him under control.'

'I haven't got eyes in the back of my head.'

'You wouldn't need to have if you kept proper discipline. What are you, some sort of trainee?'

'No,' said Jacko.

Mr Snorty Pig looked at me in disdain. 'And what have you got to say for yourself? Would it be too much to ask for an explanation?'

'Ask your son,' I said. 'He's just behind you.'

'I'm asking you.'

'All right. Every Sunday we walk past, he fires his catapult at us, and we're all sick of it.'

'My son doesn't own a catapult.'

I jerked my head towards the others, who were watching from the roadside in amazement. 'If you don't believe me, ask them. Or ask the boys he was with yesterday afternoon.'

'What boys?'

'From his school. Dave Jessop, for one.'

Mr Snorty Pig summoned his son. 'We'll soon settle this. Malcolm, do you own a catapult?'

'No, Dad.'

'Have you ever fired a catapult at this boy, or any of his friends?'

'No, Dad.'

'Yes you fucking well have,' I protested.

Mr Snorty Pig surveyed me like a heap of camel crap. 'Do I understand you to say that my son is a liar?'

'Yeah. Why don't you search his things? Then you'll see.'

There was a tense pause.

'I think...,' Jacko remarked, to my surprise, 'I think there may be something in what he says. You know what boys are.'

Mr Snorty Pig gave him a bleak stare. 'I don't believe I know your name.'

'Crofting.'

'I can assure you, Mr Crofting, I see no reason to doubt my son's word. And now I must ask you to remove this foul-mouthed little guttersnipe before I lose my temper with him. I shall expect to hear in due course that he's been suitably disciplined. You'll receive my formal letter of complaint in the morning, and the glazier's bill will follow. Good day to you.'

As the column was being hastily re-formed, Ocky hissed, 'Have you gone completely round the bend?'

'I just lost my rag. Time somebody stopped him.'

'You could have gone back later and done it.'

'It wouldn't have been the same.'

'No. You wouldn't have got caught, for one thing.'

In Church, I was made to sit two rows in front of everyone else, so that I could repent, and have pellets flicked at me. During the sermon, I consoled myself with the pleasing fantasy that behind closed doors a raid on Snorty Pig's bedroom was even now revealing all, and that as we were walking home he would be dragged out of the house and obliged to grovel. Naturally, this did not happen.

My interview with Wilkie was brief, and to the point. He said two things: first, that I should have to pay for the window; and second, that I was getting to be the absolute limit and he proposed to give me the stick, only since it was Sunday, it would have to wait until after school tomorrow. I spent the rest of the day feeling vaguely sick. The exhilaration had all gone, and the general opinion seemed to be that I was a fool.

At primary school, I'd once had a couple across the hands with a whippy little classroom cane. I knew it was going to be worse than that; much worse. I'd seen Ronnie. Even so, when the time came, and I knocked on Wilkie's door, I wasn't altogether prepared for what followed.

On the desk was a leather-bound stick a yard long and about three-quarters of an inch thick, though it tapered somewhat. There was a brass ferrule at one end, and a big silver knob at the other.

Wilkie pointed in silence to a low wooden stool. I bent over it experimentally, whereupon he stepped forward to push my head right down and place my hands firmly, one each side, so that I was gripping the edges.

It was like waiting for Jacko, except that I had my clothes on. Not that they made much difference; my shorts might as well have been made of muslin for all the protection they gave me. When the stick came down for the first time, I gasped at the sheer intensity of the pain, and gripped the top of the stool as hard as I could. The second time, it was worse, like a red-hot branding iron searing into the flesh. For the third, I had my teeth clenched and my eyes tight shut; even so, it made me catch my breath so sharply that I thought I should suffocate.

Only halfway. How I was going to survive the rest, I couldn't imagine. At the absolute outside, one more was all I could take. The fiercely throbbing pain from the first three was already forcing the tears out from behind my closed eyelids. I struggled desperately to hold them back. After all, I was a Grammar School boy. But at the fourth, they burst out uncontrollably, scalding hot, like a saucepan boiling over. I gulped frantically for air, my chest and stomach drawn in so tightly I couldn't breathe. The fifth went high, almost onto my back. One more. If Ronnie could take it, so could I. But after the sixth, which came down extra hard and right along the line of the first, my arms and thighs gave way, and I collapsed over the stool, sobbing like a six-year-old. It was a sickening humiliation, even harder to bear than the pain itself.

Wilkie stepped past me and held the door open. As I left the room, I prayed that no one would see me. But Ocky was keeping watch outside the Club Room. 'Come on, then,' he said, 'Give us a look.'

I pushed past him, and made my way upstairs. For the next twenty minutes or so, I was writhing about on the bed with my knees doubled up to my chest and a handkerchief stuffed in my mouth. I hadn't realised the effects would last so long.

Shortly before tea, Tom appeared, and stood lounging in the doorway. 'How many?'

I held up six fingers.

'You were lucky, then.' He looked me over shrewdly. 'Know what you want to do now? Pull your wire. I'm not kidding. Puts you back on top.'

Sound advice, as it turned out. A great calm settled over me as I lay in bed that night; a feeling of crisis past. At least we shouldn't have any more trouble with Snorty Pig. I didn't feel quite so bad about Ronnie, either.

As for Jacko, I thought he might have the decency to leave me alone for a bit. But the next fortnight proved to be heavy going. Nine days in a row, plus Saturday matinee. My bruises seemed to excite him considerably, and when at last they started to fade, he commented wistfully, 'I hope it isn't long before you're naughty again.'

Greatly to my surprise, he also said he would pay for the broken window, and slipped a ten-bob note into my pocket, more than enough. After such a marathon, it seemed the least I was entitled to; so I took it. But it was a bad mistake, and later I wished I hadn't. Almost without my noticing, he had managed to change the rules. Accepting cash implied consent. If I ever complained in future, people would answer, 'Well, if you've taken money...'

Besides, what did it make me?

Not that there wasn't a perfectly good word for it.

Toddy had noticed the bruise lines on the second or third day, when we were changing for football.

'Cor!' he said, lifting my shirt tail for a better look. 'Rev Ev?'

'Nothing to do with school.'

'They did that to you at home?' He sounded incredulous.

'I broke a window. Now, shut up, can't you.'

I didn't talk about Barton when I was at school. It was very important to me to keep my life in watertight compartments. Above all, I didn't want things from Barton leaking out and contaminating the time I spent at the Whitmans'. Toddy seemed quite incapable of grasping this. At the weekend, when we were up in his bedroom, he suddenly called out, 'Hey, Mike, come and see Alan's bum.'

'For Christ's sake!' I said. 'Why do you keep going on about it?'

'You don't have to be like that.'

'I've told you once already. Knock it off.'

'Who do you think you are, giving me orders in my own house?'

'Leave me alone, then.'

'If you don't like it here, why come?'

'The way you carry on, I sometimes wonder.'

'Well, that's that, then.' He flung his book down in a fury, and stormed out.

By this time, Mike had come in from the Radio Room. 'What was all that about?' he said.

I shook my head, and stared down at the floor. Another mess. I didn't want to go into it.

He sat down beside me on the bed. 'Rough week, uh?'

I shrugged, and looked away. 'A bit.'

'Toddy can be pretty irritating.'

'Oh, it was my fault, really.' I made as if to stand up. 'I'd better go and find him.'

'No.' His hand on my shoulder. 'You both need a bit longer to cool off.'

So what was I supposed to do, sit there, and count to a thousand?

Mike stood up. 'Do you want to come into the Radio Room? I could do with a hand.'

He showed me the set he was building. There was a mass of wiring to be soldered onto a valve base, with not much room for manoeuvre, and some of the wires had a will of their own.

'If you could just hold them for me, it shouldn't be too difficult.'

I held the first wire in place and watched carefully while he soldered it. He was using an electric soldering iron, which was something new to me, and a neat little roll of multicore which he unwound as he went.

'That's handy,' I said.

He looked up for a moment, and smiled. The smell of the hot flux and solder was filling the air like incense. 'Now, this one, look.'

I loved watching him work. His hands were lean and strong, with slim fingers perfectly in control. He brought the iron in at exactly the right angle, and with one quick touch, the job was done.

'Thanks. That's super. Toddy's no good at this. Too clumsy.'

I looked round the room at the circuit diagrams pinned to the wall, the tools and tobacco tins, the coils of wire and boxes of odds and ends. 'I wish we could learn this sort of thing at school.'

He held up the soldering iron. 'Do you want a go?'

'Could I?'

He found me some bits of wire and a broken valve base to practise with. After about ten goes, I finally managed to fix a wire to one of the tags, but instead of a neat, professional-looking joint, the result had all the finesse of mud-plastering done by a caveman.

'This is a mess,' I said.

'It doesn't matter. It's only junk.'

'Yes, but what am I doing wrong?'

He took a closer look. 'You're melting the solder first, and trying to put it on like paint. Hold the dry iron against the work to heat everything up, then touch the place with the solder, and it simply flows on.'

I was just getting the hang of it, when Toddy re-appeared, clutching a football. We eyed each other doubtfully.

'I'm sorry, Toddy,' I said. 'I didn't mean it.'

He nodded. 'Yeah. Okay.' He was still looking sulky, though, and you could hardly blame him. 'I'm going out,' he said, turning the ball round and round in his hands.

'Shall I come?'

'Please yourself.'

I glanced uncertainly at Mike. He nodded towards the door. 'Go on. You can do this another time.'

So Toddy and I took turns at keeping goal in front of the shed, and by tea time any residual aggression had been taken out on the ball.

After the meal, I got out my photographs to show to Mrs

Whitman. 'I took that,' I said, handing her the one of the Library.

'Did you, love? I didn't know you had a camera.'

'It was Mr Dudley's. He let me try it.'

'Let's have a look,' Toddy said. He took the picture from her, but quickly discarded it. 'It's only the Library. What ever did you want that for?'

'Nothing. Just testing the camera.'

'It's incredibly sharp,' Mike said. 'You can make out every individual brick.'

'It was a Leica.'

Mike was impressed. 'Fantastic lenses.'

'So what's the other one, then?' said Toddy.

I held it up for him to see.

'Yuk,' he said. 'That was a waste of film.'

Mike deftly removed the picture from between my fingers. 'Hey!' he said. 'This is really something. It ought to go on our board.'

Toddy looked rather surprised, I thought, but the idea was carried by acclamation. A space was made, and my portrait was pinned up next to some snaps of Mike and Toddy. To see it there with the others, you'd have thought I was one of the family.

Afterwards, when we were clearing away, Mrs Whitman stood and looked at the photo for a long time. 'It's lovely,' she said; and then quite suddenly, for no reason at all, she leant forward and kissed me.

12

As an Easter Holiday Special, one of the local cinemas was showing *Pinocchio*. I'd missed it earlier, and was keen to see it. Ocky wasn't interested; but rather to my surprise, Ronnie agreed to come. I suppose it was better than stopping at Barton; they still weren't letting him out without an escort.

And he still wasn't talking.

The Tivoli was a strange, out-of-the-way cinema we didn't normally go to. There were cast-iron pillars holding the roof up, and no curtains round the screen. The seats were threepence cheaper than anywhere else, but you lost the whole of that on the higher bus fare. I was glad we'd come, though.

'Geppetto's just like Mr Pond,' I whispered, and Ronnie looked round at me with a quiet grin. The only dubious bit was where the boys got whipped and locked in a dungeon. We glanced at each other involuntarily, and Ronnie suddenly slid down very low in his seat.

To get our money's worth, we stayed on for the B picture, a pointless story about an American sailor who rode a motorbike and was nicknamed Coffee Cup. Before long, boredom and the aftermath of a thirst at dinner time began to take effect.

'Got to go for a pee,' I said to Ronnie, and he nodded without looking away from the screen.

There was a man at the near end of the urinal, shaking himself prior to buttoning up, so I walked well past him and stood at the far corner.

'What did you think of the picture?' he said.

'All right.' I glanced towards him, saw what he was actually doing, and hastily looked away again.

'Want to make ten bob?' he said.

'Not your way.'

'Quid?'

'No fear.'

I sensed him looking me shrewdly up and down. 'Go on, you've done it before. I can tell.'

How? I shuddered, and wished I hadn't drunk so much water. It felt as if I should never finish. 'I've done it with better class than you,' I said. I really don't know why.

'Okay. Thirty bob, so long as I get what I want.'

'Let's see your money.'

He reached for his pocket, and while his hands were occupied, I made a run for it. He grabbed wildly at me as I passed, but I broke free and dashed out, slamming the door behind me.

'Time to go,' I said to Ronnie, tugging urgently at his sleeve. 'There's a bandit in the bogs.'

He shook me off angrily. 'Keep your hair on! Everyone knows that.'

I looked at him in amazement, and then saw that it wasn't Ronnie at all. I'd been in such a panic, I'd mistaken the row. I stood up for a look at the seats behind and in front of me, and several people shouted Sit Down; so I perched on the edge of my seat and peered this way and that, trying to spot him. But he wasn't there.

Having struggled past feet and knees as far as the central gangway, I walked slowly up and down it, scanning the faces by the light from the screen. In the end, I called out in desperation, 'Ronnie, where are you?'

'Ronnie, where are you?' somebody echoed in a silly voice, and a man shouted at us to shut up.

At the back, an usherette was sitting on a small seat that folded down from the wall.

'Did a boy walk out on his own just now?' I asked her.

'Couldn't say, duck, I show them in, not out.'

I asked at the box office, too, but the girl hadn't noticed him. So I went outside for a good look round on both sides of the street. There was no sign of him.

For a while, I hung around on the steps, looking at the stills, like someone stood up on a date. He might have let me know. At least we could have said goodbye. Or perhaps he'd simply seen his chance and taken it. In that case, all I could do now was to give him as long a start as possible; so I let three buses come and go, after which there was nothing for it but to return home and face Wilkie.

He heard me out in grim silence, and then said, 'Now, let's go back to the start. And this time, I want the truth.'

'But Mr Wilkinson...'

'You fixed it all up between you, didn't you? I don't suppose you ever went near the cinema.'

'Yes, we did.'

'Have you got your ticket? No, don't tell me, you threw it away.'

'I can tell you about the film.'

'*Pinocchio?* Who couldn't? Did anyone actually see you there?'

I thought for a moment. The man in the toilets. No point in mentioning that. 'I told you, I asked the box office, and one of the usherettes. They might remember.'

'But you said yourself they hadn't seen Ronald. I'll bet he was never there. That's it, isn't it? *You* really did go to the pictures, but Ronald didn't.'

'We both went. I told you.'

'I've only your word for it. And what's that worth, I wonder.'

It was hopeless.

The way he moistened his lips was full of menace. 'I'll give you one last chance, Alan. I want the truth, the whole truth, and I want it now.'

I waited in silence, doing my best to meet his gaze. After about thirty seconds, he started to drum impatiently on his desk – as if I wasn't rattled enough already. 'You remember the last time you were stupid enough to defy me because you thought it would help Ronald?'

'Yes.'

'And you still have nothing to say to me?'

'I've told you everything I know.'

He stood up decisively. 'Very well. Come with me.'

I followed him upstairs, and soon realised we were heading for the Sick Room. He opened the door, and pointed. 'In you go. I'll speak to you later, when you've come to your senses.' I heard the key turn in the lock, and the sound of receding footsteps on the stairs.

It must have been round about eight when he came back. I'd had long enough to go practically berserk and then subside again into sullen hostility.

'Well?'

I had nothing to say, and I saw no reason to move, so I simply lay there on the bare mattress with my hands under my head.

'Stand up,' he snapped. 'I'm beginning to think I didn't thrash you hard enough.'

'I've said what happened. I can't help it if you don't believe me.'

'Can't you?' he said. 'Then answer me this. If you'd known what Ronald was planning, would you have tried to stop him?'

'No.'

'And would you have told me about it?'

'No.'

'Then give me one good reason why I should believe you.'

'Because it's true.'

There was a long silence. I looked at the floor, the bed, the walls, the window. At last, Wilkie said, 'You'd better go down and get your supper. It's waiting for you in the Dining Room. And remember, there's other places I can put you, besides up here.'

That night, I lay awake for ages, thinking about Ronnie. He wouldn't be back. Pond's Law: first you learn how not to do it, then you do it right. Anyway, after the last time, he'd chuck himself under a train, sooner than get caught. I wished him all the luck in the world, of course; and I was glad, now, that he hadn't warned me, because whatever happened, I couldn't betray him. But I was sad to think I shouldn't see him again. Barton without Ronnie was something I didn't much care to contemplate.

Luckily, there was another Boys' Home that I'd taken to visiting, and I could go there every night. I'm not sure where it was, exactly, but it stood beside a lake. The boys had a little boat, and they could swim, or go fishing; and behind the house was a field, big enough for a football pitch. Every boy had his own room, or he could share with a friend if he wanted.

It was run by a big, sensible man called Andy, who never lost his temper. He looked after the boys when they needed it, and if anyone had a problem, they could tell him, and he would help them sort it out. But apart from that, he didn't interfere. Sometimes, he was married, and his wife was a bit like Mrs Whitman; but mostly he was a bachelor, only not like Jacko. He could go to Wilkie, and say, 'I order you to hand over Ronnie Pearson,' or whoever it happened to be, and Wilkie would have to do it. Then the boy would be taken in Andy's car to the Lakeside house, and pretty soon he would start to feel better. For one thing, it was always warm enough, and there were plenty of decent meals. Also, when a boy arrived, there was bound to be somebody there that the same things had happened to, so they would understand each other, and not feel so alone.

There were generally ten or a dozen boys at Lakeside, and everyone said what decent kids they were. People would gladly find them work, so they could earn some dough, and the other boys in the neighbourhood all wanted to be friends with them.

Unfortunately, there was this man who lived in a big house on the far side of the lake, and every now and then he would capture one of the Lakeside boys and lock him up there. But the others would soon find out, and then they would go and rescue him.

You could stay at Lakeside till you left school. But it sometimes came about that a boy would meet some people, probably they were the parents of one of his friends, who would ask him if he would like to go and live with them. If that happened, he would probably say, 'Yes, please', although it was not unknown for a boy to decide that he didn't want people pretending to be his parents when they weren't, and in that case he would stay on at Lakeside after all. If he wasn't certain, Andy would help him decide. Or he could talk to the friend he shared a room with, while they were waiting to go to sleep.

Next morning, at Mr Pond's, there was a big consignment of fresh stock to be checked against the original order and put away. We were short by a dozen pieces of brass rod, which meant double-checking, and then writing a giant letter on the label typewriter to complain. After I'd brewed up, there were parcels to be packed, and put out ready for Carter Paterson. Then we started a run of spacing columns for a firm in Princes Risborough that manufactured chess clocks out of kitchen timers. So I didn't have much chance to think about Ronnie.

But after dinner, I felt the need to visit our special place on the far side of the golf links – though I don't know what I thought I was going to find there. A clue of some sort? A message in a forked stick?

As I came within half a mile, I was annoyed to see a gang of intruders roaming about quite close to our hiding place. Now and again, I caught their distant voices on the wind, but I was too far away to see who they were. In any case, I probably wouldn't have known them; that was the trouble with going to Bishop Inglis. But there was no hurry. I could wait. So instead of heading for the trees, I veered off towards a patch of rough ground on the other side of the fairway.

After about three-quarters of an hour, I saw them begin to straggle away, two or three at first, the others following. They wandered rather aimlessly across the golf course, and at one point they passed close enough for me to recognise Snorty Pig. Lucky I'd kept away.

I watched them out of sight, and then headed for the trees. It was a relief to crawl in through the tangled undergrowth and reach our place of refuge. I leant back against the tree trunk, and had a fag. My last.

By the time I'd finished it, I was beginning to wonder what I was doing there. It was pointless when you were on your own. Still, there was one solace available, and the urge quickly became compelling. I felt in my pocket for a coin. Conscience demanded the strict observance of certain preliminaries.

Tails. Damn. Best of three; five; seven. No future in this. Odds and evens, then. A name at random. Ro, nn, ie, Pe, ar, so. Damn. Oc, ky, Fi, el, de. Damn! Who else do I know? Mi, ke, Wh, it, ma. Shit! I don't believe this. And then, a sudden inspiration. Mi, ch, ae, lW, hi, – Yes! – tm, an. Thank God.

Furtive glance over the shoulder, and then the usual. Spit on your hand, frantic manipulation, brief explosion of pleasure, blessed relief; and then, even before your breathing was back to normal, wishing you hadn't.

I mean, honestly, what would anyone think? The Whitmans. Mr Pond. Like this. Out here. And the stuff still trickling down the tree. It was revolting. No wonder people didn't think much of me. They could tell. Like the man in the cinema toilet knowing about Jacko. But how? Perhaps it showed in your face.

Braces. Buttons. A guilty dampness behind the flies. Get away from the place. Burn the trees down. Why did it always have to be like this? So irresistible, and yet, in the end, so joyless.

I stumbled out from amongst the bushes and half walked, half ran, for the first quarter of a mile across the golf course. A foursome on one of the greens shouted angrily, so I ran some more, till I was well away from them.

When I was crossing the footbridge, I could hear a train coming, so I looked around for some stones to drop on the carriage roofs. There was a big one resting against the girders a little ahead of me. But as I ran forward to pick it up, I suddenly saw three boys sitting at the bottom of the steps. One of them was Snorty Pig. I wasn't sure if they'd noticed me, so I crept back and stood directly over the tracks to wait for the train, and think. A good stout stick would come in handy. I thought I remembered passing one on the path that led to the bridge. But when I glanced back to check, I saw two more boys approaching from the wicket gate. There hadn't been any sign of them earlier. They must have been lying in wait.

I was trapped on the bridge. Five against one. For a second, just as the train passed underneath me, I wondered if it might be better to charge the two who were coming up from the rear; if I broke through, I could still get back to Barton the long way round. But the others would soon catch up with me. Besides, I couldn't let it be said that I'd run away from Snorty Pig. So I gripped the big stone firmly in my hand, and walked down the steps towards him.

By the time I reached the bottom, the three of them were standing in line, blocking the path.

'Well, fancy that,' said Snorty Pig as I approached. 'It's one of the Barton oiks.'

I stepped forward, weighing the stone provocatively in my hand. He stood quite still, but the two boys who were with him started to move round as if they intended to close in from the sides.

'Stay out of it,' I told them. 'This is between me and him.'

I chucked the stone at Snorty Pig, forcing him off the pathway, but before I could reach him the other two pitched into me, and dragged me to the ground. Once I was safely pinned down, he stepped forward again.

'What's the matter?' I jeered. 'Scared to take on a Barton boy without your catapult?'

'Listen to him!' said Snorty Pig. 'He says "ca'apult".' He prodded me with his foot. 'There's a T in it; or don't they teach you to spell at your oiky school?'

I glared back at him defiantly. By now, the two from the far side had crossed the bridge and were hurrying down the steps.

'Go on,' he said. 'Say it properly. Cat-a-pult.'

Following his lead, they all started to chant it, over and over, kicking me in time with the syllables. 'Cat.' Kick. 'A.' Kick. 'Pult.' Kick.

'Your dad take it off you, did he?' I taunted him. 'Serve you bloody right.'

'I didn't get flogged, though,' said Snorty Pig. 'Unlike someone I could mention.'

'I wonder if he's still got the marks?'

'Let's find out.'

There wasn't much I could do about it. Between them, they soon had my shorts and pants off, and my shirt stripped back. After that, they seemed uncertain what to do next.

In the distance, there was the sound of another train coming. 'I know!' said Snorty Pig, a sick grin spreading slowly across his face. 'You lot keep him here. Or better still, drag him up to the fence, so he can watch.' Grabbing my shorts and pants, he ran up onto the bridge, and dangled them over the parapet. As the train passed, he dropped them.

'That'll give them all a surprise at Baker Street,' said one of the four who were holding me.

To general acclaim, Snorty Pig came triumphantly down the steps. Taking advantage of the distraction, I almost managed to struggle free, but the next moment they caught me again and forced me back to the ground.

'Roll him onto his back,' said Snorty Pig, and leaning forward to examine my nakedness he added, 'Ugh, look, he's even got an oiky cock.'

He bent down and pulled off one of my shoes. There was some fresh dogshit on the path, not far away. He pressed the sole well into it and stood over me, the shoe still in his hand.

The four who were holding me down glanced at one another in malicious glee. With a violent twist of my shoulders, I broke free and managed to roll onto my side just as Snorty Pig brought the shoe down. It left a long brown smear across my bare thigh.

I thought he might be planning to do it again, but apparently he was satisfied. 'This thing stinks,' he complained, and lobbed the shoe over the fence into the long grass beside the railway cutting.

With a couple of farewell kicks, the others released me, and made their way towards the steps. Snorty Pig followed them, glancing back in case I was thinking of coming after him.

When I was sure they were gone, I stood up cautiously. How I was going to get home unobserved, I had no idea. But at least I could find my footwear and try to wipe myself with some handfuls of grass. Fortunately, there was no one about. Once over the fence – a hazardous crossing, my unprotected parts in peril from splinters – I crept along for several yards, half on my knees, till I reached the contaminated shoe. I cleaned it as well as I could, and put it on. Wrenching a clump of grass out of the ground, I set to work on my thigh; but in getting the worst off, I simply spread the rest out thinner. The stench was appalling.

Suddenly, from behind me, there came the sounds of someone carrying a bike down the steps, followed by the tick-tick-tick as it was wheeled along the path. Without thinking, I subsided hastily into the undergrowth to conceal my lower half; but the stalks jabbed sharply into the soft flesh between my legs, and I rose again with a jolt.

'Are you all right?' A boy's voice. No one I knew, though.

'Piss off,' I said, without turning round.

There was a pause. 'Your shorts are down on the line. I spotted them from the bridge.'

I looked over my shoulder to see who it was. For a moment, I couldn't place him. Then I remembered. Jessop. David Jessop. The boy who had walked away from Snorty Pig, that time with Ronnie.

He rested his bike against the fence, and climbed over. 'Stop there,' he said. 'I'll get them for you.'

'I can do it.' I didn't need any help from a St Andrews boy.

But he was halfway down the slope already. I saw him clamber up onto the ballast, hesitate for a moment, and then turn back. 'Tricky,' he said, as he came up the slope again. 'They're a bit too close to the live rail.'

'Just leave them, then.'

'No, it's okay. I'll find a stick or something.'

After a quick search, he reached upwards and broke a small branch off a sapling. 'This'll do,' he said, waving it aloft, and ran down the slope again.

From where I was sitting, I watched him lean out over the track and poke between the rails with his stick. I should have been down there helping him. After three or four goes, he suddenly flicked his hands back, and the shorts flew up and over, landing well clear of the ballast. He threw the stick down, grabbed the shorts, and ran up the slope again.

'There you are,' he said, throwing them down beside me. 'Will you be all right now?'

'Yeah. No thanks to your friends, though.'

'They're not my friends.'

I looked at him suspiciously. 'Then how come you knew what had happened?'

'I passed them, down by the gate. They were full of it. All about how they'd just de-bagged one of the Barton oi... Oh, sorry.'

I shrugged. 'Who cares?'

He looked me up and down. 'I've seen you somewhere.'

'Very likely,' I said.

We climbed back over the fence and made our way up the path in single file. David walked ahead of me, wheeling his bike one-handed by the saddle. Flashy job; drop handlebars, cable brakes, the lot. I followed, keeping my distance. He hadn't even wrinkled his nose, but I knew what he must be thinking.

When we reached the road, he flicked the hair out of his eyes, and got on his bike, ready to ride off. It was a hard thing to thank a St Andrews boy, but I couldn't just let it go. As he was pulling away from the kerb, I called after him, 'Dave?'

He stopped, and looked back in surprise.

I didn't actually say anything; but I gave him a nod and a thumbs-up, and hoped he'd know it was meant.

Ocky was never one to mince his words. 'Blimey, Alan,' he said. 'You don't 'alf pong.'

I'd run slap into him, when I was trying to sneak in through the back door.

Nothing for it, after that, but to tell him the whole story – or most of it – so it was all round the place in ten minutes. Quicker than putting a notice up. Still, I couldn't have kept it dark. If you're seen having a strip-wash at five o'clock, and dunking your shorts in a bucket of disinfectant, people expect some kind of explanation. Otherwise, they supply their own.

So far as the Wilkies were concerned, another boy had been chasing me, and I'd fallen over in the wrong place. Everyone else knew different; but they were surprisingly decent about it. I'd have preferred something less unglamorous by way of battle scars than damp thighs still raw from scrubbing, but when I walked into the

Club Room, wearing my football shorts and feeling extremely foolish, the derision was purely formal. Eddie tried to make a great production out of holding his nose, but nobody took any notice.

Tom Shales was standing next to the dartboard. Without comment, he pulled the darts out and held them up, offering me a game. 'Don't go breaking windows again,' he told me. 'Just bide your time.'

That night, at Lakeside, events followed a pattern that was becoming curiously familiar. A new boy was expected, and Andy wanted Ronnie and me to help him settle in. So we asked what his name was: and Andy said, 'David Jessop.'

On Sunday, the Whitmans asked me to dinner. They'd been away all over Easter, so I hadn't been round for a while.

Unfortunately, the visit got off to a rather embarrassing start.

At half past twelve, I arrived at the back door, and walked in as usual. Mrs Whitman was in the kitchen getting the meal ready, but nobody else seemed to be around. It turned out that someone in Harrow Weald was selling off radio parts, and the others had gone to look. 'They'll be back soon,' she said, so I sat on a stool and talked to her while she did things over the stove.

After a minute or two, she happened to drop a saucepan lid, and it rolled across the floor into a corner.

'It's all right Mum, I'll get it.'

As I was reaching down to pick it up, I realised what I'd said. Clutching the lid, I backed away in confusion.

'Thanks, love.'

She stretched her hand out, pretending she hadn't noticed, and I stepped slowly towards her, looking at the floor. 'I'm really sorry, Mrs Whitman. I don't know what I was thinking of.'

She took the lid, and put it back on the saucepan. 'Come here, you little goose,' she whispered, and gathered me into her arms.

Token resistance, after which I surrendered, yielding to the luxury of her warmth and softness. For some reason, it made me want to cry. She didn't know about Jacko, or men in cinemas, or the Snorty Pig business, or any of the other things. If she had, she'd have pushed me away in disgust. Especially if she'd known that just for a few moments I'd mentally vaporised Toddy and taken his place in the family.

By stages, I eased myself clear of her arms. 'You won't say anything, will you?' I pleaded.

She shook her head.

'I think I'll just go and wait upstairs,' I mumbled. 'Or in the living room... or... or the garden.'

She nodded. 'Yes. If you'd rather. Dad and the boys won't be long.' And then, as I was leaving the room with my head well down, she said, 'You've absolutely nothing to be ashamed of.'

Which only went to show how little she knew.

After about ten minutes, the car pulled in through the gate, crammed to the roof with cardboard boxes. Several bigger boxes had been roped to the folding luggage rack at the rear. It took us about twenty minutes to move the whole lot into the house, and by dinner time the landing outside the Radio Room was piled high with books, manuals, data sheets, dismantled radio sets, tools, meters, bundles of wire, a signal generator, and a most impressive item with knobs and dials and switches and a round glass screen at the front.

'Whatever's that?' I asked. It looked like some sort of death-ray.

'A cathode-ray oscilloscope,' said Mike, proudly. 'We've wanted one for ages.'

At dinner, the main talk was of the vast new possibilities opened up by the morning's acquisitions. Afterwards, Mike and Toddy wanted to start unpacking the boxes, so I left them to it, and helped Mrs Whitman with the washing up.

She seemed to think that Toddy wouldn't be long. 'He's not really interested; he just hates being left out. Cricket's his first love. Are you a cricketer?'

'No. I'd sooner play football all year round.'

She laughed. 'So would Mike. He thinks cricket's the silliest game ever invented. Swimming, though; he likes that.'

'Me too. When I get the chance.'

'Oh, well now,' she said, emptying the bowl and swilling the froth down the sink, 'Dad and the boys often go over to Uxbridge baths in the summer. I'm sure they'll take you with them.'

Suddenly, there were angry voices from above, and a clatter of feet on the stairs. Toddy burst into the kitchen and made straight for the back door, looking very red in the face.

'What's up?' I said, as I followed him out.

'Brothers!' he exclaimed.

We kicked his ball about in the road, and were soon joined by Jack and Charlie Messenger from a couple of doors down. I'd met them before. They were younger than us, but good company.

'Bloody thing,' Toddy muttered, kicking the ball hard at Jack.

'What?'

'Stupid oscilloscope, or whatever it's called.'

Jack passed to me, and I passed to Charlie. 'What's happened?'

'Anybody would think it was my fault.'

The ball was coming my way again, but Toddy barged in front of me and belted it back down the road, right past Jack and Charlie.

'You haven't gone and bust it?'

'I was just looking at it, and all of a sudden this thing falls off the front.'

'What thing?'

'How should I know? Some sort of dial. You could see it was only held on with Durofix.'

Jack and Charlie had rescued the ball, but were passing it back and forth to each other till we were ready.

'Well, come on,' Toddy shouted. 'Whose bloody ball do you think it is?'

But when Jack kicked it back to him, he simply ignored it.

'Look, are we playing, or not?' I said.

Without a word, he turned his back and walked off up the road. I thought he was going to fetch the ball, but he went straight past it, and left it lying in the gutter.

I shrugged helplessly at the others, and we watched him out of sight. Ten minutes later, when I went in for a pee, there was still no sign of him.

From the bathroom door to the Radio Room was only a step. Mike was sitting at the workbench, studying a manual. He looked up in surprise.

'Toddy's gone off in a huff,' I said.

In pride of place on the bench stood the oscilloscope. There was a big rotary switch at one side of the control panel; the knob was still intact, but the dial behind it had come away, leaving a few fragments of bakelite still stuck to the metal.

'Have you got all the pieces?'

Mike took a small brown envelope from a drawer, and slid the broken remnants onto the bench. They fitted together well enough to show what the plate must have looked like originally. It was the sort of thing you could easily turn up on a lathe.

'I'm sure Mr Pond could make a replacement. It'd have to be brass or alloy, but he'd make you a matching knob as well.'

Mike looked at me doubtfully. 'Wouldn't it be rather expensive?' But you could see the gleam in his eye.

'I'll tell him it's for a friend.'

He hesitated. 'I was going to try and make something out of cardboard. But it wouldn't look very...' He seemed reluctant to admit what was on his mind.

'Professional?'

He gave me a shy little grin. 'Yeah. That's about it. I suppose it's silly, really, but I like things to look... proper.'

'I'll need to take all the pieces, and the knob, and the fixing screws.'

He nodded. 'You really mean this?' As if he still couldn't quite believe it.

'Yes. Why not?'

So as not to forget it, I went downstairs and put the envelope straight into my blazer pocket. Mrs Whitman was sitting at the kitchen table, darning socks. Before either of us had time to say anything, there was a knock at the back door. It was Jack and Charlie.

'Toddy's ball,' said Charlie, handing it in. 'He still ain't come back.'

Mrs Whitman looked at me in surprise.

'He just walked off,' I said, apologetically. 'He didn't say where he was going.'

She seemed quite unconcerned. 'He'll be back when he's hungry,' she said. 'Come on in, you two.'

The three of us sat at the table, while she poured out mugs of tea and gave us rock cakes from a tin. She left space in Charlie's mug, and topped it up with cold water straight from the tap. 'There you are love, all ready to drink.' He took the mug with a happy grin and swigged the whole lot down in one long gulp. It was obviously a regular thing.

Mike came in and joined us. Not long afterwards, Toddy appeared, and sat down at the table as if nothing had happened. Mike told him about the new parts for the oscilloscope, and Mrs Whitman looked up from her darning and said, 'Oh! That's wonderful.'

We all sat round for a while, talking of this and that, and I thought: This is how proper people live, all happy and relaxed together, with everyone welcome and no one afraid. Family. Friends. Brothers. Belonging. Your little preferences remembered and indulged.

And then, instead of gratitude at being part of it all, there came a great wave of savage resentment that it was only on loan to me for a few hours a week. It should have been mine by right. I'd had it, once. Why had it all been lost? There had to be a reason, so why did nobody tell me? What was I being punished for? For God's sake, what had I *done?*

13

First thing Monday morning, I went round to the workshop. Mr Pond examined the pieces of broken bakelite, scratched at his hairline with his thumb, as per usual, and started to rummage through a collection of chain sprockets and rusty ball races that lived in an old biscuit tin. With a little grunt of satisfaction, he pulled out a battered-looking aluminium pulley. 'Try that for size,' he said.

It was exactly the right diameter. One of the flanges was badly chewed about, but the other was still in fair condition, and there was a boss on the good side for the lathe chuck to grip. If you machined off the damaged part, you'd be left with a neat disc, already bevelled at the edge. You could bore out a recess for the control knob, and then turn the whole thing round so as to machine away the boss. Tricky, but possible.

We still needed something to make a matching knob. With aluminium alloy being so scarce, there was only one piece in the oddments box. It would have been fine, except that there was a half-inch hole most of the way through. Mike's spindle was only quarter-inch.

'Doesn't matter,' Mr Pond said. 'We'll press in a bit of brass and drill it to the size you want. It won't show, and it'll take the thread nicely for the locking screw.'

'So how soon do you think the job will be finished?'

He considered the matter. 'Well, I'd say that rather depends on how soon you start.'

'Oh, but I thought... I mean, they've got to look really professional. They're for someone very particular.'

'Then you won't have to make any mistakes, will you?'

It took me all morning just to finish the disc, and another hour in the afternoon to make the knob. But I didn't mind. I wanted to please Mike, and I wanted to do something for the Whitmans that would actually make a difference, something they couldn't have managed on their own. The trickiest job of all was engraving the reference marks round the rim of the disc in exactly the right places, and filling them neatly with black enamel. The finished result wasn't exactly what I'd visualised, but it looked fairly respectable, and it didn't cost me anything, because Mr Pond said the metal was only scrap.

The enamel would take a while to harden, so I left the disc and knob on a shelf in the workshop. In any case, they were safer there than at Barton House. I didn't want Eddie chucking them round the Club Room.

I thought I might go down to the Rec and look for Ocky. But I'd scarcely left the workshop when a boy shot past on a bike, giving me a friendly nod of recognition; with a squeal of brakes, he stopped, swung round in a broad U-turn and drew up alongside me. 'Wotcher,' he said. It was Dave. Quite a jolt, meeting him again like that.

He pointed towards the hut. 'What goes on in there?'

'It's where I work.'

'Work?'

'Yeah, you know, what people do to get money.'

He seemed uncertain what to say next. I hoped he wouldn't mention our previous meeting.

'So what do you actually do? Sweep up, and so on?'

'All sorts of things. Packing, labelling; sometimes I make things. It's a light engineering shop. Lathes, milling machines, and that.'

'Gosh. Can I look?'

'I'm not sure. He doesn't like more than one boy at a time.'

Dave leant his bike against the wall of the hut, and followed me inside.

'Hallo, Alan,' said Mr Pond. 'Back already?'

'Dave wanted a quick look. Do you mind?'

'No,' he said, rather vaguely, 'I don't mind.'

Dave wandered round for a minute or two, looking at the various machines. I took the new oscilloscope parts down from the shelf to show him. 'I've just finished these,' I said.

He glanced at them without much interest. 'Oh, I see. I thought you made engines and things.'

'Small production runs, mostly, but those are a one-off.'

Mr Pond put down his hammer and ambled over towards us. 'Friend of yours, eh?'

'Yes,' I said, a little warily.

He looked at Dave and gave him a quick nod of encouragement. 'Hallo, young feller. Not at Barton, then, I take it?'

Dave looked appalled. 'Good God, no!' Then, with a flush of embarrassment, he added, 'I mean, no; no I'm not.'

There was an awkward silence. I thought Mr Pond's eyebrows

were going to disappear completely under his cap. 'Come on,' I said, propelling Dave towards the door. 'We'd best be going.'

He collected his bike, and we walked back slowly towards the road. For some reason, I was acutely aware of certain quite meaningless things about him: his belt, his wrists, his shirt collar, the little silken hairs on the nape of his neck.

'Can I ride your bike?' I said.

He looked surprised. 'Where do you want to go?'

'Nowhere. Just up the road and back.'

As I caught hold of the handlebars, I felt a strange thrill go right through my body, as if something deep inside me was about to be set free. I'd never ridden a bike with drop handlebars; in fact, for the last few months, I hadn't ridden a bike at all, apart from the lumbering old crate that Ocky used for his butcher's round.

I pulled away from the kerb, going quite slowly at first to get the feel of it. The bike was incredibly light, and the handlebars swivelled easily at the merest touch. I did a couple of circles in the road; then I put my head down, thrust hard against the pedals to build up speed, and belted flat out to the end of Welton Road, the wind fluttering my collar and gusting past my ears with a roar that blocked out every other sound. For the first time in as long as I could remember, I felt strong, and clean, and perfectly in control. This is me, I thought, this is really me; don't let this ever end. The sheer exhilaration seemed to release a year's worth of energy into my body all at once. If I hadn't burnt it up in a wild frenzy as fast as it surged into me, it would have blown me to pieces.

As the junction appeared ahead of me, I braked reluctantly, swung round to a halt on the far side of the road, and flopped over the handlebars in a limp sprawl to recover. It was one of those times, like first discovering sex, when you gradually come back down from the sky and wonder, What the hell was *that?*

A sudden thought: I'd left Dave on his own, less than a stone's throw from Barton. If anyone spotted him, there'd be a lynch mob out in no time. Oh Christ, I thought – although as a matter of fact the idea of coming to the rescue was not entirely displeasing.

There was no sign of him outside Mr Pond's. I propped the bike against the kerb and looked anxiously up and down the street.

'Dave?'

No answer; but a moment later, he stepped out from the entrance to the footpath. Of course; it was the obvious place for anyone wanting to keep out of sight.

'Are you okay?' I asked.

He looked at me as if I was mad. 'Why shouldn't I be?'

I explained.

With a contemptuous glance towards Barton, he said, 'You don't think I'm scared of that bunch of oiks?'

I turned away, and kicked a stone as hard as I could across the road. 'You wouldn't like it if anyone called you that.'

'No. But they're not likely to, are they?'

This was true. 'Okay, suppose they called you a bloody stuck-up snob?'

'Is that what you think I am?'

'No. But most of you are.'

'And most of your lot are oiks. It's a simple fact.'

'We're just perfectly normal people. Why do you have to call us names?'

'I could say the same.'

We surveyed each other uncomfortably, not wanting a row; but there were feelings involved that you couldn't control or explain.

'Anyway,' Dave said. 'What does it matter? My lot, your lot. So far as I'm concerned, you either like somebody or you don't.'

I nodded. 'Same here.'

'Actually,' he said, 'I was wondering. Do you want to come round to the house some time?'

I hesitated. 'I don't know, really. When were you thinking of?'

'I'd have said tomorrow, only we've got to go up to Town. How about Wednesday?'

I shook my head. 'We're back at school.'

'Oh. That soon?' He looked at his wristwatch. 'Well, what's wrong with now? There won't be anyone else there, if that's what you're bothered about.'

We made our way along the footpath and across the bridge. Strictly Eyes Front as we passed the spot.

'Which school do you go to, then?' he asked. 'Mount Street?'

'No. Bishop Inglis.' For once, I stood a little taller when I said it.

'That's a Grammar School, isn't it? I nearly had to go to one of those. But it's worked out okay, thank God. I'm off to Oundle in September.'

'Oundle?'

'It's a school. In Northampton.'

'Isn't there anywhere nearer?'

'What difference does it make?' he said, half over his shoulder. 'It's a boarding school.'

'Are your Mum and Dad chucking you out, then?'

'Of course not. Everyone goes to boarding school.'

'Oh. Won't you miss home?'

It was a while before he answered. 'I'm not sure. Still, there's three of us going.' He hesitated. 'One of them I could do without, though; your fat friend, Malcolm Hayward.'

At the far end of the bridge, instead of going across towards the golf links we turned left. Half a mile further on was a side road, where the Jessops lived. The house was large, and very odd. It had a flat roof with a fringe of green pantiles round the edge, a bit like a monk's tonsure, and all the corners were curved, including the windows. There was a monkey-puzzle tree in the front garden, and two entrances, with a gravel drive that went round in a semi-circle.

Just as we turned in at the gate, the postman arrived with the afternoon delivery, and handed Dave a letter. He glanced down at the address and said, 'Oh, it's for my father. It'll need forwarding.'

I was mystified. 'What's forwarding?'

'You put the proper address on, and then it goes back in the post.'

'Can you do that? Without another stamp?'

'Of course.' He gave me a rather scornful look, and then thought better of it. 'I suppose you don't write letters? You wouldn't have anyone to send them to.'

'I do Mr Pond's. Business letters. Type them out, and everything.'

'Gosh. You can type? That's handy. I wouldn't mind a typewriter.'

I thought we'd be going inside, but he pushed his father's letter through the flap and backed away again. 'It'll do later. Let's go down to the shed.'

It stood at the far end of the garden on a brick and concrete plinth. From a gap between two of the bricks, he pulled out a metal skewer with the tip bent over at right angles. This he used like a key to undo the lock. When we were inside, he pulled the door to, and fastened it with a loop of string.

All down one side, under the window, was a rough wooden work bench, strewn with old seed packets, half-used balls of twine, rusty paint tins, and ancient bottles of turps and linseed oil. Most of the space underneath it was filled with buckets stacked one inside the other, and wooden boxes covered in lime and cobwebs, but there was just room for the two of us to squeeze in side by side.

I offered him a fag, and he accepted eagerly, but you could tell he wasn't a smoker from the way he held the match. A few seconds later, he was coughing and spluttering, and trying to rub his eyes without me noticing, so I looked away and didn't say anything. After a bit, I pinched mine out and said we'd save them for later.

Dave stubbed his own out on the floor, and started to reach up for something above our heads. Glancing upwards, I noticed a neat row of two-ounce tobacco tins fixed to the underside of the bench. The lids had been nailed in position, so that with one flick of your wrist, you could unscrew the body of the tin and fetch it down. The bottom parts of the tins had all been painted black. To the casual eye, they would have been invisible.

His half-smoked fag was carefully stored away in one of them. I shot him a quick glance of admiration. 'Crafty! Who put them there?'

'All my own work,' he said. 'Nobody else comes here much. Not now. But you can't be too careful.'

'Will your Dad be away for long?' I asked.

'Who knows?' he said. And that was the end of that.

I was just wondering what he kept in the other tins, when he reached up and unscrewed one. 'Look,' he said, holding it out for me to examine.

It was packed full of eighty or a hundred small brass objects, all identical; smooth, bright, cylindrical, with a rim at one end of slightly larger diameter, and the other end crimped into a delicate eight-pointed star. They were exquisitely beautiful. I wanted to hold them, to test their smoothness, to press the ball of my finger against the star-shaped ends.

'Whatever are they?' I asked, totally captivated.

'They're .22 blanks. Pre-war. There used to be a little revolver you could get, to fire them. We must have had one once, but I don't know what became of it. I found these, lying about in a drawer.'

I picked one out of the tin, and examined it.

'Take a few, if you want. There's plenty.'

It was tempting. 'But what'll I do with them? I mean, without a gun?'

'Oh,' he said, 'you don't need a gun. I'll show you.'

We crawled out from under the bench, and Dave opened the window. Taking a blank, he pushed the crimped end down through one of the spare holes in the casement stay. It fitted beautifully, the rim at the end preventing it from falling through. He held a nail point-downwards against the percussion cap and hit it hard with a metal bar that was lying on the bench. There was a short sharp bang like a firework going off, one quick stab of sound without any echo or reverberation, but incredibly loud and powerful. It was all over in a fraction of a second, leaving a strong acrid whiff of burnt powder.

'Shit!' I exclaimed. 'Some bang.' I didn't mind letting him see I was impressed.

He grinned, and tipped half a dozen blanks into my hand. I wrapped them in a screw of old newspaper and stowed them carefully in my shirt pocket.

Another of the tins was brought out for my inspection. 'Only air-gun slugs, but at least we can actually fire them.' He reached up to a high shelf, and took down a lengthy bundle, wound round with sacking. Inside was a specially made oilskin bag, wide at one end and tapering down at the other. He undid the straps and took out a BSA airgun; not the ordinary sort where you break the barrel and push it down to compress the spring, but the really posh kind with a separate loading lever and a real breech to put the slug in. It had adjustable sights, too, and a well-oiled wooden stock with a fancy pattern on it.

'I've run out of proper targets,' he said, 'but it doesn't matter.' On a sheet of spare paper he sketched the outline of a female nude, adding the various features with practised ease. 'There,' he said, and pinned it to a wooden board which he propped at ground level against the wall of the shed. 'Five for each tit, and ten for her you-know-what.'

He paced out the distance, cocked the spring, put in a slug, and lay down to fire. I watched intently as he took aim and squeezed the trigger. There was a soft phut, and a sharper crack as the pellet hit the board. I stepped forward to check the result. A five; or strictly speaking, maybe a four.

'Okay,' he said. 'Your turn. I'll load. It's better that way, otherwise your arm shakes when you're trying to aim.'

I lay down and took the gun from him. He knelt beside me, leaning over to correct my grip.

It was incredibly exciting. Unless you count Paul's cap pistol, I'd never actually held a gun before. The feel of it in your hands; the power it gave you, as you squinted along the barrel and through the sights. Man, the Hunter. Better still, Man the Avenger. Climbing a lamp post and picking off Jacko's ornaments one by one through the open window. I squeezed the trigger, not sure how hard you needed to do it, or how far back it would go. In the end, it went off unexpectedly, when I wasn't ready.

Dave examined the target. 'You've missed. Don't worry, though. You'll soon get the hang of it.'

Once he'd shown me how to cock the spring and put in the slugs, we took it in turns to load for each other, changing places every five shots.

After about twenty minutes, he wiggled his finger between the woman's legs where the paper was all in tatters and said, 'You see? You're getting good, now. Let's make a fresh target.'

He left me holding the gun while he did another drawing. I stood up, and started aiming at various things, more or less at random. There was a bird perched on the end of a branch not far away, so I drew a bead on it, and squeezed the trigger. Almost before I knew what was happening, Dave stormed across and wrenched the gun out of my hands. 'Give that to me,' he said angrily. 'If you want to kill things, you're not doing it with my gun.'

'It wasn't even loaded,' I said.

'I don't care. Don't ever do that again.'

'All right. Keep your hair on. I'm sorry.'

But somehow, after that, it wasn't the same, and before long we went back to the shed. In complete silence, he wiped the gun all over with an oiled rag, as if to cleanse it of my profanity, and put it away in its oilskin cover. I thought perhaps I should go now, but once the package was wrapped in sacking and safely back on its shelf, he dragged a big wooden box out of a corner and arranged it in the middle of the floor. Kneeling behind it, he rested his right elbow against the top, his arm held upright in challenge. Still in silence, I knelt down opposite him, and we interlaced our fingers, gripping hard.

He was strong, and he knew it, but I managed to hold on for quite a while. To begin with, his mouth was set in a grim, straight line, but gradually, as the deadlock continued, the look in his eye seemed to soften. At last, after the best part of a minute, I felt my strength give out, and I knew I shouldn't be able to hold him. A few seconds later, with a grin of triumph, he forced my arm right down onto the box.

We sat back on our heels for a quick breather. I offered my left arm. This time, he held steady for thirty seconds, and then simply collapsed. He went down so suddenly I almost tumbled over. Afterwards, we sat there for a while, assessing each other intently.

It was odd, what happened next. I'll swear neither of us said a word. We just stood up, went outside again, and started to wrestle each other properly on the lawn. Arms, legs, everything. Not fighting; just enjoying ourselves, as if we were trying out a whole new set of possibilities. We must have been at it a good quarter of an hour. It ended with him kneeling on top of me and pinning my arms to the ground. I was exhausted, so I acknowledged defeat and let my body go slack. He showed no signs of moving, but I wasn't bothered, so we simply stayed like that.

After a while, I said, 'I need the toilet.'

He still didn't move.

'Dave!'

Reluctantly, he stood up. 'You'll have to go in the bushes. There's no one in, and I haven't a key. I'll wait for you back in the shed.'

A couple of minutes later, I buttoned myself up, and stepped out onto the lawn again.

'Who are you, and what are you doing here?'

A woman's voice, and she meant business. I spun round in surprise. She was standing ten feet away in a long blue dress with white spots all over it. Her hair was in tight grey curls, all bunched very close to her head.

'Well?' she demanded, when I didn't answer.

'I'm playing with Dave.'

'Nonsense. He doesn't make friends with your sort. What were you doing in the bushes?'

I shrugged. 'Going to the toilet.'

'You filthy little pig! How dare you come into somebody's private garden and do a thing like that?'

'We couldn't get into the house.'

'Well, thank God for that. How many of you are there?'

'Just me and Dave. Are you his Mum?'

She hesitated, and then said icily, 'Yes, I'm David's mother.'

'Why don't you ask him, then? He's only in the shed.'

Without a word, she strode across the lawn and flung open the shed door. As it swung shut behind her, I moved cautiously closer. There were voices, muffled, angry. It was only now and then that you could make out what they were saying.

'...pick people up in the street and bring them here without knowing anything about them. A boy like that? You little fool! Can't you see what he's after?'

I thought I was going to find out, but I missed the next bit.

'...this instant, and tell him you're sorry, but you've made a mistake, and will he please leave.'

All things considered, I thought I might as well save him the trouble.

That night, I badly wanted to visit Lakeside to be with Dave and Ronnie, but it wasn't possible. Ocky and Joe went nattering on for ages after Lights Out, and unfortunately Lakeside was a fragile structure, dependent on solitude, or failing that, on darkness and silence. So I just had to lie awake, and think.

It was odd how Dave and Ronnie were friends at Lakeside, whereas in real life they wouldn't have known what to say to each other. And I suddenly realised something odder still. Name anybody I knew, and I could tell you immediately, with absolute certainty, whether or not they were likely to turn up there. But I couldn't explain why. Dave and Ronnie, yes; but not Ocky, and not Toddy. Joe, yes; Snap, no. Mike was there of course; only not exactly one of us, more like a sort of assistant to Andy. Barry Anderson, yes; but not Paul. Why ever not? Of all people, surely he should have been? And incredibly, the Yes list included Philip Everard from 1B, who I didn't even like, and who had to be altered quite a lot before he could fit in. It was a total mystery. Downright spooky, in fact. How could you classify people with such complete confidence, and not be able to see what the difference was?

Sometimes it's hard to tell whether you haven't slept, or whether you've dozed off for a while and woken up again. I could have sworn I'd stayed awake the whole time, but I was suddenly aware that everything all around me had gone quiet. For a while, I hovered between sleep and waking; not clear-headed enough to think, or to reach Lakeside, but too restless and uncomfortable to drift off into oblivion. Eventually, I realised with disgust that there was nothing for it but to visit the halfway house.

I was on my way back, feeling a bit chilly just in my underpants, when I turned a corner and ran slap into Jacko. He was standing there, quite still, in pyjamas and dressing gown, right in the middle of the corridor.

'Alan?'

I caught a strong whiff of alcohol as he spoke.

'What have you been doing?' he said.

It was a ridiculous question. The Victorian plumbing may have been built to last a lifetime, but silent it was not. I mumbled some sort of answer, and sidestepped to try and get past.

He put out a hand to restrain me. 'Couldn't you sleep? Are you hungry?'

'I'm all right.'

'Come to my room. I want to talk to you.'

'But Mr Crofting...'

'Nothing to worry about.'

The only light in his sitting room came from a small table lamp. As he propelled me towards the open door of the bedroom, I noticed that one of his armchairs had been drawn up close to the gas fire; there was a crumpled newspaper on the seat, and a large tumbler balanced on the chair arm.

The bedside light was on, and the covers drawn back, but the bed had obviously not been slept in. The linoleum felt like ice under my bare feet; instinctively, I stepped forward onto the mat beside the bed.

'That's the idea,' said Jacko. 'Hop in.'

I drew back in horror. 'Oh, no, Mr Crofting,' I pleaded.

Without more ado, he simply picked me up and dumped me flat on my back on top of the bedclothes. Before I had time to protest, he slid his arm under my knees and forced my legs back over my head, leaving me with my arse in the air, as if I'd got stuck while turning a somersault. Lurching heavily against the side of the bed, he divested himself of his nightwear and clambered on top of me, back to front, with his feet somewhere down by my head. Having deftly slid my pants out of the way, he began to thrust himself downwards repeatedly with intense determination but wild inaccuracy, like W. C. Fields at 3 a.m., struggling to insert his latch-key.

Normally, he was at least quick and reasonably efficient; and through sheer force of habit, I had almost reconciled myself to what I was powerless to alter. But the present situation exceeded anything I had thought possible. It was so utterly farcical, and yet at the same time so unspeakably obscene and demoralising, that I was quite incapable of struggling or even calling for help. Not that it would have done any good. With the doors closed, you could have shouted yourself hoarse and nobody would have heard.

After a time, the thrusting ceased, but Jacko remained poised above me, as if expecting to continue. 'Sorry, old chap,' he gasped. 'Small technical hitch. Not a problem you'd be familiar with. Result of certain over-indulgences and the onset of anno domini.'

It occurred to him that he might do better if he turned round.

This he accomplished with some difficulty, and in the process forced my legs back so hard that I finally cried out in pain. 'No, Mr Crofting! Please! You're hurting.'

'Good,' he said, exactly as if I'd told him I was enjoying it; and reaching for one of the pillows he tried to thrust it down over my mouth.

I hadn't grown up with *Our Island Story* for nothing. I knew all about the Princes in the Tower and I was convinced he was trying to suffocate me. In total panic, I struggled to break free. This seemed to infuriate him, and he set about pinning me down again, grunting hard, and breathing great wafts of alcohol and tobacco into my face.

'Fuck off,' I shouted in desperation. 'You can do whatever you want, only don't keep hurting me.'

Rather to my surprise, he eased away a little, allowing my legs to fall back onto the bed. He glanced hopefully downwards, but Nature was still failing to oblige. 'Might try beating you,' he said, distantly. 'Generally does the trick in a case like this.'

But already, his train of thought had strayed elsewhere. 'I'll give you a piece of advice,' he said, and then sat gazing at me as if he was having some trouble focussing. 'The great thing in life,' he went on earnestly, 'is to find your level and sink to it. To be honest, you see, I never cared much for the better-class boys, even when they were available. On the other hand, one doesn't want something totally out of the gutter. You're the perfect compromise. There's a delicious streak of vulgarity about you, probably quite unconscious; but you came from a good home and it still shows. Do you understand?'

He shifted position slightly, and the moment his weight was off me, I managed to roll over sideways and land on the floor, with my pants still round my knees.

He looked at me in surprise. 'How d'you get down there?'

I started to shuffle towards the door, hitching my pants up as I went. He was still crouching on the bed and blinking, trying to follow me round with his eyes.

'Mushn't mind,' he said. 'Jus' a game. Be all right in the morning.'

When I was about eight feet from the door, I rose cautiously to my knees, preparing to make a dash for it.

'Not going,' he protested. 'Haven't finished. I'll get this in if it kills me.'

Reaching out to try and grab hold of me, he leant forward,

overbalanced, and took a nose dive onto the floor. Without waiting to see if he was going to get up again, I wrenched the door open and fled.

At first, I thought he might try to come after me, so I dashed back to the halfway house, bolted the door behind me, and listened hard for any sounds of pursuit. All quiet. Even so, there was no question of going back to bed. I wanted a locked door between us for the rest of the night.

Before long, I found I was shivering uncontrollably, and wished I'd had the foresight to stop and collect my clothes. There was a frayed roller towel hanging next to the washbasin. By standing on tiptoe, I was able to dislodge the roller, and free the towel; I thought I might manage by wrapping it round my shoulders. But after another few minutes, I could see there was nothing for it but to risk a journey back to the bedroom.

Arming myself with the roller, I slid the bolt back and cautiously opened the door. The stairs were still in darkness, and the whole house was silent. Leaving the door wide open, ready for a quick retreat, I tip-toed up the stairs, keeping close to the wall, and peeped round the corner. The corridor was empty, and the door of Jacko's flat was closed. I could feel my heart thumping away so hard I thought it was going to burst my chest open; but I tightened my grip on the roller, dashed into the bedroom for my clothes, and scuttled back to the safety of the halfway house.

Dressed, and behind a bolted door again, I felt a little calmer. But what now?

It was hard to see myself remaining at Barton House a minute longer. But suppose I crept downstairs and climbed out of a window, where would I go? As Ronnie had found out, you couldn't afford to make mistakes. Imagine hammering on the Whitmans' door at four in the morning and telling them Jacko had tried to kill me. They'd think I was crackers. Worse still, they'd deliver me straight back, and then I should be completely at Jacko's mercy.

Nobody else was likely to believe me either. And who could blame them? I scarcely believed it myself. There was no mental slot in which to accommodate the night's experiences, no way of interpreting them in terms I could make any sense of. I needed some expert advice. But who to ask? It was the old, old problem. Choosing the wrong person could be far more disastrous than biding my time and pretending nothing had happened.

Meanwhile, there was the rest of the night to get through. Using the folded towel as a cushion, I sat on the floor, propped more or less upright in the corner beside the washbasin; and eventually, with the roller resting across my knees in case of emergencies, I drifted off into a shallow and fitful sleep.

I awoke, stiff and aching, round about six, with the thick, sour feeling you get from sleeping in your clothes. But for all that, my brainwheels must have been turning busily during the night. Because while I was running some cold water into the basin to splash my face with, I suddenly realised that whatever else had gone wrong during the last twenty-four hours, a happy chance had unexpectedly shown me how I could get in touch with Dudley.

It was going to require Mike's help, which meant waiting until he'd seen the new parts for the oscilloscope. But on Saturday morning, while I was typing some labels for Mr Pond, I was able to take the first step.

'Could I have an envelope and a stamp? I'll leave the money in the tin.'

He nodded. 'Oh, and by the way, that boy was here, asking for you. I told him you were back at school.'

'What did he want?'

'He didn't say.'

I slipped the plain manilla envelope into the machine and typed Mr Dudley's name, followed by the school address. Then I put Would You Please Forward, underlined, in the bottom left-hand corner. The huge lettering looked rather peculiar, but Mr Pond's was the only typewriter I had any access to, and it wouldn't have done to write the address by hand. My writing might be recognised, and even if it wasn't, it would still look like a schoolboy's. So I stuck the stamp on, and hoped for the best.

But on Sunday afternoon, when I went upstairs to the Radio Room, my insides were tying themselves in knots again.

'Your parts,' I said. 'I hope they'll be all right.'

Mike looked up in surprise. 'Gosh, that's quick. Has he finished them already?'

I watched nervously while he undid the tissue paper and laid the dial plate and the knob side by side on the bench. For several minutes, he sat staring at them with a puzzled frown. Once or twice, he picked them up, and turned them over and over between his fingers.

'What's the matter?' I said. 'Won't they do?'

He didn't seem to have heard me. For a while longer, he gazed at them in silence, gently shaking his head. At last, he slowly turned to face me. 'They're... they're *beautiful*,' he said, as if he could scarcely believe it.

'Shall we fit them on, then?'

A couple of minutes' work was all it took. As we stood back to admire the result, I could see his eyes were shining. He reached forward again, and clicked the knob back and forth through its various positions.

'The reference marks line up perfectly,' he said. 'Your Mr Pond must be a real craftsman. How much does it come to?'

'Nothing. They were only made out of scrap.'

'Well yes, but what about his time? It must have taken him ages.'

I looked down at my shoes, and started counting the eyelets. 'Actually, it wasn't him that made them. He was too busy.'

Mike frowned. 'Well who, then?'

I gave him a nervous little grin.

'You? You – made those?' He rested his hands on my shoulders, and gently tickled the back of my neck with his thumbs as if I was his favourite kid brother. 'You clever little monkey.'

After which, he couldn't resist turning back to the oscilloscope and clicking the knob some more. I left it a moment or two longer, and then took a deep breath.

'Mike? Can I ask you a favour?'

He spread his hands wide, offering the whole world.

'There's someone I need to write to. It's very important. Only the thing is, all our letters are opened. So could I tell them to send the answer here, to you, and then you could pass it on?'

He gave me a knowing look. 'You're starting young. What's her name?'

It might have been simpler to let him go on making a joke of it, but I didn't want it to be that way between us. No lies to Mike. 'It's not what you think. I wouldn't ask if it wasn't really important.'

He could see he was out of order. 'No, I'm sure you wouldn't.'

'But you still haven't said if you'll do it.'

'Of course I will.'

'And not tell anyone?'

'Cross my heart.'

That evening, when I left, Mr Whitman gave me five bob for making the oscilloscope parts. It was decent of him, and kindly meant, I'm sure, but I didn't know whether to be glad or sorry. The money would certainly come in handy for my escape fund; I reckoned I needed to save up two pounds at least. But the parts had been meant as a gift, and getting paid for them not only put me back in the Whitmans' debt, it seemed to reduce my status from semi family member to the sort of person you didn't accept presents from.

For once, I was almost glad to get back to Barton. At last, I could write my letter.

In the relative safety of the Quiet Room, I pulled the centre sheet out of my rough note book, the least likely to be checked for missing pages, and wrote Mike's name and address at the top. The rest of the wording had already been well rehearsed.

> Dear Mr Dudley, thankyou for the photorgraphs, I
> hope you are well, you did not put your address.
> Things have not been very good recently, please would
> you send me your address as I would like to write to
> you propally and ask your advise. Very important, our
> letters are opened so please please do not write to
> where I live which you may remember but send to
> name and address above who is a good friend, and
> oblige, Alan (C).
> P.S. Please please write, otherwise I don't know how I
> can keep on.

The sealed envelope spent the night in my blazer pocket. Next morning, on the way to school, I posted it. And for the moment, at any rate, I decided to start believing in God again, because I thought it could do with a prayer to speed it on its way.

14

On Friday the same week, Ocky arrived home very late with his right arm in plaster, and a vague story about an accident in the gym. But he muttered darkly about getting even, as if someone had done it on purpose.

From the set of his face, you could tell the pain was worse than he let on, and for several days, I had to cut up his food for him. What seemed to bother him most, though, was the likelihood of losing his butcher's round if he couldn't provide a substitute. There hadn't been time to find someone at school, and everybody at Barton was either too young or had a Saturday job already. In the end, I said I would ask at the workshop if I could switch to the afternoon, so as to fill in at Shipstone's for him during the morning.

Mr Pond was less than enthusiastic. 'I hope you're not going to make a habit of this. I can't do with unreliable boys.'

'No. I promise. It's a real emergency.'

'Just this once, then.'

So at eight-thirty the next morning, I was waiting on Shipstone's doorstep. Precisely as the Post Office clock was striking the half hour, Mr Shipstone appeared and unlocked the doors from the inside. He still had his bowler hat on, that he always wore to Smithfield.

'Who are you?' he said in surprise.

'I'm here instead of Ocky. He's broken his wrist.'

'Very well. Make yourself known at the cash desk.'

This stood at the back of the shop, like a fortress built out of solid mahogany. Within it, side by side, sat the two Miss Shipstones, in identical print frocks, with neat black sleeve protectors elasticated at the wrists and elbows. In front of each was a rack of steel-nibbed pens, a set of three glass inkwells, for black, red, and blue, respectively, and a hefty ledger with broad pages ruled into dozens of columns. On a shelf to one side stood an old-style daffodil telephone, and behind them, set into the wall, was the door of a huge walk-in safe. To judge from their faces, you couldn't have smuggled a farthing out of the place without them knowing.

I presented myself before them, as instructed. Uncertain which to address, I positioned myself half way between them. Silently, the younger one motioned me towards her sister with a small movement of her pen holder. I stepped smartly sideways, and waited.

'Yes?'

'I'm here instead of Ocky. He's broken his wrist.'

'Ocky?'

'Fielden,' said the other, without looking up.

'And you are...?'

She wrote my particulars in the Wages book, and nodded towards a large trap door in the floor next to the cash desk. 'Down there. Goddard will show you where the bicycles are. And remember, all your deliveries are to Account customers. You don't ask for money, and if it's offered, you don't accept it. Is that clear?'

The trap door provided the only access to the basement, which housed the cold store, and also the workroom where things were done which it wouldn't be suitable for the public to catch sight of. On delivery days, men would stagger in from the street, their backs bent under huge carcases wrapped in muttoncloth with the meat hooks still attached at the top. Scattering the customers with a great shout of 'Mindjabacksthere', they made their way to the trap door and lowered the sides of beef with a block and tackle that swung out on a hinged arm fixed to the wall. Those with lighter loads simply turned round, and disappeared down the hole with the uncanny agility of steeplejacks.

I was about to try my luck on the ladder when Mr Shipstone called me over. 'You can do this first,' he said, handing me a cardboard box full of sawdust for the floor. 'Use plenty behind the block. There's always a lot of blood on Saturdays.'

The street door opened and Pete Goddard walked in; he was whistling, and his boots clattered noisily over the quarry tiles.

'Silence!' came a withering voice from the cash desk.

The tune died on his lips, but he shot me a wry grin. He was a friend of Ocky's, and I'd met him several times down at the Rec. He glanced round expertly at the floor. 'That'll do,' he said. 'C'mon.'

From his method of negotiating the ladder, he was clearly a professional. Once he was far enough down to hold the sides, he slid the rest of the way like a brickie on a building site, his toes ratcheting lightly against the rungs.

'I told you not to do that,' came a peevish voice from below.

I followed him down, one rung at a time. The basement room was bigger than I had expected, and except for the metal-clad double doors that led into the cold store, it was tiled all round like a public lavatory. In the middle stood a vast butcher's block, and behind it was a man in a striped apron and a coarse blue coat of vaguely nautical appearance. Round his waist was a stout leather belt, worn rather slack, from which there hung three or four different sharpening steels that jangled together as he moved. He was boning out the joints with incredible dexterity, and tying them round with smooth white string that hung down from a cob in a wire cradle fixed to the ceiling. Every fifteen or thirty seconds, he would throw down his knife and select another, giving it a quick wipe up and down the steel before using it. The moment one joint was finished, he started on the next, flinging the meat about with frenetic speed, juggling with his knives, yanking the string down from above his head, and tossing bones into a bin. He looked as if he had no time for boys. A smaller man, with a bald head and bandy legs, was wrapping the joints and pinning ready-prepared labels to them with tiny metal skewers, referring constantly to an Order Book with tall narrow pages.

Pete beckoned me over to a stone slab on the far side of the room. Some of the finished parcels had already been placed there, grouped to suit our various journeys. He reached under the slab and dragged out two rectangular wicker baskets with handles across the top.

'There you are,' he said, pushing one of them towards me with his foot. 'Yours are the ones with F on the labels. Mine say G.'

'So who's V?' I asked, pointing to one of the parcels.

'Van.' He indicated the bald man. 'Fred takes those.'

The bikes were kept in a shed at the end of a little alley that ran alongside the shop. They were trade bikes, the sort with a small front wheel and a shallow cradle above it to hold the basket. Under the cradle was a pair of hinged legs that folded down to make a stand. Compared with Dave's bike, they were slow and clumsy, a bit like pedalling a wheelbarrow. There was a big metal plate with the shop name on it clipped inside the frame, and you had to ride with your knees apart or the fastenings kept scraping your skin.

Ocky had told me which streets he delivered to, and I thought I knew where most of them were. But some of them hadn't got signs up, so I kept on having to stop and ask, and quite a lot of the houses didn't have any street numbers or names. If I'd been king, I'd have made a law that everyone had to paint their house number at least six inches high, and the fines would all have been shared out by the local delivery boys to make up for the time they'd wasted.

'I thought you'd scarpered,' Fred commented sourly when I got back to the shop. 'I told Miss Shipstone, "That isn't a boy you've taken on, it's a tor-toyse".'

My second journey was more successful. Within the half-hour, I was back again, and loading up for the third. By this time, the man with the knives was upstairs in the shop, serving alongside Mr Shipstone, and Fred had switched over to making sausages.

It was little wonder they kept the machine downstairs. You couldn't have used it in public without being had up for gross indecency, especially the bit where you greased the protruding nozzle with your hand, and slid a length of empty sausage skin over it. But the whole process was so enthralling you could have sold tickets to watch. As the pinkish-grey snake leapt wriggling off the machine like something alive and angry, Fred would bring it under control with astonishing sleight of hand, pinching it into six, knotting them up in a neat bundle, and slipping the paper band on, all in a single movement.

Conversation was impossible while the machine was running; it made a noise like a thousand ball bearings being rattled about inside a petrol can. But as soon as he switched the motor off, Fred remarked, 'Are you going to stand there the rest of the morning?'

Hastily, I got on with re-loading my basket. 'I was just interested.'

'You're not paid to be interested.'

'It's clever, the way you do it. It's like...' I was going to say, like magic, but I thought it sounded a bit silly.

By this time, he was greasing the nozzle again. 'I know what it's like,' he said, with a lewd sneer. 'I don't need an errand boy with a dirty mind to tell me.'

The third journey took me into unfamiliar territory again. Some of the roads weren't even properly made up, nothing but mud and stones, with huge potholes everywhere. It's a wonder the bike didn't shake itself to pieces. They were mostly big houses, too, with separate side gates saying 'Tradesmen's Entrance'. You'd think that if people had that much money, they could have run to some decent tarmac. And it was the same old business of no names or numbers. You were simply supposed to know.

It was gone eleven-fifteen by the time I got back. The workroom was deserted, and the big pile of van parcels had gone. Fred must be out on his rounds. Pete's pile had dwindled, but Ocky's still looked enormous. I couldn't see how I should ever finish on time.

Journey Four went better again; the good and the bad seemed to alternate. Even so, it was after twelve by the time I walked into the shop with my empty basket. Pete was loading up for his last trip. 'Running a bit late, aren't you?' he said. While I was explaining about the delays, he looked at the labels on my remaining parcels. Greatly to my surprise, he said he would take a few of them for me, so I could manage with only one more journey. 'Don't worry,' he said. 'I'll make sure Ocky pays me back.'

As it happened, the one parcel I least wanted to deliver would have taken him right out of his way, so it went in my own basket after all. It was for the Haywards. I left it till last, with the vague idea that if I hung about near the house, I might finally succeed in waylaying Snorty Pig as he came home from school.

Once the other deliveries were taken care of, I pedalled cautiously along his likely route to see if I could spot him. I thought I was out of luck, but suddenly, as I turned a corner, I saw him ahead of me, walking quite slowly, swinging his satchel aimlessly to and fro. By dodging back, and making my way through a network of side streets, I managed to reach one of the turnings ahead of him and lie in wait. It was the perfect ambush, with a high fence at the corner, so he wouldn't see me till it was too late.

After about a minute, there was a curious sputtering sound from the direction of the main road, and round the corner came one of those ridiculous little three-wheel vans that had the front end of a motorbike sticking out from under the windscreen. Painted along the side in flowing script was the wording: Shipstone & Sons, High Class Butchers & Poulterers. And seated in the front was Fred.

As quick as I could, I turned my back and stood close to the fence, hoping he wouldn't spot me. But my apron was a giveaway, and the bike was standing propped up on the pavement with the nameplate clearly visible. I heard the van lurch to a halt with the engine still running, and a moment later, Fred's voice.

'You've got dirty habits, then, as well as a dirty mind.'

I jerked two fingers at him over my shoulder, but there was no sign of the van moving again. Snorty Pig was due any second. In desperation, I turned to glare at Fred, silently mouthing 'Fuck off' as vehemently as I could.

The engine revved a little, and then died back again. 'You needn't think I won't report you. We don't employ delivery boys who piddle in the street.' With a further revving noise, he engaged the gears, and eventually the van jolted off into the distance.

Snorty Pig was so long coming, I thought I must have missed him. But just as I was beginning to give up hope, he appeared at the corner and started to cross the road. Before he was halfway over, I moved in quietly behind him and brought my knee up hard under his arse. As he turned to face me in angry surprise, I landed him one straight in the mouth. His head jerked back and slightly to one side. But instead of coming for me as I'd expected, he simply stood there, staring at me, his face deathly pale and his chin streaked with blood.

'Wotcher, Malcolm,' I said.

He cringed. Tears dribbled out from the corners of his eyes, and he started to sag like a great fat blancmange. It was revolting. I hit out at him a couple more times, and he held his arms up feebly in front of his face, but apart from that he didn't move.

There was black hatred bubbling up from inside me, but I couldn't go on with it. If he had cut and run, I should have chased him and brought him down; if he had lashed out at me even once in return, I should have let rip with everything I'd got. I'd beaten him up a thousand times in my imagination, but I hadn't allowed for anything so one-sided. In baffled contempt, I backed off a couple of paces and spat in the road at his feet. 'Well, come on then,' I said. But he still didn't budge.

At that moment, a lorry swung round the corner and sent us both scuttling for the pavement. I pushed Malcolm against the fence, grabbing his tie by the knot and jerking him backwards and forwards.

'Don't,' he said, feebly.

'You and me have got things to settle.'

Still shaking, he started to edge his way along the fence. When he was about two feet away from the bike, he reached out with his foot and kicked it over. As it crashed to the ground, the basket fell from the cradle, and the Haywards' parcel was tipped into the road. The paper wrapping unrolled as it went, leaving the meat resting on the bare asphalt.

'That'll teach you!' he sneered triumphantly. 'Barton oik.'

When I told him whose meat ration it was, he refused to believe me, so I pointed to the label, which was still pinned to the wrapping paper. He tried to stare me out, but eventually he gave up and knelt down for a closer look. When he rose to his feet again, his lips were drawn tightly back against his teeth.

'It's all your fault,' he said.

'Who kicked the bike over?'

'You attacked me.'

'That's right. And what would your Mum and Dad say, if they knew why?'

His mouth twitched. 'You think they'd believe you?'

Time for my trump card. 'It wouldn't be me that told them.'

His chin jerked up in surprise.

I let him puzzle it out for a moment or two. 'One of your own lot,' I said. 'Dave Jessop. Him and me are like that.' I twined two fingers together and held them in front of his face. 'You didn't know, did you? I even go to his house. He saw what you did. And when he tells them, they'll believe it.'

Malcolm's bottom lip was quivering. After a long time, he said lamely, 'What are we going to do?'

'For a start, you'd better get all the stones out.'

He knelt down on the kerb and picked the joint up as if it was a dead rat. 'Ugh,' he said, turning it over, 'it's all bloody.' He peered down at the surface, and prodded it gingerly with the tip of his finger, trying to loosen the grit.

We were so preoccupied that neither of us noticed the Shipstone van returning till it was practically alongside. We glanced up to see Fred staring in disbelief through the curved porthole at the side of the cab. I thought he was going to get out, but after about thirty seconds he turned his head away, gripped the steering bar with righteous disdain, and drove off round the corner.

'Now you'll cop it,' Malcolm said.

'I wouldn't count on it. I've got nothing to hide.'

Not strictly true, of course. I didn't want it getting back to Ocky that I'd messed his job up, and I didn't really want the dogshit business resurrected. But the longer I kept Malcolm sweating, the better.

He passed me the joint for inspection. 'D'you reckon that looks all right?' he asked, doubtfully. His hands were stained all over with the meat juice.

'I suppose so. You'd better wrap it up again, and I'll deliver it. And remember, if your Mum complains, you're for it, so you'd better make sure she doesn't.'

With the package safely returned to the basket, I pedalled down to the Haywards' house and made for the back door. But there was a tall wooden fence across the path, and the door through it seemed to have been bolted on the far side. So there was nothing for it but to ring at the front.

'Yes?' A woman. Malcolm's mother, presumably. I hoped she wouldn't recognise me.

'Shipstone's,' I said, holding out the parcel.

She looked as if she didn't know what things were coming to. 'You don't deliver meat at the front door. Take it round the back.'

'I tried. Your garden door's locked.'

'Nonsense.'

'Well, I couldn't open it.'

'You lift the latch, and push,' she said. 'You're also extremely late.'

'It's not my fault. We've got a boy off. Broken his wrist.'

I was still holding the parcel out, but instead of taking it, she stepped back and started to shut the door.

'Well, do you want it, or not?' I said indignantly.

Before I could even finish the sentence, the door slammed in my face, with an extra little rattle as the fancy wrought-iron knocker swung out and back again.

I had another go at the side door, but it was definitely fastened. There was no sign of Malcolm yet, or I'd have told him to take the parcel himself. After a minute or two, I rang the bell again, but nobody came, so I left the joint on the front step and made my way belatedly back to the shop.

The slab in the window had been completely cleared, and sheets of greaseproof paper were hanging on hooks, neatly spaced along the meat rails. The plaster pigs that stood in the corners had nothing left on their trays but packets of stuffing. I knocked hopefully at the door and rattled the handle, but nobody came. Peering in through the panes of thick, uneven glass, I could see that the shutter was down in front of the cash desk. The shop was plainly shut for the weekend.

The bike shed was locked as well, so I left the bike in the alley, with the basket still in the cradle and my apron folded up inside. It was the best I could do. As for my money, it would simply have to wait.

When I finally got back home, dinner was long finished and cleared away. Ocky had gone out, and so had most of the others. I thought Hurly might have saved me something, but when I poked my head cautiously round the kitchen door, I could see there was nothing on the Aga. Hurly was sitting at the table, doing her figures for Fancy Madam. I caught her eye as she looked up, but she shook her head and nodded silently in the direction of the scullery. A moment later, Mrs Wilkie emerged.

'It's no use, Alan. You've been told often enough. You come to meals at the proper time, or you go without.'

'Yes, Miss.'

'Where have you been?'

'Doing Ocky's round for him. Because of his arm. It took me a long time to find all the houses.'

'I can't help that. Rules are rules.'

She turned away to look in one of the cupboards, so I jerked a quick V sign at her back. No point in arguing, though. Besides, it was gone two by the kitchen clock; time I was getting across to Mr Pond's.

He glanced round impatiently as I let myself in. 'Ah, there you are. I'd almost given you up.'

'I'm sorry. I came as soon as I could.'

'If you don't want to work here, I can soon find someone

who does.'

'I've said I'm sorry, Mr Pond.'

There was a pause. 'Yes,' he conceded, rather more graciously. 'So you have. So you have.'

But I was left in no doubt that things weren't right between us.

So altogether, it was a bad afternoon: and Ocky didn't improve it. 'You prick!' he said at tea. 'I saw Pete down the Rec.'

'And?'

'Fred's been telling tales. Trust a Grammar School boy to fuck things up.'

'What tales?'

'All sorts.' He shrugged sardonically. 'I wouldn't hardly know where to begin.'

Ever since posting my letter, I'd been trying to calculate how soon I could realistically expect an answer. I had caught the eight-thirty collection on Monday morning. With luck, the letter might even reach the school the same afternoon. Failing that, it would certainly be there in the morning. But how long would they take to find Dudley's address and put the letter back in the post? At the very, very best, it could even happen by Monday evening; Tuesday was more likely, though, in which case, Dudley would get it on Wednesday morning. He wouldn't have time to write an answer until the evening, so unless he went out to the pillar box the same night, he couldn't post it till Thursday. Even so, and allowing for various unforeseen delays, there seemed a really good chance that when I went to the Whitmans' on Sunday, the reply would be waiting for me.

As soon as I arrived, Mike beckoned me upstairs, and I followed him eagerly into the Radio Room.

'There you are,' he said, proudly, pointing to the workbench.

'What? Where?' I couldn't see any letter.

'The oscilloscope. I've rigged it all up to show you.'

'Oh. Oh, I see.'

He sat down on one of the stools and started flicking switches. A bright green line appeared on the screen, jumping about and changing shape each time he made an adjustment.

'Now, that's a thousand-cycle tone straight from the signal generator. As you can see, it's a pure sine wave. But...', he turned another knob, '...there it is after it's been through this amplifier.' The wave pattern had degenerated noticeably, with little spikes and kinks spoiling the smoothness of the line. 'You see? Distortion. Needs investigating.'

'But wouldn't you have known just by listening?'

He frowned. 'Well yes, probably, in this case. But sometimes, it can seem as if everything's okay, and underneath, there can be something badly wrong.'

'Can there?' I felt strangely uneasy.

He nodded. 'Besides, it helps you locate the fault. You see, if we try the same thing, only at ten times the frequency...' He broke off with a rueful little smile. 'I'm sorry. I thought you'd be interested.'

'Yes. Thank you. It's very good.'

He switched off the various instruments, and turned slowly away from the bench. He wasn't huffy or angry, the way most people are when they say they're sorry like that. We sat facing each other on the two stools, with our heels hooked over the cross bars and our knees almost touching. After quite a long time, he said quietly, 'No letter. Is that it?'

'I suppose it's a bit soon, really.'

All the same, I'd been counting on it. The prospect of having to hold out for even a day longer suddenly seemed unbearable. Without warning, I felt tears brimming up behind my eyelids, so I leant back against the wall and looked up at the ceiling.

'Perhaps they're away for a few days,' Mike suggested.

This hadn't occurred to me. But it was obvious, when you came to think of it. Or Dudley might simply have waited until the weekend before he wrote. He might have run out of envelopes. Or stamps. There were a thousand reasons for the delay. Even so...

Mike leant forward. I thought he was going to slide his hands onto my knees as part of his big brother act, so I jerked my legs sideways out of his reach. When I was first on my own, I used to long for someone to show me affection; but once you get out of the way of it, you don't know what to do with it when it's offered.

'Look,' he said. 'I promise you'll have the letter as soon as it comes. I'll bring it to school with me.'

'But you mustn't tell Toddy.'

'Don't worry. It's between ourselves.'

I'd really have liked to stay, and maybe help with some soldering or something. But Toddy called out to me, so I thought I'd better go down and see what he wanted.

He was waiting at the bottom of the stairs with a football under his arm. 'Anybody would think,' he remarked tartly, 'it was

Mike you come to see.'

On Monday, Wilkie collared me as soon as I came home from school. 'Did you call in at Shipstone's this afternoon?'

'I couldn't. They close at four on Mondays.'

It turned out they'd rung him up that morning with a whole catalogue of complaints, including one from the Haywards.

'That wasn't my fault,' I said. 'The Hayward boy kicked my bike over and tipped the meat into the road.'

'And what did you do then?'

'I made him pick the grit out and wrap it up again. Then I delivered it.'

He looked at me sharply. 'But you didn't. The Haywards say they never received it.'

'They're lying.'

Wilkie pursed his lips fastidiously. 'Don't speak like that.'

Indignantly, I gave him a summary of events.

He heard me out in silence, his eyebrows poised in provisional disbelief. 'Now I'll tell you what really happened,' he said. 'You don't suppose I've forgotten how all this started? You broke the boy's window and you were punished for it. Ever since, you've wanted revenge. When you were out on your round, you saw the Hayward boy and attacked him; he probably kicked the bicycle over in self-defence. Yes! I can see it from the look on your face. You knew the whole story was bound to come out if you delivered the joint in that condition, so you threw it away somewhere and made up this preposterous tale about what happened at the house. Then you deliberately kept away from the shop till after closing time in case there'd been a complaint.'

'It's true I attacked him, but he had it coming.'

'Ah! So you admit it?'

'Only that. All the rest is lies.'

'Then where is the joint?'

'How should I know? Malcolm Hayward probably hid it.'

'Why would he do that?'

'He knew it was his fault. Anyway, he probably wanted to get me into trouble. He's always had it in for me.'

It was beginning to look as if I should have to explain what happened at the railway bridge; but I wasn't given the chance.

'Your sordid squabbles with other boys in the neighbourhood are beside the point. You were entrusted with a valuable piece of merchandise. Whilst in your possession, it was damaged and then lost. Shipstone's and the Haywards are very properly insisting that you pay for it, and I intend to see that you do.'

I could feel my knees beginning to shake with rage. 'But why? I didn't damage it, and I did deliver it. If you don't believe me, why don't you ring up Mrs Hayward and ask?'

He turned away dismissively. 'I don't like your tone, Alan. You still have a lot to learn about what's expected of you, and it's high time you were taught a lesson.'

I fully intended to call at Shipstone's after school next day, but the Rev Ev kept me in for only getting one out of ten in a test – again – and the shops were shut by the time I came out of the station. Wednesday was early closing. So the earliest I could manage was Thursday.

It was about twenty to five when I walked into the shop. There weren't any customers left, and the knife man was swabbing the block down ready for closing time, the four steels jangling noisily at his waist. The elder Miss Shipstone was sitting by herself in the cash desk, examining her fingernails. As soon as she saw me, she started flicking through the pages of her ledger with an air of great pre-occupation.

I didn't see why I should stand and wait like a penitent, especially as they owed me money, so I turned my back and leant against the ledge of the cash desk to watch the knife man while I was waiting. But he held his arm out imperiously and moved his extended forefinger in a semicircle, directing me to face the desk again.

After an interval, Miss Shipstone closed the ledger and treated me to a cock-shrivelling glance. 'So you're here at last?' And immediately, she launched into a comprehensive indictment. Point the first: I was lazy, slow, inefficient, irresponsible, and indecent. Point the second: the joint had cost practically seven shillings, nearer eight if you threw in all the telephone calls she'd had to make, on top of which I had done incalculable damage to the firm's reputation. Point the third: as I hadn't been worth the going rate, she would only allow one shilling for my morning's work. Therefore – point the fourth – I owed her six shillings and sixpence, and she would like it now; or failing that, not later than the end of the week.

'But Miss...' I protested.

'And another thing,' she went on. 'You didn't wash your basket or clean the parcel slab. So you can set to work this instant and scrub the floor to make up for it. You'll find the bucket downstairs under the sinks.'

I stared at her defiantly. 'I'm not scrubbing your sodding floor, or anything else.'

The knife man's jangling stopped abruptly.

But my blood was up. 'I worked overtime, Saturday morning, and I want my proper money. I did all the deliveries, including Mrs Hayward's, and if she complains about her joint, ask her why she wouldn't take it off me when I was stood on the doorstep holding it out to her.'

For several seconds, nobody moved. I could feel my heart thumping, and my face all hot and flushed.

'Well?' I demanded.

She made no attempt to answer, so I turned and headed for the door. But the knife man was standing in front of it with his legs apart and his arms folded. It was clear that I wouldn't be leaving.

The pair of them watched in grim silence as I swept up the sawdust and went round on my knees with the scrubbing brush and a bar of yellow soap. When I reached the entrance, the knife man lifted each of his thick boots in turn to allow me to scrub underneath them; otherwise he remained exactly where he was, staring at me impassively. A suicidal impulse to throw my bucket of water over him came and went.

By the time I'd been all round again with clean water and a cloth, it was nearly half past five. I put my blazer on, hooked my arms through the straps of my satchel, and stood silently in front of the cash desk.

'Very well,' Miss Shipstone said. 'You may go.'

'What about my money?'

I heard the knife man coming up behind me, and turned to face him. He caught hold of my tie close to the knot, jerked it upwards, half throttling me, and pushed me all the way out into the street. When we reached the pavement, he held me against the wall beside the doorway, with his huge hand pressing against my throat.

'You cheeky little sod,' he said. 'In twenty-seven years, I've never heard anyone speak like that to Miss Shipstone.'

He raised his other hand; I closed my eyes, and gritted my teeth for the blow. Instead, I heard the steels jangle, and felt him thrust something roughly into my hand.

Even after he'd gone, I hardly dared to open my eyes and look.

It was half a crown.

15

Waiting to hear from Dudley, day after day, had made me tense and anxious. On Saturday morning, I was apprehensive in case Mr Pond was still in a bad mood, but the smell of suds and the rhythmic slapping of the drive belts were reassuring. Like wearing your own clothes again after borrowing somebody else's.

He gave me a lock to mend. It only needed a new spring and a drop of oil, but when I'd put it all together again, he said I was a useful chap. After the Shipstone episode, I could have done with having that in writing.

'By the way,' I said, 'We seem to be getting awfully low on stock. Steel flats are right down, and there's none of the brass hex.'

He nodded. 'I know.'

'And there's none on order, either. I checked.'

'That's right,' he said, over his shoulder.

Not my business, of course, but I couldn't help feeling he owed me an explanation. It came, quite suddenly, when I was doing the parcels.

'Notice to quit,' he muttered. 'That's what.'

'Notice? But I don't understand. I thought all this was yours.'

'Not the land. It was sold off as a building plot, but then the war came and everything had to stop. I leased it for the duration. Now it's wanted again, so I have to go.'

It was like feeling your armour melt, or the solid ground cracking under your feet.

'But what will you do?'

He shrugged. 'Finish, I suppose. Not before time.'

'Stop working? But what about all the machinery, and the tools?'

'Sold for scrap, I shouldn't wonder. It's all old stuff.'

I was still kneeling on the floor beside the box, with the string held taut in my hand. For the sake of something to do, I finished tying it round and stuck the label on. But already, it was starting to seem pointless. 'Couldn't you find somewhere else?' I said, struggling hard to keep the future alive. 'Surely there must be other bits of land.'

He eased his cap back and scratched at his hairline. 'Maybe. If I was younger, perhaps.'

'What about all your customers?'

'They'll manage.'

'Couldn't you set up a workshop at your house? Just a little one?'

'At my age, don't you think I'm entitled to put my feet up?'

I started another box, checking the items against the delivery note. Two thousand brass retaining screws, 4 B.A., with specially milled ends. Five hundred quarter-inch brass plates, both ends radiussed. 'How long have they given you?'

'I'm here till Quarter Day. After that, it depends on the building permit.' He flicked vaguely through one of the trade calendars that hung next to the typewriter. 'I'll keep you on as long as I can, if that's what's bothering you. But if something better turns up, take it. Don't mind me.'

My hands and forehead were starting to feel clammy. 'Oh no, I'll stay, Mr Pond. I promise. I wouldn't want to work anywhere else.'

'Wanting hasn't got much to do with it,' he said.

After dinner, Ocky needed his nails cutting, a difficult job to do for somebody else. The positions we got ourselves into, it was a good thing nobody saw us, or they might have mistaken what we were up to.

'How did you manage at Shipstone's?' I asked him.

'So so. But after last week, they'd have taken a stretcher case, as long as it wasn't you. I told them you was a Grammar boy, so what could anyone expect.'

He must have liked getting scragged, he asked for it so often; but the plaster gave him an unfair advantage. 'How long till you get this off?' I said.

'Dunno. I ain't bothered, really. Only you get fed up of having to wank left-handed. Don't feel the same, somehow.'

Once the manicure was completed, we went down to the Rec with Joe and Snap. Some of their friends from Mount Street were there, with a proper football, so we all joined in.

After about half an hour, I happened to glance towards the road, and saw a familiar figure biking in through the Park gates. He stopped a little way off, and sat watching us. I whistled, and he waved back.

'Who's that?' said Ocky suspiciously.

'Dave Jessop. He's all right. I told you about him, remember?'

Ocky shrugged. 'Class bike, I'll grant you that.'

'I know. He lets me ride it.'

'Lucky you,' he said, and turned back to the game.

Dave leant his bike against one of the rusty iron seats, and we sat down on the grass, close by. It was good to see him again. After a while, he said cautiously, 'What's all this I hear about you and Malcolm Hayward?'

I filled him in on the Shipstone saga, and added hopefully, 'You wouldn't happen to know anything I don't, like what became of the parcel after I left?'

'You're still in trouble, then?'

'I could be. It's hard to say. If you do catch wind of anything, I'd really appreciate a tip-off. I might even need to call you as a witness. You know, that day at the bridge. Would you mind?'

He frowned, and leant back on his elbows. 'You think I'm the sort to go round telling tales?'

'I'm not asking you to. But the Haywards wouldn't believe me on my own. You know that.'

He stood up, and started to do something unnecessary to his bike.

'Well?' I said.

He clearly thought I should have known better. 'It'd be rather off, don't you think? Especially when Malcolm's going to Oundle with me. Or had you forgotten?'

'You've changed your tune,' I said, getting to my feet. 'Last time I saw you, you hadn't a good word for him.'

'Yeah. Well, I'm sorry, but there are certain things that simply aren't done. Even you can see that, surely. And unfortunately...' He looked down at the grass, pushing a small stone to and fro with his foot. 'You see, it's bound to get back to my mother. After you came to the house that time, I was made to promise...' He broke off, horribly embarrassed.

I nodded. 'All right, if that's the way you feel.'

'I'm sorry. Really.' He fished a tube of wine gums from his pocket, and held them out to me.

'No thanks,' I said.

The football game seemed to be on the point of breaking up. Two or three of the Mount Street boys were walking away, and everyone else was standing about uncertainly. Ocky shouted something to me which I couldn't make out; eventually, he gave up and came across to where we were standing. With a glance of undisguised hostility at Dave, he repeated his message. It turned out that the boys who owned the football were leaving, and he wanted to know where our tennis ball had got to. I told him it was in my blazer pocket, and pointed to one of the piles of coats that were serving as goalposts.

Instead of going for the ball, he stood waiting a couple of paces off, clearly expecting me to follow. When I didn't, he came and stood beside me, resting his hand possessively on my shoulder, and eyeing Dave as if he was trespassing on private property. Dave stared back at him in scornful silence.

'Well?' Ocky said to me at last, 'Are you coming? Or not?'

'If you don't mind,' Dave said, affronted, 'Alan and I were talking.'

'I won't be very long,' I said to Ocky.

He hesitated, then turned his back contemptuously and went in search of the ball.

'My God!' Dave said. 'He's pretty basic, whoever he is. One of your lot?'

'My best mate, actually.'

The way Dave looked at me, you'd have thought a dog I owned had just pissed on his shoes.

It shouldn't have been like this. I wished we could start again, and get things right. The trouble was, we simply didn't belong in each other's worlds. There was no future for us except on neutral territory. We needed to be alone together, just the two of us, doing the elemental things like tree-climbing, or having a friendly wrestle, or lying side by side in the long grass.

'I'd better be going, then,' Dave said, wheeling his bike onto the path.

I thought I might walk beside him as far as the Park gates, but he swung his leg over the saddle and rode off without giving me the chance.

When I got back to the game, Ocky stood watching him for a moment. Then he spat on the ground and said resentfully, 'Beats me what you see in a bloke like that.'

Wilkie grabbed me as soon as we got home. Apparently, Shipstone's had rung to complain that I hadn't paid them the six shillings and sixpence. He said he was getting pretty tired of the whole business, and I said, so was I, which didn't go down too well.

Dilating his nostrils as if he was itching to pick his nose, he said, 'I'm responsible for you in the same way as a father. If you owe money, I have to make sure it's paid.'

'If you were my Dad,' I said, 'you'd stick up for me, instead of letting Shipstone's and the Haywards treat me the way they have.'

'If I was your father,' he said, with a look that was meant to turn me into a pillar of salt, 'I'd take a strap to you.'

My only option now was to dig in and leave him to make the running. So I simply stood there and said nothing. I tried to look him in the eye, but I couldn't hold his stare, so I fixed my gaze on the brass paperweight next to the telephone, an ugly little statue of an elephant with a howdah on its back.

When he got tired of waiting, he said, 'Very well. I can see I shall have to collect the money from you and send it down myself.' He glanced at a Cash Book. 'I notice you have nothing deposited. Turn out your pockets.'

'It's my money. You've no right to take it.'

He got up from behind the desk and stepped briskly towards me. 'I'm not prepared to discuss this any longer. Turn your pockets out. All of them.'

When I didn't budge, he stepped half a pace back and fetched me a blow to the head that sent me careering sideways against the bookcase. The impact dislodged a small china jug that sat on the top shelf, and sent it crashing to the floor where it broke.

'You'll pay for that as well,' Wilkie said. 'Now, for the last time, turn your pockets out.'

He was clearly ready to batter me into submission, so it seemed like a good idea to give in.

Still feeling slightly dizzy, I reached into my trouser pockets and placed the contents one at a time on the desk. A handkerchief, the knife man's half crown, two bob and a tanner from Mr Pond, a piece of string, a cigarette card I'd forgotten about, a pebble, and a collection of pennies and halfpennies.

'Now your jacket.'

I added the tennis ball, a bottle opener, a pen, a pencil, a six-inch wooden ruler, and a pen-knife.

'Inside pockets.'

My season ticket and a tuppenny notebook with some engine numbers in it.

He riffled the notebook pages and slid the season ticket from its holder in search of banknotes, but he was out of luck. Fortunately, the rest of my money was safely hidden away in a tin at the workshop. He swept the coins into his hand and totted them up. 'There's five and fivepence ha'penny here,' he announced. After a moment's thought, he put the coppers down again and only kept the silver. 'So you still owe me one and six, not counting the jug.' He ran his eye over my other possessions and selected the penknife. 'Meanwhile, I shall hold on to this as security. You'll get it back when you've finally settled up.' Indicating the shards of pottery, he added, 'Clear those away, will you; then take the rest of your things and go.'

I left the room in mutinous silence. My cheek and ear were burning, but there was a hard, cold ache in the bone itself, all down one side of my skull. At tea, I hardly noticed what I was eating. Afterwards, I was drifting away from the table feeling strangely disoriented when Mrs Wilkie called me back.

'Aren't you on washing up tonight?'

'Oh. Am I?'

'Don't come the innocent with me, my lad.'

I wheeled the trolley down to the scullery, and started lifting the stacks of dirty plates onto the draining board. Hurly stood watching me with her hands parked on her hips.

'Are you all right, Alan?' she said, doubtfully.

'Yeah. I'm okay.'

I wasn't entirely clear about what happened next. But Mrs Wilkie bustled in and started telling me off. I'd left some mugs behind, or something. I thought she said I should take the trolley and fetch them, but there didn't seem any point until it was unloaded, so I went on shifting the crockery off it.

'*No!*' she shouted, in total exasperation. 'What did I just tell you?'

I stood there, confused, holding a stack of ten or a dozen plates; thick white ones, and quite heavy.

'My God, you're the limit!' she said.

What with Dave, and Shipstone's, and the workshop closing, and still not hearing from Dudley, I'd had enough. So I simply let go of the plates, and dropped them onto the floor. It wasn't an accident; I did it quite deliberately. But there was no malice intended: I felt the need to be rid of them, and took the easiest way. And afterwards, I stood quite still, with the broken pieces lying there at my feet.

I was vaguely aware that Mrs Wilkie had left the room and that Hurly was starting to clear away the wreckage, but I had no proper sense of the passing of time. Eventually, Wilkie appeared. He had clearly been told what had happened.

'I can see there's only one thing to be done with you,' he said, grabbing hold of me by the collar and propelling me out of the room in front of him. I thought we were probably heading for his office, in which case I should be getting the stick again. But we stopped at the cellar door. Still holding my collar, he felt in his pocket for the keys with his spare hand, and undid the lock. Pausing only to snap the lights on as we went, he pushed me through the doorway, down the steps, and all the way along the passage at the bottom.

When we reached the door of the bomb shelter, he finally let go of me, and said curtly, 'Strip. Everything.'

I was past arguing. More than anything, I wanted to be on my own. So I did as he said, dropping my clothes in a heap on the brick floor. I felt his knuckles against the skin of my back as he pushed me into the dark shelter; then the door scraped shut behind me and I heard the key turn in the lock. There were duckboards on the floor inside the doorway, awkward to stand on in bare feet. As I wobbled round in search of a better footing, I heard the snap of a light-switch, and the lines of yellow light around the door were extinguished, leaving me in total darkness.

For two or three minutes, I stood quite still and listened, expecting faint echoes of the continuing life upstairs to filter down to me; distant voices, muffled footsteps. But there was nothing; only the sound of my own breathing. The room had a disused, mouldy smell, like damp sacking. I wondered if there were really rats about, and whether their eyes would glow red in the dark. Anyway, I thought, I'm bigger than any rat. But supposing I fell asleep? They went straight for your cock, that's what everyone said. You were dreadfully vulnerable, without any clothes.

Ronnie had been given a blanket; I was sure of that. So why not me? Perhaps it was somewhere in the room, and you had to find it.

I stepped cautiously forward, with my hands held out in front of me. Almost at once, I was off the duckboard and felt the concrete floor under my feet. After four or five paces at the most, I touched a brick wall ahead of me, and ran my fingers over it, back and forth; it was solid and featureless, from ground level to as far up as I could reach. The room seemed very narrow, with the side walls so close I could almost stretch from one to the other. Like the wall at the end, they were of bare brick, clammy and cold to the touch; but about eighteen inches above the floor on both sides, rough wooden benches had been fixed. I explored them, inch by inch, and groped systematically into the space beneath them, but I didn't find anything. There wasn't even a bucket. I wondered how I should manage, if the need arose. Perhaps they weren't planning to keep me there for long.

I sat down on one of the benches. The bricks felt rough and cold against my shoulders, so I leant well forward, with my arms across my knees. It surprised me, how calm I was keeping. For weeks, I had lived in silent dread of being shut up like Ronnie. Anything would have seemed preferable; Jacko; another beating. But now I was actually down there, it wasn't so terrible.

The Lakeside Story. Technicolor, of course. Alan's been captured by the man who lives on the far side of the lake. Immediately, the others swing into action. Mike taps out a message in Morse Code. Ronnie and Joe and Dave crawl unseen through the bracken, armed with...

On second thoughts, probably not Dave. Faithless Dave, who let his friends down because he was afraid of his mother.

No, not fair. True, perhaps, but not fair. Pond's Second Law: Before you judge a person, you should walk a mile in their shoes.

Anyway, for the first time in months, I was back at the Studio. Big scene: this boy's been locked in the cellar to make him tell where the diamonds are. He escapes, of course; but today we're shooting the bit where he sits there, all on his own, and wonders what to do. Like using the duckboards to batter the door down; only it turns out they're nailed to the floor. At which point it strikes him all of a sudden that he's up against something he really can't cope with. And as a result...

Only so many tears inside you, people said, and better out than in; like being sick.

All the same, Ronnie hadn't sat here crying. You could be sure of that. Why wasn't I born tough, like Ronnie?

Counting, that was the thing. Counting seconds. Counting your own breaths; anything would do. One... two... three... Once, when I was just a kid, I set myself the stupendous challenge of counting all the way to a hundred with no mistakes. It took me fifteen minutes, and for years afterwards, I used to think that if I counted up to a hundred that was a quarter of an hour gone.

'While one with moderate haste might tell a hundred.' Shakespeare. And guess what. Incredibly, an actual use for Hedger's poetry. Everybody should learn some, in case they got locked in a cellar. The whole repertoire. Hours' and hours' worth. Now is the winter of our discontent. To be or not to be. Would that we now had here but one ten thousand of those men in England who do no work today. Earlier items, too; from Junior School. Amazing what comes back to you. A chieftain to the Highlands bound says Boatman do not tarry, and I'll... And I'll...

Tunes: plenty of mileage in those, too. Tapping out the rhythms with your fingers. 'Workers' Playtime'; 'Lillibulero'; 'Parade of the Tin Soldiers'; 'Policeman's Holiday'; 'Roll Out the Barrel'; 'It's a Lovely Day, Tomorrow'.

Definitely getting a bit chilly. A few drill exercises, modified to suit the confined space.

What time was it? Eight o'clock? Nine, even; or ten? Not too long now, if they were going to let me out for bed-time.

Some more counting. One... two... three... four... Why hadn't Dudley written? I'd said it was urgent. Didn't he believe me? Pouring his tea at breakfast, opening the paper. Headlines: 'Boy Found Dead In Cellar'. 'Oh my God,' he says, racked with remorse.

No. Scrub that.

A thought: One day, all the main leaders got together to see about making the world a better place. But no one could think of the answer. Finally, they asked Alan what they should do. And he said: It is very simple, you divide everyone up into three groups, the nice people, the nasty people, and the in-betweens. Then all the nasty people are put in crates and dropped into the Atlantic. The in-betweens are sent to live in Australia, or somewhere like that, where it wouldn't matter. And then there'll only be nice people, and everything will be fine. So the leaders went away and did what Alan suggested; and everyone was delighted, only they wondered why it had never been thought of before. The End.

I was starting to shiver; and once I'd started, I couldn't stop. Before long, my whole body was shuddering and jolting as if my joints were likely to fly apart at any moment. I tried to do some more exercises, but I couldn't stand up for shaking, so I rubbed my hands along my legs and arms to generate some warmth. From now on, it wouldn't just be a matter of filling time. If someone didn't bring me a blanket, I should have to start thinking seriously about survival.

Perhaps the whole idea was to let me freeze to death. It was probably much the easiest way for the Wilkies to get rid of me. Which, after all, was what they wanted. To try and conserve my body heat, I swung my legs up onto the bench and sat hunched together, hugging my knees. How long did it take you to die of cold? How would it feel? The numbness would creep upwards along your legs and arms, and downwards from your head, spreading over your whole body, like mould; and when all the separate numbnesses met in the middle, you would die. A slow, lingering death. Better to go quickly, all at once, bang. Like Paul. Or Mum. Dad, too, probably. Compared with all the recent perplexities, there was a welcome simplicity about dying. It solved everything, and without any hard decisions. All you had to do was sit there, and wait for it to happen.

In the meantime, an urgent practicality. There was, as I knew, no bucket. From habit or instinct, I went through the usual repertoire of restraints, but I could feel my resolution slowly weakening, until, with a strange exultation, I accepted the inevitable and let go. The feel of the warm fluid coursing over my body was strangely reassuring; I wanted it to go on and on. When it ceased, the loss of its comforting caress brought a sense of absolute desolation, as if the very last of my strength had been drained out of me, my last resource used up.

Gradually, I came to see that by shifting to the opposite bench, I could obliterate the past and start afresh as somebody else. I could even say all the poems again, hum all the tunes. I was just on the point of moving when I thought I detected a faint sound in the distance. To begin with, I discounted it, for fear of disappointment, but before long there could be no doubt. Someone was coming.

Footsteps, cracks of light, a jingle of keys, wood scraping on brick.

Silhouetted in the doorway stood Mrs Wilkie. She glanced down with distaste at the puddle on the floor, which was clearly visible in the light from the passage. 'You filthy little tyke.'

'There wasn't a bucket.'

She didn't answer.

'There isn't a blanket either.'

'Do you want one?'

'Yes.' A statement, rather than a request.

'Stand up, and ask me properly, then.'

My joints were stiff and painful. With some difficulty, I swung my legs down to the floor, and stood up, keeping a hand against the wall to steady me. I realised I was standing in the puddle.

'Well?' she said.

'Can I have a blanket, please?'

She surveyed my nakedness with contempt. 'I didn't hear you.'

'Please, Mrs Wilkinson, can I have a blanket?'

Again, no word or movement by way of answer. Then she said, with grim satisfaction, 'Kneel down, right where you are.'

I lowered myself to my knees.

'Right down, with your head touching the floor.'

When my face was about six inches above the puddle, I hesitated.

'Make up your mind,' she said. 'Do you want the blanket or don't you?'

It was the best part of a minute before I could bring myself to do it. When my nose and forehead were touching the wet ground, she said, 'Now, what was it you wanted?'

'Please, Mrs Wilkinson, can I have a blanket?' My voice, husky and half-choked, resonated oddly against the floor below me.

Something soft and loose flew over my head and landed behind me.

'There,' she said. 'And it's more than you deserve. You're evil, you and your kind. Evil. And well you know how to use what the Devil gives you.'

The door slammed shut, and I was left on my own again. As her footsteps died away, I raised my head and reached out behind me for the blanket.

One day, I thought, I will kill you for this, Mrs Wilkinson.

The blanket stank and was full of holes. But by placing it diagonally on the bench I could lie at full stretch with the four corners folded over me and only my face uncovered. As warmth gradually returned, I became exceptionally clear-headed. The next time somebody came, I'd be waiting for them behind the door, and I'd have the blanket over their head before they knew it. With any luck, they'd have left the door unlocked at the top of the cellar steps. Even without my clothes, I could make it into the street and as far as the workshop. Easy enough to force an entrance. After that, with a sharp chisel in one hand and an iron bar in the other, I could start dictating terms. And while I was waiting, there was a gas ring, and tea and milk and sugar and biscuits.

Paul, sitting on the opposite bench, nodded his approval. 'Now you're talking, Alan.'

'Remember Rex Watkins?' I said, and we laughed.

Rex used to lie in wait for us on the way to school. The day we finally overpowered him, we left him there in the street with his arms around a lamp-post and his thumbs tied together. After that, people thought twice about taking liberties with the Carey brothers.

I must have fallen asleep, or dozed at any rate. The light was on again in the passage, and someone was opening the door. I lay still, raising my head just far enough to see who was coming in.

It was Jacko, in a thin dressing gown, with bare legs showing below the hem. In his hand was a short length of cord; clothes-line probably, or heavy duty electric cable. It was about two and a half feet long. Enough to tie somebody up. Or strangle them.

I disentangled myself from the blanket as quickly as I could, and backed away from him towards the end wall. When he got close, I jumped onto the bench again, hoping to dodge past him and make for the open door; but he drove me back to the far corner by lashing out forehand and backhand with the cord. I felt it cut sharply down across my thighs and shoulders, and cowered against the wall with my arms above my head. For a few moments, he stood in front of me, panting slightly, and swinging the cord gently to and fro. Then he spun me round and started forcing my shoulders downwards as if he was trying to cram my body into a sack. There was a waft of sour sweat from his armpits, and the usual scent of Brylcreem. For a few seconds I writhed about desperately, trying to break free; but it was useless.

I think I may have blacked out for a short time. At any rate, I became aware that although we were still in contact, his grip had slackened and the motion of his loins had ceased. He was leaning heavily against me, gasping from exhaustion, and, as I soon discovered, dribbling profusely.

When he finally disengaged himself and stood up, I subsided in limp terror onto the floor and lay there, perfectly still. After a little while, he picked me up in his arms and placed me gently back on the bench. Retrieving the blanket, he wrapped it carefully round me, and began to stroke my forehead with infinite tenderness.

'There,' he whispered softly, like a parent comforting a sick child, 'it's all right now.'

It was, I realised, the only time that either of us had spoken throughout the entire episode.

The sound of the door closing reached me without inducing any particular emotion. For an hour or more, I scarcely moved, as if by keeping still I could hold time in suspense, and prevent anything else from happening. At last, I decided to risk experimenting with a few small movements. When no harm befell, I eased myself by stages into a sitting position and slid along the bench to the far end, so that I could prop myself in the corner.

Little by little, as the mental block unfroze, various thoughts began to trickle into my consciousness. I wondered, in a detached sort of way, what Mrs Wilkie had meant when she said I was evil. And what was this thing the Devil had given me? It must be something to do with going to Grammar School. Or perhaps she was mad. Not that it mattered, now. I was marooned in a place from which there was no route back to normality. One thing was certain. If they ever unlocked the door, I should refuse to budge. The world I had come from was no longer there on the other side, so I was better off where I was, in the dark, in the silence. I had no future, except as an exile from the human race.

I must have slept again, I suppose.

When Wilkie finally came to let me out, I hadn't the least idea what time it was, and I didn't ask; soon after breakfast, I imagined. He told me to fetch my clothes from upstairs and then go for a bath. 'Not more than six inches of water, mind,' he added.

While the tub was filling, Ocky appeared in the doorway. 'Heard you was out,' he said.

I nodded.

'Blimey!' he exclaimed, stepping into the room. 'Have you seen what you look like?'

I climbed rather unsteadily into the bath and started to wash off the grime; there were long streaks of blood, too, from cuts on my knees and elbows. The hot water was making me sting all over.

'What time is it?' I said.

'Four.'

'It's afternoon, then?'

'No, arsehole, it's the middle of the night; that's why it's dark and we're all in bed.'

I struggled to make sense of this, but my mind had switched itself off.

He reached forward and pointed to a long purple weal across my thigh. 'What's that, for Christ's sake?'

I didn't see any point in discussing it.

'There's more!' he announced, inspecting my shoulders and arms.

When I still didn't answer, he backed away and sat on the rim of the other bath. 'Bloody 'ell!' he said. 'That makes two of you. What goes on down there, that you won't even talk about?'

At tea, we had Sand Cake, one of Hurly's specialities. It was a dirty yellow all the way through, being made without benefit of currants. Ocky and some of the others sitting beside us broke off bits of theirs to give me, which I was glad of, not having eaten since the previous day.

Pretty soon, I was bringing it back up, and shaking violently all over. I felt light-headed and extremely cold. Over the next fifteen minutes, the shaking got worse and worse, until it was completely out of control. I had the vague impression of being carried upstairs, though I couldn't have said who by, and when I came to, I found myself in bed in the Sick Room, wearing an outsize pair of pyjamas with the legs and sleeves rolled over at least six times.

And there I remained, on a diet of Bovril, dry toast, and leftover slices of Sand Cake, for the next two days.

Something Ocky had said kept coming back to me; about not talking.

All at once, with a violent physical shock, a simple fact was suddenly made plain to me. A thing too disturbing even to contemplate, but the harder I struggled to shut it out, the more impossible it was to deny.

I knew exactly what had happened to Ronnie, down in the cellar. If the truth were told, I had known it all along, but the knowledge had managed to conceal itself till now.

Jacko.

So that was it – the thing he'd been hoping I'd guess. If only he'd said. Why hadn't he?

Daft question. Because you don't, that's why. Because you can't. Because there isn't a way.

16

At school on Wednesay morning I watched from the sidelines as Monday's Latin homework was given back. After a lengthy and sarcastic post-mortem, the Rev Ev looked at his watch, and frowned as if we'd wasted the time on purpose. 'For what's left of the lesson,' he remarked, pointedly, 'you'd better finish the exercise you started yesterday.'

Several minutes later, he noticed me sitting at my desk with my arms folded.

'Carey?'

'I didn't know what to do, sir.'

'My instructions were perfectly clear.'

'Please, sir,' said Barry, who was Form Captain, 'he's been absent.'

The Rev Ev glanced at me in exasperation. 'Then why didn't you say so?'

Various answers occurred to me, but I couldn't be bothered

with them. I was present, as the law demanded; co-operation wasn't in the contract.

Barry said, 'I don't think he's very well, sir.'

'When I want your comments, Anderson, I'll ask for them.'

And there you had it. If that's how he spoke to a boy with three fountain pens in his top pocket and Scout tabs on his garters, you could see there wasn't much hope for the rest of us.

Fortunately, the bell rang, so the matter went by default. As we were leaving, Toddy remarked casually, 'Oh, by the way, I nearly forgot. Mike wanted you.'

My letter!

Visiting other form rooms was a high-risk activity; people became immensely territorial during breaks. Nevertheless, at the start of the dinner hour, I positioned myself in the corridor outside 3A's room.

Eventually, Mike appeared, laughing and joking with a couple of other boys. I was hoping that when he stopped to speak to me, they'd go on without him; but they didn't. It was rather awkward talking to him with his friends staring at me.

He produced an envelope from his inside pocket. 'I'm not sure if it's what you were hoping for,' he said.

What else would it be? I snatched it eagerly and made my getaway.

'Was that your bro?' one of the others asked as soon as my back was turned.

'Him?' I heard Mike answer. 'Christ, no!'

Locked safely inside one of the toilet cubicles, I took the letter out of my pocket. Dudley had thriftily re-used my own envelope with an economy label. There was no mistaking the huge typing; it wasn't completely covered. I ripped the top open and withdrew the contents.

Dear Mr Dudley, thankyou for the photorgraphs, I hope you are well, you did not put your address...

I stopped, puzzled. It was my own letter. Why would he send it back to me? If he couldn't be bothered to answer it, he'd simply have put it in the bin. I turned the envelope this way and that in search of an explanation. Something about Mike's name and address caught my eye. They weren't in Dudley's handwriting; I could see that now. Had someone intercepted the letter? It had certainly been opened, but who by? The school office? Oh God, no, please not that.

The label was well stuck down, but I managed to lift one corner. There was a handwritten address next to my typing. The letter had been forwarded, then. So what had gone wrong?

By and by, half concealed under the label, I discovered a stamped notice, very pale, as if the ink pad had been almost dry. 'Undelivered for reason stated: Return to Sender.' There was a tick against Gone Away.

I stared blankly at the envelope, unwilling to take in what had happened. All that futile hope to come to terms with.

I flushed the torn-up letter and envelope down the toilet and wandered outside. I ought to have been in the dining hall by then, but I wasn't hungry. I wasn't anything. My mind had shut itself down again. I was vaguely aware of walking out of the school gates in the direction of the shops. There were plenty of other boys doing the same, so I simply followed them. I hadn't the least idea where I was going, but I felt the need to keep moving. After a while, I realised that from force of habit my feet were taking me down the station approach.

It wasn't the right time for boys in green blazers to be walking through the barrier, but I held out my season ticket and nobody questioned me. The same island platform did for both directions. As it happened, the first train to arrive was for Baker Street, so I got in. It was one of the old sort they still used on the Watford line, with slam doors and separate compartments.

Most of the way I was on my own. I sat in the corner, gazing blankly out of the window. The glass still had a faint criss-cross pattern left from the wartime anti-blast netting. There used to be little pictures of a Silly Man tearing the netting off, and a Sensible Man saying 'I trust you'll pardon my correction, that stuff is there for your protection.' At least, that's what he was saying when the notices were printed.

At Finchley Road, two or three people got into the compartment and sat down on the opposite seat. As the train was leaving, I remembered too late that I ought to have changed to the Bakerloo. In the southbound Metropolitan tunnel were the ghostly remains of three abandoned stations which had been closed down in the early days of the war. They had long since been obliterated from the tube maps, but in spite of that, they were still there in the tunnel, folorn and derelict, like the remnants of a lost civilisation. Or rather, and this was the real horror, sometimes they were there, and sometimes not. Paul had explained patiently that the northbound tunnel bypassed them, but their dim deserted platforms, lit by the pale gleam from the windows of passing trains, had continued to haunt my most harrowing nightmares.

From their sinister elusiveness, and a half-memory of seeing them still in use during those early visits to my grandmother's, I had gradually woven a strange fantasy in which, like Atlantis, they occasionally came to life again for a single day. One chance was all you would ever get, but if you were there at the right moment, and managed to step out onto the platform, you would enter a world in which life had gone on as it ought to have done, with no war, and the family still alive – though of course there was always the risk that unwittingly you would do the forbidden thing, and find yourself suddenly all alone in the dark, with the magic broken and no way of escape; for the trains never stopped there now, and iron grilles had been welded over the exits that led up into the street.

As a small child, I always tried to keep my eyes closed as the trains went through the forgotten stations, but such was their hideous fascination that I could never manage it. For years afterwards, they still gave me the horrors, and even at the exalted age of twelve and a half I was far from immune.

On that particular afternoon, they had the same effect as a razor blade touching a taut string. As we came to the old Swiss Cottage station, I swore that this time I would keep my eyes shut. It was hopeless, of course; but luckily, the platform was on the far side from me, so I managed by staring hard at the tunnel wall. But the Marlborough Road platform would be on the near side. If the carriage had still been empty, I'd have moved to a different seat, and then moved back again in time for Lords. But I couldn't do it with people watching me; they'd have thought I was crackers.

You could tell by the change of sound when the tunnel was opening out for another station. As we approached Marlborough Road, I gritted my teeth; after all, it only took ten seconds or so to travel through. But then, quite unexpectedly, the brakes came on and the train slowed down to a walking pace. With a sudden jolt, it braked again, and I realised with a thrill of horror that against all precedent it was actually going to stop.

One chance, that's all you ever got. I reached for the handle, and as the train came to a halt, I opened the door.

Just as my foot touched the running board, a hand reached out from behind and caught the hem of my blazer. At the same moment, the signal must have changed, and the train started to move again, gathering speed very quickly as if to deny the fact that it had ever stopped. For several seconds I strained forward through the open doorway while the dim outlines of the empty station slid past in the gloom; then, just as we reached the end of the platform, my rescuer caught hold of the door by the leather window strap and pulled it shut.

Whatever he had to say, I didn't hear him. A clammy sweat had broken out all over my forehead, and for the rest of the journey I sat slumped in the corner with my eyes tight shut and my mind blown all to pieces.

At Baker Street, without any conscious effort, my feet followed the well-remembered route, and I found myself on the Westbound platform, letting a Circle train go on without me, because it was a Hammersmith one we needed. It came. I boarded it. After that, it was easy. We were going home.

Ladbroke Grove was always the 'not-long-now' station. By then, the back of the journey was broken. Latimer Road, Shepherds Bush, Goldhawk Road; then Hammersmith, and only the bus ride left.

A quick flash of my season ticket. Through the booking hall; out into the street; across Broadway and a couple of other streets to the bus stop. There was a Coal Office right beside it, with a beautiful model railway wagon displayed in the window; it had real coal in, and its own little length of track. But they must have lowered the windowsill, because I could see in, now, without Paul having to give me a leg up.

The bus came, and I got on. Fivepence-ha'penny in my pocket: more than enough. Over Hammersmith Bridge, with its great suspension chains swooping up and down outside the windows. Castelnau. Barnes Bridge. Our stop. Walking past the greengrocer's, turning left. Not far now.

I'd never been back since I left the hospital. The street looked quite familiar, and yet oddly different, as if the shapes had been distorted by a clumsy artist.

For some time, I stood gazing blankly at the ruined terrace, wondering why the sight of it affected me so little. Some of the debris must have been cleared away, but there were still piles of rubble everywhere, well weathered by now. Even the rubbish people had dumped there was overgrown with weeds. A spindly fence of wire and split palings had been draped across the gap, but it had been trampled flat in several places, so I wandered in off the pavement and sat down amongst the old mattresses and rusty buckets.

It was a pointless thing to do, but I couldn't just go away again after coming so far. They say that if bees go back to the hive and find it gone, they pitch on the ground where it used to be, and stay there till they die. Same sort of instinct, I suppose.

Idly, I pushed some fallen bricks aside with my foot, and uncovered a fragment of linoleum. I remembered the pattern, although I'd completely forgotten about it until that moment. It's what we had in our toilet. For some reason, it made me very uneasy. How could you forget a thing, and it still be there in your memory? What else was lying buried that I might remember?

On a sudden impulse, I started trying to tear the piles of rubble apart with my bare hands as if I were searching for survivors. But I only managed to pull aside a few small lumps, and all the time I was hoping there wouldn't be anything underneath them.

There's no sense to this, I thought; and I must have spoken the words out loud, because a man who was passing by nodded and said, 'You're right, mate, no bloody sense at all.'

I'd been wondering whether to knock at some of the street doors and see if anyone recognised me, but I thought the better of it. It suddenly seemed important to get away. There was no route back to the past, and if there was, I didn't want one. The question now was what to do next.

Threepence in my pocket, and the clothes I stood up in. Not promising, but it was more than I'd had down in the cellar. The nearest main line station was Paddington. I could certainly make it as far as that. Get on a train for Bristol, Exeter, Penzance, Anywhere. Find someone to work the toilet trick with, when the ticket inspector came.

And then?

Time enough to think about that when I got there. For the moment, the chief thing was to keep moving.

Best to walk back to Hammersmith and save the bus fare. Just as well I did, too, because at the station things suddenly turned sticky. I waved my season ticket, holding my thumb across the middle, but the inspector called me back. In an ordinary black blazer, I'd have been invisible, but he must have known the green one wasn't local. He kept me standing beside his hutch while he dealt with a rush of other passengers, and when I saw the train was about to leave, I lost my nerve and bought the cheapest ticket I could from one of the slot machines. Stupid, really. Waste of precious resources. I should have gone round to the other station and tried my luck on the Piccadilly Line.

Till the last minute, I really meant to get out at Paddington. But there were ghosts there; it's where we used to go engine spotting. Better to stay put. A few stops further along was King's Cross. Less familiar, but the name had always appealed to me, and it seemed a promising gateway to the future. You could even get to Scotland, which was almost a foreign country.

Besides, King's Cross had another advantage. Thanks to the war, they never properly finished the new Circle Line station when it moved from Pentonville Road. For years, there was a bit of the old tunnel left between the platforms, and if you knew your way about, you could use it to bypass the exit and avoid showing your ticket. All it took was a short crawl under a couple of barricades when no one was looking, and you were out, or in, as the case might be. So I could make it to the Main Line station without any risk of a surcharge or awkward questions.

As I'd expected, it was easy. Having emerged safely into the concourse, I roamed about for a good five minutes, looking at destination boards and wishing I'd paid more attention in Geography. Which was further away, Peterborough or York? They both had cathedrals; I knew that much. And Doncaster? Where the hell was that?

According to the station clock, it was nearly ten to four. Time to be on my way. There was a train for York at 4.15. That would do. Meanwhile, I had other needs. Not having eaten since breakfast, I was finding it harder and harder to forget how hungry I was. Unfortunately, if I kept a penny back for a platform ticket, total resources came to one ha'penny.

I made my way towards the station buffet with very little idea of what I was going to do.

'How much is tea?' I asked the woman at the counter.

Silently, she pointed to a tariff on the wall behind her.

'And how much for a cup of hot water?'

She gave me the sort of look you'd get if you ordered beans on toast at the Ritz. 'I couldn't say, I'm sure.'

'Couldn't you ask, then?' I ventured.

Under protest, she called over her shoulder to someone unseen. An older woman, vaguely reminiscent of Hurly, appeared in the doorway.

'Hot water?' she said in surprise, when the case was put to her. 'We don't sell it.'

'Is it free, then?' I asked, hopefully.

The two women exchanged glances.

'Well, you're a one, and no mistake. How much have you got?'

'A ha'penny.'

She waddled forward to the counter and looked inside the big enamel teapots. Selecting one, she held it briefly under the boiler tap and released a cupful of hot water into it. After vigorously sloshing the contents round and round for thirty seconds, she poured the resulting gnat's piss into a cup and pushed it across the counter. 'Christmas Day in the Workhouse,' she said, when I gave her my ha'penny.

The coloured hot water was better than nothing, but afterwards, I felt hungrier than ever. My eyes kept straying to the Tariff. Sooner than torture myself, I took my empty cup back to the counter and walked out again towards the platforms.

They still weren't letting people onto the train, so to kill time I looked at all the derelict slot machines that stood close to the barriers. Chocolate dispensers, empty since 1940, and looking as if they were rusted up inside. I rattled the drawers on the off-chance, but they didn't budge. There was a big cast-iron weighing machine, coloured dark green, with a notice above it saying, 'I Speak Your Weight'; underneath, someone had scratched 'Liar' into the paintwork. Over by the far wall was a squat red machine with all the letters of the alphabet arranged in a circle round the top. For sixpence, it said, you could emboss your name on an aluminium strip. But the handle was padlocked, and there was a metal plate fastened over the coin slot. You got the feeling the country was still closed down.

A double row of telephone kiosks looked promising; all those Button B's. But people were queueing to use them, so it was no good. Out of sheer boredom, I nicked an *Evening Standard* from W. H. Smith's. Ridiculously easy, but a waste of time; the afternoon editions only had racing in. So it soon went in the bin.

Without any conscious intention, I found myself heading back to the buffet, and after a moment's hesitation, I slipped cautiously inside. What for, I hardly knew. Perhaps I hoped for a few leavings.

The buffet had two entrances. The one that led straight in from the platforms was round a corner, where the women who were serving couldn't see me. As I came in, a man with his back to me was putting a tray down on one of the nearby tables. He was about to pull out the chair when he made a little gesture of annoyance as if he'd forgotten something, and walked back to the counter again. On his tray was a cup of tea, and a plate with a sandwich on it. No one was looking my way. In two seconds, I had grabbed the sandwich and dodged back out again.

It was a miserable, thin, dried-up little affair with three small slivers of tomato in it. I folded it in half and wolfed it down in two mouthfuls, so as not to be caught with the evidence.

By now, they were letting passengers through the barrier for the York train. I said I was only engine spotting, but the bloke gave me a sour look and told me to buy a platform ticket. I was glad I had kept my last penny.

Halfway along the train, I spotted an empty compartment, and settled down in a corner seat facing the engine. So this was it. Goodbye Barton House. It was a moment to be savoured, although I shouldn't feel really safe till the train was actually moving.

Only another seven minutes. Soon, I should have to give serious thought to dodging the ticket inspector, which mightn't be quite as easy as I'd hoped. To work the toilet trick, you had to go in with someone who actually had a ticket to pass out round the door. But you could hardly ask a total stranger, except maybe another boy, who would understand. If I said I'd lost my ticket, no one was likely to believe it; I couldn't even say what colour it had been, or how much it cost. I could always stand in the corridor and say my Dad had got our tickets, somewhere up near the front of the train. But unless I could hide when the bloke came back, the truth would soon catch up with me.

What did they actually do, I wondered, if they caught you with no ticket and no money? Turn you off at the first stop and hand you over to the police? Maybe that was what had happened to Ronnie, his first time. At the recollection of his return, and the events that followed it, I shuddered.

The compartment door slid open, and a man came in carrying a suitcase. He hoisted it onto the luggage rack, took off his hat, and sat down opposite me. He was wearing brown shoes and a grey suit with narrow chalklines. He made a show of opening a paper, but I sensed him looking at me and preparing to speak.

'All on your own?'

'Yeah.'

'Far to go?'

'York,' I said. The name had a good solid ring to it. After all, York had its own archbishop.

'York? Ah.' He nodded approvingly. 'Do you live there?'

'No.'

He smiled. 'I thought not. London born and bred by the sound of you.'

'That's right.'

'So what takes you to York? Staying with friends?'

I nodded. It sounded plausible, but a little embroidery wouldn't be amiss. 'With my uncle, actually.'

'Really? Where does he live? We might turn out to be neighbours.'

I thought for a minute. 'I don't know, exactly.'

His eyebrows lifted a fraction. 'Then how will you find the house?'

'He'll meet me. I hope.'

'Yes, of course. Silly of me.' He gave a deprecating little laugh and glanced out of the window at the guard, who was just outside on the platform, talking to someone.

I thought he would probably settle down to his paper, now. But no.

'Planning to stay long? In York?'

I shrugged. 'I don't know. A few days, maybe more.'

He looked at the rack above my head. 'Without any luggage?'

I was caught completely off my guard. 'What's it to you?' I demanded, but he must have seen the confusion on my face.

He sat back with a little private smile, as if he had just proved something to his own satisfaction. After a momentary glance at his paper, he looked up again, assessing me shrewdly, his head held at a slight angle. 'I'm sorry,' he said. 'I expect you've been warned against talking to strangers.'

'Yes. Often.'

'Very wise.' He paused. 'But since I already seem to have bought you a meal, I thought it was time we were better acquainted.'

'Bought me a meal?'

'An exaggeration, perhaps. But you stole my sandwich. Don't I get anything in return?'

Jesse Owens himself couldn't have reached the platform faster.

Now what? I thought about boarding the train further along, but the man was a mind-reader, and I wouldn't have put it past him to come looking for me. If I left the platform altogether, I should lose the ticket, and that would be that. So I made for the outermost end, and sat down on the slope, intending to let the York train go, and settle for whatever came next.

I stared fixedly at the entrance to the approach tunnel, and tried hard to think. But the cogs wouldn't go round. I'd made a mess of things, as usual. You needed money, and food, and a properly worked-out cover story that could stand up to interrogation. I should have told the man my luggage was in the van, or that I kept some things at my uncle's.

Actually, some genuine luggage wouldn't have come amiss. How long could I last with nothing but what I stood up in? And supposing I got to York, what would I do? Beg? Steal? Get a job? What? Where? Hang around in cinema toilets and wait to be picked up? Bloody hell!

That was the real catch. You could walk out of school, or Barton House, whenever you wanted to; there was nothing to stop you. But what was the point, unless you had somewhere to go? You were like a dog with its lead clipped to a fence wire; a few feet in either direction, and that was your limit.

Behind me, doors slammed and a whistle blew. As the train slowly pulled out past me, something at one of the carriage windows caught my eye. It was the mind-reader, smiling sardonically, and raising his folded newspaper in salute. I looked away. By the time I'd changed my mind, it was too late, and he wouldn't have seen me waving back. I was sorry, because it suddenly struck me that in a curious way, he'd actually been on my side.

For a time, I stayed where I was at the end of the platform, staring at the rails and struggling to shut out the growing certainty that I wouldn't be boarding the next train after all. Too much sense – or not enough guts. Take your pick; it came to the same thing. I wasn't equipped for escape. The moment had arrived, and I hadn't been equal to it.

At first sight, there were various options open to me. I could go back to Barnes again, and hope to find someone who remembered me. I could call at the Nicholsons', or the Pascoes'. But what could any of them do except give me a bed for the night and hand me over to the Wilkies in the morning? If I was going to end up back at Barton House, it had better be sooner rather than later. If I had to be dragged there, the least I'd get was a beating, and maybe the cellar again.

The only other serious possibility was to go to the Whitmans'. But I should have to tell them everything, and I shrank from the shame and degradation of it. In any case, with nothing to hope for now from Dudley, I needed their good opinion more than ever.

After about a quarter of an hour, I got to my feet and made my way slowly towards the Underground. With the rush hour about to start, I could easily lose myself amongst the crowds, and no one would look too closely at my season ticket.

There was a westbound Circle train waiting at the platform as I came down the steps. I didn't hurry. Let it go if it wanted. But it was still there when I reached the platform, so I got on. A few minutes later, we were at Baker Street. I was intending to get off, but I still hadn't decided where to go next, so I stayed where I was and let the train carry me on to Edgware Road. I could always get out at any stop and go back to Baker Street.

After two or three more stations, I was no nearer to making up my mind, and before long I gave up any pretence that I was going to get out. It was a Circle train. All I had to do was sit tight, and eventually I should arrive at Baker Street again. Time enough for any decisions then. Or if need be, I could go round again. And again. Perhaps I could spend the rest of my life travelling round and round, never arriving, never having to risk making a decision.

But the train I was on didn't travel the whole circuit. At Aldgate, everyone had to get out, and it drove off empty, leaving us all on the platform to wait for the next one. When it came, it was full already, and in the scrum that followed I was swept onto the train with my feet hardly touching the ground. Not being tall enough to reach the strap handles, I tried to stay close to the doors and cling to one of the vertical hand rails. But at every stop, the two conflicting tides of passengers threatened to drag me from my moorings. By the time we arrived at Baker Street, I was quite glad to get off.

By now, it was almost six o'clock. Time to reach a decision. So, which was it going to be? Barton House or the Whitmans'? As I crossed the concourse and fought my way down the steps to the Metropolitan line, I made up my mind to get into whichever train was leaving first. Uxbridge Line; Barton. Watford Line; the Whitmans'. I looked at the indicator. The first train was for Uxbridge. Very well, so be it.

I could always change, of course, anywhere up to Harrow. But I knew I wouldn't. For the moment, a strategic retreat was all I could face; and as for what might happen when I got back to Barton, I was past caring.

'Where on earth have you been?' Mrs Wilkie demanded. 'It's nearly seven o'clock.'

'Bomb on the line,' I said. The standard wartime excuse for lateness. It just slipped out.

'*A bomb!*'

'That's what they told us. Unexploded bomb, close to the tracks.'

She scanned my face with her lie-detector eyes. What she saw, I couldn't say, but she must have presumed me innocent, because I was packed off to the kitchen in search of supper.

'In trouble again, is it?' Hurly said as I appeared in the door-way.

'Not exactly. It's a bit complicated.'

'Don't go telling me, then. I can't be doing with it.'

The leftovers from tea having been declared unfit for human consumption, she opened a tin of M & V, my favourite. After heating the contents in a saucepan for several minutes, she poured them into a soup plate and put it down in front of me.

'There, now,' she said, patting my shoulder reassuringly. 'When a boy's worn out and hungry, he needs feeding. I don't care what he's done.'

M & V was a rich, spicy stew meant for the troops, and came to us by a route that was left discreetly unexplained. By Barton standards, it was a rare treat, next best thing to a fatted calf, and that night it tasted better than ever.

'Hurly,' I said, on a sudden impulse, pausing for breath about halfway through the plateful. 'Do you think I'm evil?'

'Evil?' She looked at me in surprise. 'I doubt it. No more than average.'

'Mrs Wilkie says I'm evil. Me and my kind.'

Hurly directed a shrewd glance at my flies. 'When a boy finds out what he's got down there, he'll use it, one way or another, and there isn't a saint in Heaven would tell you different.'

'Oh, I don't think that's what she meant.'

With a wave of her hand, she dismissed the subject impatiently. 'Eat your supper now,' she said, 'and don't be letting people with sick minds ruin your appetite.'

17

By all accounts, we were having the finest summer since 1940 – God's apology for the bad winter – but after my day adrift, a private patch of fog seemed to travel about with me wherever I went.

On Saturday, at the workshop, I even set the lathe running with the key still in the chuck. Fortunately, when it flew out, all it broke was a window; but it cost me the price of the glass and got me banned for the rest of the morning.

'Put somebody's eye out, doing a damn fool thing like that,' Mr Pond said sharply. 'Can't think what's got into you.'

Neither could the Whitmans. At tea on Sunday, they kept swapping significant glances that I wasn't supposed to see. Afterwards, Mrs Whitman steered me into the front room and sat me firmly on the sofa. I sensed a Little Talk in the offing, so I kept my eyes down, and waited. What had they found out? Earlier, during the meal, I'd noticed that my photo had been removed from the board in the kitchen and replaced by a family snapshot; so I thought she was probably working her way round to saying they couldn't do with me coming there any more, or anyway not so often.

She gave me a skein of wool to hold while she wound it into a ball. 'Do you feel like telling me what the matter is?' she said, all of a sudden, her hands orbiting busily in front of me, like a demonstration of the solar system.

I shrugged. 'I'm all right.'

'I was wondering...' she went on, pausing to hitch some loose strands back onto my fingers. 'I was wondering whether you might be coming up to an anniversary?'

'Oh, no. I was born in February.'

But she wasn't to be put off. 'You're probably trying not to remember, but it might be better in the end if you faced it.' She hesitated. 'Wasn't it about this time of year when you lost your family?'

'That was ages ago.'

'Yes, but people are often sad when the time comes round again. Sometimes, they don't even realise why.'

I closed my eyes, the only defence available. 'If I tell you something, will you promise to keep it dark?'

'Of course. With two sons and a husband, I'm an expert at that.'

'The other day, I wagged off school and went to look at the house. Well, the place. I never meant to. I just got in a train, and that's where I finished up.'

She went on winding as if nothing had happened, so after a bit I cautiously opened my eyes again. When the ball was finished, she sat down beside me and drew me close to her. I'd been hoping she wouldn't; it felt rather undignified. But all the same, I was glad.

'Was it the first time you'd been back?'

I nodded as best I could with my face resting against her shoulder. As I moved my head, I could feel her blouse rustling back and forth over her underwear.

'You poor love. You must have felt very upset.'

'Not really. I thought it would help me remember the blank bits. But I still can't.'

'So what did you do?'

'Nothing. Hung around for a bit. Then I came home.'

'And knowing you, you never said a word to a soul.'

'Why should I? Who'd want to know?'

She ran her hand affectionately across the top of my head. The Sam Barnett haircut seemed to encourage this; people were always doing it. 'It's not good to bottle things up,' she said. 'One of these days, you'll explode.'

A week or two later, Mr Whitman took the three of us to the open-air pool at Uxbridge. I thought at first that I shouldn't be able to go, not having any trunks, but Mrs Whitman found me an ancient costume from the thirties, with a bib at the front and cross-over shoulder straps.

'You'll look a right twerp in that,' Toddy said.

But I wasn't bothered. Anything legal would do. I hadn't been swimming properly since 1943.

As we went through the turnstile, the whiff of chlorine and the distant sounds of splashing and boynoise jolted me suddenly out of the fog and back to life again. It was like in *The Wizard of Oz*, when Judy Garland opens her door, and everything outside is in Technicolor.

The cubicles were ramshackle affairs, made out of canvas and scaffolding. There weren't many, so Toddy and I had to share. Within about ten seconds, I was changed, with my clothes stacked in my wire basket ready to hand in at the counter; but Toddy had barely taken his shoes and socks off.

'Get a move on,' I said, but he was obviously in no hurry.

Mike hauled himself up on the dividing rail and looked over the top into our cubicle. 'Ready?'

'You go on if you want,' Toddy said. So Mike and I went out to the pool together. The sight of the water sparkling in the sunshine sent a thrill of pleasure all through my body as if I'd been kept on a lead for months and someone had just unleashed me. I dived straight in off the pool side, and swam a couple of widths as fast as I could. It was even more satisfying than pounding up Welton Road on Dave's bike.

Dave. For a moment, I felt a pang of regret that he wasn't there in the pool beside me. We'd have been good together, Dave and me. Like when we wrestled. I'll bet he was a good racing swimmer. Just the type. He could have given me a few tips. Pity. Still, Dave was history. He wasn't even at Lakeside any more.

When I got back, Mike was sitting on the edge of the pool, dabbling his legs in the water. I grabbed the hand rail, shook the wet out of my hair, and looked around.

'Where's Toddy?' I said. The pool was shaped like a cross, with two long arms and two short ones. I thought he was probably somewhere round the corner.

'He likes to take his time. Race you across and back?'

I had a job to keep up with him, especially on the return lap. He cut through the water rather stylishly with his head well down, and won by at least three seconds.

We hauled ourselves out and sat on the edge, side by side. 'You're not bad,' he said, with a little nod of approval.

'I lost a lot of time at the turn. There's a special way, but I can't get the hang of it.'

'It's not difficult,' he said. 'Come on, I'll show you.'

He was a good person to learn from. 'Forget about speed. Just concentrate on getting the actions right. You're still turning sideways as you touch. The trick is to go straight down, and then twist yourself the right way up as you come to the surface. Look.' He demonstrated the movements with his hand. When I still couldn't get it right, he caught hold of me and manoeuvred my body down, round, and up again with a twist, to give me the feel of it. After another couple of goes, he called out, 'That's it. You've got it.'

I tried it a few more times, quite slowly, just to make sure, and then for some reason I duck-dived and swam down between his legs, wriggling my way through because they weren't very far apart. He moved his feet outwards for me, and I did it again several times. We tried it the other way round, too, only I was a bit short in the leg for him, and halfway through he rose up underneath me like a whale, lifting me bodily out of the water. I fell forwards on top of him and we splashed around for a while in a hopeless tangle, spluttering and giggling, until we finally made it back to the side.

Toddy was standing on the edge, still dry, and watching us with a left-out look. He dipped a toe in the water and withdrew it hastily.

'Jump straight in,' I called. 'It's much the best.'

He shook his head and wandered off towards the shallow end. I started to follow, splashing some water up at him from below, but Mike stopped me. 'He doesn't need that. Just leave him alone.'

I suppose I must have looked rather surprised.

'Something you should know,' Mike said quietly, when Toddy was safely out of earshot. 'One day when we were small, we went for a walk along the canal at Harefield. Toddy ran on ahead a bit, and found a body face down in the water.'

'Drowned?'

Mike nodded. 'A little girl.'

'Oh, shit,' I said. 'I didn't know.'

'For months, he used to wake in the night, screaming. So don't go taking the piss because he's scared of the water. And incidentally,' he rested a finger across his lips, 'I haven't told you. Get it?'

'Yeah, sure. But if he learnt to swim, wouldn't he feel safer?'

'Very likely.'

'So why won't he try?'

'You know your trouble?' Mike said, scooping some water up in his cupped hands and baptising me. 'You're too bloody logical.'

Mr Whitman had been stolidly doing lengths, making his way through the water with purposeful efficiency but not much sign of enjoyment. Catching sight of Mike and me, he took a break and waded over towards us. He was bulkier than I'd realised, and amazingly hairy; there were even tufts on his shoulders and down his back. As the water drained out of them, they began to spring up and stand away from his body.

'Enjoying yourselves?' he asked with a genial smile, stooping a little and resting his arm round my shoulder.

'Super. It's the best pool I've ever been in.'

He gave me a little squeeze. 'Good. I'm glad.'

I'm sure he only meant to be fatherly, but an extremely distasteful thought came into my mind. It was a good thing Jacko wasn't so hairy.

'Where's Toddy?' Mr Whitman said. 'Time for his swimming lesson.'

I pointed towards the ramp at the shallow end. Toddy was standing there, quite still, and only in as far as his ankles.

Mr Whitman looked across at Mike. 'Give us fifteen or twenty minutes. Then we'll all join up for a bit.'

'How far can you swim without stopping?' I asked Mike, when we were on our own again. 'Carpenter swears he can swim a mile. I don't know whether to believe it.'

Mike looked thoughtful. 'It's possible. If he's built up to it. What about you?'

'Dunno,' I said.

So we did widths together, non-stop, swimming side by side at a nice comfortable pace. I only managed eight.

'Never mind,' Mike said. 'Each time we come, you'll find you can do a few more.'

Each time we come. Four words that promised a whole wonderful summer.

I glanced at the clock on the far wall.

'We'd better give them a bit longer,' Mike said. So we climbed out and lay face down on our towels in the warm sunshine.

All around us were families, blokes with their girl friends, young kids, clusters of other boys, everyone shouting, laughing, swimming, diving, larking about, or lying stretched out lazily in the sun just like ourselves; and it suddenly struck me that here, in this one particular place, I wasn't a Grammar snob, or a Barton oik, or Jacko's bum-boy, or the Rev Ev's slight, unmeritable man. I was simply myself, and nobody was objecting. I didn't have to pretend to be something I wasn't, or feel ashamed of anything I was. And all these other people around us, that was exactly the way they felt about themselves: only they felt it all the time. It wasn't a precious gift bestowed on them for a single afternoon. They took it for granted, as if it was everyone's birthright, and it probably never occurred to them that it was something a person could lose.

I sat up a little and glanced at Mike. Luckily, his eyes were closed, so he didn't realise. It was odd how somebody special could magic the world into seeming a better place. I wished I could be more like him. Not in a slavish way; no question of copying his hairstyle or the exact sound of his voice, although they were both just right, like all the rest of him. The real thing was to feel the same inside, to be confident of belonging, and able to think about tomorrow without being afraid.

After a minute or two he opened his eyes and saw me looking at him; but I couldn't tell what he was thinking.

Down at the shallow end, amongst the inner tubes and water wings, we found Toddy doing a rather ungainly breast stroke while his father held him up with a finger hooked into his trunks.

We jumped in and waded towards them. Mr Whitman winked at us and gently removed his finger. Toddy swam on for about five seconds, then splashed about wildly, trying to touch bottom, and stood up coughing and spluttering.

'You did four or five strokes completely on your own,' Mike

told him.

'I didn't.'

Mike appealed to me for confirmation.

'It's true, Toddy,' I said. 'Honestly. You were really swimming.'

He gave me a sour look, as if he thought I'd been bribed to lie to him.

'Come on,' Mike said. 'Piggyback tournament.'

He bent his knees a little so I could climb onto his shoulders, and Mr Whitman did the same for Toddy. I was glad we paired up that way round, although it gave Toddy a definite advantage. Before long, he'd managed to topple me twice.

'Two nil,' he shouted triumphantly.

I swam a couple of strokes back to Mike. We'd been moving gradually towards the deeper water, so his shoulders were easy to reach, now. 'Hang on tight,' I told him, as I remounted.

This time, I was determined to score. But while I was giving Toddy an extra hard tug, Mr Whitman lost his footing and they both collapsed on top of us. A moment later, we were all thrashing about in a tangle underwater.

The rest of us surfaced more or less at the same time, but I could feel Toddy somewhere down round my ankles. When he didn't appear, I called to Mike, and dived under to help. Between us, we brought him up to the surface, and Mr Whitman caught hold of him round the waist to make certain he didn't sink again. 'It's all right, old son, it's all right.'

As we reached the side, Toddy clung desperately to the rail, spewing out mouthfuls of water and retching violently. With a look of sheer hatred, he gasped, 'You shit, Alan, you did that on purpose.'

'Oi!' said Mr Whitman curtly. 'That's enough of that.'

I looked at Mike in dismay. He shook his head dismissively.

'I could have drowned,' said Toddy angrily.

'No you couldn't,' Mike said. 'Not with all three of us here. Anyway, you can swim now. Remember?'

'That's right, take sides against me. I'm only your bloody brother.'

'Out!' said Mr Whitman. 'I'm not having this.'

We all clambered onto the pool surround, Mr Whitman pushing Toddy from below, and then hoisting himself out of the water with surprising agility.

'I didn't mean you two,' he said, turning to me and Mike. 'I'll deal with this.'

Toddy looked round at me. 'Go on, then,' he said. 'You heard. Get back in.' Without warning, he stepped forward and lunged into me as hard as he could, sending me flying backwards into the water with a gigantic splash.

'Sod it!' I shouted. 'You didn't have to do that.'

Mr Whitman marched Toddy off under arrest. Mike dived back in and drew me discreetly round to face the other way. 'Just ignore him, all right? You can dive between my legs some more if you like.'

Later, obviously at gun point, Toddy mumbled an apology. But on the way home, it was Mike who sat in the back of the car with me, leaving Toddy to sulk in the front, and we all spent the journey trying a bit too hard to pretend that nothing had happened.

On Monday, by tacit consent, Toddy and I avoided each other, but when I was kept back after school, he gave me a quick glance of encouragement. I was glad of that. Hedger was looking decidedly hostile.

I had to wait for several minutes while he adjusted the knobs on his deaf aid, a ticklish business, and settled the bakelite headphone securely over his vast, fleshy ear. Eventually, he rested his hands flat on the table and looked me hard in the eye. 'I'm getting a lot of complaints about your work,' he said. 'Low marks, poor attitude. What have you got to say for yourself?'

'I'm doing my best, sir.'

'What's the matter, then, been ill?'

'No, sir.'

'At your age, you can't be in love. So what is it – trouble with the police?'

'No, sir.'

'Family problems?'

'Family, sir? I'm at Barton House, sir.'

His eyebrows shot upwards. 'Ah! Yes.'

I waited patiently, hands behind my back.

'Mmmnnh,' he said, eventually. 'I dare say that accounts for it. No father to kick you up the backside. Anything else you want to tell me?'

'No, sir.'

'Daily Report, then. Best cure for slacking.' He slid a duplicated sheet towards me. There were columns for Conduct, Effort and Achievement, with enough spaces to last for forty periods. 'You get this signed at the end of each lesson and show it me every evening. Understand?'

Next morning, everyone wanted a good look at the sheet. 'Too many crosses in one week, and you get the cane,' Naylor warned me with a salacious grin.

All of which meant that it wasn't the ideal moment for another head-on collision with the Rev Ev. However, thanks to a poisoned finger, Mrs Dooley fell behind with her darning, and it turned out in the middle of the week that I hadn't got any socks. In summertime, we only ever wore them for school and Sunday best, so it hardly seemed to matter if I did without. But the Rev Ev chose to regard it as a calculated insult.

In the Latin lesson, he waited until we were all sitting down, then called me out to the front. 'What is the meaning of this?' he demanded, glancing down at my legs. 'Are you some sort of street arab?'

Best to say nothing, I thought.

'Answer me.'

'No, sir.'

'Then *where – are – your – socks?*' he said, whacking me round the calves with a ruler.

'I haven't got any, sir.'

'Don't be ridiculous. You'll be telling us next you haven't got any underwear.'

The others were all staring hard at their desks.

'Let me give you a piece of advice, Carey,' he went on. 'When a boy like you is fortunate enough to come to a school like this, he should make it his business to be as inconspicuous as possible. And if he can't or won't conform to certain minimum standards of decency, he should remove himself, and go to the sort of establishment where he belongs. Do I make myself clear?'

'Yes, sir.'

'Next time you enter this room, I shall expect to find you dressed like everyone else.'

As it happened, we had him for Scripture later the same day.

'What does he expect you to do?' Naylor said. 'Knit yourself a pair of socks in the dinner hour?'

'If we all took our socks off,' Carpenter suggested, 'you'd be dressed the same as the rest of us.'

Barry turned pale. 'Evans'd go up the pole.'

'I wouldn't worry,' Naylor said. 'We'd never get everyone to do it.'

At the start of the Scripture lesson, I was called out to the front again.

'I see you've chosen to disregard my instructions. Five hundred lines by tomorrow morning. "I must attend school properly dressed".'

A voice came from the back. 'That's not fair, sir.'

Heads turned, and the Rev Ev slowly raised his chin in a supercilious stare. 'Take care, Whitman. If you involve yourself in other people's affairs, you can expect the same punishment.'

There was a brief silence. 'It still isn't fair, sir.'

It must have taken a lot of guts, but I wished he hadn't done it. It wasn't necessary.

The Rev Ev eyed him coldly. 'Very well, Whitman. See me at the end of the period.'

Next day, still sockless, I travelled under diplomatic protection in the form of a note, extracted with some difficulty from Mrs Wilkie.

'What is this?' the Rev Ev enquired with disdain, when I handed it over instead of my five hundred lines.

'A note, sir.'

'No, Carey, this is not a note. It is a scruffy half-sheet of paper, with no date, no address, and apparently written by somebody semi-literate. I imagine you either produced it yourself, or persuaded one of your cronies to do it.'

'No, sir.'

'Who is...' he peered at the signature, '...Mrs Wilkinson?'

'The wife of Mr Wilkinson, sir.' It was the only way I could think of to describe her.

There were audible sniggers from the back.

'And may we know who Mr Wilkinson is?'

'He's the bloke where I live, sir.'

'The bloke where you live?' He dangled the phrase in front of the class, inviting ridicule. None came. This obviously annoyed him. He glanced contemptuously at my legs and haircut. 'And where is it you live?'

He knew perfectly well. He just enjoyed making me say it.

'Barton House, sir.'

'I see.' He looked slowly round the room, compelling everyone's attention. Then he picked up the note, tore it in two, and handed me the pieces. 'Lines that are not produced on time are automatically doubled,' he said. 'One thousand, by Monday morning.'

At that rate, somebody calculated, in another ten days I should owe him a million.

On Sunday, when we were lying beside the pool again, Mike said, 'So it's total war now, with the Rev Ev?'

'That's up to him.'

We had just completed fourteen consecutive widths, side by side, including the proper turns; and this time, I was wearing some rather smart maroon trunks which Mrs Whitman had bought for me specially at a sale. Toddy was down at the shallow end, having another lesson, and with any luck, this was to be the day when he really and truly learned to swim.

'From what I hear,' Mike said, 'you've got a cast-iron case. You ought to really fight him on this one.'

'I will. Besides, there's nothing to lose. He's put three crosses on my report already.'

Mike pulled a face. 'It stinks, the way he picks on you.'

'I wish I could see the sense of it. I mean, just because I'm at Barton...'

Mike propped himself on one elbow. 'Alan! Barton's got nothing to do with it.'

'Well what, then? What makes me so different?'

A smile seemed to hover just behind his face, as if he couldn't be sure whether to take the question seriously. 'Do you honestly not know?' he said at last, a hint of incredulity in his voice.

'Why else would I be asking?'

But the moment I caught his eye, he looked away. 'I've told you. He's warped. He likes persecuting decent kids.'

'That's not an answer. Tell me, Mike. I really want to know.'

He stood up abruptly. 'Oh, come on, we've got better things to do than discussing the Rev bloody Ev.' And after standing poised for a moment with his toes curled over the edge, he dived back in.

Some boys we met in the pool told us there were Smith's Potato Crisps at the kiosk, and when we were leaving, Mr Whitman bought us a bag each in honour of Toddy's debut as a swimmer, which was now official. It was the first time I had ever tasted them, although I was careful not to mention the fact for fear of seeming ridiculously inexperienced. Actually, they were stale and slightly rancid, but simply to open the glacé packet with its red and blue printing, and sprinkle the salt from the twist of blue waxed paper, was like joining the champagne classes. Dave, I guessed, would prob-

ably eat potato crisps as often as once a fortnight.

Over tea, there was a sudden lull in the conversation. As if at an agreed signal, Mr Whitman turned towards me. 'There's something we thought we'd ask you, Alan.'

I hadn't the least idea what to expect.

'We're off to Cornwall for about ten days in August. How would it be if you came with us?'

I was too excited to bother much with the details; but there was something about a caravan, and the three of us sleeping in a tent.

'What if they won't let me go?' I said, in sudden alarm. You never could tell. Regulations. Or spite.

With a disdainful smile, Mr Whitman reduced the Wilkies to dust. 'Oh, I think you'll find we can very soon take care of that,' he said.

When I got back to Barton, Ocky was sitting at one of the tables, examining his right arm with disgust. The plaster had only been taken off on the Friday, and the flesh was still slack and flabby.

'No strength,' he said, flexing his fingers and twisting his arm this way and that. 'They promised it would be as good as new.'

'Give it a week or two. You'll be all right.'

I cupped my hands around his fist, and told him to try and force them apart by opening his fingers.

'By the way...' he said, in the middle of his second attempt, and jerked his head towards the far side of the room.

There was a boy sitting there on his own, slim, fair-haired; about eleven, I suppose. I'd never seen him before.

'Billy Webb,' Ocky said. 'They've given him Ronnie's bed.'

I'd always known we'd seen the last of Ronnie, but this made it somehow very final.

'What's he like?'

Ocky shrugged. 'How should I know?'

Billy was sitting quite still, with his shoulders hunched and his fists between his thighs, as if he couldn't believe he was where he was. Every now and then, he looked vaguely round the room on the off-chance that things might have changed for the better, only they hadn't. I knew the feeling.

'Where's Tom?' I said, suddenly apprehensive.

'Don't ask.'

'I only meant...'

Ocky nodded shrewdly. 'Yeah. I know.'

At bedtime, I was too busy thinking about the holiday to fall

asleep. I didn't know much about Cornwall, but it clearly offered unlimited possibilities – including the chance that once away from Barton, I might somehow contrive not to come back. But in the meantime, I couldn't afford to put a foot wrong. Whatever Mr Whitman said, a threat to stop me going would be a terrible weapon in the hands of Jacko and the Wilkies. It didn't bear thinking about.

Best to fix my mind on something else. Mike, at the pool side, preparing to dive. A sight so intensely pleasurable, it almost hurt. But why wouldn't he tell me what I needed to know? What was it, this one defining fact about me that everyone else could see so clearly, and refused to believe I wasn't aware of?

I rolled over onto my back and lay with my hands under my head. I wasn't the only person who couldn't sleep. Somebody else was twisting and turning on the far side of the room. Billy, at a guess. Small wonder. Your first night; that's when it really started to hit you.

Ten minutes later, I could still hear him. You want to help, but the trouble is, if people are really down, they often prefer to be left alone.

In the end, I slipped out of bed and padded across the room.

'Billy?'

He curled up in a ball, and pulled the sheet close around his shoulders. 'Fuck off.'

'Yeah, okay. Do you want a wine gum?'

Total silence for a moment; then he unwound himself a fraction. 'I don't mind.'

I slipped back to fetch the packet from my blazer pocket.

'I've got the black one,' he said guiltily, as he started to suck. 'Do you want it back?'

'No. You're okay.'

I would have left him to it, only he sat up a little and peered at me through the semi-darkness. 'You're Alan, aren't you?'

'That's right.'

He sucked for a while in silence. I couldn't think of anything to say. Pointless to ask what the matter was.

'Do people get beaten up a lot?' he asked eventually.

'It depends. Watch out for Tom and Eddie.'

'Is it true the last bloke ran away?'

'Yeah.'

But don't ask why, I thought. You wouldn't want to know.

'What time do we get up?'

'Half six, seven. You won't need to hurry. I have to get off

Ken Shakin
REAL MEN RIDE HORSES

Cowboys and Indians, outlaws and inlaws, Mormons and other strange bedfellows in the pink desert

Ken Shakin's *Love Sucks* was a new kind of gay writing. Sexy and in-your-face with a vengeance, but with a sharp edge of social comment that dug its way through the entrails of New York's big-city anomie. In *Real Men Ride Horses* Shakin turns his acerbic gaze on a very different America: the plains and deserts of the West, past and present. This mythical landscape has always been home to all kinds of male bonding: from the Indian botes through cowboy pardners and Mormon bedfellows, to the drifters who haunt the bars and gas stations of the West today. This new selection of stories — "Real Men Ride Horses", "A Virgin in the Desert", "A Communist in Montana", "How the West Was Won" and many more — will make you laugh and cry, as Ken Shakin uncovers the lusts and pains that lie beneath the macho facades.

ISBN 0 85449 285 2
UK £9.95
US $14.95
AUS $24.95

early, though, to catch the train.'

'Oh,' he said, as if two bits of the jigsaw had just fitted together. 'You're the Grammar boy.'

Already, he'd labelled me.

'I'll get back to bed, now,' I said.

Just as I dozed off, an anxious thought jolted me briefly back into consciousness. Pretty soon, someone had better warn Billy about Jacko.

Next morning, the Rev Ev demanded my thousand lines, and the room grew suddenly quiet as everyone waited to see what would happen next. When I failed to produce them he remarked with prim satisfaction, 'Very well, Carey, you leave me no choice. I shall place the whole matter in the hands of Mr Cobban.'

He might have added, 'And may God have mercy on your soul.' Soft swishing noises came from the back of the room. The Deputy Head had a reputation.

I waited all day to be sent for. Every time I heard someone approaching along the corridor, I thought they were coming to fetch me. But nothing happened. At the end of afternoon school I half expected Hedger to keep me back, but he glanced briefly at my report form which now had four crosses on, thanks to the Rev Ev, and told me to go. A last-minute arrest as I walked out of the gates remained a possibility, but I reached the railway station without incident. In a way, it was almost a disappointment. I was ready for the showdown; delay could turn me stale.

Wilkie was lying in wait when I got home. My first thought was that the Rev Ev had rung him up from school.

'You're a lucky boy,' he said, almost resentfully, as if I didn't deserve it. 'A very lucky boy.'

It turned out that Mr Whitman had telephoned during the day, and the trip to Cornwall was all fixed.

'I don't want you boasting about it to the others, mind,' Wilkie went on. 'And don't go getting any ideas.'

What ideas? As for telling anyone, why should I? It was none of their business. Nearer the time, I should mention it to Ocky; but that was all. Good fortune was best kept to yourself.

Next morning, my name was read out in Assembly to see the Deputy Head. Carpenter nudged me and whispered, 'Now you're for it.'

Mr Cobban was short, and heavily built, with thinnish dark hair slicked well down. He looked humourless, and hard as ironwood.

'You are...?'

'Carey, sir.'

A slight, unmeritable boy.

He glanced at a clipboard. 'Been dodging lines, I see.'

'No, sir.'

He looked put out, and referred to the clipboard again. 'But Mr Evans tells me you've twice failed to produce lines for him.'

'Yes, sir.' I moistened my lips nervously. 'I didn't see why I should, sir.'

He looked me up and down severely, as if he was X-raying my mind. 'Suppose you tell me what all this is about?' he said at last.

I explained.

'Yes, but he told you to have some socks by your next lesson, and you didn't.'

'I couldn't. It was the same day, sir.'

He stood up and examined a large timetable on the wall. 'Mm,' he conceded. 'So it was. But you came without any socks the next day as well, didn't you?'

'They hadn't been mended, sir.'

'Then it's about time your mother got herself organised.'

I gritted my teeth, and looked at the floor.

'If you really hadn't any socks,' he went on impatiently, 'why didn't you bring a note?'

'I did, sir. Mr Evans tore it up. He said I'd written it myself.'

'And had you?'

'No, sir. Mrs Wilkinson wrote it.'

I thought he was going to ask who Mrs Wilkinson was, but instead of that, he suddenly banged the side of his head several times with the flat of his hand and exclaimed, 'Aaaah! I know who you are, now.'

The tension seemed to have gone down a notch, but he was soon back on the attack. 'When Mr Evans set you the lines, you shouldn't have simply disobeyed him.'

'I couldn't see what else to do, sir.'

'You could have told your Form Master. Who is that, by the way? I'll want a word with him.'

'Mr Hedger, sir.'

'Ah.' A wry smile flitted across his face. 'Able, Baker, Charlie. Are you receiving me? Over and out.'

There was a long pause. Then he looked at the clipboard again, and said crisply. 'This whole ridiculous business has gone on quite long enough. I'm going to settle it here and now.'

'But sir...'

He reached behind him and withdrew a book from a long shelf. 'I'm cancelling the lines; you can learn me some repetition.' He flicked through the pages, selecting something suitable, and held the book out. Instead of Shakespeare, which I'd expected, there was the narrowest poem I had ever seen. 'First two lines of that, I think.'

'Two, sir?' I queried in amazement.

'Yes,' he said, in rather an odd voice.

'When for, sir?'

He consulted his watch. 'Oh... I should think about thirty seconds from now. Does that sound reasonable?'

I read the words through twice, handed the book back, and repeated them for him on the spot.

'Good. I'll tell Mr Evans I've dealt with the matter appropriately.' He put the book down. 'And Carey, another time, instead of getting yourself in a mess like this, come straight to me.'

18

I'd barely spoken to Billy since his first night, but he seemed a decent enough kid. On Saturday, after dinner, I found him mooning about outside, so I said, 'Do you want to come out on the golf course?'

'Yeah, okay.'

As we crossed the railway bridge, I asked him casually, 'Anyone told you about Jacko?'

'Your mate Ocky says he wants watching.'

'It's true.'

'One o' *them*, is he?'

Thin ice. I should have kept my mouth shut.

'Jacko has nasty habits,' I said. 'Like burning people with lighted fag ends. Take care, that's all.' Come to think of it, though, it was pointless warning anyone. What could they do about it, even if they knew?

We walked on again in silence. It was sunny and hot. My shirt suddenly seemed itchy and intolerable, so I pulled it off and tucked it into my belt. After about five yards, it fell out, so I tried knotting it round my shoulders instead, but the sleeves were too short. I wished I'd left it behind. Luckily, just where the path came out onto the golf course, there was a patch of woodland. 'Half a mo,' I said, and climbed over the fence. A little way into the thicket, I found a tree with a handy fork. 'D'you want to leave yours here too?' I said.

Billy tugged his shirt off and passed it over the fence. As we moved into the open, he ran ahead, bowling imaginary cricket balls, his body lithe and graceful in the sunshine.

'Where are we going?'

I pointed. 'Under those tall trees in the distance. It's a good place. I've been there several times.'

At first, it was hard to find. With the leaves all grown again, everything looked so different. But eventually, I spotted the proper way in through the bushes, and a few moments later we emerged into the tiny clearing. It was cool and green, with odd little patches of dappled sunlight filtering through from above.

Billy looked round approvingly and settled back with his hands under his head. 'So what do you and Ocky do when you come here?'

'Me and Ronnie, it was. Wouldn't be Ocky's style, a place like this.'

He shrugged. 'You and Ronnie, then. What did you do?'

'This and that.'

'Nothing special, then?'

'Why? What did you expect?'

He looked puzzled, let down. 'What's the big idea, then?'

'To get away from Barton, of course.' It seemed too obvious to need explaining.

He sat up, and reached over his shoulder to brush the leaf mould from his back. There was clearly something else he was waiting to ask.

'Is it true about people getting locked in the cellar?'

'Yes.'

'Has it happened to you?' There was a note of challenge in his voice, as if he thought it was just a story, something to scare the new kids.

'Yes, if you must know.'

'And Ocky?'

'I don't think so. He's never actually said.'

Billy sat for a while hugging his knees and sorting out his opinions. He still seemed restless, dissatisfied.

'Tell you what,' I said, glancing upwards. 'Let's climb this tree.'

Billy was good; much better than me; better than Ronnie, even. We went about halfway up, and sat side by side on a thick branch, sharing a fag, and dropping bits of loose bark into the clearing below us.

'You've got a hard on,' Billy remarked confidently, glancing at my flies.

'What if I have?'

He reached forward. 'Come on, then. Give us a look.'

'Fuck off!' I pushed him away in surprise.

'Suit yourself,' he said.

Before long, he started to make his way down again, finding his footholds with effortless assurance. You'd think he'd been climbing that particular tree since he was six. Sooner than have him watch me, I stayed up on the branch for a couple of minutes before I followed him down.

As I crawled out through the undergrowth, I could see him crouching on the ground, intent on something close in front of him. He was building a miniature African hut out of twigs and pieces of long grass. It was quite small, only about a foot in diameter, but intricate and cleverly made. He worked quickly and efficiently as if following a well-established routine.

Hearing me approach, he looked round in mild irritation and crouched protectively over his handiwork.

'That's good,' I said. 'D'you like making models and things?'

'No.'

He turned away again. Clearly, I was intruding, so I stepped aside and watched him from a distance.

After a few moments, he stood up and took a pace back. The hut was evidently finished. He walked slowly all round the little structure, and then felt in the pocket of his shorts. As he withdrew his hand, I saw he was clutching a crumpled book of paper matches. Without so much as a glance in my direction, he knelt down in front of the model, struck a match, and held it under the roof edge till the thatch had caught. Then he sat back on his heels and watched intently as the hut went up in flames. When there was nothing left but a few charred remains, he reached forward and scattered them this way and that with his bare hands.

For some time, he crouched over the spot, scanning it carefully to make sure that every trace of the hut had been obliterated. His body, bare to the waist, was taut and rigid, the muscles tensed, the vertebrae projecting in sharp relief all down his back. At last, he relaxed a little, looked up, and caught my eye. 'There,' he said, with quiet satisfaction.

So Perish All Mine Enemies.

He stood up abruptly and said, 'Can we go now?'

As we were walking back, he asked casually, 'Do Tom and Eddie go housebreaking?'

'First I've heard of it. Who told you?'

'Ocky.'

'He should know,' I said.

We paused to let some golfers drive off one of the greens. Billy picked a handful of wild grass and used it to tickle my back and shoulders. 'Ocky says you're nuts,' he commented.

'Yeah. He would.'

'He thinks a lot of you, though.'

'Tell us another!'

He shook his head. 'No. It's true.' And the corners of his mouth twitched upwards into a little private smile.

When we were putting our shirts on, he glanced back over the golf course. 'Shall we come here again tomorrow?' he said.

'I can't. There are these people I go to on Sundays. The Whitmans. He's a boy in my class at school.'

'Whitmans?' He gave me an odd look. 'The printers?'

'Stationers. They've got branches all over the place. Why?'

He didn't answer. For some reason the shutters had come down, and the rest of the way home, he scarcely said a word.

At tea, Ocky was in a strange mood, as well. 'You've been for walkies with Billy, then?' he said accusingly, as if I'd pinched his personal property.

'Any objections?'

'I should think he was bored out of his mind with all your Grammar School crap.'

Let it go. I didn't feel like rising to it. 'There was one odd thing, though. He clammed up completely when I mentioned the Whitmans.'

Ocky gave me a scornful glance. 'Yeah, well he would, wouldn't he? His Ma used to work at their printing place. And you know what? Apparently, your Mr Whitman's a real shit.'

I could feel my face burning. 'That's not true.'

Ocky shrugged dismissively.

'I know the Whitmans a bloody sight better than Billy does,'

Will Aitken
TERRE HAUTE

'I'm going home and I'm going to tell my father exactly what you did to me'

A poetic novel of sexual awakening in the American Midwest, tracing an adolescent's journey from introspection to perilous desire. Set in the Indiana town of that name, *Terre Haute* is the story of one very memorable year in the life of Jared McCaverty, a boy who has just discovered sex but has yet to discover what it means. Spoiled by his rich family, he lives in a fantasy world filled with films, art and daydreams. But he soon comes to realize that sex can be a powerful weapon — especially when used against a married man.

"Forceful, sexually graphic, and dark — an unusual and intelligent debut" — *Kirkus Review*

ISBN 0 85449 279 8
UK £8.95
AUS $22.50
not for sale in North America

Peter Szabo
DOES JOE DURVA STILL EXIST?

The quest for a 1950s gay model leads to a metaphysical adventure

A middle-aged English painter, quite successful in the fashionable art world, is thrown into existential angst when he turns up an old photo from *American Physique* that had represented all the erotic yearnings of his youth. He resolves to track down the model, Joe Durva, though he can hardly explain to himself why. From Los Angeles to New York, through a trail of seedy porn shops and city gyms, Lewis follows the traces of Joe's life, which seem increasingly weird. Was Durva really abducted by aliens? And what hold over him do the DeMarcos have, a couple of "psychic healers" that the FBI suspect of serious crimes? Lewis's quest peels back layers of the American past, from the McCarthy era through the Vietnam war; but whether Joe Durva still exists or not, Lewis at least succeeds in finding himself.

ISBN 0 85449 284 4
UK £9.95
US $14.95
AUS $24.95

I told him angrily. 'They've been very good to me. I'm even going on holiday with them.'

'Holiday!' Ocky said with a sneer. 'Be different if you had to work for them.'

After tea, everyone crowded into the Club Room to hear the report from Lord's on the first day's play in the Test. But I wasn't in the mood, and finding the workshop deserted, I drifted by easy stages down to the railway bridge.

I could hear a train in the distance as I went up the steps, so I ran to the top and leant over to watch it go by. For a few moments, the noise blotted out all other sounds, so I didn't hear anyone approaching. But when the train had disappeared, I happened to glance round and noticed Billy standing at the end of the pathway. He hesitated for a moment, then came slowly up the steps.

'Wotcher,' he said, leaning over the parapet a little distance away. I wasn't sure if he'd followed me, or whether we'd met by accident.

We must have been there for about five minutes, each busy with our own thoughts, when something hurtled past my ear and hit one of the side girders with a clonk. I looked up in surprise. A few seconds later, another missile hit the edge of the parapet and ricocheted onto the wooden planking at our feet.

'Shit!' said Billy. 'We're under fire.'

At the end of the further pathway, under the trees, stood two boys in cricket whites and St Andrew's caps. One of them, unmistakably, was Malcolm Hayward.

'Right,' I said to Billy. 'You piss off. This is a private fight.' Retrieving the stone from where it lay on the planking, I chucked it back at Malcolm as hard as I could.

'But there's two of them,' Billy said.

'There's only one that counts,' I told him, looking around for some more stones. 'Hop it. I've been waiting for this.'

Billy still looked doubtful, but I hadn't got time to waste arguing. I turned my back on him and began gathering up some stones as fast as I could. When I'd collected half a dozen or so, I advanced to the end of the bridge and loosed them off quickly, one after the other. I had the advantage of height, but Malcolm, as I now saw, was armed with his catapult. The other boy was scrabbling about on the ground and handing him stones. My own supply was going to be pretty limited. There might be a few more lying on the bridge, but I couldn't count on it.

I turned back and shouted to Billy, 'You can get us some stones if you like.'

He nodded and ran back to the pathway on our side of the bridge. I found a few pebbles lodged in the planking, and stepped forward to throw them, only this time I was more economical, and between shots I crouched down to dodge Malcolm's fire. Several stones hit the girders on either side of me, but most of them spun away and dropped onto the tracks below. I hoped Billy wouldn't be too long.

The next time I stood up to loose off a couple of shots, I saw Malcolm nod to the other boy, who glanced briefly in my direction and then dodged back towards the road. So now it was just the two of us.

Billy came running across the bridge with a fresh supply of ammunition, which he put down within handy reach. 'I'll be okay now,' I said. 'He's on his own.' A stone hit the girder next to Billy, and he ducked down in alarm. 'Get back,' I said. 'I've told you, it's not your fight.'

As soon as the next stone hit the bridge, I stood up and sent Malcolm a couple in return. I think one of them actually hit him.

'Barton oik!' he shouted.

'Come on up here,' I called back, and he gave me a big V sign.

For the time being, neither of us had any intention of moving. It looked like a stalemate. I chose a large and especially well-shaped stone from Billy's pile, and turned it this way and that in my hand to get the best grip. After a tense pause, I sprang up suddenly and chucked it with all the force I could manage. Malcolm ducked, but the stone went wide and landed among the trees.

Just as I crouched down again, I noticed a blur of white on the pathway. The other boy was back, and it looked as if he had brought some reinforcements. I crept cautiously towards the end of the bridge to reconnoitre. Four of them now. Damn. They must have been coming away from their sports field after a match. If they rushed the bridge, I shouldn't have much of a chance on my own. I should simply have to retreat.

Without exactly meaning to, I glanced round to see if Billy was still there. He certainly wasn't on the bridge. But perhaps he was out of sight at the foot of the steps. It might be as well to find out. At least he could gather some more stones, and maybe fetch me a long branch or something I could use in self-defence.

Keeping my head well down, I crawled back to our own end of the bridge. 'Billy?' I called softly. He didn't answer, so I peeped cautiously over the edge. There was no sign of him. Oh well. It was no bad thing. I didn't really want him getting involved.

Glancing towards the left-hand side of the steps, I noticed that part of the wooden handrail was coming away. There probably hadn't been anyone round to mend it since 1940. It turned out to be fixed a lot more firmly than I'd thought, but after struggling for a couple of minutes, I managed to wrench away a piece about five or six feet long. It would make a handy weapon for when the stones ran out.

I crawled back to the far end of the bridge dragging the piece of railing, and peeped over the edge to see what Malcolm was up to. Already, he and his three friends were cautiously advancing towards the foot of the steps. I could hear them arguing about whether I'd gone or not, so I settled the matter by standing up suddenly and pelting them with four or five stones from the dwindling pile. They scuttled back in surprise, and went into a huddle under the trees. After a little while, I saw Malcolm take aim, so I ducked down again. A second later, there was the usual clonk as a big stone hit the end girder. Then another, and another.

The volley continued almost uninterrupted for several minutes. Then it suddenly ceased, and I heard a rumble of footsteps running upwards towards me. They must be trying to rush my position. Leaving it as late as I dared, I advanced to the middle of the top step, gripping the piece of handrail with one end thrust well out in front of me. As soon as I appeared, they stopped dead. There were only three of them. Malcolm had stayed behind to give them covering fire.

For a while, we all stood motionless. The handrail was a pretty effective deterrent. When they'd had time to take the situation in, I said, 'You three bugger off. This is between him and me.'

They stood there for a moment, still uncertain.

'D'you want the end of this between your legs?' I said, jerking the splintered tip of the railing towards them.

They moved down a couple of steps. The biggest looked at the others and said contemptuously, 'Trust a Barton oik to fight dirty.'

'Why don't you tell Malcolm to come up here on his own?' I said. 'Let's see if he's got the guts.'

For a moment, I thought they were going to try and rush me again; then they backed cautiously down the steps and along the path to where Malcolm was standing. I took advantage of the respite to put some stones in my pocket. If I had to retreat in a hurry, I didn't want to be left unarmed.

It was a while before anything more happened, although I noticed one of them darting back to the road for a moment before rejoining the others. I could see they were arguing. So much the better. Then all four of them started to walk slowly towards the bridge, with Malcolm in front and the rest in a group close behind him. I took a comfortable grip on my piece of railing, and waited.

When they got to the steps, they came about halfway up, with Malcolm still in front, and then paused.

'Well?' said Malcolm, leering up at me.

'Get rid of them,' I said. 'You and me have got things to settle.'

Nobody moved.

'Go on, tell 'em to scarper.'

Malcolm shrugged, and nodded to the others behind him. Just when I thought they were going to back off, they all reached in their pockets and pelted me with a shower of stones. As I raised my left arm instinctively to shield myself they leapt up the remaining steps towards me. I still had the rail in my right hand, but it was too heavy to wield properly without a two-handed grip. By the time I had stepped back and got both hands on the rail again, they were on top of me. I managed to trip one of them and send him flying down the steps, but I had to let go of the rail to defend myself, and before I knew it, the other three had rolled me onto my back. I writhed about desperately, but two of them forced me down while Malcolm picked up the rail and held it upright with the splintered end about six inches above my flies.

'Now,' he said, 'what was it you wanted to settle?'

Lying flat on my back, I felt the bridge structure suddenly start to vibrate. Another train, perhaps, still too far off to be heard. Then, all at once, there were running footsteps pounding across the bridge towards us.

'Fuckin bastards!' Ocky's voice, unmistakable.

There was a blur of legs all round me, and the grip on my feet and arms was suddenly relaxed. I crawled out from amidst the mêlée to find about half a dozen Barton boys laying into Malcolm and Co with grim efficiency. For the moment, I seemed almost superfluous. Billy was there, head down, fists flailing wildly, with Joe and Snap on either side of him. And towering above them was Tom, his red hair vivid in the evening sunlight, and his lean pale face twisted into a snarl as he landed a straight left into Malcolm's stomach.

I caught Billy's eye and gave him a quick nod of thanks for

summoning the cavalry. But just then, I noticed a flurry of white under the trees as some more St Andrews boys came running towards the bridge.

'Look out,' I shouted, 'there's more of them.'

The new arrivals put fresh heart into Malcolm's lot, and between them, they drove us part of the way back towards our own side. There must have been seven or eight of them, now, but fortunately, the bridge was too narrow for them to have any chance of surrounding us.

Pretty soon, I lost all track of time. The battle flowed this way and that across the bridge as one or other side gained a temporary advantage and then lost it again. At least twice, we drove them right back to the very edge of the steps, only to lose control and find ourselves in retreat. But it hardly mattered. This was the Day of Reckoning, and a quick finish wouldn't have suited us.

There was a tall boy with his back to me, landing a punch in Ocky's mouth and dodging away again with an arrogant toss of his head. I knee'd him in the arse as hard as I could and grabbed his shoulders to try and drag him down. He spun round angrily, but lost his balance and fell on top of me. With a hand on my throat, he drew his fist back. Then, at the last minute, he froze.

It was Dave.

We stared at each other blankly. 'What's this all about, anyway?' he said.

'If you don't know, what are you doing here?'

'I could see our blokes were in trouble.'

Already, the main battle had drifted a little away from us. He let go of me, and I stood up angrily. 'Why should you want to stick up for a bunch of turds like them?'

His fists clenched, and then relaxed again. 'I was wrong about you. I thought you were different, but you're not, are you?'

'This isn't your fight,' I said. Why don't you just go?'

'How can I?' He gestured helplessly in the direction of the others.

Until that moment, I'd been wishing the battle would last for ever, but the exultation had suddenly evaporated, leaving only a sour disgust.

'Then keep out of my way, that's all.'

I could see Billy's face contorted with pain; one of them was twisting his arm right round behind his back. So I left Dave standing there, and ran forward to intervene.

Soon afterwards, the main action split in two. The St Andrews boys outnumbered us, but a couple of them were starting to look as if they'd had enough. With a bit of encouragement, they might decide to quit. We managed to isolate them at the far end of the bridge, and two or three of us started to drive them down the steps. By the time they reached the pathway, they'd made up their minds.

'Piss off home,' I said.

With a barely perceptible nod, one of them turned away, and the other followed. You could tell they wouldn't be back. From now on, we should have the upper hand.

I was about to climb the steps again, when a warning shout came from behind. 'Alan, watch out!'

I jerked my head upwards and saw Snorty Pig on the top step, holding my piece of rail like a javelin, poised and ready to throw. Instead of trying to dodge aside, I stared up at him defiantly, almost as if I was daring him to hurl it at me. Maybe I had some crazy notion that the masterful look in my eye would force him to put it down, and that would be the end of him. If so, it didn't work. I saw him raise his arms and then lunge downwards with a massive effort, launching the rail towards me like a harpoon. I froze, and watched it coming.

Through the brain fog, I was vaguely aware of a sudden movement to my left; then somebody lunged into me, knocking me sideways with tremendous force. As we fell to the ground in a heap, the railing hit the pathway where I had been standing, and clattered harmlessly back against the lower steps.

It seemed like an age before anyone moved. I lay there, perfectly still, conscious only of somebody's weight on top of me, and the smell of dust and sweat.

Slowly, we disentangled ourselves.

'You all right, Alan?'

It was Tom.

Only just for a split second, it hadn't been Tom at all.

A street. A face at a window. An endless moment of paralytic terror. Shouts. Get down, Alan, get down! A clatter of boots on the roadway. Somebody kicking the legs from under me. Grit on bare knees. A warm, familiar body lying on top of me, forcing me urgently down against the pavement. An eternity spent holding my breath.

And then?

They brought me Snorty Pig to see what I wanted done with him. He stood in front of me, grey faced and sagging. The whole scene had a strange air of unreality and I was suddenly feeling rather sick, the way you do when you've just had gas at the dentist. It should have been a moment to savour, but now he was finally mine to do as I liked with, it scarcely seemed worth the trouble. Pointless even to force a confession out of him.

'Strip him bare and chuck him in the nettles,' someone said.

But there was unconditional surrender in his eyes, and that was all I cared about.

After his near-miss with the rail, the battle had virtually ceased of its own accord. By the time I started to climb the steps, the other St Andrew's boys were already making their way down, examining their elbows for scraped skin, or tucking their shirts resentfully back into their trousers, as if getting thrashed by the Barton oiks was the sort of thing that could only have happened under a Labour government.

We stayed on the bridge till nearly supper time, in the pride of undisputed possession, seated at the exact centre, three on each side, with our backs against the girders and our legs stretched out in front of us.

'We saved you this,' Tom said.

Snorty Pig's catapult.

I couldn't think what to do with it. My brain had gone on strike.

Strange irony that after so many years it should have been Snorty Pig who gave me back my memory. An equivocal gift, if ever there was one. Because now, when I needed to talk to him more than ever, the special place I kept in my mind for Paul was dark and empty. He wasn't there any more. He'd simply packed up and gone, without a word. I couldn't even remember what he looked like.

Ocky, Joe, Billy, Snap, Tom. As an experiment, I said to myself: These are my brothers, now. But they weren't.

'For Christ's sake!' Ocky exclaimed. 'What are you doing?'

With the elastic at full stretch between my hands, I worked it against the edge of the nearest girder till it broke. Then I stood up, and hurled the catapult as hard as I could over the parapet, and we heard it land in the distance, somewhere along the tracks.

'You *prick!*' he shouted angrily. 'What did you do that for?'

'I'm off now,' I said. 'See you.'

Sunday tomorrow. Uxbridge. The sun warm on my back, and the blue pool beckoning.

Could so much water fail to wash me clean?

But when I arrived at the house next afternoon, Mr Whitman had gone out, and Toddy was upstairs, lying in a darkened room.

'Is it his asthma?' I asked.

'More the pollen, I think,' Mrs Whitman said. 'Mind you, it could be his nerves as well.'

'Nerves? What's wrong?'

'He won't say. But strictly between ourselves, it's probably the exams.'

'They aren't for another couple of weeks.'

'I know, but he wants to get into the 'A' stream, and he's worried he won't do well enough. Mike's in the 'A' stream, so Toddy has to be. It's often the way with younger brothers.'

'Oh,' I said. 'Is it?'

She leant towards me and ran her finger gently across my forehead. There was a scab there from yesterday. 'What's all this, then?' she said, looking me over in case there were any more.

'Nothing. Just a scrap. Shan't we be going swimming then, if Toddy's ill?'

I knew the answer before she spoke. 'Dad's gone in to the Office, I'm afraid. There are things he can only get done when there's peace and quiet.'

'Oh. Well, that's that, then.'

'I'm sorry, love. Are you dreadfully disappointed?'

Mike was out in the garden, weeding.

'You look like a wet weekend,' he said. 'What's up?'

'I thought we'd be going swimming.'

'Yeah.' He stood up and wiped the back of his hand across his forehead. 'Actually, we still could, if you're that keen.'

'Your Dad's got the car.'

'It's just about bikeable. You could borrow Toddy's.'

We arrived hot and dusty from the journey. So much the better, though. It made the water that much more inviting.

'Shall we be swimming in Cornwall?' I said, when we were sunbathing after my widths. Fifteen, this time.

'Of course. Not like this, though. In the river.'

'Every day?'

'Twice a day, if you like.'

Apparently, these friends of theirs had bought up a derelict country mansion not far from Falmouth, and were turning it into a hotel. For the time being, they were living in a caravan parked in the grounds, and the Whitmans had been offered the use of it while they took a break.

'Tight fit, with all five of us,' I said.

'Only Mum and Dad. We'll be in the tent. And the tent's only a stone's throw from the river. We'll be able to get up in the morning and dive straight in.'

I could have hugged him, for sheer pleasure. 'I've never slept in a tent,' I said.

He suggested going for ices, and said he would pay. I waited for him outside the changing place while he went to collect some money. It seemed to take for ever, and when he finally reappeared, I could see that something was wrong.

'My wallet's gone,' he said. 'I know it was still in my pocket when we were changing.'

'Perhaps it fell out of your basket on the way to the counter.'

'I've looked all over.'

'Was there a lot of money in it?'

He shrugged. 'Some. And one or two other things.'

'Perhaps someone will find it, and hand it in.'

He gazed out unhappily towards the pool. 'You won't say anything at home, will you? Dad's weird about money. Spending it's one thing, but losing it's quite another.'

Back in the water, we tried to pretend we were having fun, but it was hopeless. It should have been really good, just the two of us, without Toddy to get in the way, or Mr Whitman with his horrible hairy shoulders. But losing the wallet had made the sun go in.

I glanced at Mike uncertainly. 'Do you want to go?'

He nodded. 'May as well. Long ride home.'

We made our way to the cubicles in silence. As we claimed our baskets, the man at the counter reached up to a shelf above his head and held out something towards us. 'Yours?' he said to Mike.

'Yeah! Thank God for that. Where was it?'

'Couldn't say.'

Mike reached out for the wallet, but the man snatched it away. He was wearing a string vest, and his arms and neck were leathery brown and muscular, like an army PT instructor. 'How do I know it's yours? Got your name in?'

'No.' Mike looked suddenly very vulnerable. 'But it's mine all right.'

'It is his,' I said. 'I recognise it.'

'Anybody could say that. Suppose you tell me exactly what's in it?'

Mike looked horribly embarrassed. 'A ten-bob note. Some loose change. A few bits and pieces.' He hesitated. The man still wasn't satisfied. 'And there's a photograph.'

The man gave him a knowing leer. 'Girl friend, eh?'

'No,' Mike said, looking down at the floor. 'Just my cousin.'

Flicking his fingers rapidly through the wallet, the man drew out a photo. 'Oh, yes,' he said, glancing at me. 'Very good likeness.'

With the place so crowded, we had to share a cubicle.

'Since when have I been your cousin?' I demanded.

'I thought it would save explaining.'

'Explaining what?'

He didn't answer.

'Anyway,' I said, stripping my wet trunks off. 'What on earth is Dudley's picture doing in your wallet?'

He turned away and started to rummage amongst his clothes. 'It fell down. I was going to pin it up in the Radio Room. Just didn't get round to it, that's all.'

In which case, he needn't have trimmed the top and bottom to make it fit his wallet.

We dressed in silence. As we made our way out through the canvas flap, he said, 'Did you want it back, your picture?'

'No, why?'

'You don't mind if I keep it then?'

'Do what you like with it. It's no use to me.'

We handed our empty baskets in. 'Look,' he said. 'It's not what you think. I promise you.'

This wasn't a lot of help, because I didn't think anything, really, apart from wondering what all the fuss was about.

Most of the way home we rode like brothers cycling to school; the elder in front, the younger, unacknowledged, a suitable distance behind. The tyres made an interesting humming sound on the hot road-metal.

As soon as we got back, Mike went straight upstairs and locked himself in the bathroom. Toddy had ventured down to the living room, so I sat and talked to him for a bit. But it wasn't a success. Without warning, he sneezed twenty-seven times non-stop and fell back exhausted. He looked so wretched his mother told him to go and lie down again.

'And what about you?' she said to me when he'd gone.

'Me?'

She sat herself down beside me. 'You've got that look on your face. You haven't been back to Barnes again?'

'N-no,' I said. 'Not exactly. But...' And without meaning to, I found myself telling her about Paul. 'I killed him, you see. If I hadn't just stood there... If he hadn't had to come back...'

There was a long silence, during which I reviewed my entire life to date, and still had time left over.

At last, she said, 'Suppose it had been the other way round. Would you have wanted Paul to worry about it all the rest of his life?'

'No. But if I was dead, what I wanted wouldn't have much to do with it.'

She tried a different tack. 'You were only nine,' she said. 'Would you blame Toddy or Mike for something they did when they were nine?'

'No.'

'Why blame yourself, then?'

I knew there must be an answer. She was being – as Mike had said of me – too bloody logical. There were certain things you had to go on and on getting punished for, because you could never be forgiven. Only Paul could forgive me, and Paul was dead. But at least everything finally made sense; Barton, Jacko and the Rev Ev. They were simply what I deserved.

Mike appeared in the doorway, his eyes wide with alarm at the sight of me obviously spilling beans. But he caught my rapid headshake, and visibly relaxed. 'When's tea?' he said.

'When Dad gets in. Are you going to finish that weeding?'

We heard him go out through the back door.

'I'll see if he wants a hand,' I said.

'All right, love. He'll be glad of that.'

I wasn't too sure, though, so I squatted on the grass a little distance away from him. 'Which bit shall I do?'

'This isn't your job,' he said, without looking up.

'I don't mind helping.'

He glanced round cautiously. 'You're not still mad at me, then?'

'Was I ever?'

I couldn't see what he was on about. Then it clicked. He'd half-suspected me of pinching the wallet; after all, I was a Barton boy. And now he was feeling ashamed.

It was late when I got home, and something was obviously afoot. At the very least, Hurly must have distinguished herself again.

'Heard the latest?' Ocky muttered, looking uncomfortable.

'Tom and Eddie. They've only gone and got themselves bloody nicked.'

19

A few days before the end of term, we spent one of the Rev Ev's lessons addressing envelopes for our reports – a waste of time, you might have thought, since we should be taking them home with us anyway. But envelopes were ambassadors, he said, and it was necessary to learn how things were done. There would be a diagram on the board, showing the precise positions and measurements of the preliminary pencil guide-lines; there would be further detailed instructions regarding approved and non-approved forms of wording, use of capitals, etc. We had only to follow them meticulously for success to be guaranteed; consequently, anyone spoiling their envelope would have to pay for another.

As we set to work, he patrolled ceaselessly up and down the rows, pointing out error after error with haughty sarcasm; guidelines ruled too heavily, in the wrong places, crooked, or even – a surer sign of damnation than any other – with the flap of the envelope pointing to the left instead of to the right. Before long, even confident boys like Barry Anderson had turned into nervous wrecks.

From the start, I was reconciled to the inevitable humiliation of producing envelope after envelope, only to see each one held up for public ridicule and ripped contemptuously to pieces. But it was not for nothing that I'd been handling Mr Pond's correspondence for the last six months. Addressing envelopes had long ceased to be the terrifying novelty which most of the others seemed to find it. I was also well accustomed to working from drawings. So for once I found myself sitting with my arms folded and the job done, whilst everyone else around me floundered helplessly.

In due course, the Rev Ev paused in front of me, a suitably acid comment ready on his lips, and held his hand out for my envelope. For fifteen or twenty seconds, he examined it in silent disbelief and then, with a curt nod, replaced it on my desk.

I'll say this for him: he rallied splendidly. Within seconds, his script had been re-written. Glancing at Carpenter's envelope with fastidious scorn, he announced, 'Those of you who have had the advantages of a decent upbringing might well ask yourselves how it is that when it comes to the carrying out of a simple task, a boy from an Institution puts you all to shame.'

If someone had given me a gun and a single bullet, I think I'd have shot the Rev Ev sooner than Jacko. But as he turned towards me again, I caught his eye, and for the first time ever, I managed to hold his gaze. In the end, it was he who looked away. Hardly a famous victory; but a hairline crack had appeared in the solid steel.

Except for people like Toddy, or Barry Anderson, who scooped most of the honours between them and had nothing to worry about, sending a boy home with his school report was like making the messenger deliver his own death warrant. But for once, I was better off than most. So far as Wilkie was concerned, school was merely a place where somebody else, thank goodness, was responsible for me. So the chances were that when I handed over the famous envelope, he would scarcely even bother to look inside.

I wasn't far wrong. For form's sake, he glanced through the report, looked at the back to check that he wasn't missing anything, and then passed it across to me. 'Here,' he said. 'You'd better read what your precious Grammar School thinks of you.'

It was an impressive document, sumptuously printed on thick, watermarked paper, with abundant use of Old English type and a crest ornately embossed in the top left-hand corner. Pre-war, you could have passed through international frontiers on the strength of it.

Most of the teachers had confined themselves to a monosyllable: Poor, Fair, Weak. But the Rev Ev's disparaging comments filled his spaces completely, and even trespassed into the adjacent rectangles. 'He shews neither the aptitude nor the attitude that I look for in a member of this school.' Etc, etc.

'Shews.' The prim archaism could almost have been predicted. Not so the summing up in the section headed Form Master. Fair and square across the page, in a hand of magisterial authority, Hedger had written: 'A good start, considering.' And this was positively the last word on the subject, since the space for the Headmaster's comment was totally blank, apart from a signature done with a rubber stamp.

Pinned to the bottom of the report was a tiny hectographed slip, obviously cut with scissors from a larger sheet. 'Please note: On attaining a height of five feet two inches, it is customary for boys in the Second Form and above to attend school in long trousers.' As if to remove any lingering doubts about my qualifications, my height and weight had been interchanged; according to my report, I was seven and a half feet tall.

Clearly, as Wilkie remarked in a moment of rare humour, there wasn't a minute to lose.

Still three weeks to go till we left for Cornwall. In the meantime, I was counting the days.

Not that I lacked for occupation. Mr Pond had work for me whenever I wanted it. With the business due to close on Michaelmas Quarter Day, all the regular customers hurried to stock up while they had the chance. I was glad of the money; but the magic had all gone. You can't put your heart into something with no future.

There were jobs to be done at Barton House as well, a sort of delayed spring-cleaning; floors to be scrubbed, cupboards to be turned out, windows to be polished on the inside with vinegar and water sprinkled on pads of newspaper. Then there were all our mattresses to be taken down to the yard and propped on their edges for an airing, while the bedsteads were swabbed over with disinfectant. Another day, a detachment of us were marched down to the Church Hall to sweep it out ready for the Parish Supper, to which, of course, we were not invited. Just when we thought we'd finished, the Reverend Hawkhurst arrived with half a dozen sacks full of fresh peas which he wanted shelling, also for the Supper. As a small token of his appreciation, he presented us with a coloured photograph of Princess Elizabeth and her husband to be, taken from the *Illustrated London News*. Jacko decided that someone had better frame it, and gave me the job because I was good with my hands – a doubtful compliment, considering what he generally wanted me to do with them.

Afternoons were spent down at the Rec, or wandering over the countryside with Billy. I didn't mind him tagging along; most of the time, he was quite good company. I used to find it fascinating, simply to watch him move. He was lithe and agile, slipping between the rails of a fence with sinuous, cat-like ease, or moving stealthily through the undergrowth with the sheer animal grace of a panther stalking its prey. It often used to make me wish I could draw. But it was hard to fathom him. He developed the strange habit of sitting beside me with his thumb hooked into my belt or his fingers gripping the neck of my singlet: and yet there was nothing intimate about the physical contact; I'd felt closer to Ronnie when we were a hundred yards apart. Besides, there were lines ruled all around him that you weren't allowed to cross. Once, I asked him about his mother working at Whitmans. 'What's it to you?'

he said, and that was that.

Every so often, as if by prior arrangement, he spent an afternoon with Ocky instead. There would be an exchange of glances and off they would go together, with a warning look in my direction that told me to mind my own business. Not that I needed to ask what they were up to. With Tom and Eddie still on remand, Ocky was working the shops on his own account, and he needed an accomplice. It used to bother me a bit, Billy getting involved. I don't know why, really. I suppose I was still a shopkeeper's son at heart, and somehow it seemed to put us on opposite sides of the fence. I did once make a guarded comment to Ocky, but he stared back at me, granite faced, and said, 'You don't own him. It's up to him what he does.'

One day, all three of us went to watch the narrow boats on the Grand Union, and we hung about at one of the locks for most of the afternoon, hoping that someone would let us help. Or better still, offer to give us a ride. Filling or emptying the lock took about fifteen minutes. In the meantime, there was plenty to talk about.

'What you got, then?'

'Aluminium ingots.'

Aztec treasure...

'Where're you heading?'

'Birmingham.'

Timbuktu... Samarkand...

'D'you travel all night?'

'No.'

'What's your headlights for, then?'

'Tunnels.'

'Is there any tunnels on this bit?'

'No. Further north.'

I wanted to know about journey times, where did the boats tie up for the night, how were the sheets fastened, would there be rats in the holds?

No idle chatter, this. We weren't so very far from the cinema where Ronnie and I had seen *Pinocchio*. The canal! So obvious, now. I pictured him concealed in the bushes beside the towpath, waiting for nightfall; choosing his moment to wriggle under the sheets of a moored butty; lying in the dark on top of the cargo for days on end; and then, at Birmingham, when the sheets came off, dodging frantically between people's outstretched arms, and running like hell. Smoke. Dark streets. Freedom.

That evening, after tea, Wilkie kept us all back for one of his

219

long blasts. Evidently, there'd been complaints again about shop-lifting. He didn't say where from, but it was usually Woolworth's. They were a pushover; all the goods spread out in front of you.

'And be assured,' he told us, 'I mean to get to the bottom of this, once and for all. That isn't a threat. It's a promise.'

We all sat very still and stared hard at the tables, in case our eyes should swivel magnetically in certain particular directions.

Ocky was good at appearing unconcerned. 'Soon blow over,' he said, and left it at that. But at bed time, I noticed him deep in conversation with Billy, and at one point they both glanced at me warily over their shoulders. All done in a second, but that was as long as it took me to realise a simple fact that should have been obvious from the start, considering Billy's grudge. There were other shops besides Woolworth's where the goods were all displayed within easy reach. Stationers' shops, for example.

It was a complication I hadn't bargained for. I hoped Ocky was right about things blowing over. But in case he wasn't, the less I found out, the better; and please God when the awkward questions started I should be out of reach, three hundred miles away.

We were planning to set off really early for Cornwall, so I spent the previous night at the Whitmans', on one of the kapok mattresses we were going to use in the tent. It had been spread out on the floor between Mike and Toddy's beds, with a folded sheet and blanket arranged on top of it like a rudimentary sleeping bag.

Mike tested it doubtfully. 'It doesn't look very comfortable.'

'Don't worry,' I said, 'it'll suit me fine.'

My first night ever away from Barton. I'd have slept on the bare floor if they'd asked me to.

Toddy watched in amazement as I stripped my clothes off and slid between the two halves of the sheet. 'Don't you wear pyjamas?' he said.

We were up at six, and away by eight, with a huge pile of cases roped to the luggage rack, and the rolled-up kapok mattresses strapped to the roof. The idea was to travel as far as Exeter, and stay the night with an old army friend of Mr Whitman's. Nearly two hundred miles, all in a day: an astounding prospect, when you'd never been out of London in your life.

The journey itself surpassed my wildest expectations, with a fresh surprise waiting round every corner. Things known only from pictures were suddenly there in front of us; a half-timbered house, men harvesting, cows. And it was really true that the colour of the soil kept changing as you went from county to county. Teachers were always telling you things like that, but until you saw for yourself, you simply couldn't imagine what they meant.

More important, each additional mile was taking me further and further beyond the reach of Jacko and the Wilkies; far enough, in the end, to escape completely from their gravitational pull. At first, the relief was so overwhelming that I scarcely noticed the subtler implications. But when we stopped in Salisbury for a dinner break, it struck me all of a sudden that during the morning my status had quietly altered. At home, whatever the Whitmans did to make me welcome, I was only a visitor, a Barton boy on a half-day release. There was always a line, with me on one side and them on the other. But from now on, we should all be visitors, and we all belonged together on the same side of the line.

After dinner, the heat became almost unbearable, and travel began to lose some of its glamour. Our arms and thighs kept sticking sweatily to the seat leather, and with three of us crammed in the back, tempers shortened. It was hard to decide if our regular drink and pee breaks were a welcome respite, or merely prolonged the agony. By late afternoon, when we finally reached Exeter, the journey was coming to seem more like an endurance test.

The Palmers lived a little way out of town. Quite a big house; solid, and old, with creeper growing on the walls. As we scrunched to a halt on the gravel drive, a boy with nothing on but a pair of swimming trunks came round the corner of the house, riding a bike.

'Wotcher,' he said, leaning in through the car window. He looked younger than Mike, but older than me and Toddy.

Mrs Whitman greeted him with a smile of recognition. 'You must be Raymond.'

'Yeah. The others are round the back. I'll tell 'em you're here.' His voice had a lovely warm West Country burr to it.

In fact, his parents must have heard us arriving, because they appeared at the front of the house as we were all getting out. They looked a bit posher than us, but not in a way to make you feel uncomfortable. There was a girl, too, much the same age as Raymond.

Introductions all round. The twins, Raymond and Rowena. Our turn. I felt suddenly apprehensive, and realised I was wondering what the Whitmans were going to say about me. Nothing, as it turned out. Mr Whitman simply pointed to each of us in turn. 'Mike. Alan. Toddy.' Presumably, it had all been explained in advance; besides, it wouldn't be hard to spot the odd one out.

Or so you might have thought. But when we were taking our overnight luggage into the house, I heard Rowena hissing to Raymond, 'No! I'm telling you! It's the one with the very short hair.'

'It can't be,' he insisted. 'I heard him calling her "Mum".'

Gosh. Had I? Again?

Afterwards, the five of us sat about on the grass, cautiously sizing each other up. 'What do you want to do?' Rowena said.

A pointless question, when you don't know what's on offer. Toddy shrugged vaguely, and Mike looked as if he felt rather out of things. It wasn't for me to answer; but ever since Raymond first appeared in his swimming trunks, I'd thought longingly of the Uxbridge Baths, and when nobody else spoke, I reckoned I might as well.

'I know what I'd like,' I said, dreamily, stretching out on the lawn. 'I'd like to dive into a huge swimming pool, just to cool off.'

'Yeah, well, we could have, if you'd got here earlier,' Raymond said. 'But there wouldn't be time, now.'

'It was just an idea. I wasn't serious.'

Mike caught Raymond's eye. 'Oh yes he was!'

'It's all he ever thinks about,' Toddy said in disgust.

'I just like water. What's wrong with that, especially on a day like this?'

Raymond was sitting next to me. 'C'mon, then,' he said, and stood up.

'Where are you going?' Rowena called after us, but he didn't answer.

I followed him into the house, and he took me upstairs to the bathroom, which was all done out in black and white tiles, the latest thing in about 1930; you felt as if you were standing inside a three-dimensional crossword puzzle. Mounted centrally over the bath was a shower head as big as a dinner plate, with a pipe running up to it from a mixer tap on the wall. A bulky rubberised curtain hung from the ceiling, bunched together at one end of its track.

'Not quite what you had in mind,' Raymond admitted. 'But if you really want to cool off...'

My singlet, plimsolls, shorts, and underpants hit the floor in five seconds flat. I stepped into the bath, a huge affair with room for at least three people in it, and Raymond started to draw the curtain round.

I experimented with the control lever, but nothing happened. 'How do you get it to work?'

'Oh, is it stuck again? Just a minute.'

He slipped his trunks off, and stepped in after me, closing the curtain all the way round us.

'Like your hair,' he said, with a quick nod of approval. 'Just right for swimming.'

His middle, where the trunks had been, was so pale compared with the rest of him that you couldn't help noticing. I ran my finger along the line where the colour changed, and he laughed. 'I know,' he said, 'I'm striped.'

He rattled the big handle back and forth a number of times. Suddenly, without warning, a deluge of icy water dropped from the shower head with incredible force. I gasped in surprise, and leapt back out of the way. But after the first shock, it was rather fun. Taking a deep breath, I went back under again, and stood quite still for about thirty seconds, letting the water pummel my head and shoulders and course down all over my body. It was like standing out in a hailstorm.

'It's super,' I said, stepping back a little to let him join me. The shower head was so enormous that two people could share it easily.

After a minute or two, he motioned me to one side and lay on his front with his bottom directly under the downpour. For twenty or thirty seconds he remained there, with his arms and legs stretched out ecstatically. 'Try it,' he said.

It was an amazing sensation.

I was about to stand up again when he stopped me. 'No, stay there, and turn over.' So I did, and that was more amazing still. As I lay there letting the sharp little needles of water tickle my cock and thighs, he stood at the end of the bath looking down at me with a broad grin. 'Good, isn't it?'

When we got tired of that, we knelt down facing each other, and horsed around for ten minutes or so, sliding to and fro under the downpour in various different positions. You'd have thought we'd known each other half our lives.

Eventually, when we were both starting to shiver, he pushed the lever back, and the deluge stopped instantly, leaving an eerie silence. The water still in the shower head started to gather into a blob that hung poised above us, waiting to drop. Ray got a hard on, and tried to position himself so that the falling water would bomb the end of his cock. We stood there, gazing upwards with rapt attention as the blob gradually swelled and distended itself further and further downwards.

'We're going to be here all night,' I said.

But still it refused to fall. After about a minute, I caught his eye and we both burst out laughing. With a wry grin, he reached upwards on tiptoe to dislodge the hanging droplet; it broke immediately, and ran all down his arm.

While we were drying ourselves, he said, 'You know, I don't get it. Which of you three are brothers?'

'Mike and Toddy.'

'And you're their cousin?'

'Well... yes,' I said, slightly at a loss. Since when had the cousin business become official?

He frowned. 'But I thought... Oh well, it doesn't matter.'

I was glad he'd dropped the subject. People always tried to define you in terms of your family. What does your father do? How many brothers and sisters have you got? As if you couldn't exist in your own right, and there weren't any other ways of belonging. Not that I minded, exactly. It was nice to be part of a family again, even a substitute one. But questions were tricky. It was always difficult with a new person, knowing how much to admit.

We got dressed in his bedroom; he had it all to himself, of course. There were Dinky toys arranged on the windowsill, and some rather classy model planes hanging on thin wires from the ceiling.

'Did you make these?'

He nodded, and showed me one that was half-built, so I could study the way it was done. I told him about the workshop, and Mr Pond. We were just discussing the exact differences between helicopters and autogiros, when there was a shout from below for us to go down and eat. He said he had a book that explained it all, and we could look at it after tea.

But while we were downstairs, it came out that he had an electric model railway up in the attic. He warned me that it wasn't working, but I said I would really, really like to see it. So after the meal, we all went up for a look.

There was a special ladder that pulled down from the ceiling. As you emerged through the trap door, the layout was all around you, arranged on trestles. It was very elaborate, with scenery and tunnels and everything. The coal trucks even had little pieces of blackened cork in them that looked amazingly realistic. But the current had gone dead, so the trains wouldn't run.

The others soon drifted away, but Ray and I stayed on in the attic. It seemed a dreadful pity the railway wasn't working. I asked what the trouble was, and he said he thought there was something the matter with the controller. He was right, too. It was one of those little transformers with a lever on top and a row of studs in a semicircle. You could tell from the feel of it that something was loose inside.

'Got a screwdriver?'

It took us about three-quarters of an hour, plus a visit downstairs to the garage where there was a vice. Then we reassembled the controller, and climbed up the ladder again to try it. By around eight o'clock, the Great Western Railway was back in business.

'Hey, Dad!' Ray called out the news from the top of the ladder. Two or three minutes later, Toddy and Mr Palmer appeared through the trap door, so we gave them a demonstration.

'Clever chap,' Mr Palmer said, and tickled the back of my neck with his finger.

I thought Toddy would probably stay for a bit, now there was something to see, but he didn't seem interested, and the two of them left together.

After they'd gone, Ray brought the 8.25 to a stylish halt at the station platform, and without looking up, he said, 'Alan?'

'Mm?' I was busy marshalling a goods train.

'Have you got a girl friend?'

'No. Why?'

'Just wondered. I bet your brother has.'

'Uh?'

'Cousin, I mean.'

'What, Toddy!' I found it hard to imagine.

'No. The nice one. Rowena's potty about him.'

'Really? How do you know?'

'She said. Anyway, you can tell by the way she looks at him.'

'Oh. Can you?.'

'Of course.' A moment later, he added, 'I think they've gone for a walk.'

About ten o'clock, Mike came up the ladder, and stood with only his head and shoulders showing. 'Alan. Mum says Bed. Early start again tomorrow.'

In the lounge, the Palmers were pushing furniture back to make room for our kapok mattresses.

'Oh dear,' Mrs Palmer was saying. 'I'm afraid it's going to be rather a squash for them.

Ray and I glanced at each other, and without more ado it was settled that I should take my bedding up to his room.

'Well, those two have certainly latched onto each other,' I heard Mr Whitman commenting, as we went upstairs again.

I thought I should get to sleep without any trouble, but it was hot, and I was over-tired from the day's excitements.

After about ten minutes, Ray sat up in bed, his bare shoulders silhouetted against the window. 'I hate hot nights,' he said. 'You can't get to sleep.'

He climbed out of bed, dropped his pyjama bottoms to the floor and kicked them into a corner. Then he lay stretched out on top of the bedclothes completely naked.

'D'you want to try something?' he said. 'It's really good, I promise you.'

'What sort of thing?'

'Bit like the shower, only better. You do it with hairbrushes.'

'I'm pretty tired, really.'

'Go on. You'll like it. I guarantee.'

'Not just now.'

'Suit yourself. You don't know what you're missing, though.'

Actually, what I'd really have liked was to wrestle with him, the same as I'd done with Dave; only right there on his bed, just as he was. He was like Dave, in a way, but without the drawbacks.

He yawned, and settled himself more comfortably. 'Hey, we never looked up about autogiros. Shall we do it now?'

It seemed a pity to waste time sleeping when there were so many things to talk about. But I'd travelled a long way since morning.

'Let's leave it,' I said. 'It'll keep.'

'Ray's going to miss you,' Mrs Whitman said to me, as we drove away.

'Yeah, me too. I thought he was really nice, didn't you?'

'We didn't get much of a chance to find out,' Toddy remarked sourly.

Mr Whitman glanced over his shoulder. 'I reckon Rowena's going to be missing somebody, too. Eh?'

'I wouldn't know,' Mike said after an icy pause, and gazed rather pointedly out of the window. 'She's not my type.'

'Didn't you think she was pretty?' Toddy asked him.

'Did you?'

Toddy shrugged. 'I suppose so. I didn't notice, really.'

Mr Whitman gave a knowing laugh. 'You will, boy. You will.'

20

Cornwall was a land of exotic vegetation, and peculiar saints that no one had ever heard of: St Pinnock; St Veep; St Ingunger. There were palm trees growing out of the pavements, and from time to time, in the far distance, we caught sight of the sea.

Beyond Falmouth, as we left the main road for the last few miles to Penskerrick, we drove along steep, narrow lanes with tall hedges on either side, or dark, silent woodland where the tree trunks were buried up to their knees in rhododendrons.

Soon after two o'clock, we came round a narrow bend and saw a rough, unmade track that ran downhill to our left through a dense tangle of foliage. Mr Whitman stopped the car and reversed for a closer look.

'This *can't* be it!'

We studied the map the Luckhursts had sent us. It showed the bend and the track, but there ought to have been a signpost. On the other hand, we hadn't passed anything else the least bit likely, and despite the air of dark, brooding neglect, there were fresh wheelmarks in the beaten earth.

In the end, we decided to risk it, and set off cautiously down the uneven track as if we were venturing into the Amazon jungle. Far above our heads, huge fronds hung over us like monstrous relics from a primeval forest. Every few yards there were clumps of bleached and dessicated cow parsley, seven or eight feet tall, and what appeared to be giant rhubarb, with leaves like elephants' ears, and stalks you couldn't have closed your fist round.

After a good half mile, the track suddenly twisted to the right through gateposts tilting drunkenly apart, and opened out into a gravelled yard that was overgrown with weeds. Along one side stood a row of brick-built stables, with their wooden half-doors cracked and peeling. On the other was the rear portion of the house, stone-built, and semi-derelict, but obviously in the process of refurbishment. Sand and bricks and fresh timber were stacked by the open doorway, and a stout plank for wheelbarrows led up and over the sill.

There was no one about, so Mr Whitman sounded the horn.

We all got out of the car, and waited to see what would happen.

By and by, a woman appeared round the far corner of the house, with her head done up in a brightly coloured scarf. At every step, as she strode confidently towards us, her bulging thighs seemed likely to rupture her shorts which were green and perilously tight, and her huge tits bounced hypnotically up and down beneath her jersey.

'Not wearing a bra,' Mike muttered, out of the corner of his mouth. And from closer to, you could see in fascinating detail how the taut material was moulding itself to her form.

With terrifying enthusiasm she kissed Mrs Whitman firmly on both cheeks. 'How wonderful! You've made it! And in such good time!'

Her legs and arms were bronzed to an almost impossible shade, and her voice was deep and resonant, like a man's.

'And these are the boys!'

Instinctively, we all took a pace backwards.

'Shall we start unloading?' Mike said.

She pointed to the far end of the yard, where the drive curved round the house and out of sight. 'You'll need to be at the front, my love, next to the caravan.'

Apparently, we'd arrived by the back entrance. A bit further along the road, we'd have come to the proper one, which wouldn't have taken ten years off the car springs.

As we reconvened in the forecourt, Mr Luckhurst appeared at the door of the caravan, which was parked in a shady corner under a tall tree. He was wearing cavalry twill trousers and a checked shirt with a Paisley silk cravat.

Leaving the two women to discuss old times and domestic arrangements, he took the rest of us on a tour of the grounds. We followed him down some steps and along a broken pathway through what had once been an ornamental garden. Its upkeep must have been a full-time job for at least two people, but now, like everything else, it was overgrown and neglected. At the far end, a hundred yards or so from the house, we went through a squeaking wrought-iron gate, and out onto a patch of grassland surrounded by trees. At one side of this stood a small brown tent.

'You can always move it,' Mr Luckhurst said. 'But that's where the nephews generally pitch it. They like to have it a fair way from the house.'

At the far side of the clearing, a narrow pathway led steeply downwards through the trees. After thirty or forty yards, it opened out into another clearing, which ran right down to the edge of the river. Jutting out from the bank was a small stone quay with the top turfed over, and a rickety wooden landing stage projecting a few yards further out. Two small rowing boats were moored to iron rings set in the stonework.

The only thing lacking seemed to be water.

The boats lay high and dry on a vast bank of smooth oily mud, which stank of rotting seaweed and looked like the sludge from all the drains in the world. Beyond it, the water ran in a narrow channel, completely inaccessible from where we were standing. On the far side was another mudbank running right up to the trees on the opposite slope.

'But how do you get the boats into the river?' Toddy said in dismay.

Mr Luckhurst looked at his watch. 'It's only about an hour to low water. When the tide's in, it comes right up to the quay.'

'What about all the other times?'

'This is only a branch creek. If you miss the tide, you wait till it comes back. The main creek's down there.' He pointed away to the left. 'The other side of that headland, there's a little shingle beach. You can get to it quite easily. It's not private, but there's always water there. So long as you leave the boats on their trip anchors, you'll be able to go out whenever you like.'

'What's a trip anchor?'

Mr Luckhurst laughed. 'Ask Dad. He'll explain.'

'Will he?' said Mr Whitman with a doubtful smile.

We made our way back through the trees, feeling rather deflated. At the upper clearing, the three of us stopped behind to examine the tent.

'If you ask me,' Toddy said, 'this place is a real chiz.'

'It'll be all right, though,' said Mike. 'There's the beach. And the tent's going to be super.'

I nodded enthusiastically. 'Yeah. Down here on our own, we can do whatever we want.'

But Toddy seemed unconvinced, and I suddenly realised rather guiltily that when I'd said it, I'd been thinking of me and Ray.

At about half past five, we saw the Luckhursts off. For a while, it looked as if they would never leave. They kept remembering things they ought to have told us: which pubs to go to; the way to the little beach; what to do about the builders; what not to do about the Elsan in the far-end stable; and how to cope with Mrs Farthing, who had a screw loose, but would sell us eggs.

From things we'd brought, and what the Luckhursts had left for us, Mrs Whitman made us an evening meal, which we ate outside with our plates balanced on upturned buckets or piles of bricks, a bit like after an air raid.

Then the three of us set off to explore the proper approach road, which was certainly less rutted and overgrown than the other. After about a quarter of a mile, it curved round to the right and ran uphill towards what appeared to be the Falmouth road. We decided to follow this round and return to Penskerrick by the back entrance. At a guess, the two turnings couldn't be more than half a mile apart.

But after at least a mile, there was still no sign of the other drive, and the road was obviously taking us further and further from the house. At last, we came to a crossroads. Mike thought we should take the turning to the right, but Toddy was all for going back.

'Come on,' I said. 'It can't be far, now.'

'That's what you said before.'

'Well I'm going on,' Mike announced. 'You two can suit yourselves.'

'I'm going back,' said Toddy.

Mike shrugged, and set off along the road to the right. 'See you later,' he called over his shoulder.

Toddy started to go back down the hill again. After about a hundred yards, he glanced round and shouted, 'Well? Are you coming?'

'I'm sure this is the best way,' I shouted, pointing to the road Mike had taken.

For at least a minute, neither of us looked like budging.

'Come on, Toddy,' I said at last. 'Don't be a twerp.'

'Why do you always have to side with Mike?' he said, as he stumped his way uphill towards the crossroads.

'I'm not siding with anybody. It's common sense, that's all.'

Fortunately, in less than half a mile, we came to the jungle turning.

Back at the house, practically opposite the gate, I noticed a narrow footpath leading away to our left.

'That's how you get to the beach,' Mike said. 'Shall we take a look?'

'What's the point?' Toddy snapped. 'It'll still be there in the morning.'

To cheer him up, we played French cricket in the clearing beside the tent, but the ball kept disappearing amongst the trees. After about half an hour, we lost it down the slope that led to the creek, and spent a good ten minutes searching. Just as Mike finally spotted it, we heard Toddy calling us from below.

'Hey, come and look.'

We ran down the path and out onto the little grass-topped quay to find the whole scene miraculously transformed. The two dinghies, afloat on the incoming tide, were tugging gently at their mooring ropes, and in place of the mudbanks there was water lapping almost up to our feet and stretching across the creek from side to side, all bright and golden in the evening sunlight.

Mike caught my eye, and together we raced back to the tent for our trunks and towels.

He was into the water a few seconds ahead of me. As I ran out onto the landing stage, he surfaced, spitting vigorously. 'It's salt!' he called.

I dived in after him, and we gradually made our way out to the middle, splashing each other, dodging this way and that, and duck-diving to find out what we could see beneath the surface, which wasn't much because our antics had stirred the mud up.

After a couple of minutes, we looked back towards the quay. Toddy was still sitting there, fully dressed, with his arms clasped tightly round his knees.

'Aren't you coming in?' Mike shouted.

He shook his head.

'Why not?' I called out. 'It's super.'

We swam back to the quay to try and persuade him, but it was no good.

'By the time I've fetched my things, you'll be getting out.'

'Come in without any, then,' Mike said. 'No one's to see.'

'I said No. Don't you understand plain English?'

So we left him there and swam out into the creek again. Next time we looked, he'd gone, and we caught a distant glimpse of him, walking slowly away uphill amongst the trees.

In the morning, Mike settled down to study the tide tables, while Toddy and I explored the way to the beach. The pathway took us uphill, then down again and across a couple of fields, till we came quite suddenly to the edge of a steep drop. Below us was a shingle beach, curving round from the headland on our right to a line of rocks that jutted out on our left. A little distance away, in the deeper water, three or four dozen boats were moored; cabin cruisers, some quite big yachts, and a number of sailing dinghies with canvas covers on.

We scrambled down quite easily, and ran across the shingle looking for flat stones to skim on the water. I thought the rocks would be good to dive from, but I didn't mention it. The previous night, after our swim, Toddy had barely spoken to us. It was worse still in the tent. Mike and I lay side by side, with Toddy across the end because he was the shortest and that was the best way of fitting us all in. It seemed perfectly sociable; but the moment he lay down, he turned his back on us and refused to say a word. By morning, we seemed to have been forgiven, but even so, I thought the subject of swimming was best avoided.

'Look,' he said, pointing to the headland. 'That's where our creek comes out. Dad says we'll be rowing the boats round later.'

'Is it difficult – rowing?'

'I shouldn't think so. D'you want to go back, and try?'

One of the boats was a proper dinghy, but the smaller one was a pram, with blunt, swept-up bows and no keel. According to Mr Luckhurst, this meant it would float in less than a foot of water and was easy to beach and re-launch. It also meant, though he hadn't pointed this out, that you might as well have been rowing a saucer. Mike had been practising while we were down at the beach, and seemed to be getting the hang of it pretty well; but when it was our turn, Toddy and I took an oar each, a bad mistake, and we set off across the creek with the boat going round and round like a chairoplane at a funfair. The others, watching us from the quay, were reduced to helpless laughter.

We got on rather better with only one of us rowing at a time, but Toddy soon gave up in disgust. 'Stupid thing. What's the point of a boat if it won't go where you want?'

'Try the proper dinghy,' Mike suggested.

It certainly went straighter, because of the keel. But it was too heavy to row for very long. The pram was a lot handier, once you'd learned the knack of keeping an equal pull on both oars.

To take all five of us round to the beach, with our packed dinner, our swimming things, and various other bits of baggage, we should clearly need both boats. After a certain amount of argument, Mr and Mrs Whitman went in the big dinghy with Toddy and the luggage, leaving me and Mike to follow in the pram. He said he thought he could manage it if somebody else came with him in case he needed a rest.

'Toddy's lighter,' said Mrs Whitman.

'Alan can row better,' said Mike.

So the matter was settled.

Once we were clear of the little Penskerrick creek, I thought we'd be able to see the beach. But the intervening headland was deceptive; there kept on being more and more of it. By the time our destination came in sight, Mike was looking distinctly fed up. He shipped the oars and examined the palms of his hands.

'Blisters,' he said.

'D'you want me to row for a bit?'

'No. I'll manage.'

'Dip your hands in the water. Gives you a better grip.'

I don't know where that came from. Something overheard on the Barnes slipway, perhaps; in another life.

'Mm,' Mike said in surprise, a couple of minutes later. 'It works.'

Safely ashore again after our first voyage, I watched intently as Mr Whitman balanced the anchor across the bows of the big dinghy and pushed the boat out backwards into the deeper water. The tripping system was delightfully simple. The anchor had two ropes: the dinghy's own mooring rope was hitched to the ring at the top, but round the flukes was a longer, thinner rope which he kept in his hand and paid out carefully as the boat moved away from us. When it finally stopped, a quick tug on the trip line toppled the anchor into the water, and it lay far enough out for the dinghy to stay afloat, even at low tide.

'There,' he said, unwinding the rest of the coil to a spot above high water mark, 'Barney Luckhurst would be proud of us.'

By the time the pram had been anchored likewise, we felt we were almost on nodding terms with Columbus. At the very least, we reckoned we'd earned our picnic.

Towards the end of the meal, Mrs Whitman said she was thinking of going to Falmouth the next day for a few things, and should she pop in quickly on her own, or should we all go, and make a day of it?

Opinions were divided. Mike and Mr Whitman were all for spending the day there, but Toddy said he wanted to stay at Penskerrick.

'And what about you, Alan?' Mrs Whitman said, handing me a slice of cake.

'I'd quite like to see Falmouth; but I don't really mind.'

'Well, it's not your decision anyway,' said Toddy scornfully.

'It's our holiday, and it's up to you to do whatever we say. You're only here because we invited you.'

There was an uncomfortable silence.

'Toddy!' Mrs Whitman said at last. 'That wasn't very nice.'

'Well, it's true. I thought you were supposed to tell the truth.'

Mr Whitman intervened. 'You speak like that again to your mother, and you'll feel my belt across your backside. Now, apologise to Alan.'

Toddy stared back at him defiantly.

'We're all waiting, Toddy.'

I stared down at the ground between my knees, and started counting the pebbles, the cake still untasted in my hand.

'Sorry,' Toddy muttered sourly, after a further pause.

'I should bloody well think so,' said Mr Whitman. 'And you can go without the rest of your dinner.'

'Didn't want it anyway,' Toddy said, and walked off haughtily along the beach.

Mr Whitman put his cup down. 'Take no notice, Alan.'

When the picnic things had been put away, Mike reached for the bag with our trunks and towels in. 'Come on,' he said.

It was a good beach for swimming. Before long, Mr Whitman joined us, but he soon struck out for the open water, zooming powerfully round the cove like a speedboat, while Mike and I stayed nearer the shore, using the dinghy as a diving platform. With no mud around, the water was fascinatingly clear, and the sun shining down through the little waves on the surface sent a vivid pattern of bright, rippling lines dancing about beneath us. We stayed well clear of the rocks because Toddy was sitting there, right at the end, as far out as he could get; he was apparently engrossed in something, though it was hard to imagine what. At one point, I noticed Mrs Whitman making her way rather precariously towards him, but after staying a couple of minutes, she went back to the beach again without him, and got on with her knitting. He was clearly there for the duration.

We explored the rock pools on the headland side, played golf with limpet shells and pieces of driftwood, swam some more, got dressed, ate our tea, checked the trip lines, and packed up ready to walk home; and still Toddy was sitting there all by himself, far out on the rocks.

'Come on, Toddy, we're going now,' Mr Whitman called. But he took no notice.

'This is ridiculous,' said Mike.

Grimly, Mr Whitman started to pick up the luggage. 'He can find his own way home.'

As we set off up the steep path from the beach, I caught Mike's eye, and together we glanced back. I whistled; but it was still no good.

He shrugged. All the same, I sensed that something more was expected of me. I held out the bag I was carrying, and he reached forward to take it. 'You go on,' I told him.

I made my way over the rocks without the least idea of what I could do or say. Toddy was sitting there all hunched up, with his chin on his knees, staring out across the open water.

'Wotcher,' I said.

He nodded without looking up, so I sat down beside him and gazed out across the water as well. After about five minutes of total silence, I said, 'Shall we go now?'

He stood up slowly, stretching his arms and legs. 'Yeah,' he said. 'Might as well.'

The rowing had given us all stiff shoulders by the morning, so the trip to Falmouth proved to be no bad thing.

Down in the little harbour where the St Mawes ferry was taking on passengers, some kids were diving in off a big flight of stone steps that led down from the pier.

Toddy said to Mike, 'We'd better hang on to Alan, or he'll be down there joining them.' So they locked arms across my shoulders, and Mr Whitman took a snap of us, all in line, with me in the middle. A man who was passing smiled and said to him, 'Three fine boys you've got.'

Everyone bought postcards, so I chose some too, and sent one to Ocky and one to Ray.

Next to the postcard place was a model shop. I thought it might be nice to build some miniatures of our two boats. I didn't know how I was going to set about it, but with holiday optimism, I bought some sheets of balsa wood, a knife, and a tube of cement. Further along, down a side alley, we came to a ship's chandler, where the air was thick with the pungent smells of new rope and nautical ironmongery. Mike discovered a proper marine chart by Imray, Laurie, Norrie and Wilson, which showed our own river in full detail, with all the rocks and mudbanks and even the little Penskerrick creek; so Mr Whitman bought it. I decided to buy something too, just as a momento, and chose a hank of whipcord; it would do to make ropes and fenders for the models, but the best thing was that it seemed to have soaked up all the different smells of the place, and one good sniff would bring it all back to me whenever I wanted.

On our way home, Toddy suddenly said, 'You know, I was thinking, our boats ought to have names.'

So we christened the pram *Nipper*, because it went round and round like the dog on the gramophone records. Mrs Whitman suggested calling the proper dinghy *Rowena*, which I thought was brilliant; but it proved to be unacceptable in certain quarters, and was dropped in favour of *Patsy*, the name of a cat the Whitmans had owned pre-war.

The following day, when we carried our things down to the beach again, I was relieved to find the boats were still there. I thought they might have been pinched during the night.

'This is Cornwall,' Mr Whitman said, 'not London.'

But for various reasons, we thought it might be a good idea if we kept *Nipper* at the landing stage in future, even though there wouldn't always be water enough to float her. To avoid having to row against the tide, it was agreed that Mike and I should take her back immediately after dinner, while Toddy and Mr Whitman went out in *Patsy*. Mike and I would walk back from Penskerrick and we should all meet up again on the beach in time for tea. Mrs Whitman wasn't too keen on boating, and said she would stay put to mind the baggage.

It was surprising how much easier the journey seemed, compared with the first time. We rowed about half the distance each, and found ourselves at the landing stage a lot sooner than we'd expected. There was no reason to hurry back to the beach, so we took our shirts off and stretched out in the sunshine on the little quay. It was nice, just the two of us on our own.

After a while, Mike said, 'Something on your mind?'

It was hard to know where to begin. Too many feelings I couldn't even give names to. 'Will you tell us something, true?' I said at last.

He stiffened slightly. There was a long pause. Then he nodded.

'D'you think I've been getting my feet a bit too far under the table?'

Whatever he'd been expecting, that wasn't it. 'No,' he said, relaxing again, 'I don't. I think it's where they belong. And if this is about that business the other day, for God's sake just ignore it, like the rest of us.'

'That's easy for you to say. But if I fall out with Toddy, what happens then?'

'We all sit tight till it blows over, like any other family row.'

'But I'm not family, am I, that's the point.'

'Yes you are. As good as.'

There was a grass stalk right in front of me, so I picked it, and started twisting it round my finger. 'Three can be an awkward number,' I said. 'I thought perhaps...'

'Toddy's the awkward number. Always has been. Mum says he's highly strung: most people call it being a pain in the arse.' He hesitated. 'The truth is, he envies you.'

'Don't be daft! Who wins the prizes? Who gets picked for all the teams?'

It was a while before he answered. 'This is between ourselves, all right?' When I nodded, he went on, choosing his words with care. 'Toddy's actually older than you, but no one would ever guess.'

'Because I'm taller?'

'Well, that – and other things. But it's more to do with the way you think, the sort of person you are. You make him realise there's more to life than scoring runs or coming top in Latin. And that scares him, because those are the only things he knows. Whereas you do real things in the real world; you work with lathes, you make things, you mend things. Toddy's never had to work for his money, or fend for himself, or do anything useful.'

'He's lucky then. Most people have to.'

'I don't think lucky is how he sees it.'

I was utterly bewildered. 'Well,' I said, 'if ever he feels like changing places, you can tell him from me, he's on.'

Meals at Penskerrick were a revelation. Cornwall was too remote from London to be troubled much by the Ministry of Food. There were tales of government officials with false moustaches trying to gull the locals into selling them eggs, but you could spot them a mile off, and nobody ever fell for it. The Luckhursts had made sure that everyone knew who we were, and supplies of various kinds would simply appear without even having to be asked for. One day, we got back to the caravan to find two rabbits hanging by their feet from the door handle, dead of course, but otherwise all present and correct. Converting them into stew involved some disturbing processes for which my morning at Shipstone's had not prepared me.

Fruit and vegetables were almost unlimited, and Mrs Farthing appeared every second day. She was quite barmy, just as the Luckhursts had warned us; she dressed mainly in pieces of sacking, and never failed to ask me if all my teeth were my own. But from under the straw in her wicker basket came more eggs than I had ever seen in my life. One evening, when Mrs Whitman made scrambled eggs for us, I nearly passed clean out from the shock of seeing a whole dozen broken into a basin one after another.

Most days, we called in at the village shop, four or five miles away. It was also the Post Office, though the brass grille that was meant to separate His Majesty's business from Mr and Mrs Honeycott's was almost obscured behind packets of soap flakes, crockery, kitchen utensils, nails, clothes-pegs, buttons and boot-laces, and a couple of uncut Cheddar cheeses. On one shelf was a row of books; on others were stacks of tins – soup, baked beans, macedoine of vegetables – with alien brand names and unfamiliar labels. Crates full of apples, celery, tomatoes, occupied much of the floor; and leaning against the dark mahogany counter were two or three hundredweight of dried beans and peas, in hessian sacks with little shovels in them and the tops rolled down like socks. Other items hung from the ceiling; sides of bacon, kippers, kettles, galvanised buckets, coal scuttles, netting, broom handles, and hanks of clothes line. I could think of a lot worse ways of spending a morning than simply to stand there amidst this chaotic profusion, and listen to Mr Honeycott, whose voice was so warm and friendly and reassuring, you could have wrapped it round you like a blanket.

The morning after we brought *Nipper* back to Penskerrick, a chance remark while we were waiting to be served prompted the Honeycotts to mention that someone they knew had a motor boat for hire. Having studied the chart, Mike was keen to explore the whole river, so Mr Whitman took down the particulars, and that afternoon they set out together to pay a call on the owner.

While they were gone, Toddy and I looked in on the builders. One of them was a caustic little man, who wanted us out of his way; but the other, whose name was Eric, an easy-going, friendly man of about forty, seemed glad of someone to talk to, and didn't mind answering questions. We found him upstairs, ankle deep in shavings and sawdust, fitting a timber architrave into a newly cut-out doorway. After my laborious attempts at picture-framing, I was much impressed by his ability to cut perfect mitres entirely by eye.

He picked up a length of moulding and threw it down again contemptuously. 'Look at that,' he said. 'All warped.' He pronounced it wawrrped. 'Fancy sending unseasoned timber. I'll bet it had roots and leaves on it a couple of months ago.'

'I thought seasoning was to do with salt and pepper,' Toddy said.

Eric laughed. 'You're no carpenter, then, not like your brother?'

Toddy bridled visibly. 'Him? He's not my brother.'

Some of the floorboards had been taken up, because the house was being re-wired. According to Eric, there had been no electricity anywhere near Penskerrick before the war, and sooner than use oil lamps, the people who lived there had generated their own. I could scarcely believe this. It seemed roughly equivalent to mining your own coal.

Eric gestured vaguely towards the back of the house with his hammer. 'You go and look out yonder,' he said. 'Behind the stables. All still there, see? Dynamo; little diesel engine; storage batteries.'

'Come on,' I said, turning excitedly to Toddy.

But he wasn't there.

I got no answer when I called, and there was no sign of him outside, so I went to look for the generator house on my own. It stood well back behind a clump of trees; a proper brick building with a tiled roof, though not much bigger than a toolshed. Unfortunately, the door was locked and the window was all grimed over, but I could make out the vague shape of the engine, and something else beyond it which I took to be the dynamo.

There was nothing more to be done there, so I went back to the caravan. Mrs Whitman was sitting outside in a canvas chair, reading a paper.

'Where's Toddy?' I said.

'I don't know. I thought he was with you.'

'I'll do some more of my model, then.'

I spread the things out on the caravan table. I had made a start already, but I couldn't see how to shape the planks correctly. Before long, I realised I needed to study a real boat to see how it was done. *Patsy* was at the beach, but *Nipper* was only down at the landing stage, so I went to have a look.

She wasn't there.

I knelt down on the quay, half expecting to find a frayed end of rope still attached to the metal ring. Nothing. Either someone had taken her, or Mike and I hadn't moored her properly the day before, and she had drifted away.

'Oh, Christ!' I thought, and wondered how I should break the news to the Whitmans.

I was about to go back to the house, when I thought I heard someone calling. I stopped to listen, and it came again. 'Al-lern!'

I turned in surprise, and looked towards the head of our little creek. Forty or fifty yards upstream, was *Nipper*, stuck fast on the far side of the channel; and leaning frantically over the stern, wild-eyed and daubed from head to foot with mud, was Toddy.

'You prune!' I called back in amazement. 'What are you *doing?*'

'What's it fucking look like?'

I managed to work my way through the trees till I came out almost opposite him.

'How long have you been stuck?'

'Half an hour, three-quarters.'

I guessed it must be about four o'clock. As far as I remembered, low tide that day was around seven, so he was going to be marooned there till ten or eleven at night.

'I can't stay here till then,' he protested.

'What else?'

'There must be something you can do.'

I thought about it. 'I know!' I said. 'Chuck us your trip line. I'll make it fast, then you can lie flat on the mud and haul yourself across.'

'I'm not doing that. This mud stinks. It'd be like crawling through shit.'

'Well, throw it anyway. I'll get you some food, and you can pull it across.'

But unfortunately, the line wasn't long enough, and I couldn't reach it. The only other thing I could think of was that Eric might have some planks we could borrow.

'But you won't tell anyone?' Toddy said, anxiously.

'I can't get you out of there on my own.'

'I'll stop where I am, then.'

'And if people ask where you are?'

'Tell them you don't know.'

'You're being a real prick, Toddy.'

'Piss off, then, and leave me alone.'

'All right,' I said. 'I will.'

By the time I got back to the caravan, Mike and Mr Whitman

were home again. They had seen the motor boat, and it was fixed for us to have it for two days the following week.

Mike was clearly delighted. 'She's much bigger than *Patsy*. We'll be able to go the whole length of the river. Even round to Falmouth, and out to sea.'

While Mrs Whitman was getting some tea ready, I showed him my model. When I explained the problem about the planks, he suggested making patterns first out of paper, to save wasting the balsa. It seemed like a pretty good idea, and I was glad.

'Where's Toddy?' he asked.

I said we'd both been talking to Eric, and then he'd slipped away without me noticing.

Mr Whitman looked up sharply. 'He hasn't been making remarks again?'

'No. Nothing like that.'

'And you've no idea where he's gone?'

'I looked all round the house, but I couldn't find him.'

My cheeks were burning. The Whitmans didn't deserve to be lied to.

After tea, Mike said he'd like to see the dynamo and the engine. Once we were out of sight behind the generator house, he gave me a shrewd glance and shoved me gently back against the wall. 'Okay. Cut out the crap. Where is he?'

So I told him the story to date.

He laughed. 'Serve him right, stupid little twerp. But we can't just leave him there, whatever he says. We'll have to tell Dad.'

Mr Whitman heard us out in silence, and gave me a look I found it hard to interpret.

'I'm sorry,' I said. 'I ought to have told you earlier.'

He nodded. 'Yes. That would have been a lot more sensible.'

By this time, Toddy was glad to see us. Ladders and planks were considered again, but rejected after a site inspection; the mud wasn't flat enough.

Mrs Whitman had packed some bread and cheese in the waxed paper out of a cornflakes packet, but the distance was too far to be sure of throwing the parcel accurately. If it landed out of reach, that would be that.

'Worth a try,' said Mr Whitman. 'Not much else we can do.'

I stopped him just in time. For some reason, I'd happened to think of Ronnie, marooned in the Sick Room. String!

We tied the end of my Falmouth whipcord round a suitable stone, and after five or six goes, Mike managed to land it close to the boat. Within a couple of minutes, Toddy had hauled the package of food across and hoisted it on board. Later, we wrapped his pullover up in newspaper, and sent it across to him by the same method.

It was well past eleven before he set foot ashore. The worst part of the wait came at the very end; *Nipper* had been surrounded by water for more than an hour before she floated off. By the time Toddy could row her back to the landing stage, it was quite dark, and the scene by torchlight had a vaguely sinister feel. Black water, and the creak of oars approaching out of the night. Like the Resistance. Or a scene from a smuggling film.

He was filthy, of course; and by now, everybody was hungry again. So what with one thing and another, we didn't make it to bed till round about half past one. Even then, it was hard to sleep. The moment we settled down, Toddy began to wheeze and cough; and it went on practically non-stop till morning.

In spite of which, I had a confusing dream about canals, where people had all been roped together in pairs; except for me. Why had I been left out? The system was clear enough: each pair had to be made up of a motor boat and a butty.

'Yes,' said the mind-reader from King's Cross with a sardonic smile. 'But the thing is, which are you?'

21

On our way to collect the motor boat, we called in at a pub for our Sunday dinner. The sign over the door said 'The New Inn, by J. Crossley', as if it was a book title.

We all went into the Bar, and Mr Whitman bought us glasses of shandy, but pretty soon we had to come out again, because the atmosphere was turning Toddy into a medical emergency. His chest had been growing steadily worse since the day he got stuck on the mud, and after a couple of minutes in the smoke-filled room he was coughing like a consumptive. Out in the fresh air, he soon recovered, but there could be no question of him going back inside, so a table was carried into the yard and we ate al fresco.

Our meal had been ordered in advance, courtesy of the Honeycotts, whose shop boasted the only telephone for miles, and in due course a trayload of plates appeared, with cold roast chicken on them – an amazing treat. In London, chicken was rarer than champagne; I hadn't even had sight of it since before the war.

Mike was eager for us to eat up and be on our way. With high water around four, he was sure the tide would already be far enough in for us to fetch the boat. I helped him to carry the empty plates indoors while Mr Whitman settled our bill at the Bar, and we came out into the yard again through the back entrance. On the ground outside was a wicker basket with an old cushion in the bottom and two cats curled up on it, fast asleep. Their bodies were so completely intertwined that you could scarcely tell where one ended and the other began. Instinctively, we glanced at each other, and squatted down for a closer look. Mike reached out cautiously to stroke their fur, and one of the cats stirred a little, stretched its legs for a couple of seconds, and then settled back luxuriantly against its companion.

'I wouldn't mind being a cat,' Mike said.

The motor boat was moored to a stone quay. Her bows were decked over to make a storage locker; otherwise she was quite open, except for a squarish wooden structure in the middle which housed the engine. She looked as if she had recently been re-painted; brown on the inside, white on the outside. Screwed to the stern was a little plaque with the name *Marge* done in bakelite letters, the sort people had on their gates.

I thought the four of us were going to return by water while Mrs Whitman drove back on her own. But Toddy was still coughing a bit, and she said he'd better come with her, in case he had another attack. He seemed rather cut up about this, so I said I would go in the car as well, to keep him company. In any case, I suspected Mike and Mr Whitman wanted to try the boat out on their own, with nobody watching.

Mr Whitman started the engine with one deft flick of the crank handle, and sat back near the stern holding the tiller while Mike cast off. They backed slowly away from the quay in a graceful curve, and then shot ahead rather suddenly as Mr Whitman engaged the Forward gear. Mike nearly lost his balance, but he gave us a thumbs-up over his shoulder as *Marge* set off towards the mouth of the creek, and we watched them safely out of sight.

'Who'll be home first?' Toddy said.

It was hard to judge. The car was a lot faster than the boat; but it wasn't far by water, whereas the road snaked its way laboriously for miles round all the creeks.

Discussing the pros and cons of it started Toddy coughing again.

'We'll have to get you some linctus,' Mrs Whitman said.

But that wasn't the end of it; by the time we reached Penskerrick, ahead of the boat party as it happened, she had announced a major policy decision.

'Where's Toddy?' Mike said, as *Marge* came chugging up to the landing stage.

'Moving his things up to the caravan,' I said. 'Mum reckons it's doing him no good, sleeping in the tent.'

'Poor old boy,' said Mr Whitman.

Mike nodded. But I caught his eye, and I knew what he was thinking. For once, we'd be able to get a decent night's sleep.

Over tea, the talk was all of the motor boat; how she handled, how fast she could go, how far to the gallon. Ought we to tow *Nipper* behind her to row ashore in, or could she be beached? Where should we go tomorrow? Mike pored over the chart and the Tide Tables, trying to work out how we could visit the maximum number of places in the two days we had her.

But one thing was certain. She would have to be taken round to the beach without delay, and while she was being moved, it seemed a pity not to go for an evening trip on the river. Mr Whitman said all five of us should go; but to Toddy's fury, his mother vetoed it and said the two of them would stay behind together.

'He needs to get some air into his lungs,' Mr Whitman said.

'He needs rest. Otherwise, he'll only be worse tomorrow.'

'No reason for Alan not to come,' said Mike.

In no time at all, we were out beyond the headland, and making straight for the main river. Mike held the chart across his knees, locating the various beaches and land formations, and pointing them out to me excitedly, as if he owned them all.

'There's a big reef of rocks there,' he said, pointing over to our right.

Nothing was visible. 'Where?' I said, bewildered.

'Still submerged. You only see them at low tide; but you can still go aground on them. That's why you need the chart. You have to know what's under the surface. Up-river, it's mudbanks; out here, it's rocks and shallow places.'

Suddenly, without warning, the engine noise changed completely, and we slowed down almost to a stop.

'What's happened?' I said.

'Weed round the propeller.'

'What do we do now?' It would take us till midnight to row *Marge* home from where we'd got to.

'Dead easy. Just go into Reverse, and it unwinds.'

At the stern, Mr Whitman was grasping the gear lever, swinging it quickly from side to side. All at once, there was a violent threshing sound and a mass of white froth came bubbling up to the surface behind the boat. A moment later, the engine noise was back to normal and we were under way again.

'You see?' Mike said, delighted.

'How come you know all this?'

'The man told us. It's always happening. We did it several times this afternoon.'

There was rather a nice beach near the mouth of the river, so we landed there and spent about half an hour looking at rock pools. On the way home, Mr Whitman sat at the front, and Mike and I took it in turns to steer.

'Remember,' Mr Whitman said, 'ships pass port to port. And keep your eyes open for floating weed.'

We anchored *Marge* at the beach ready for the morning, and strolled slowly back to Penskerrick.

'Well?' Mike said to me. 'What do you think? Isn't she beautiful?'

'Yeah. It's going to be really good. There's far more things to see out there than I'd realised.'

'D'you reckon you could make a model of her?'

I was doubtful. 'Maybe. I'll know better when I've finished the other ones.'

Toddy and Mrs Whitman had supper ready for us. Afterwards, we played pontoon. Toddy won, which pleased him, but it was hard work trying to keep him cheerful and I wasn't sorry when Mrs Whitman said we could all do with an early night.

As Mike and I made our way to the tent through the derelict ornamental garden, I said, 'It's rough on Toddy, having to sleep in the caravan.'

'Rough on Mum and Dad, too.'

'Perhaps if he doesn't cough so much, he won't keep them awake.'

Mike let the gate swing to behind us. 'I meant, fat chance of a decent screw when Toddy's lying six feet away with his ears flapping.'

'Oh,' I said. This hadn't occurred to me.

We got into bed, and lay for a while in silence. It was too early to go to sleep.

After a minute or two, Mike said, 'Keep this to yourself. Nobody knows yet, not even Mum or Toddy.'

I wondered what was coming.

'Dad and me have decided to try and build a television.'

'Television?'

'It's like the wireless, but you get a picture as well. There's a little screen next to the loudspeaker.'

I tried to take this in. 'Won't it be very difficult?'

'I'm not sure. We may need your help. One or two of the bits will have to be specially made.'

'You'll have to hurry, then. The workshop's closing down.'

'I know. You said. Bound to be other places, though. Are you on?'

'You bet.'

Whitman and Carey Ltd.

Hard to guess what a television set would look like. The Andersons' big radiogram, perhaps, with the oscilloscope somehow perched on top of it. But in spite of a certain vagueness over matters of detail, I'd got it all built and running by the time I fell asleep.

Somehow or other, during the night, I must have rolled over without knowing it, and maybe Mike had done the same, because I awoke to find him lying half on top of me. It was beginning to grow light, but everything outside was quiet and peaceful. He was fast asleep, so I stayed quite still, enjoying the gentle pressure of his body against my side. But after a while I needed to change position, and although I was very careful, I felt him stirring. I froze immediately, but it was too late. He yawned, stretched, and looked round in surprise.

'Sorry,' I muttered.

With a sleepy grin, he wriggled his pyjamas down, and pulled me close to him. If I resisted, it wasn't for more than a second or two, and only from sheer astonishment. I loved the feel of his hands on my bare skin, and the warmth of his naked body against my own.

'Like the cats,' he murmured contentedly, as I snuggled up to him.

Only not like the cats, as it turned out.

But not like with Jacko, either; not in the least. The sheer joy of it, for one thing. Whenever Jacko touched you, he was taking something away from you, and the contact left you dirty; but with Mike it was like being given a wonderful present, something you'd vaguely longed for without even knowing it existed. I loved being able to do things back to him, too, things I had secretly wanted to do without knowing how to admit it, even to myself. At first, I was timid about it, apprehensive; but the look on his face and his long voluptuous gasps of pleasure reassured me. And when he came in my hand, instead of it being revolting, the way it had been that time with Jacko, it was the most exciting thing that had ever happened.

'Now you,' he whispered, taking hold of me.

At the touch of his hand, the ecstasy seemed to come welling up from somewhere impossibly deep and far away – as if my body had merged with the whole earth, and the molten core of it was surging relentlessly upwards, ready to burst out in a climax of incomparable magnificence. Who would have guessed it could possibly feel so good with another person? Not just the rapturous cockthrill, better by a million than anything you could have managed on your own, but the miraculous sense of being made whole again, and emerging strong and clean into the sunlight.

Afterwards, as we lay for a while in a loose tangle, still breathless with amazement and delight, the whole pattern was suddenly clear to me. At last, everything fitted. Lakeside. Wrestling with Dave. Me and Ray. Me and Ronnie, too; because that's what it had been, the thing between us – I could see that now. Everything made sense. And what I'd been doing with Mike seemed the most right and proper and natural thing in the world. It had bound us together, like blood brothers; and that would make all the difference, because when you were a Barton boy, the thing you needed above all else was somebody really special.

At last, Mike eased himself away from me and sat up.

'What's the time?' I said.

He looked at his watch. 'Ten to six.'

Crouching at the far end of the tent, he undid the flaps and poked his head outside. The morning looked bright and sunny.

'Swim?' he said.

'What, now?'

'There'll be plenty of water.'

'But our things are up at the caravan.'

'Who cares?'

So we made our way down to the landing stage, just as we were, and dived naked, laughing, into the cold bright waters of the creek.

It was my perfect day; as sweet and pure and crisp and sharp as sinking your teeth into a big green juicy apple.

We set out early in *Marge*, and made straight for the estuary, with the wind and the salt spray beating against our faces. There were big yachts under sail, some with huge spinnakers bellying out at the front, others beating into the wind and heeling over at dangerous-looking angles. As the day wore on, we kept meeting cruisers out from Falmouth, laden with trippers, and steered by bored, leathery characters in greasy yachting caps, who pointed out the sights to their passengers without even bothering to look.

At dinner time, we selected a beach, and landed. Toddy, who had spent a happy morning in charge of the bilge pump, even came swimming with us. We built huge cairns out of pebbles, fed crusts to the gulls, and at last discovered a way of dislodging limpets from the rocks, which was to take them by surprise and fetch them off with one good thwack before they could anchor themselves down.

In the afternoon, we went right out to sea.

'How long would it take us to reach France?' Toddy asked.

On our way home, we made for a beach just south of the estuary. It proved to be rocky and rather shallow, so we dropped anchor a little way out and ate our tea afloat. Afterwards, Mike and I waded ashore. The beach was strewn with boulders, and everywhere, lying on the pale sand, were shapeless lumps of a strange green rock, veined with black.

'Serpentine,' Mike said.

We found an especially fine specimen resting in a pool, half concealed under a long frond of seaweed; it was a flattish, oval lump, two or three inches long, worn perfectly smooth. As we fished it out, the rich mottled green glowed in the sunlight with a wild, exotic beauty.

'We should keep it,' I said.

So we carried it back to the boat. By then, of course, it had dried, and lost its lustre. But we could always wet it again, whenever we liked. I tucked it carefully into the pocket of my shorts, and all the way home, I kept checking to make sure it was still there, letting my fingertips dwell on its smooth surface.

That night, in the tent, with the flaps closed safely behind us, Mike suggested rearranging the mattresses and blankets into one wide bed for us both. I consented eagerly. All day long, I'd been looking forward to lying beside him again, all snug and peaceful, like the cats. Or even not like the cats.

But once we were under the covers, he flung himself onto me with a brusque urgency that I hadn't expected. As I rolled away in surprise, he brushed against me in a fashion that put me sharply in mind of Jacko. The shock was nauseating.

'Shit!' I said, fighting my way out from under him. 'What are you doing?'

He paused, breathing heavily. 'You were keen enough this morning. Practically begging for it.'

'It was different this morning.'

'Different? How?'

'I don't know. But it was. It just – happened.'

He slid away from me and rolled onto his back. 'You let other people,' he said bitterly. 'Why not me?'

'I don't let them. You can't always stop them.'

'Oh yeah? Like Raymond? You didn't really need to sleep in his room.'

'What's it to you?'

'Christ, Alan! How can you say that?'

'We didn't do anything, if that's what you think. Not that it's any of your business.'

He sat up, with his fists clenched and his forehead pressing hard against his knees. 'Alan, please, I'm busting for it. It's worse than that time at the swimming bath when we shared a cubicle. Remember? You stripped off and stood there, right in front of me. I practically...' He threw his head back with a kind of stifled sob, as if he was gasping for air.

'If you're that desperate, why don't you use my picture? Isn't that what you keep it for?'

'No!!' He was appalled. 'You don't do that when it's some-one you really care about.'

'Well, if you care that much, just leave me alone.'

I woke in a muck sweat from a nightmare about the cellar, sur-prised to find that I must, after all, have fallen asleep. It was dark outside, and there wasn't a sound. Apart from that, I had no idea of the time. Mike slept with his watch on, and I couldn't have looked at it without disturbing him.

I sat up, and tried to think. Yesterday, it had all made perfect sense. But if Mike wanted the same things as Jacko, what then? How could anyone want to do that to you, if they really cared? On the other hand, if he did want to, wasn't it pretty mean of me not to let him? Not much to ask, after all he'd done for me, and it mightn't be quite so bad with someone you liked. Or perhaps it was all a dreadful misunderstanding from start to finish. What about Mike and Rowena? Or if not Rowena, surely some other girl? Ray had been certain about that. And what about Ray himself, lying there naked on top of the bedclothes? His scheme with the hairbrushes: I could guess now how we'd have ended up. Maybe Mike hadn't been all that wide of the mark. Even so, why should he be so jealous? Perhaps – it was a sickening thought – he'd wanted Ray for himself.

I knew I had no chance of sorting it out unless I could be on my own. Cautiously, I felt around in the darkness for my clothes. Shorts, plimsolls, singlet, pullover. No sign of my underpants. They must be somewhere down inside the bed. Too bad. I thrust the bundle quietly through the tent flaps and crawled outside.

When I was dressed, I made instinctively for the path down to the quay. There was a faint greyness about the night sky which made the trees stand out in silhouette, so I found my way without much difficulty.

Reaching the quay I paused briefly, uncertain what to do next; then I walked out to the end of the landing stage and sat down with my legs hanging over the edge. The creek, all black and oily between the overhanging trees, seemed eerie, menacing even. You could imagine a ghostly ferryman rowing towards you out of the darkness. If you stepped into the boat and sat down, it would glide away softly into the night and you would never be seen again.

I shuddered. I could really have done with a fag, but I hadn't brought any. I didn't think I'd be needing them at Penskerrick. How wrong can you be?

It was all so incredibly confusing. Problems you couldn't precisely put into words. These things were never explained, that was the trouble. Evasions instead of answers. Even disinformation. As if you were being kept in the dark on purpose.

It started when you were just a kid. A particular kind of disapproving look, and dependable people lying to you. 'If you keep on doing that, it'll drop off like a tadpole's tail.'

And then this chart we had at Junior School. Your Body. Heart, lungs, a muscle or two; just the basics. A boy and a girl were shown in outline, side by side, and amazingly, in the place where you naturally looked first, the boy had nothing. Not wearing little pants, or holding his hands in front of him. Actually drawn with nothing. And you thought: How does he manage? But for all you knew, the better sort of people had a way of doing without; like girls. Did angels have them? Did Jesus? It was crucial to find out. Imagine asking, though. 'Please, Miss...' There'd be nothing left of you but a charred place on the floor.

Later, there was a change of tactics. Instead of pretending that there was nothing to know, and if there was you certainly oughtn't to know it, they assumed you knew it already. They dropped hints, and made veiled comments. You and your kind. So you were none the wiser, only you daren't admit it. To ask would have been indecent; worse still, if you didn't know, you were obviously a fool.

It was baffling. During the war, you were taught to recognise mines, and warned against kicking strange objects you found lying in the street. Nobody tried to pretend they didn't exist. Here are the facts, and this is what you do. So why not explain about Jacko, and things like that? And then you would know, instead of having to puzzle it all out as you went along.

I couldn't think what I should do. There seemed to be no solution, except perhaps to start walking, and keep on going till I somehow managed to walk right out of the world. If the ferryman came, perhaps I should step on board.

Without much sense of purpose, I made my way back to the tent, and then on through the ruined garden towards the house. If I was heading anywhere, it was to the Falmouth Road. The quickest way was via the back drive, but in order to reach it, I should have to go past the caravan. If the Whitmans were awake, they would hear my feet on the gravel. So I chose the other route, the one we'd explored on our first evening.

It was dark and spooky. I slid my hand into my pocket and let my fingers wander over the piece of serpentine. It was a comforting shape; something good to hold on to.

At the end of the drive, I turned to the right and set off towards the crossroads. How far to Falmouth? I wasn't sure. Five miles? Ten? I could manage that. I had plenty of time, and a decent surface under my feet.

There was something hypnotic about walking: no conscious effort, merely the soft pad, pad of my plimsolls on the deserted road, the cool night air blowing gently against my face, and every now and then, the smooth encouraging feel of the serpentine at my fingertips. I felt free, unthreatened, insulated by solitude and darkness.

I must have passed the crossroads, because after a while I realised I was approaching the back drive to Penskerrick. No question of going down it, though. I walked straight on, heading for

Falmouth.

By the time I'd gone another half mile, a part of me knew precisely how it would end. It was going to be King's Cross all over again. But it took me a while to come to terms with it. By then, the sky was growing paler. Before long, it would be dawn. My pace began to slacken.

If you could press a button, and be wherever you wanted, where would you choose?

Well?

I turned half round, and stood facing across the road. Pointless to go on; unthinkable to go back. Perhaps if I stayed there long enough I should turn to stone, and be marked on the Ordnance Survey.

Walking home was like trying to clear up a mess before anyone notices. The back drive in the dark was nightmare country, but I forced myself not to run, in case the noise woke something up, and it came after me.

When I reached the yard, I realised that the obvious way to avoid disturbing the Whitmans was to go straight through the house. I remembered the layout, and managed to feel my way in the dark without much difficulty. But as I emerged, and came within sight of the caravan, I stopped dead. The light was on, and a shadow was moving to and fro across the blind. Had Mike reported my disappearance?

I stood still for several minutes, uncertain what to do. Then the light was suddenly extinguished. No one had come outside. Perhaps Toddy had needed a drink, or something. I waited a while for whoever it was to get back to sleep, and then made my way cautiously towards the entrance to the garden, one step at a time.

As I crawled into the tent, Mike rolled over and propped himself up on his elbows. 'Alan?' There was a click, and the torch snapped on. 'You're dressed! Where the hell have you been?'

'For a walk. Any objections?'

'It's the middle of the night!'

'I couldn't sleep.'

I crawled forward and lay down on top of the blankets, still in my clothes.

Mike switched off the torch. 'Look, Alan, I really don't understand, but if I've upset you, I'm sorry.'

'Let's just forget it.'

'I mean, the last thing on God's earth I want is to...'

'I said, Okay.'

I felt quite sleepy, now, so I adjusted the pillow, and curled up at the far edge of the mattress.

'Aren't you going to get into bed?'

'I'm all right.'

'I wish I could believe it. Look, I promise I won't lay a finger on you.'

'It isn't your fingers I'm bothered about.'

A cheap crack, and not called for. I was ashamed as soon as I'd said it.

Mike withdrew into icy dignity. 'I've made you a promise. Isn't that good enough?'

It was almost too much trouble to move, but in the end, I levered my plimsolls off with my toes, wriggled quickly out of my clothes, and slid in under the covers. We lay back to back, as far apart as possible, like the people in one of those medieval legends who sleep with a sword between them.

Mike was already dressed when I woke, so he went up to the caravan ahead of me. By the time I arrived, a heated discussion was taking place. Toddy had coughed all night, and Mrs Whitman wanted to take him to Falmouth to see a doctor and get him some proper medicine. There was talk of them going to the pictures, too. *Up in Arms* was showing, with Danny Kaye in, and Toddy was keen to see it. God knows why.

Mike sounded very put out. 'What's the point of hiring a family motor-boat and then not using it?'

'There's nothing to stop the rest of you going out in her,' his mother said.

But Mike still wasn't satisfied. 'You haven't forgotten we've got to take her back this afternoon?' he said crossly. 'We'll need the car to come home in. Or do you expect us to walk?'

'It's Tuesday. Toddy and I can go on the bus.'

Mr Whitman frowned. 'Hang on a minute, though. If I'm driving the car round, who's going to deliver *Marge*?'

I could see exactly what was coming.

'Me and Alan, obviously,' Mike said, suddenly enthusiastic.

'Oh – no,' said Mrs Whitman. 'I don't think that's a very good idea.' She turned to Toddy. 'I'm sorry, love. No pictures. We'll have to take the car and come straight back.'

'Mum!' Mike protested. 'What's the matter? Do you think Alan and me can't handle *Marge* on our own? If Toddy wants a day in Falmouth, you go. We'll manage.'

Mr Whitman gave him a shrewd look. 'Do you really think you're up to it?'

Mike bristled. 'Of course! I'm not completely incompetent.'

'Alan?'

'It's up to Mike, really.' Not a lot else I could say.

'That's settled then.' Mr Whitman glanced at his watch. 'Look here! If you're going to catch that bus...'

To get our money's worth out of *Marge*, we spent the morning and early afternoon cruising relentlessly all round the estuary; but it was a bit like eating your way through a pudding that isn't as nice as you'd thought. For Mr Whitman's benefit, Mike and I were studiously polite to each other. But he wasn't fooled.

'You two had a tiff?'

'No,' I said.

We arrived back at Penskerrick around four, and took our belongings up to the caravan. Then it was time for Mr Whitman to see us off. I stood at the bows, ready to haul in the mooring rope, while Mike started the engine. I thought he looked very capable, sitting in the stern, with one hand on the tiller and the other on the controls. We backed away from the landing stage quite professionally, waved Goodbye, and chugged along towards the main creek.

With the tide in our favour, the journey up-river should take us about an hour. I spent as long as possible coiling the rope neatly on the little foredeck, and then sat down on the seat at the front, facing forward.

After picking our way past the boats moored in the creek, we swung round in a gentle curve and began to head up-stream. I gazed bleakly at the broad, empty expanse of water ahead of us, and the steep, wooded slopes on either side. It was surprising to find the river was still so wide so far inland. And we had it all to ourselves. We only saw one other boat, and it passed us well out of hailing distance, right on the far side.

It seemed a very long time before the creek we were heading for came in sight. I glanced back at Mike for confirmation. He nodded, and eased the tiller over to swing our nose round. A few seconds later, there was a strange, muffled clonk from the stern, and the engine suddenly cut out.

We looked at each other in alarm. Mike swung the lever to Neutral and slid the crank handle onto the shaft. Much to our relief, the engine started at once. But as soon as he put it into gear, it stalled again. Three more times, exactly the same thing happened. I moved back towards the stern, and we gazed in perplexity at the engine cover, wondering what to do next.

'We haven't run out of petrol?' I said.

'We can't have. I checked.'

'Dirty plug?'

'Shouldn't think so. It runs sweetly enough in Neutral.'

All the same, we decided to take a look. I fetched the plug spanner from the locker while Mike tackled the magneto lead. 'Shit!' he exclaimed, jerking his hand away. 'It's red hot!'

Eventually, he got it off using his handkerchief, and then tried to remove the spark plug. It seemed to be jammed solid. We nearly gave up, but after one final blow to the spanner with the heel of his hand, he felt it loosen. We examined the points, but there was no dirt on them.

'It's a good thing this didn't happen when we were out at sea,' I said.

'Yeah.' He glanced up, and swung his head round in amazement. 'Look how far we've drifted, though.'

Already, we were past the entrance to the creek.

'Do you think we should anchor?'

'Too deep.'

He re-fitted the plug and magneto lead, and tried the starting handle. Once again, the engine ran in Neutral, but not in gear.

I looked round in all directions to see if anyone was coming. Not a soul in sight.

'We'll have to try and row,' Mike said.

We unshipped the oars and took one each, sitting either side of the engine cover. But rowing *Marge* was a very different thing from rowing *Nipper*. It was all we could do to hold her against the tide. Before long, we gave it up as a bad job, and sat for several minutes in hopeless silence.

'Somebody's bound to come eventually,' I said.

Mike glanced at his watch. 'Oh God! Look at the time. I'm going to get crucified for this.'

'It's not your fault.'

He caught my eye, and gave a bitter laugh. 'All this, for the sake of Danny Kaye.'

We had drifted well past the creek now, but the tide was slackening as high water approached. It wasn't likely to take us much further. But when it turned, what then?

A vague idea was beginning to form in my mind. I stood facing the engine, fitted the crank handle, and set the gear lever to Forward.

Mike was scornful. 'It'll never start like that.'

'I know. But I think the propeller shaft must have got jammed. Turning it over in gear might loosen it.'

We tried, but even between us we couldn't shift it. One way, it was stuck fast; the other way, the handle simply freewheeled on the ratchet.

'It's jammed all right,' Mike said. 'But how could it have happened?'

'Weed?'

'It wouldn't have stalled completely.'

'What about driftwood?'

'Yeah! There was a thump, remember?'

Mike sat right in the stern, bared his arm, and reached into the water to feel for the propeller. After several anxious minutes, he sat up again and shook his head. 'It's no good. Too far under.'

Obviously, there was only one thing for it. I started to strip off.

'For God's sake! What are you doing?'

'It's the only way to reach it.'

'But you can't. I mean, right out here?'

'Someone's got to, and I can't turn that handle; but you might, if I can loosen things a bit.'

I kicked my shorts and pants off. Nude bathing was getting to be a habit.

'Alan, I really don't think you should do this.'

'Any other suggestions?'

I dived in and swam round to the stern. The rudder was very much in the way, so Mike unshipped it, and hauled it carefully inboard. Hanging onto the stern with one hand, I reached about under the boat. The propeller was much further forward than I had imagined, but at last my fingers encountered the edge of one of the blades. There was a mass of weed all round it, and something hard that wasn't the propeller and couldn't be weed either. I surfaced, spluttering, to tell Mike what I'd found.

He stood in the bows so as to lift the stern as much as possible, and I went under again to try and pull the weed away; but it was difficult when you couldn't see what you were doing, and you couldn't breathe, and you only had one spare hand.

'Got a knife?' I said.

Mike felt in his pocket and handed me a clasp knife, the sort with a knobbly black handle and one big blade; everyone had them at that time. We looped some string through the hasp and tied the other end round my wrist in case I dropped it.

This time, I got on better. After a while, I felt the propeller shift a little. I could turn it back and forth about an inch, then it would jam again. But with some of the weed stripped away, I was able to get a firmer grip on whatever the hard thing was. It felt like a lump of stone. Letting go of the boat, I made another attempt with both hands, and found I could shift the lump as well as the propeller. I hacked at the weed again, wishing the knife was three times the size, and felt a big piece come away. Everything shifted a lot more freely after that, so I concentrated on cutting through whatever was holding the lump in place. After a couple more goes, it came away in my hand and I brought it up to the surface.

It was a piece of rock, with fronds of seaweed still firmly attached to it. It must have broken off, somewhere nearer the mouth, and drifted upstream on the tide, the weed bladders keeping it afloat just below the surface.

With the stone gone, the rest of the weed should come away pretty easily, so I went down one last time to free as much as I could. The rest we could probably shake off by running the propeller in reverse.

'Try the engine now,' I said, and swam well clear of the boat.

It started easily. I saw Mike put it in gear, but he must have left the throttle at full, because the boat shot forward suddenly so that he lost his footing and fell backwards. I saw him reach wildly for the tiller as he disappeared into the bottom of the boat; but of course it wasn't there, because we had unshipped the rudder.

For a long and dreadful moment, I imagined him knocked unconscious, and the boat surging away at top speed, leaving me all alone in the middle of the river. Mentally, I divided the distance to the shore by the width of the Uxbridge swimming baths, and found the result discouraging. In desperation I struck out towards the boat, but she seemed incredibly far away. By the time Mike brought her chugging alongside, I was only about thirty seconds away from panic.

As I reached up to haul myself out of the water, my strength suddenly failed. Mike grabbed me under the armpits and lifted me half over the side so I could hang there and get my breath back. With one final effort and another heave from Mike, I made it safely into the boat, and lay sprawled on the bottom boards, surprised to find myself shivering and shaking.

Mike crouched down beside me, looking extremely anxious. 'Are you okay?'

'Yeah,' I gasped. 'Let's get going.'

I watched him settle in the stern and steer us towards the creek. Then I dried myself as well as I could, using my pants, and struggled into the rest of my clothes.

After about ten minutes, the quay came in sight. Mr Whitman, unmistakable even at a distance, was pacing furiously up and down. When he saw us coming, he stepped forward to the very edge. We waved, and he gestured angrily at his watch.

'Where in God's name have you been?' he shouted, as we drew alongside. 'I thought you'd both got drowned.'

'Engine conked out,' Mike said. 'It took us ages to get it going.'

'I suppose you'd been messing about with it?'

'No. It just cut out. In the end, we discovered the propeller was jammed. Alan had to go overboard to free it.'

Mr Whitman turned on him, spitting the words out savagely. 'You made Alan get out of the boat in the middle of the river?'

'It was the only way,' Mike said indignantly. 'One of us had to.'

'I rather doubt it. But if anyone had to, it should have been you.'

'It's all right, Mr Whitman,' I said. 'It was my idea.'

'All right?' he said. 'All right? Look at you, boy, you're shaking.'

He sent Mike to sit in the car. Then he put his arm around my shoulders, and said, 'I want to know exactly what happened out there.'

So I showed him the piece of stone and told him the whole story. By the time I'd finished, he seemed to have calmed down a bit. He rumpled my hair, smoothed it flat again, and sent me back to the car while he settled up with *Marge*'s owner.

Mike looked at me anxiously.

'It's okay now,' I said.

We drove all the way to Honeycott's in silence. Toddy and Mrs Whitman had been waiting there since a quarter to six, and were not best pleased. The journey home was electric with unspoken I-told-you-so's; and Toddy didn't improve things by insisting, between coughs, that from now on he didn't want to be called by his baby name and would only answer to Robert. Fair point, I suppose; but it wasn't the moment.

That evening, Mike seemed very subdued. I guessed there'd been a row. After a while, he wandered off on his own, and when

I got down to the tent, he was already in bed.

A clear gap had been left between the mattresses. I lay down, still in my clothes, and without shutting the flaps. 'You and your Dad,' I said. 'Is it okay now?'

He nodded a little uncertainly. 'Yeah, I reckon so. More or less.' There was a long silence. Then he said, 'You were terrific this afternoon, you really were.'

'It wasn't anything special.'

'Oh, come on!' He hesitated, steeling himself. 'Look... About last night...'

I rolled onto my side, quite close to him. 'I know, I'm sorry; it wasn't your fault. Yesterday morning was really good. Honestly. And it's fine by me, whenever you want. Just so long as you don't...'

'Don't what?'

With an outstretched finger, I mimed Jacko's method.

You'd think I'd spat in his face. 'Christ!' he said angrily. 'What the hell do you take me for?'

I wished I'd kept my mouth shut.

Suddenly, his whole demeanour changed. With a gasp of horror he sat up and said, 'Is that what happens at Barton?'

I didn't want to think about Barton; not at the moment.

He shook his head in disbelief. 'Oh God! That's disgusting! If I'd had any idea...'

'Let's just drop it.'

I wanted to reach out and touch his bare shoulder, but he made a sort of choking sound, and curled up in his blanket, facing away from me.

'Mike?'

No answer. I was contaminated. Not fit to be one of the family.

In silence, I shut the flaps, undressed, and slid into bed. For a long time, I lay awake, oppressed by the sense of something precious slipping away, and being powerless to prevent it. We had, as I realised with an unwelcome shock, only three more days at Penskerrick. Soon, I should be back at Barton, with nothing settled, and Mike's opinion of me damaged beyond repair.

At last, yielding to an absurd impulse which I fought off for as long as possible, I reached out in the darkness for my shorts, and felt in the pocket for our piece of serpentine. When I fell asleep, I was still clasping it firmly in both hands.

22

There wasn't time to finish the model of *Patsy*. When we were packing, I nearly chucked it out; it wouldn't have lasted five minutes at Barton House. But Toddy – he'd forgotten about being Robert, apparently – said he would keep it for me. So it travelled home with us after all, balanced on people's knees.

The drive to Exeter was pretty subdued. There was one consolation, though. I was very much looking forward to seeing Ray again. Only it turned out that he and Rowena had gone to stay with some cousins. 'He's so sorry to miss you,' Mrs Palmer said, when she saw my face fall. 'He thought you were rather special.' I wished she hadn't said it while Mike was listening. Upstairs, I peeped into Ray's bedroom, but it was like looking at someone's things after their funeral. From then on, the whole day seemed to collapse in ruins. We even had to have baths.

The rest of our journey back to London was about as cheerful as a march to the scaffold. But shortly before we left, I copied down the Palmers' telephone number from the receiver in the hall, and I was pleased I'd thought of it. If the worst came to the worst, Exeter was as easy to reach as York, and when I arrived I'd be able to contact Ray.

Another thing on the plus side was that right in the middle of Yeovil, I suddenly reached an important decision regarding Jacko. I knew now precisely what I would do next time he sent for me – that is, assuming I had the nerve – and it was so simple that I couldn't imagine why it had never occurred to me before.

It was a dismal experience, walking back into Barton House on the Monday morning. All the squalid details you learned to ignore stood out again as if seen for the first time. For a while, I felt like a stranger. The Club Room furniture had been shifted round. There were jokes I wasn't in on, and the talk was of things that had happened while I'd been gone. 'You've seen the last of Tom and Eddie,' Ocky said. 'We thought it'd only be probation, but...' He shrugged. Apparently, this place they'd broken into, the owner had caught them at it, and Eddie had kicked his head in. Even Ocky himself seemed changed; harder somehow, and more resentful, as if he'd been messed about with once too often.

After dinner, Jacko wanted to see me. When I walked into the room, he was sitting behind his desk. As usual, he simply pointed.

So this was it. I stood quite still, with my feet apart and my hands behind my back.

'Well?' he said at last.

'I'm not going on with this, Mr Crofting.'

He hardly moved a muscle. 'As you wish,' he said, with just the faintest inclination of his head.

I waited, but nothing happened. 'Can I go, then?'

Without a word, he waved me out of the room. The whole thing had taken less than a minute. I was jubilant. To think it was that simple!

It wasn't, of course. Next morning, he sent for me again. There was a shoe box on the table with various items in it.

'I want you to have a look at these. Take your time. Sit down, if you like.'

There was a comb in a leather case, a cheap penknife, a note-book, a couple of unstarted pencils, things like that. Oh, Christ, I thought. I knew where they must have come from. I'd have to find Ocky, and warn him. In the meantime, I could stall. I put the things back in the box and looked at Jacko blankly.

'Are they yours?' he asked.

'No.'

'Do you recognise them?'

'No.'

'They were found in your cupboard, while you were away.'

'They can't have been.'

'It's true. I do assure you.'

'But I've never seen them before.'

'Are you suggesting somebody else put them there?'

'They must have done.'

'Who?'

'How should I know?'

Jacko rested his chin on his hands and glanced across at me quizzically. 'Do you know what I think? I think we've finally found our shoplifter.'

'It's nothing to do with me. I never took those things. If I had've, do you think I'd have left them where you could find them?'

Crocodile smile. 'Oh, come on, Alan. Your fingerprints are going to be found all over them.'

'Well of course. I've just been looking at them. You told me to.'

'Did I? When was that?'

I couldn't believe it. 'Just now. In the box on the table.'

'Box?'

I glanced round indignantly. The box had gone. Turning back, I found him gazing at me impassively. After a brief pause, he reached for the telephone. 'I think we'd better send for the police.'

Let him. I could tell them a thing or two.

He must have read my thoughts. In a tone of gentle reproof, he added, 'And since it's me that's shopping you, they'll know exactly what to think of any spiteful little stories you might make up in revenge.'

We stared at each other in silence.

'Do you know what happens to boys like you at the sort of place they'll send you?'

Without warning, he caught hold of my hand and dragged me across to the bedroom doorway. Thrusting my fingers into the narrow hinge space, he swung the door shut with a jerk. A split second before the bones cracked and the flesh was crushed to pulp, he stopped the door with his foot.

'Look at you,' he said contemptuously. 'Ready to pee in your pants, and you haven't even been hurt. The sort of lads you'll be up against, the late lamented Tom and Eddie will seem like a couple of spring lambs. What chance do you think you'll stand?'

He let go of my hand and reached for the telephone. 'I can protect you, Alan. Or I can throw you to the wolves. It's up to you.'

My knees having unaccountably given way, I slid to the floor with my back pressing against the doorframe. My fingers were bruised and throbbing and my balls had gone numb from shock.

'Well?' he demanded. 'Which is it to be? Do I ring the police?'

I shook my head.

'I want to hear you say it. Yes or no?'

'No.'

He glanced at me shrewdly, then lit a cigarette and passed it across to me. 'I think your need is probably greater than mine,' he said. 'Just at the moment.'

So ended my rebellion. And he pressed home his advantage by doing a new thing to me in the bedroom, something I'd never even have thought of. Then he said I should do it to him as well.

'No!' It was out of the question.

'You haven't forgotten, Alan? I hold all the cards.'

'I can't.'

'Of course you can.' He smiled. 'Just pretend you're sucking a stick of rock.'

When I left the room, I spent the next twenty minutes throwing up in the toilets, and then set out in search of Ocky. As I'd expected, he was down at the Rec with Pete and some other boys.

'There's something I need to know,' I told him. 'When I was away, did you and Billy use my cupboard for stashing some of your stuff?'

He gave me a stone-wall stare. 'What stuff?'

'Look,' I said. 'Someone's landed me right in the shit. One false move, and you'll be in it as well. So just give me some straight answers. Did you leave anything in my cupboard?'

'Wasn't it locked?'

'Do us a favour!'

For a while, he tried to freeze me out. Then he said, 'No. I didn't put nothing in your cupboard. Satisfied?'

'Billy?'

'No.'

'Anyone else you can think of?'

'No.'

'This is important, Ocky.'

'I said, No.'

'Well, somebody did. And it's all stuff from Whitman's.'

'Yeah, I see. Tricky.' He thought for a minute. 'Well, just say you don't know nothing about it.'

'It's all got my prints on, now. Jacko tricked me into handling it.'

Ocky groaned. 'You arsehole! Will you never learn?'

We sat down on the grass with our backs against the chain-link fencing. I couldn't explain what Jacko was really up to. Ocky knew nothing about that, and I didn't intend to tell him. Luckily, there was no need. 'You know what he's trying to do?' I said. 'He thinks if he pushes me far enough, I'll end up shopping someone. You, probably. Or Billy.'

'Less you know, the better, then.'

'I want to know who's dropped me in it.'

Ocky chewed his lip. 'Okay. I'll need exact descriptions. Everything you can remember.'

After tea, he beckoned me to follow him outside. 'That stuff you was on about. Definitely not ours.'

'Well whose, then?'

'No one's,' he said, with a puzzled sniff. 'I've asked all round.'

'Then who the hell dumped it in my cupboard?'

He shrugged unhelpfully. 'How would I know?'

'D'you think I nicked it myself?' I demanded angrily.

He backed away a little. 'I didn't say that.'

But he gave me a very strange look, as if I was either a lot cleverer than he'd thought, or a lot stupider, and he couldn't decide which.

Next morning, I had to go to the sewing room to try on some long trousers for school. Term didn't start till the following week, but the Wilkies were going away for a day or two, and if alterations were needed, Mrs Dooley would have to be given instructions before they left.

As it happened, the pair that fitted me best were nearly new; even so, they had wanker's pockets, so I was glad things hadn't been left till the last minute. Even a handkerchief would have fallen through.

Mrs Wilkie said she would get them seen to. 'But apart from that, they're fine,' she commented, as I rotated slowly in front of her. 'As a matter of fact, you'll really look rather smart.' So far as I could remember, it was the first time she had ever paid me a compliment.

Afterwards, I called round at the workshop in search of occupation. There was no one there, but peeping in through the windows, I could see that the whole place was now practically empty. I was making my way back to the road again when Mr Pond appeared.

With a sigh, he opened the door and let me in. 'Not much left, I'm afraid.'

The machines had all been taken away and sold, leaving only their outlines on the bare floor and the fixing bolts protruding, bent and useless, from the concrete. The stacks of dusty boxes had dwindled almost to nothing, revealing patches of bare wall never before seen, the paint incongruously pristine, but swagged with clusters of cobwebs hanging in strange patterns. An old workbench stood abandoned in the middle of the room, with a few hand tools scattered about on it, and one vice still in position. Some stock ends lay in a box on the floor beside it. The far corner, where the office had been, was ankle deep in rubbish, broken cartons, ancient screwed-up newspaper, and squares of cracked linoleum that had stood under some of the cupboards. And all around, wherever you looked, there were hundreds and hundreds of dead woodlice, some on their backs with their legs in the air, others curled up into hard little scaly balls.

I mentioned the scheme for building a television.

Mr Pond scratched at his hairline under the peak of his cap. 'You can use the bench. Till Michaelmas Quarter Day. There's nothing else.'

'What if you aren't here?'

He took me round to the back of the hut and showed me a broken paving slab that lay close to the wall. 'We'll leave the key under there.'

'Do you mind if I look through the oddments box?'

'Go ahead. Anything you need, take it.'

Back inside, he rummaged about for a minute or two, found what he wanted, and made for the door. I stayed behind for a while, sorting the stock ends. It was simply something to do. Then I left the key under the slab and took myself off to the kitchen.

'Any biscuits going?' I asked.

Hurly had evidently been celebrating the Wilkies' imminent departure. 'Will you look at your long face,' she said, putting the biscuit tin down with a certain amount of difficulty, as if the table was constantly changing height. 'Are you not with Ocky, now? Or Billy?'

'I've been at the workshop.'

'Hiding, is it?' she said, accusingly.

'No. Just doing a few odd jobs.'

'My arse! You think I'm a stupid old woman who wouldn't know what's the matter with you?' She scrutinised me with her head at an angle, like someone coming to terms with modern sculpture. 'The day you walked into my kitchen,' she went on, 'didn't I say to myself, Now there's a little parcel Jack Crofting'll be itching to get the wrappers off?'

'You *knew*?'

'Would a person's eyes and ears not work as well one side of a kitchen door as they do the other?' She stuck her hands on her hips and settled her vast bulk against the Aga. 'And wasn't I only fourteen myself when Father Corcoran came murmuring in my ear, and me so innocent, I thought it was God's work he wanted doing.'

'Did you tell?' I needed to know.

'I did, so. And they gave me the strapping of a lifetime for the wicked, wicked lie. Nine months later they gave me another for proving them wrong. Poor thing couldn't have looked more like his daddy if he'd been born in a biretta.'

'What happened then?'

'People thought if I had any decency I'd die from the shame of it.' Her eyes hardened. 'But it wasn't myself that had any call to be doing a thing like that. Nor a young boy, neither. Do you hear, now?'

'What should I do about Mr Crofting, then?'

'Do?' she repeated, as if it was a daft question. 'Count your blessings. He'll not go getting you pregnant, that's for sure.'

After dinner, when I was clearing away, Jacko said he wanted to see me.

'I can't. I'm on washing up.'

'As soon as you've finished, then. Twenty minutes?'

I nodded, and went on stacking the plates. One thing was certain. Nothing on earth would induce me to face a repetition of yesterday. So in twenty minutes from now, I'd better be long gone.

The need for immediate action simplified everything marvellously; I scarcely had to bother with making decisions. There was only one place I could go.

I wheeled the laden trolley along to the scullery, and slipped unnoticed out of the back door. The thing was to get myself out of sight in the shortest possible time. I had coppers enough for the bus fare, but using the normal stop was out of the question. Welton Road was so straight you could see from one end to the other, and I might have to wait for up to fifteen minutes. The route over the railway bridge and back to the shops on the far side was a good deal longer, but at least it was safe.

I was tempted to make a dash for the pathway, but anyone looking out of a window would see me, so instead, I went straight over the fence into the patch of rough ground where the workshop stood. It was so overgrown that by crawling on hands and knees, I could stay completely hidden. At the far side, still crouching low, I pushed my way through a thinnish place in the hedge and out onto the path that led to the railway.

And then I ran.

Nothing like being a delivery boy for getting to know the district. Not too far away, I remembered, there was a bus stop with a shelter. Easy enough to stay hidden there, at least from a casual glance. It stood close to a hedge, too. Extra cover if necessary.

I'll swear it was half an hour I waited; and every moment, I was expecting Jacko to arrive with a screech of brakes and take me prisoner. I slouched down low behind a panel of wired glass with posters stuck to it, and tried to persuade myself that with any luck, no one had missed me yet. By the time the bus finally arrived, I was shaking so much I could hardly climb on board, and when I was paying, the coins jumped out of my hand, and rolled away in all directions to lodge in the slatted floor.

I liked buses, though, especially double-deckers. Snug. Friendly. So many things to hold on to, and all gently vibrating. You could never be anything but all right on a bus.

There was half a mile to walk after I got off. I took it slowly. No risk of interception, now, and I needed time to think. What was I actually going to say to the Whitmans? I could picture myself stepping into the house, and the door closing behind me. After that, the screen went blank. Like trying to imagine how it felt to be dead.

I went round to the back door, and knocked. No answer, so I tried the handle. But the door was shut fast. Fighting down panic, I knocked again. I knew it was useless, though. All the windows were shut. Everyone must be out.

A moment of sheer desperation. Then, absurdly, I felt reprieved, as if a risky operation had been postponed. I could even walk away and pretend I'd never been near the place. No future in that, though. I'd made it safely ashore; why put to sea again? It was only a matter of waiting till somebody came. And it mightn't be long; there was washing pegged to the line.

I sat down with my back to the wall and my legs stretched out in front of me, as tired all of a sudden as if I'd been running for miles and miles and miles.

The drone of a bi-plane crawling across the sky jerked me suddenly awake. I looked round in alarm. Footsteps. Jacko! He'd guessed, and come after me. Christ! Nowhere to hide. I tried to stand up, but I'd lost control of my legs.

'Alan?'

It was Mike.

'Wotcher,' I said.

'What's happened? You look terrible.'

I shrugged. Impossible even to begin.

He felt in his pocket for the key, and opened the door. Somehow, I made it into the house, and sat down at the kitchen table with my face buried in my hands. I heard him closing the door and fitting the key back on the inside.

'You'll lock it, won't you?' I said.

'Why?'

'Please. And the bolts.'

They made a very comforting sound.

'Is the front door locked as well?'

'Of course it is. I've only just got back.' He drew up a chair, and sat down close beside me. 'Alan, what have they done to you?'

I came within an inch of telling him. But it was an inch of armour-plating, which only telepathy could have penetrated. 'It's all so complicated.'

'Don't you think you should talk to Mum and Dad, then?' he said.

'Are they here? Nobody answered.'

'Everyone's out, I'm afraid. Toddy's playing in some sort of cricket match. Mum's gone over to watch. They'll pick Dad up from work on the way home. Probably not till six or seven, though.'

'Can I stay till they come?'

'Of course.' He sat back a little, surveying me anxiously. 'How long has all this been going on?'

'A while.'

'I wish you'd said.'

'I meant to, when we were away. But I kept putting it off.'

A small movement of his hand caught my eye, and I thought: If he touches me, it'll mean it's all right again between us. And miraculously, it was. His arm around my shoulders. I'd needed that. I'd needed it more than anything in the world.

At last, it felt safe to relax a little. All I had to do now was wait. Three hours; four at the most. Once the Whitmans had heard the whole story, they would say I could sleep on their floor for the night, and not go back to Barton. Then, in the morning, Mr Whitman would sort everything out, and Jacko would be made to leave me alone. I might even stay at the Whitmans' till the Wilkies were back, just to be on the safe side.

'Do you want to work on your model?' Mike suggested. 'It's still up in our room.'

It hardly seemed worth the trouble; but I followed him upstairs. I'd got to do something, after all.

The boat, half-finished, was lying on top of the chest of drawers, just as I'd left it. Anybody could see it was a hopeless mess.

'It'll look all right when you've finished it,' Mike said. He was only trying to cheer me up, though.

I sat down wearily on the end of his bed. 'It should have gone in the bin. That's all it's fit for.'

He didn't argue the matter. 'Do you want to go over to

Uxbridge, then?' He looked at his watch. 'There's time.'

I thought about it. I wouldn't have minded being there, but it wasn't worth the going and coming back. If we could just have walked down to our little quay, and dived into the creek...

'You know what I wish?' I said. 'I wish we were back at Penskerrick.'

'Don't we all!'

'In the tent, I mean. Just you and me.'

This time, he didn't rush things. Safe at last inside a cocoon of legs and arms, I snuggled close to him, letting his healing hands perform their magic. I could imagine what Ocky would have to say, or Carpenter, or any of that lot. But what did they know? To each according to his needs. Besides, this thing with Mike was a totally private matter, nobody's business but ours. I couldn't have said what he was to me: lover, brother, saviour, friend – what use were categories invented by other people? But I was where I belonged. He made me feel like a human being again, with a right to the air I breathed.

By and by, I was aware of him coming a second time. So soon? I hadn't realised you could – or perhaps we'd been lying there longer than I thought. When he was done, I curled up underneath him, and dozed off for a while in blissful contentment, wondering vaguely what he would tell his mother about the sheets. I should think he probably slept as well. He lay quite still, at any rate.

After a time, we began to surface through a tranquil haze of drowsiness. I was just stretching experimentally amidst a loose tangle of limbs when there were suddenly footsteps on the stairs and Toddy burst into the room with a wild war whoop.

'Hey, Mike! I got my fifty!' He was still in his cricket whites.

For a few moments, he stood there motionless, with his mouth wide open; then he backed slowly out of the room, still gaping at us in horror as if he'd found us lying there with our throats cut. We heard him scampering down the stairs again, and a confused sound of voices came from below. We both sat up in alarm, slipped out of bed, and started to dress. Within seconds, heavier footsteps came pounding up the stairs, and Mr Whitman strode into the room.

He gazed at the scene with a mixture of loathing and disbelief. Mike was only in his underpants; I had nothing on but my shirt. For a very long time, nobody moved. Then he stepped swiftly towards the window with his arm raised, and hit Mike across the face as hard as he could with the back of his hand, sending him reeling against the windowsill. I wanted to cry out, but couldn't. I thought he was going to hit me too, and I wished he had, in a way. Instead, he gave me a quick, contemptuous glance and said brusquely, 'Alan, get dressed, and wait for me downstairs.'

I pulled on my pants and shorts, and scuttled onto the landing with my plimsolls still in my hand. Immediately, the bedroom door slammed shut behind me. As I waited down in the hall, I could hear muffled voices raised in anger, but I couldn't make out the words, except once, when Mr Whitman gave a bitter laugh and shouted, 'You don't even know the meaning of the word.' Through the kitchen doorway, I could see Mrs Whitman standing at the sink with her back to me, gazing rigidly out into the garden. Toddy was nowhere to be seen.

A door slammed on the landing. Mr Whitman came downstairs, and told me to get in the car. Without a word, he started the engine, and backed out of the drive.

After we'd gone the best part of a mile, he still hadn't spoken. Glancing round at him nervously, I said, 'Mike's been very good to me, Mr Whitman. It wasn't his fault.'

For some time, he didn't answer. His lips were tightly compressed, and he kept his eyes fixed grimly on the road ahead, as if looking at me would infect him. At last, he said with barely concealed disgust, 'I'm afraid there's a lot more to this than you probably realise.'

I could have said the same. But we drove the rest of the way in silence.

At Barton, he wanted to see Wilkie. But the Wilkies had left during the afternoon, so he had to settle for Jacko, whose normally suave composure barely survived the shock of finding us side by side in the hall. He obviously thought I'd blabbed.

What passed between them, I had no way of telling. I hung about for nearly an hour, expecting to be sent for, but my presence was evidently not thought necessary. Eventually, Mr Whitman emerged, and left without even saying goodbye, although he strode right past me on his way to the front door.

I sat in the Club Room, pretending to listen to the wireless, till nearly a quarter to ten. But still Jacko didn't send for me. At lights-out, after the usual 'Goodnight, animals,' he paused briefly with his hand poised over the switch, and just for a second or two, our eyes met. To begin with, his expression remained completely impassive; but then, with a faint smile of disdain, he raised his chin a quarter of an inch in triumph.

23

On the first morning of term, as I walked to the station with the promised long trousers flapping strangely around my shins, it occurred to me vaguely that I was now a second-former. But it was only a passing thought; there were more important things on my mind.

I still hadn't been sent for, even when Wilkie returned, and for days I'd been sick with worry at not knowing what had been said. I kept seeing the look on Mike's face when his father hit him, and feeling ashamed of how little I'd said and done to stick up for him. But no one had bothered to ask for my side of the story.

It felt like weeks and weeks since I'd last seen him. Obviously, I hadn't gone over on Sunday. Back at school, though, they wouldn't be able to stop us seeing each other. So I'd been ticking the days off impatiently, and all the way on the train, I was wondering how soon we'd be able to meet.

When I got out, I ran into Carpenter on the platform.

'Hm,' he said, looking me up and down. 'Like your longs. Trez smart.'

The sight of some new boys waiting nervously at the school gates reminded us of our altogether superior status. Poor little sods; they looked as vulnerable and innocent as new-born foals in a field. 'We were never as wet behind the ears as that,' we reassured each other with lordly confidence, as we made our way to the 2B form room.

It was interesting to see how people had changed during the holidays, their faces somehow not quite as you remembered them. The form list had a different look as well. Toddy and Barry Anderson were in 2A now, and Everard had been banished to 2C. In place of them, there were aliens in our midst, a clear affront to our tribal integrity. All the same, the chance of a fresh start seemed rather appealing. Previous mistakes could be quietly buried. And this year, thank God, there'd be no Hedger, and no Rev Ev.

What with the timetable to copy down, and a new desk to personalise, it wasn't until the dinner hour that I had a chance to go in search of Mike. Fortunately, I caught sight of him in the Fourth Year corridor as I reached the top of the stairs. He was looking in my direction, so I called out to him, but he couldn't have heard, because a moment later he turned away and walked into one of the form rooms. When I got to the door, somebody else was just going in.

'Is Whitman there?' I said.

I waited at least two minutes, but nobody came. I didn't really want to knock if it could be avoided, so I stood there till the next person arrived, and tried again.

After a moment or two a head came round the door. 'Are you Carey?'

I nodded.

'He says: Piss off, and don't come back.'

'But...'

'You heard. Now, beat it.'

The long trousers were no help at all; it felt as if I'd been stripped naked and everybody was jeering.

In the blessed privacy of the toilets, there came the thought that Mr Whitman had probably told Mike he wasn't to talk to me. I'd need to catch him alone. Not too difficult, though, if Toddy would act as go-between; and he certainly owed us that much.

I found him chatting to Barry Anderson in 2A's form room. As soon as he saw me, he turned his back.

'Toddy?'

'That's not my name. Anyway, what are you doing here?'

'Could you tell Mike...'

'No,' he broke in. 'I couldn't.'

'I tried to see him, but he wouldn't talk to me.'

'I don't blame him. You're a real turd, Carey.'

His vehemence took me aback. 'That's a bit strong, isn't it?'

He ignored the interruption. 'To think Dad went to Barton House to apologise! Your Mr Crofting soon put him right. Quite a reputation you've got, apparently. They reckon you were even doing it with Dudley.'

'Toddy! That's –'

'I've told you not to call me that. And by the way, were you pinching stuff from our house, or only out of our shops?'

'What the hell are you on about?'

'You needn't try and deny it. Dad saw the actual things. You knew they were onto you, so you legged it straight round to our place to con us into protecting you. And poor Mike fell for it.'

I took a deep breath, and tried hard to keep my temper. 'I never pinched anything out of your shops. If Jacko told you that, he was lying.'

'Oh, really?' said Toddy sarcastically. 'You'll be telling us next he framed you deliberately, just out of spite.'

'Yes,' I said quietly, as much to myself as to Toddy. The whole picture was suddenly clear to me, in living colour.

He gave me a look of utter contempt. 'God, you make me sick!' He started to turn away, but changed his mind. 'And I'll tell you another thing.' Whatever it was, he'd been saving it up specially. 'You're not just a thief and a disgusting little... tart. You're *common*. I mean, look at you! Your hair. The way you talk. The way you sleep in your underwear.'

I spent the rest of the dinner hour wondering why I hadn't clocked him one.

The moment I got home, I knocked on Wilkie's door. Jacko had lied to Mr Whitman, but he couldn't have said the same things to Wilkie, because in that case, I'd have been sent for straight away. It was obvious, really; he wouldn't dare mention the stolen goods or the way I'd scarpered, in case I came back at him with a few facts of my own. He'd probably mentioned the bust-up at the Whitmans', but that would be all. If I could just get Wilkie to listen, I could still bring Jacko down in flames.

Wilkie looked up in surprise.

I pitched straight in. 'You know Mr Whitman was here?'

'So I understand.'

'What exactly did Mr Crofting tell you?'

'I beg your pardon?'

'What exactly did Mr Crofting tell you?'

Wilkie leant forward on his elbows, his expression glacial. 'Oh, I heard you the first time, Alan.'

'Only he told Mr Whitman a pack of lies about me, and it's not right, because now the Whitmans won't even speak to me.'

He went through his usual routine of showing restraint under provocation. 'Now just you listen to me, my lad. The Whitmans treated you with remarkable kindness. They fed you, they opened their house to you, they even took you on holiday. And a pretty strange way you seem to have had of expressing gratitude. So don't come whining to me if they've shown you the door.'

'But what am I supposed to have done, exactly?'

His lip curled in disgust. 'You know very well.'

'No. I don't. Why won't you tell me?'

'I'm not prepared to discuss this any further.'

'Don't I have a right to know what's been said about me?'

He stood up. 'One more word out of you, and the only thing you'll have any right to is a damn good thrashing.'

I stood my ground defiantly. 'You never believe me, do you? Never! But you believe the lies. I want to know what Mr Crofting told you, and I've a right to an answer.'

'Very well, Alan,' he said grimly, taking his coat off and unlocking a tall, narrow cupboard, 'you shall have one.'

But it turned out to be no answer at all.

'Eight!' Ocky exclaimed afterwards, counting the marks. 'Bloody hell! What was all that in aid of?'

'Mind your own.'

'It wasn't for nicking all that stuff?'

'I said, Mind your own.'

Naturally, it wasn't long before Jacko sent for me. 'My dear boy,' he said, 'you do believe in making life difficult for yourself.' Then he smiled, and rubbed his hands together with relish. 'Still, I suppose I shouldn't complain.'

Once again, I launched straight into the attack. 'I know you lied about me to Mr Whitman, but what did you tell the Wilkinsons?'

He looked at me impassively. 'You're angry. But believe me, we all have your best interests at heart.'

'That's rich!'

He shrugged. 'You and the Whitman boy – that sort of thing isn't suitable, not suitable at all.'

'Why not? He was like a brother to me.'

With a wan smile, Jacko demurred. 'Hardly that, by all accounts.'

'Better than a brother. And you still haven't told me what you said to the Wilkinsons.'

Pointing to the Brylcreem jar, he remarked, 'I really did think you'd managed to grasp the simple fact that I hold all the cards. I'll see you come to no harm. But only so long as you don't do anything silly.'

I didn't have much time for a scheme of things which obliged me to put up with Jacko but denied me Mike. I thought about going to Exeter, and asking the Palmers to speak to the Whitmans for me. As a last resort it was worth considering. But there was something more important on the agenda just at present, thanks to a timely discovery in one of my secret hiding places. If Jacko wanted a dirty war, he could have one.

'Look,' I said to Ocky, and opened my fist just long enough for him to see the handful of .22 blanks that Dave had given me.

'What will you do with them?' he said.

And somehow or other, between us, we hatched a scheme for planting them in the burners of Jacko's gas fire. The government ban on the use of gas for heating had been lifted on the first of September. It was in the papers. So all we had to do was conceal the blanks in the radiants, and wait for some cooler weather.

We didn't enquire too deeply into each other's motives. It wasn't necessary. But it surprised me that Ocky was so co-operative, considering what he generally thought of my schemes. Then he happened to let drop something I'd never realised.

'Old scores to settle,' he muttered, and flapped his right arm like a bird with a broken wing.

'Jacko?' I said in amazement. 'But I thought you broke it at school.'

'Well, now you know different,' he said flatly.

'And you kept quiet about it?'

'He's got plenty of ways to put pressure on you. You know that.'

The main question was how to get into Jacko's flat. He always left the door locked when he was out.

'I'll soon take care of that,' Ocky said.

'How? It's a Yale.'

'Dead easy. Strip of celluloid.'

'D'you know how to do it?'

The look he gave me, you'd think I'd asked if he knew what his prick was for.

On Sunday, when Jacko was safely installed at the Welton Arms and the Wilkies were busy downstairs, we left Billy on guard at the top of the staircase, and set to work on the lock. Ocky slid the celluloid into the crevice between the door and the architrave, and applied some gentle pressure.

'How long does it take?' I whispered.

'Couple of seconds.'

I waited. Ocky was cursing quietly, and trying to wiggle the celluloid far enough in to reach the bolt. After two or three minutes, he took it out and tried again from the beginning.

'I thought you knew how to do this,' I said, impatiently.

He pulled the celluloid out again. 'If you're so bloody clever, do it yourself.'

'You're the expert. But I thought we'd have been in and out again by now.'

'Don't rush me. It's a tough one.'

'Pity we can't ask Tom.'

'D'you think I don't know what I'm doing?'

But the door remained obstinately shut.

'Must be deadlocked,' Ocky said in disgust.

'Meaning?'

'The bolt won't push back. You can only get in with a key.'

'Now you tell us!'

'Well, how was I supposed to know?' he snapped.

Billy wanted to let the blanks off with a hammer and nail, but I wasn't ready to give up yet. Somehow or other, I was determined to find a way of getting into the room.

Ocky shook his head. 'You won't do it without a key.'

'All right. I'll get one.'

'I suppose you think Jacko's going to lend it to you?'

But I wasn't to be put off. 'We only need to get our hands on it for long enough to take an impression; then I could make a copy.'

'Don't be daft. They're done on a special machine.'

'I could do it by hand. It'd just take longer.'

'No chance. They've got to be dead accurate.'

'I'll need a Yale blank. Can you get us one?'

'Waste of time. I keep telling you.'

'I thought you were in on this. What's up? Can't you manage it?'

Ocky bridled. 'I should bloody well 'ope so. Might be a day or two, though.'

No matter. We had until Quarter Day. And first of all, there was the impression to take.

Somewhere in the back of my cupboard I still had a piece of the modelling wax from Christmas. At normal temperature, it was fairly hard, but a little warmth soon made it soft and pliable. Just the job. Much better than chewing-gum, which we thought of first.

The really difficult part would be getting hold of the key, which lived on the end of a chain in Jacko's trouser pocket. To separate Jacko from his trousers was simple enough; I accomplished it with depressing regularity. But on these occasions I was not – as the civil service would put it – in a position to borrow the key. No end of ingenious schemes occurred to me, but they belonged to the realm of pure fantasy, and served no purpose except to pass the time during train journeys and tedious lessons.

Around the middle of the week, Ocky sidled up to me and palmed something surreptitiously into my blazer pocket. 'What you wanted,' he said.

The key blank was as bright and sharp as a newly minted coin, and as thrilling to the touch as a pistol or a Bowie knife. Once, in secret, I even held it lightly against my lips, as a man might kiss a dagger blade to consecrate it to vengeance.

The mere contemplation of the power it gave me would have sustained me for the next six months. But with barely a fortnight, now, till the workshop finally closed, the need to obtain the vital pattern was becoming a matter of urgency. As for the method, though, my mind was still as blank as the key.

Ocky was no help. 'I took a lot of trouble getting you that. I 'ope I wasn't wasting my time.'

In the end, it was almost too easy. On Saturday afternoon, the last weekend before Quarter Day, I made for the toilets as a matter of some urgency, and found them paperless. The Wilkies were out, and Hurly wasn't in the kitchen; so there was nothing for it but to apply to Jacko, whose company, as it happened, I had only recently left.

I could hear him speaking as I knocked, but he didn't answer. 'It's urgent!' I shouted, and he called out crossly, 'Very well. Come in.'

He was on the telephone. 'Yes?' he said, bringing his hand down over the mouthpiece.

I explained.

'Odd sort of time to want it.'

'Certain things have that effect on me.'

'I'm busy. You'll have to wait.'

'I can't.'

'Make do with newspaper, then.'

'Mrs Wilkinson said we mustn't.' This was true. A blockage of titanic proportions earlier in the year had been followed by a strict ban.

'I can't come now. This is long distance.'

'What am I to do, then?'

He gave a lengthy sigh of exasperation. 'You know where they're kept?' he said. 'In the cellar?'

I nodded. He fished his keys out of his trouser pocket, unclipped the ring from the end of the chain, and threw me the whole bunch. 'Straight back.'

'It'll have to wait till I've finished.'

'Yes, yes.' He waved me away irritably.

Locked safely in the toilets, I examined the keys. There were three of the right general type. Which was the one? I couldn't copy them all. Fortunately, the first was a Union, not a Yale, and one of the other two was extremely old and worn; also, I noticed, it belonged to a lock with only four tumblers instead of five. The chances were that the lock on Jacko's door had been fitted quite recently. So it must be the third key we wanted.

The wax was in my pocket, but my body heat wasn't enough to soften it. There was always the Aga, but what if someone came in? Luckily, there was no need to risk it. Lying on its side at the end of the yard was an old galvanised water tank; it had sprung a leak, but was still being kept in case it should come in handy. The afternoon sun had been falling on it for an hour or more, heating the metal right through. A few seconds' contact with the surface rendered the wax soft and pliable.

I took the impression, slipped the wax back in my pocket, and ran upstairs with the keys so as to arrive suitably breathless. Jacko took them back without a word. It was a pity he knew I'd had them, if only for five or six minutes, but the chances were he would never guess what had happened. In any case, depending on the weather, it might be a week or two before he lit his fire. By that time, it would have slipped his mind.

A few minutes later, I let myself into the workshop. The first job was to scribe some guidelines across the key blank to mark the centre of each notch; a ticklish job, with no room for inaccuracy. When I was satisfied, I selected a triangular file from the jumble of old tools left on the bench, fixed the blank in the vice, and set to work. The worst possible thing would be to file too much away; so once the notches were nearly down to size, I had to proceed very slowly, constantly checking against the wax impression. It took about half an hour to rough the shape out, and another hour and a half of tinkering to get the profile absolutely accurate.

I brushed the brass filings away as well as I could, but a good many were still lodged accusingly in the scored surface of the wooden bench. So to cover my tracks, I found a brass offcut in the oddments box, and spent a couple of minutes filing the end of it. Sherlock Holmes would have noticed that the key brass and the turning brass were of different compositions; but nobody else was likely to. I left the wax impression amongst the rubbish in the corner, hidden inside an artistically screwed-up twist of newspaper. The finished key I slipped back in my pocket. If anyone found me with it, I could say it was a spare for the workshop that Mr Pond had given me.

At bedtime, I beckoned Ocky into the washroom. 'We're in

business,' I told him, and slid the key a little way out of my pocket.

'About time,' he said. It was against his principles to be impressed.

In the morning, after Church, we left Billy on guard again at the top of the stairs and made a second attempt on Jacko's door. I slid the key into the lock and twisted it gently to the right. It wouldn't turn, so I tried twisting it to the left instead. But it was no better.

Ocky muttered scornfully, 'I told you. They have to be done on a machine.'

I eased the key very slightly outwards, and tried again. At first, nothing happened; then, quite suddenly, I felt something give. With a little scrunching sound, the key turned a degree or two to the right. Then it stuck.

'We're getting there,' I whispered.

I tried to ease it back again, but there was no shifting it. I pushed, pulled, and twisted, till the key handle was slippery with sweat, but it wouldn't budge.

A low whistle from Billy warned us that someone was coming. A moment later, there were adult footsteps on the stairs.

'For Christ's sake!' Ocky hissed. 'Get a bloody move on.'

I was still struggling with the key. 'I can't. It's jammed.'

'Leave it, you prick.' He tugged at my sleeve.

'No.'

'You're on your own, then,' he muttered, and darted away round the corner.

By the sound of it, the footsteps were already passing the halfway house. I glanced frantically round, and saw Billy starting to go down the stairs. There were voices. Billy's. Then Wilkie's. Billy was buying me time. I had one last go at the key, but it was stuck fast.

While Billy was still talking, the footsteps started again, so I had no choice but to make a dash for the corner, and flatten myself against the wall alongside Ocky. We held our breath, straining to hear what was happening. Thank God it was Wilkie coming, and not Jacko. But the key handle stood out like a flashing light, all bright and sparkling against the dull patina of the lock face. Nobody glancing in that direction could fail to notice it.

The footsteps reached the top of the stairs, and ceased again. Billy and Wilkie were still talking. Then the voices began to recede. Wilkie was heading towards his flat, with Billy still chattering away to distract him. At last, a door slammed in the distance, and we heard the soft pad of Billy's plimsolls as he hurried back to join us.

'Shit!' said Ocky, with a gasp. 'This is the last time you catch me working with a bloody amateur.'

I stared glumly at the jammed key. We couldn't simply abandon it. But there was no knowing when Wilkie might come back, and the moment he stepped through his door, he'd see us.

'Got your knife on you?' I asked.

'Knife? What fuckin use is a knife?'

It was the marlin spike I wanted. With a gesture of resignation, he felt in his pocket and held the knife out.

I snatched it from him and fitted the spike through the hole in the key handle. If I was lucky, the extra leverage would loosen the key. If I wasn't, it would snap the end off. Then we'd really be in a mess.

For the best part of a minute, I tried every possible combination of twisting and pulling and levering. Suddenly, without any warning, the key sprang upright and slid clear of the lock. It was so unexpected that I almost fell over backwards.

I gave Ocky his knife back, and he took it without a word.

'Sorry about that,' I said. 'Needs a bit of adjustment, that's all.'

He didn't deign to reply.

I went straight back to the workshop to try and find out what was wrong. A careful study of the impression revealed a place where the wax had been scraped a little, along the edge of one of the deepest grooves. For fear of filing away too much, I must have left the key a little bit oversize; in testing it, I'd worn the wax down. Too late, now, but I should have made two impressions and kept one for checking the final adjustments. As it was, I should have to make do, and guess. Very cautiously, I filed away a little more of the brass along the suspect edge. This time, the key slipped snugly into the wax.

At dinner, there was still no sign of Jacko. It looked as if he'd be stopping at the Welton Arms till closing time.

'I'm ready for another go,' I said to Ocky.

'You needn't think I'm coming. Scared me out of a year's growth, you and your bloody key.'

'I'll do it on my own, then. I thought you wanted to be in on it, that's all.'

Billy agreed to keep watch again, so we slipped away from the Club Room at a convenient moment, and made our way upstairs.

I was about to slide the key into the lock when Billy gave a warning cough, so I slipped smartly out of sight round the corner. A few seconds later, he gave me the All Clear. But I could still hear footsteps coming. Peering round the corner, I saw Ocky arrive at the top of the stairs. He made no attempt to join me, but stood there, next to Billy, with his hands firmly in his pockets. I ignored him, and approached Jacko's door again. Just as before, the key refused to turn till I eased it out a little; but the moment I found the right position, it twisted round without any trouble at all. I pushed the door, and it swung open.

As I took the blanks out of my pocket, it occurred to me that I ought to have darkened them. If they caught the light, Jacko might see them glinting. But fortunately, the latticework of the radiants didn't reach all the way down to the bottom. The fronts were solid for nearly an inch above the burners. I dropped in four blanks – one for me, one for Ocky, one for Ronnie, and one for luck – and jiggled the radiants a little till the bright brass casings settled into positions where they were virtually invisible. The whole job took about thirty seconds.

Once I was safely out again, I walked past Ocky without a word, and started down the stairs.

When we were all back in the Club Room, he said, diffidently, 'D'you want a wine gum? Have a couple, if you like.'

I only took the one, though.

By rights, with the job done, we should have chucked the key into the canal. But I couldn't, not after all that work. Besides, we might have a further use for it. There was a loose floorboard in our bedroom, so we reached in as far as we could, and fastened the key to the underside of one of the other boards with a drawing pin. Safe enough. It would never be found by accident, unless the entire floor was taken up.

'So what do we do now?' Billy said.

'We keep an eye on the weather forecasts,' I told him. 'And wait.'

24

When Jacko sent for me after tea a few days later, I was more than usually apprehensive. Had the blanks gone off already? Surely not; he showed no signs of injury. Perhaps he'd spotted them lying there, and guessed.

He pointed silently to one of the big armchairs, and went into the bedroom to fetch the Brylcreem. With nothing to lose, now, I saw no point in co-operating, so I simply stood there and waited.

After a while, he rested his cigarette in the ash tray and started undoing my buttons. But the feel of his hands caressing my thighs was more than I could stand, and I shuddered violently.

'Are you cold?' he said.

'No!' I blurted out, glancing in alarm at the ash tray.

'Because if you are,' he went on, 'we can always light the fire.'

I felt my stomach suddenly contract as if it had been sucked empty and flattened against my spine. 'No, I'm all right,' I protested, swallowing hard.

But the moment he touched me again, I started shaking.

'I'm sure you must be cold,' he said.

I shook my head, but he stepped across to the hearth, and knelt down in front of the gas fire. I heard the scrape of the match, and the pop as the burners ignited.

How long before the blanks went off? I hadn't the least idea. But surely it must be very soon. Would he even have time to start? With eyes closed and teeth gritted, I waited for the blast.

From behind me, there were soft thuds as Jacko's clothing fell to the floor, and the familiar hollow sound of the metal lid being unscrewed from the jar.

As he eased me into position over the chair, I thought I was going to be sick, and when he gripped my waist, his right hand sticky with the Brylcreem, I let out a gasp of terror. To keep me quiet, he pushed my head down, forcing my nose and mouth deep into the soft upholstery. It was one of his energetic days; as his urgency increased, I found myself being flung about beneath him like a rag doll. For the moment, I even forgot about the blanks, and gripped the chair as hard as I could to avoid being thrown to the floor.

He had slowed down again to a standstill, and seemed about to let go of me, when the first of the blanks went off. There was a single staccato burst of sound, like someone exploding a paper bag, only hugely amplified; then silence. No rumble or echo, as I had half imagined. Jacko leapt back suddenly, leaving me draped exhausted over the chair. I closed my eyes still tighter, and waited.

The second bang came almost immediately. 'Down!' he shouted. 'Get down!' and flung himself full length on the floor. Seeing that I did not follow, he reached up and dragged me down beside him. We lay flat on the carpet, our heads protected by the armchair, our feet sticking out beyond. A second later, the other two blanks went off, virtually together.

Instinctively, after the fourth explosion, I made as if to stand up again. Jacko dragged me down at once. 'Stay where you are,' he hissed. 'There may be worse to come.'

For about a minute, we lay quite still behind the chair. Already, the Brylcreem scent was overlaid by an acrid whiff of gunpowder, but if Jacko noticed it, he made no comment. Eventually, he crawled forward and peeped round at the fire. 'I'll have to try and turn the gas off,' he said. 'Don't move, whatever you do.'

Keeping his body pressed close to the floor, he slithered cautiously towards the hearth, his shrivelled buttocks rising and falling alternately under his shirt tail. Except that he was minus his trousers and crawling over a carpet, you'd think he was creeping up on an enemy trench to lob a grenade in.

For a couple of minutes, the situation hovered uncertainly between calamity and farce. By the time he had managed to reach the gas tap and retreat again to the shelter of the armchair, I was shaking uncontrollably with a confused mixture of relief and hysterical laughter.

'It's all right, old chap,' he said, with surprising tenderness, putting his arm around me. 'Just shock. Perfectly understandable. I expect it brought things back to you, eh? But it's all over, now, and nobody's hurt.'

I looked round at him blankly, wondering what would happen next. It seemed to me that everyone in the building must have heard the explosions, so why had nobody come? Surely not even the fortress architecture of Barton House could have muffled the sound completely. Suppose they came rushing in to see what the matter was, and found us, just as we were. Not even Jacko could talk himself out of that one.

We stood up, rather shakily, and I glanced towards the fireplace, expecting to see the radiants blown to smithereens and the hearthrug strewn with shattered fragments of fireclay. But there didn't seem to be that much damage. I suppose the force of the blast had escaped through the open latticework and dissipated itself quite harmlessly. Luckily, Jacko misinterpreted my look of surprise. 'Must have been a blockage,' he muttered. 'I expect some rubble came down the chimney during the summer.'

I nodded, still feeling slightly dazed by the whole experience. 'Hurry up and get dressed,' he said, with a nervous glance at the door. 'There's a good chap.'

But I took my time.

At the foot of the stairs, I ran into Wilkie. 'Where have you been?' he snapped.

'With Mr Crofting. He wanted to see me.'

'I heard a noise. I thought it was a car backfiring. But somebody said it seemed to come from upstairs.'

'Mr Crofting lit his fire, and it blew up.'

'You were there when it happened?'

I nodded.

'And is he all right?'

'Yes,' I said, with barely concealed regret, and went in search of Ocky.

With the gas bang a failure, and nothing left to look forward to, it was difficult not to think about the Whitmans. Soon, I was forced to acknowledge that waiting for Jacko to light his fire had merely been a distraction. What had really sustained me all this time was the absurd and unspoken hope that somehow or other I might be restored to favour. But it wasn't likely to happen without an intermediary. Dudley would have been ideal. He was the one person I'd have been able to talk to, and still look in the face after I'd told him everything; and the Whitmans would probably have listened to him, too. But it was pointless even to think about it.

Several times, I'd tried to engineer a meeting with Mike. Once, outside the dining hall, I saw him heading towards me, but he had some friends with him, and he walked straight past, pretending not to notice. Another day, in the dinner hour, I followed him at a distance all the way to the shops, and then lost him again before I could catch up. In desperation, I finally sent him a note; but there was no reply.

It was obviously no good bothering with Toddy, but the more I thought about it, the more I came to feel that I might just possibly manage to get a hearing from Mrs Whitman. The day after the gas bang, I decided to stake everything on this one last chance.

It was a Friday, and we had games in the afternoon; it was easy enough to slip away when the others set off for the changing rooms. At the station, a Watford train was the first to arrive; it seemed like a good omen, and with any luck, my green blazer would get me through the barrier at the far end without anyone bothering with my ticket.

During the journey, I rehearsed my opening sentences a hundred times, with different versions to suit the various attitudes that I might encounter. 'Mrs Whitman, I know you think...' Or, 'Please, Mrs Whitman, listen to me for thirty seconds before you say anything.' Or even, the faintest of possibilities, 'Mum?'

For a time, I felt my confidence increasing. But two or three hundred yards from the house, I suddenly realised that I couldn't go through with it. Not face to face. Not yet. Anyway, supposing she wasn't in?

There was a call box not too far away. All I needed to do was to ring the number. If she answered, I could ring off again without having to say anything. But I'd know she was there.

I dialled, and stood there biting my lip, my finger twitching gently against the cradle, ready to push it down at a moment's notice. After seven or eight rings, I heard the receiver being picked up, and her voice saying the number. I waited, quite still, not even breathing; I wanted to hear her voice just once again. She said 'Hello' and repeated the number. I hung up. Well? She was there.

In the old days, I'd have gone round to the back, and walked straight in. But events had made me a stranger, so I rang the bell at the front door, and stood there with my back turned, hoping it might be a moment or two before she saw who it was. Perhaps I ought to have taken my blazer off; the green was a give-away. Or maybe she'd think it was Toddy, home early for some reason. Except that he wouldn't have come to the front door.

Waiting there on the step, I discovered what people meant by 'dying a thousand deaths'. Then came the sound of someone undoing the latch and swinging the door open behind me. I clenched my fists, digging my nails hard into my palms, and turned round.

We both froze. It was Mr Whitman, in posh clothes, but only half-dressed, as if he was getting ready to go out for the evening. His collar was skewed round at an angle, only held by the back stud, and his shirt sleeves were gripped above his elbows by a pair of blue elastic armbands.

Nothing was said; one look at his face was all I needed. As I backed away, he moved forward to keep pace with me, driving me down the path one step at a time. Halfway to the gate, I turned and fled.

Billy was lying in wait for me, outside the clothing factory. 'Don't go in. Ocky wants you, down at the bridge. Urgent.'

At first, when I approached from the pathway, nobody seemed to be there, but hearing my footfall on the planking, Ocky peeped cautiously over the top of the far steps.

'Jacko's onto us,' he said, when I joined him. 'He's found the cartridge cases. I was given the third degree when I got 'ome.'

'Why pick on you?'

'He knows I can slip a lock.'

'He doesn't realise about the key, then?'

Ocky frowned. 'I'm not sure. There's one thing though, he ain't said nothing to Wilkie. He said, why didn't we settle it privately, just him and me.'

'What did he mean by that?'

There was a long silence. Ocky stared blankly ahead, his mouth twitching from time to time as the words struggled to escape. At last, without looking round, he muttered, 'You wouldn't believe what he tried to make me do.'

It was now or never. 'Something to do with the Brylcreem jar?'

He shook his head. 'No. Jam.'

'*Jam?*'

Ocky looked down at his feet. 'Spread it on. Lick it off.'

I felt my gorge rise. 'Oh, shit! Surely you didn't...'

'Course I bloody didn't!' he said, angrily. 'I told him straight out: I've got more on you than you've got on me, so you needn't think you can try anything.'

'I'd really like to have heard that,' I said.

We sat in silence, side by side on the step. After about a minute, Ocky made a strange noise, and leant forward with his shoulders heaving and his face right down between his knees.

'Ocky?'

With an effort, he raised his head an inch or two, but it was no good; a moment later he collapsed again, sobbing uncontrollably. It was a terrible thing to see.

'He made you do it, then?'

'Didn't have no choice.'

He reached behind him, pulling his shirt tail out of his shorts, and holding the waistband down for me to see. There were three circular burns in a neat row.

'Bastard!' I said. 'Fag end?'

Ocky nodded. 'Thought I'd better warn you.'

'You mean he knows it was me?'

He braced himself as if he thought I was going to hit him. 'I couldn't help it, Alan. Honest. I just couldn't take no more. Not after the third.'

'Look. It's okay. I'd have done the same.'

He shook his head. 'No, you wouldn't. That's the difference between us.'

'Of course I would. Jacko makes people do whatever he wants.'

Ocky sat up, turning his head so that I shouldn't see his face. 'Anyway,' he said with a long sniff, 'how come you know so much? About the Brylcreem, and that?'

'How do you think?'

'You too?' He frowned, unable to take it in. 'Since when?'

'Since ever.'

'You never said.'

'Neither did you.'

His lips parted, but it was a while before the words came. 'I never thought he'd dare. Not with a Grammar boy.'

And for once, he wasn't taking the piss.

He sat for a while with his knuckles pressed hard into his open mouth, shaking his head from time to time in despair. 'What are we going to do, Alan?' he said at last. 'What are we going to do?'

Jacko sent for me after tea. 'You'd better sit down,' he said. 'While you still can.'

I perched awkwardly on the edge of an upright chair and watched him remove a matchbox from the middle drawer of his desk. He tipped the contents into his cupped hand and held them out for my inspection: the four blank cartridge cases, discoloured, now, by the heat, and with the crimped ends blown open. I examined them with interest, and asked him what they were.

'Don't be silly, Alan. Oliver has admitted helping you plant them in my fire.'

'He told you that?'

Jacko nodded, tilting his head a little to one side, as if he sympathised with my predicament.

I looked him straight in the eye. 'After what you did to him, he'd have said whatever you wanted.'

'I can't imagine what you mean.'

'I've seen the burns, Mr Crofting.'

With a quick, reptilian smile he said, 'Burns? Dear me. The things you animals do to each other. Mind you, I suppose it's natural. A friend gives you away, and you take revenge.'

'That's not what Ocky will say.'

He raised his eyebrows. 'Of course not. He'll say whatever

you tell him to. I'm sure you know some inconvenient things about his various little activities.'

Holding the matchbox against his palm, he tipped the four blanks back inside, and put the box away again. I noticed he didn't lock the drawer. From his chair behind the desk, he looked across the room at me. 'Don't let's play games, Alan. We can either settle this ourselves, or I can show the cartridge cases to Mr Wilkinson.' He paused. 'And this time, it'd be the cellar again, not just another thrashing.'

I steeled myself to stare back at him, expressionless.

'So you really want me to tell Mr Wilkinson?' he said at last.

'You can do.'

'I think you may regret this, Alan.'

As I was leaving, I paused for a moment, with one hand on the doorknob. 'Oh, by the way, Mr Crofting,' I said, 'I went to see the Whitmans this afternoon.'

'Yes?'

'I thought you might like to know.'

He was good, Jacko. You had to hand it to him. But for just one tiny fraction of a second, I'd seen the look in his eye.

It was risky, of course, mentioning the Whitmans. Suppose they rang to complain about me turning up there? But they were either out for the evening, or expecting guests, so the chances were, if they did ring, they wouldn't do it till morning.

I was pretty sure that Jacko would wait as well. For several reasons, he'd be reluctant to tell Wilkie. It would suit him a lot better to threaten us into doing whatever he wanted. So the best thing was to call his bluff. He might tell in the end; but in that case, with Ocky's burns to explain away, and the two of us backing each other up, we could make some pretty sizeable waves. At a pinch, I could even bring Hurly into it, although I couldn't depend on her. It was obvious, now, how she managed to keep her job, and she might prefer to hold her cards in reserve.

In the meantime, we still had one or two cards of our own to play. The key, for example. Suppose the cartridge cases were to disappear during the night?

'We should have done it before he found them,' Ocky said. 'He knows now, and he'll know who's taken them. Besides, it could be a trap. What if he's waiting for us?'

'It's worth the risk. If we get rid of the evidence, we can both swear blind he's making the whole thing up.'

'And who's Wilkie going to believe?'

'If he tells Wilkie, show him your burns. We'll back each other up.'

Ocky shook his head. 'It's pointless, if you ask me.'

'It isn't you that's going to end up in the cellar.'

'You do it, then.'

'I'll think about it.'

By lights-out, I'd pretty well made up my mind. Earlier, I'd retrieved the key and hidden it in my shoe. I'd also drunk six glasses of water at bed time, so as to be sure of waking during the night.

I slept fitfully, and heard a distant clock striking three. It was as good a time as any. There was no point in dressing; with so many ornaments round the room, a loose sleeve could be dangerous. Underpants and bare feet seemed the ideal burglary outfit, but I put my socks on over my hands so as not to leave fingerprints.

Before inserting the key, I stood quite still at Jacko's door, listening for the slightest sound. It was both a precaution and a delaying tactic. My last chance to turn back. Finally, with my heart thumping hard enough to burst out of my chest, I slid the key into the lock, withdrew it the necessary fraction of an inch, and slowly turned it. Pushing the door open, I peered inside and listened. Still no sound, so I slipped noiselessly into the room and closed the door behind me, dropping the sneck to hold the latch open. I might have to leave in a hurry. Besides, if the worst happened, and someone came in from the corridor, I could slip my socks onto my feet, with the key hidden under my instep, and say I'd knocked for an aspirin and found the door unlatched.

The room was almost completely dark, but after a time, I was able to make out the vague shape of the desk on the far side. The trick would be to reach it without knocking anything over, but at least I knew the layout after so many visits. I gazed intently in the direction of Jacko's bedroom door for any sign of a light, and then set off across the room one step at a time, feeling my way past the various little tables till I reached the desk.

The drawers had drop handles with brass finger-plates behind them. With my socks over my hands, I was rather clumsy, and in grasping the handles I let one of them slip. It fell back against the brass plate with a loud metallic rattle which seemed to echo all round the room. With a sharp intake of breath, I froze, straining to hear the slightest sound from the bedroom. It was two or three minutes before I dared to move again.

At the second attempt I was able to slide the drawer open. So far as I could remember, Jacko had put the matchbox close to the front and fairly well to the right. Probing gently with my finger-tips, I soon encountered something promising. To make certain, I slipped my right hand sock off and felt with my fingernail. To judge from the tiny rasping sound, it was definitely a matchbox. Here goes then. Very gingerly, I lifted it out of the drawer and slid open the tray. With a gentle sideways motion I rattled the contents. Matches. Damn. I felt a sweat break out on my brow as I tried to replace the box without disturbing anything.

A torch would have come in handy. I even wondered whether to strike a match, but it seemed too risky. Never mind. Stay calm, that was the thing. I did some slow, deep breathing to steady my hand and arm, and started exploring the drawer again. At last, under a loose sheet of paper, I found another matchbox. This time, the rattle was more encouraging. I slid the tray out and felt inside. At once, my fingertip encountered the rough crimped edge of one of the brass cases.

One by one, I transferred the four exploded blanks into my right fist and drew the sock back over it. The box I replaced, as accurately as I could, but sooner than leave it empty, I put a few matches in from the other box.

With the drawer safely closed again, I prepared to make my escape. All went well until I was six feet from the door. But then, as I took my next step forward, I heard a faint thud as if a button had fallen to the floor. What could it have been? I hadn't bumped into anything.

Anxiously, I sank to my knees and started to feel about me in the darkness. There didn't seem to be anything there. But something had definitely dropped. One of the blanks? But how? Even if it had slipped, the sock would have caught it. Unless... I checked. Shit! Mrs Dooley must have been behind with her darning. And now one of the blanks was lying there on the carpet, God knew where, as damning a piece of evidence as Jacko could wish for. Better all four of them still in the box, than three gone and one of them found on the floor. I began to regret having drunk so much water.

There was one thing, though. You couldn't leave fingerprints on a carpet. So I bundled the socks into a ball, with the key and the other three blanks stuffed safely inside it, and left it next to the door. Unencumbered, I could search more easily, using both hands.

I must have been half an hour, squatting on Jacko's floor, working systematically to and fro, feeling for the missing blank. It had to be there somewhere; it was simply a matter of patience.

Having searched several complete arcs, I moved forward a little and started on the next. Still finding nothing, I slid my knee to the left and rested it on the floor again. As I put my weight on it, I felt a violent stab of pain as the open end of the little brass case dug into my skin. It was all I could do to keep from crying out. My whole body felt burning hot, then suddenly cold and damp. Still, at least I'd found what I was looking for.

All that remained was a visit to the halfway house. Apart from anything else, it was quite a relief simply to lock the door and put the light on. I flushed the blanks away with the aid of the toilet brush, and held some paper against my knee to stop the bleeding. I hoped there wouldn't be stains on Jacko's carpet.

In the morning, Ocky muttered, 'Have you made your mind up yet? About them blanks?'

'Blanks?' I said, tapping the side of my nose. 'What blanks?'

After dinner, Jacko cornered us. 'Upstairs. Both of you. Now.'

He pushed us unceremoniously into his bedroom, locked the door and pocketed the key. We glanced at each other uneasily.

'I thought we'd have a little party,' he said. 'Just the three of us. You two are going to entertain me.'

It was a while before I caught his drift. When I did, I felt a cold, clammy sweat breaking out on my brow.

'I'm not doing it,' I said, the sound of my voice echoing strangely in my ears.

Jacko spread his hands, full of sweet reason. 'Oh, come now, it wouldn't be the first time. During the big freeze, you even slept in the same bed.'

Ocky gasped.

'I said I'm not doing it, Mr Crofting, and that's that.'

'What's wrong? Don't you fancy Oliver as much as the Whitman boy?'

I seemed to have lost the power of speech and movement, and could only stand there, paralysed, waiting for the whole world to disintegrate around me.

Without warning, Jacko seized Ocky from behind, forcing him down over the end of the bed, and wrenching his shirt and shorts apart to expose bare skin. 'Well?' he said, his cigarette end hovering half an inch from Ocky's waist, 'which is it to be?'

The floor seemed to be tilting back and forth under my feet like the deck of a ship at sea.

Jacko brought the cigarette down onto Ocky's back, held it

there for a moment, and then withdrew it. Ocky gave a yelp and gasped in terror, 'I can't take no more burns.'

'You heard him, Alan,' Jacko said. 'It's up to you.'

Somehow, I managed to shake my head.

This time, Jacko held the cigarette down longer, stifling Ocky's screams by pressing his face against the bedclothes.

'For Christ's sake, Alan,' Ocky pleaded, twisting his head free for a moment. 'Do it.'

Silently, Jacko pointed to the Brylcreem jar.

Only one hope remained. I tried all the usual tricks like saying the alphabet backwards, and thinking of ugly people. But it rather conspicuously didn't work. And so in the end the thing had to be done, after a fashion, with Jacko scrutinising our every move.

When it was over, and I withdrew, all sticky and streaked with brown – a horror for which imagination had somehow failed to prepare me – it turned out that Jacko still hadn't finished with us. 'Right!' he commanded crisply. 'Now change places.' The way he said it, you'd think he was taking a PT lesson.

As we were leaving, he caught hold of my arm. Nodding towards his desk, he said, 'Congratulations appear to be in order. You almost deserve to get away with it. I'll see you don't, of course; but I'd love to know how it was done. Perhaps one day you'll tell me.'

I waited.

With a strange gleam in his eye, he went on, 'I do like a boy with spirit. It's so much more satisfying when you finally break him.'

By tacit consent, Ocky and I made for the railway bridge, and sat at the far end with our legs stretched out in front of us, almost touching. Nothing was said. We needed each other's company, but speech was no longer possible. Events had shocked us into a terminal silence, as if we'd been forced to inject each other with poison, and there was nothing left, now, but to wait till it took effect.

After about half an hour Ocky stood up and walked away, with a curt glance that warned me not to follow. It was a moment for thoughts and feelings to harden into attitudes. The world and I had nothing left to say to each other. It had forfeited any right to have its opinions listened to or its judgments held in respect; and since it refused to hear me, why should I waste my breath? I would have walked barefoot for twenty miles to make things right again between me and Mike. But failing that, I should manage without a special person. I could manage without a replacement family, too;

if the Whitmans were so ready to think the worst of me, perhaps I was well rid of them.

Our piece of serpentine was still in my pocket. I suppose it ought to have gone back into the sea, where a mystic hand would have caught it, like Excalibur. Instead, I dropped it over the parapet onto the track, to lie there amongst the ballast, a single fleck of colour against the grey, until such time as the dust from passing trains had dulled its brilliance, and it was finally lost to sight.

Matters had clearly reached some sort of crisis, but how it would all end was beyond imagining. Now that the whole order of things had broken down, it was impossible to see more than a few seconds into the future. When a train went under the bridge, you couldn't even be sure it was going to reappear on the other side. If it didn't, it would be no surprise; the old certainties had simply ceased to apply.

As it turned out, though, the last act had a stark simplicity about it. I suppose it could even have been foreseen.

Later that afternoon, when Jacko was safely out of the way, Ocky broke into his flat – using our key, presumably – barricaded the door with furniture, and proceeded to do the whole place over. By all accounts, he made a thorough job of it, smashing glass, tearing up books and papers, flinging the china ornaments into the hearth, ripping open the soft furnishings, and wrenching the legs off the chairs and the little tables. By the time the Wilkies arrived and broke the door down, he'd finished the sitting room and was making a start on the bedclothes, slashing the sheets to ribbons and strewing handfuls of mattress stuffing across the floor.

That evening, he was taken away in a car, and we didn't see him again.

Jacko was said to be very upset by the vicious and unprovoked attack on his personal property, and went away for a short holiday to get over it. But it was the longest short holiday in living memory, because I stayed at Barton House till I was fifteen, and he never came back. Instead, we had Miss Scantlebury, a committed boy-hater, who must have been to the same charm school as Fancy Madam. 'You keep away from Billy,' she warned me darkly. 'He doesn't want your sort hanging around him.' After that, whatever she said to me, I simply stared her down like Ronnie with Ma Wilkie, and pretty soon she settled for armed truce.

The morning after Jacko's departure, Wilkie sent for me, and said, very stiffly, 'I gather one or two incidents may have occurred concerning yourself and Mr Crofting.'

With due caution, I acknowledged the possibility.

'I rather think it might be best if we said no more about them. Don't you agree?'

I thought he was probably talking about the gas bang, so naturally I said Yes. And that was the end of it.

So one way and another, I got by. And in those austerity years of power cuts and bread rationing, whalemeat sausages and snoek, I doubt if Barton House was a worse place to be than anywhere else.

I missed Ocky, though. There didn't seem to be much left after he'd gone. In time, the memory of those final twenty-four hours came to be softened by a merciful oblivion, but I often used to recall a thing that happened a few days earlier, not long before he went. It could even have been in his last week, though I wouldn't swear to it.

For some reason, I woke in the night and found him standing at the window between our beds, gazing up at the sky.

'What are you doing?'

'Lookin at the moon.'

'Why?'

'Good friend.'

'Whatever do you mean?'

'Dependable. Not like people. People let you down.'

'Not all of them.'

'Oh yes. You'll see. Like your Whitmans. It's fine to begin with. But once they discover you shit and fart like any other bugger, they lose interest. Where I was before, this couple come round one Battersea Dogs' Home Day. "Ooh, Oliver, that's a nice name." All sorts they was going to do for me.' He turned his head away. 'One postcard. From Bournemouth.'

'I'm sorry. I didn't know.'

'I'm telling you,' he went on, hurriedly, 'you can't rely on nobody, not ever. You're on your own. There's only three things you can trust to stay the same, no matter what – the sun, and the moon, and the feel of your cock in your hand.'

At twelve and a half, it seemed like a pretty sound philosophy. I thought it would do me fine to be going on with; and then as the years went by, I never saw any particular reason to change it. The siege mentality, once acquired, has a way of becoming permanent. It's as if you were one of those stop-watches with two needles; one of them keeps going, while the other stays behind at a particular moment in the past, till someone releases it. Only they never do.

Strange as it seems, I'm not even sure I'd want them to. As boys, we thought of childhood as something you had to live through before you could qualify as a real person. But nowadays, when I see kids playing in the street, or think about us all and the way we were, it often seems to me that we got it wrong; that it's children who are the real people, and adults only the worn-out empty shells of them, washed up onto the beach.

* * * * *

Recent quality fiction from The Gay Men's Press

Robert Rhodes
NONSTOP NEUROTIC CABARET

The zany adventures of a drugged-out, dragged-up British student in the American Midwest

Paul Davenport — pronounced 'cocksucker' — sits with a pierced ear tilted to the sounds of Halowe'en: a harvest of white noise. The Mayflower Residence Hall is shaped like a tuning fork; room 201A is on an outer limb, where vibrations collect. A cigarette filter blackens between fingers pink with dye. Paul sits like a rabbit, spotlit on the road; like a child, hearing its mother beaten. Quite a party, up on — 7? 8? In the two months since, as a (s)exchange student, he first minced over Iowan soil, Paul's been beaten up twice. And here is is, all queered up, going out for more.

ISBN 0 85449 278 X
UK £8.95
US $14.95
AUS $19.95